An Inspector Saralkar Mystery

THE KID KILLER

SALIL DESAI

NATIONAL BESTSELLING AUTHOR

FiNGERPRINT!

Other titles by Salil Desai published by Fingerprint!

THE SANE PSYCHOPATH

Inspector Saralkar Mystery Series:
3 AND A HALF MURDERS
MURDER MILESTONE
THE MURDER OF SONIA RAIKKONEN
KILLING ASHISH KARVE

LOST LIBIDO AND OTHER GULP FICTION

Published by

FiNGERPRINT!

An imprint of Prakash Books India Pvt. Ltd.

113/A, Darya Ganj, New Delhi-110 002,
Tel: (011) 2324 7062 – 65, Fax: (011) 2324 6975
Email: info@prakashbooks.com/sales@prakashbooks.com

facebook www.facebook.com/fingerprintpublishing
twitter www.twitter.com/FingerprintP

ISBN: 978 93 5440 732 1

Processed & printed in India

Praise for Salil Desai's Books

3 and a Half Murders

'Twisted Thriller, Quirky Characters.'

–**Sriram Raghavan**, Director, *Andhadhun, Badlapur*

'The book impresses the reader with the final revelation.'

–*The New Indian Express*

'Realism is never too far in Desai's book . . .A non-regulation twist turns the saga on its head.'

–*Bangalore Mirror*

Murder Milestone

'Enthralling mystery, exciting narrative!'

–**Subodh Bhave**, acclaimed actor, who plays Inspector Saralkar in forthcoming web-series adaptation, *Kalsutra*

The Sane Psychopath

'Terrific plot, a horrific crime! A disturbing story, narrated superbly.'

–**Sujoy Ghosh**, Director—*Badla, Kahaani*

Killing Ashish Karve

'This is the best murder mystery by an Indian author so far.'

–Sunday Tribune

'The book is a real page-turner. . . . An original Indian police procedural.'

– DNA

Lost Libido and Other Gulp Fiction

'Desai's writing is energetic and contemporary.'

– Shobhaa De

'Intriguing, ingeniously plotted and wickedly contrived.'

– Dr. Shashi Tharoor

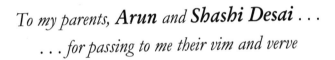

*To my parents, **Arun** and **Shashi Desai** . . .*

. . . for passing to me their vim and verve

PROLOGUE

January 2015

"Mom, what must I say to teacher and my classmates when I offer these sweets?"

"You have to say, *'Tilgul ghya, god bola',*" the pretty, thirty-five-year-old replied as she turned her scooter onto the main road.

"Okay! I keep forgetting. It means *'Take these sweets and speak sweetly', no?*" her son, riding pillion, asked.

"Correct! You should start practising Marathi, kiddo, we are not in the US anymore," his mum remarked.

The boy didn't reply, busy committing the Marathi greeting to memory. His mother gave a quick half-glance behind.

"You should mix with other boys, beta," she said gently. "Why didn't you go kite-flying yesterday with the neighbourhood kids? It's so much fun . . . that's the way to celebrate *Makar Sankrant.*"

"Hmmm. Next time," the kid replied.

"Promise?"

"Promise!"

"Aargh . . ." the mother suddenly gasped, in a strangled voice.

"What happened, Mom?" her son asked, alarmed as the vehicle wobbled and his mother brought it to a jerky halt.

"Get down . . ." his mother spluttered, gesticulating frantically with one hand, the other hand clutching at her throat, barely able to keep herself astride, her feet planted on the ground, losing strength by the second as she struggled to retain balance.

The boy alighted from the two-wheeler quickly. No sooner had he done so, his mother staggered away, letting the scooter fall, making no attempt to put it on the side-stand.

She tottered a few shaky steps, turned around to look at her son, her face contorted, her eyes blinking rapidly and randomly, and then collapsed on the road with a sickening thud. The boy saw blood spurt from her throat, her nose, her mouth, and the spot where her un-helmeted head had hit the tar.

Her body began to writhe and twitch, and a bewildered croak emanated from her mouth, as her eyes glazed over with fear and pain.

The boy watched, terrified. "Mom!" he screamed and began to sob and tremble, as the trickle of blood formed a puddle beside her.

*****

Chapter 1

July 2022

Like all rivers, Pune's Mutha River gulped down copious amounts of human waste in its depths, but perhaps it drew the line at corpses. Not all corpses but those of children perhaps. Especially murdered children!

That's probably why its waters loosened the hold on the block of cement weighing down the body of eleven-year-old Pranjal Bhatti and let it float to the surface, framed by the green carpet of water hyacinth, so that someone would notice it.

And someone did. From a bridge. The Rajaram Bridge, connecting the upper middle class, predominantly Marathi locality of Karvenagar with Sinhagad Road, one of the busiest thoroughfares in Pune, that could take you to the famous hill fort of Sinhagad, if you wished to go there.

Pranjal Bhatti had gone missing just three days earlier, clad in a smart yellow t-shirt and blue jeans, wearing his favourite Crocs, his trendy bag slung over his shoulders, a Fitbit on his wrist and his precious mobile in his pocket, astride his bicycle.

All of that had been missing when he was found and his mutilated body hauled into the rescue boat.

*****

"Do you think he is one among them?" Saralkar remarked, his eyes sweeping a glance at the swarm of curious onlookers, gathered atop the bridge and the riverside embankments on both sides. "Watching his handiwork with relish?"

PSI Motkar shrugged distractedly, his distressed gaze fixed on the boat making its way back to the bank with the boy's remains. "I guess it's a possibility, sir."

"Hmm. I've often been tempted to round everyone up whenever I see ghouls staring at corpses, as if it were a spectacle to behold."

There was a dangerous wistfulness in his boss's tone that made Motkar steal a glance at him. "We can't do that, sir."

"Why not?"

Motkar's eyes shot up. "I mean they are not obstructing police investigations, sir . . . they are just watching . . . out of harm's way."

Saralkar grunted, continuing to glare at the crowd thoughtfully. "Look at so many of them trying to shoot clips with their mobile phones—to upload on WhatsApp and Facebook—*Dead body of murdered kid salvaged from river* . . . and they'll get their kicks from their clips going viral."

"You are right, sir. Shall I get an alert across to the Cyber Cell to monitor and block graphic visuals and videos?"

"Yes, might be useful," Saralkar said, his eyes now moving to the approaching boat, which was minutes away from the embankment.

As Motkar made a call to the Cyber Cell, Saralkar braced himself for the sight and smell he was likely to be confronted with soon. Why did dead bodies decay and putrefy, turning into something loathsome and revolting? He, of course, knew the science behind it—escaping gases and decomposition.

But why did life have to heap this ultimate indignity on living creatures by turning them into disgusting carcasses once death claimed them, if left undiscovered and unattended? Why indeed did life entrust a human being's dignity after death to the hands of others, when all one's life one was burdened with securing one's own dignity? The bloody irony of it!

The first whiff of death hit his nostrils as the boat touched the shore. Saralkar's right hand was quick on the draw, as it reached inside his right trouser pocket and swiftly transferred the handkerchief to press it against his nose.

He almost choked, for Jyoti's perfume, which he had quickly sprayed on the handkerchief in anticipation of this moment when Motkar had called to apprise him of the kid's body, was also overpowering. Saralkar was allergic to all strong smells. But for now, he would tolerate it and hope it would shield him a little from throwing up and survive the next few minutes.

PSI Motkar had finished his call. "The Cyber Cell will keep an eye out, sir." He began walking towards the docked boat, then looked at his boss, who stood rooted to his spot, trying hard not to look queasy as always.

It was the trilling of his mobile that came to Saralkar's rescue. He grabbed it like a desperate man clutching at a lifeline. "Hullo," he said, answering the call of his car service advisor, with the alacrity and gravity of receiving an important tip-off. "Yes."

He gestured to Motkar to carry on and strolled away towards a quieter spot, determined to patiently engage in a conversation with the car service advisor about oil change, acceleration problems, and other sundry issues his vehicle faced.

Saralkar was no coward but he'd learnt from bitter experience that his stomach wasn't his most reliable ally. Five minutes later, it let him down once again when he stared at the grotesque state of little Pranjal Bhatti's corpse.

*****

THREE DAYS EARLIER

"What, Mamma?" Namita asked, picking up the phone. Her tone was as unwelcoming and resentful as that of any teenager her age.

"Is Pranjal back home?" her mother asked.

"No!"

"He isn't home yet?" Smita Bhatti asked, a tinge of worry in her voice now.

"That's what I just said, Mamma," Namita replied, preparing to cut the call, "I'm not going to give him any message. You call on his mobile directly!"

"Namita, he isn't answering his phone, beta," Smita said, "I've tried a couple of times. It's 5.45 p.m. He should have been home half an hour ago . . ."

Namita clicked her tongue. "He'll come, no, Mamma. What's there to worry?"

"But why is his phone unreachable?"

"Stop fretting, Mamma. Maybe he's just down below chatting with a friend and his phone is on silent . . ." Namita said.

"Yes," Smita conceded, "look, I'm going to be a little late at office. Will you please go down and see if he is around, in case he does not turn up in fifteen-twenty minutes?"

Namita blew up. "No, Mamma, no! Why must I have to look after him? You come back early from office and look for him if you want to. I don't have time."

She cut the phone with impunity.

Smita knew there was no point in trying to call back. Her daughter would probably just ignore her call. Instead, she called up Pranjal's number one more time. This time no rings passed. *'The number you are trying to reach is currently switched off'* came the automatic response, which was hardly comforting.

It was so unlike Pranjal to not answer his phone or at least call back within a few minutes. But Smita had work to complete and there was no point in worrying unduly. She decided to get on with her incomplete task and finish it within half an hour.

Twenty minutes later her mobile rang. But it wasn't Pranjal. It was Namita.

"Mamma, he hasn't come yet," Namita said, "I am just going down to check."

"Please do that, beta," Smita said, her anxiety deepening but relieved that her daughter was being responsible. "Meanwhile, I'll just call at a few of his friends' houses."

Smita packed up her things for the day, then started making phone calls. The office had begun to empty. Some colleagues were leaving, others still completing their day's work. Her cubicle had no real privacy, but there was nothing she could do about that.

Another twenty minutes later, she was close to panicking, for none of the phone calls had yielded the whereabouts of her son. She dialled her daughter's number again.

"Namita beta, did you find . . .?"

"No, Mamma," Namita replied, "he's not there. How can he be such an idiot? Doesn't he know you'd be worried?"

Smita's heart sank. "Listen, Namita, I'm leaving office now to come home. Meanwhile, will you please call Daddy?"

"Why?"

"Tell him Pranjal's not home and his phone is unreachable. Ask Daddy what we should do. Ask him if we need to go to the police station," Smita said.

"Why don't you talk to him no, Mamma? Why me?"

"Just do as I say, Namita," Smita snapped, "stop arguing. I'll get further delayed trying Daddy's number if it's busy or he's in a meeting. I'm leaving for home now . . . so you call him. He'll have time to think and tell us what to do by the time I reach home. Understood?"

"Okay," Namita said morosely, "but he's travelling. What if I can't reach him?"

"Then just drop him a message that he should call back urgently."

Her mother disconnected and Namita grudgingly scrolled down her phone, then dialled the number saved as SD Mohnish Bhatti.

There were a couple of beeps and then instead of rings she heard the recorded message—*'The number you've dialled is outside the coverage area. Please try again later.'*

Namita sighed and dialled the number again and again.

*****

Chapter 2

"Sir, prima facie it certainly looks like Pranjal Bhatti. Of course, positive identification from the family is still awaited," PSI Motkar said. "A missing complaint was filed by his mother three days ago at Bavdhan Police Chowky at around 7.30 p.m. in the evening . . ."

Saralkar nodded, still wallowing in humiliation at having thrown up, right in front of Motkar, the constables, and the forensic team. It would be the subject of considerable amusement and snickering, he reckoned— *'Saralkar saheb puked . . .!'*

Maybe he was finally getting old. "When had the boy actually gone missing? The same day?" Saralkar asked, trying not to dwell on his embarrassing mishap.

"He left home for his coaching class around 3.00 p.m. in the afternoon and was expected to return by 5.15 p.m. as usual," Motkar said. "After searching and looking for him on their own, his mother and sister finally approached Bavdhan Police Chowky at around 7.30 p.m."

"The lad doesn't have a father?" Saralkar queried.

"The father was out of town in New Delhi on some work, I think," Motkar replied. "He somehow managed to get a ticket and flew back to Pune on a late-night flight."

"I see. So did the family or police suspect kidnapping?"

"Not initially, sir," Motkar said, "but there was a ransom call to the father the same night and so almost immediately it turned into a kidnapping case."

"To the father? But wasn't he travelling back by air from Delhi? What time did he receive the call?"

Motkar referred to the papers in front of him and searched for the detail. "Around 10.30 p.m., sir."

*****

Three Days Earlier

"Yes, Smita . . . I've finally got a confirmed seat on the 10.45 p.m. flight," Mohnish Bhatti told his wife, as he scrambled to collect his cabin baggage that had cleared the security check, "I am rushing to board the flight. Are you and Namita okay? Did the police say anything more?"

"They . . . They immediately sprang into action . . . but . . . but they haven't told me anything so far . . ." Smita replied, her voice choked with anxiety. "I am so scared, Mohnish! Why is this happening to us? Where could Pranjal have gone? The police kept asking me if something happened at home . . . whether Pranjal failed some exam . . . or perhaps we had scolded him . . ."

"What? What do they mean?" Mohnish asked. "Are they saying Pranjal might have run away from home?"

"Yes, they said it's quite likely. Many children of this age go missing on their own because of some problem or some incident. They said, often it's just to teach parents a lesson for scolding them. Children can be very sensitive . . . or it could be an attention seeking tactic."

"That's ridiculous. Our Pranjal would never do that!" Mohnish replied, anger and anxiety in his tone, as he scampered towards his gate and saw that the boarding for his flight had already commenced. He joined the queue.

"That's what I told them," Smita said, "and I said nothing whatsoever had happened at home to make Pranjal want to do something like that. To that this Constable Dhanak said that sometimes parents don't even realize what's bothering their children . . . or they often don't even know something's wrong. I am so worried, Mohnish. Where's our boy? It's night, and he must be alone somewhere, scared . . ."

She broke into a sob.

"Don't . . . Don't cry, Smita darling," Mohnish said helplessly. "Everything will be alright. I'll be there in a few hours. Don't worry . . . Pranjal will be fine . . . God will look after him . . ."

He knew it all sounded so inadequate when he just received more sobs in response from his wife. "Smita . . . Smita . . . please be okay . . . have you had something to eat?"

Smita sniffed. "No. How can I?"

"Have something please . . . please . . . I need you to be strong," Mohnish coaxed her. "I am on my way—the flight is boarding, so I've to go. You eat a little and rest. Is Namita around? Just give the phone to her."

His wife said, "Okay," then called out to their daughter, "Namita! Daddy wants to talk to you."

A few seconds elapsed before Namita came on the line. Mohnish had embarked on the apron bus now that was to take passengers to the aircraft.

"Hullo," said Namita.

"Namita, beta . . . are you okay?" Mohnish asked.

"Yes," came the cryptic reply.

It disconcerted Mohnish as always. "That's good. Will you please get Mummy to eat a little? Something . . ."

"I'll try."

"Okay. And you also eat something. I'll be there around 1.30 – 2.00 a.m. Please look after her, Namita . . ." Mohnish said.

"Okay," Namita said and before he could say anything further the call disconnected. Mohnish wasn't sure if it was a call drop or Namita had cut the call.

He considered redialling but decided he needed to clear his own head a bit. The last two hours had been just one long scramble—first the shock of being told his son had gone missing by Namita and then Smita, then the chaos of first digesting the news and trying to figure out what to do, then the mad and excruciating rush to arrange an air ticket to fly home on an evening when all direct flights seemed packed. The frantic calls to a few contacts who might get him a seat, the packing of bags, checking out of the hotel, the taxi to the airport amidst heavy traffic—all the time texting and talking to Smita, then following up with airlines and contacts, while also attempting to find some contact who knew someone higher up in the Pune police force.

Thank God he was on his way finally. He needed a moment now to gather his thoughts and calm his jangling nerves. He shut his eyes tight trying to regain his composure and took a deep breath. Pranjal's face immediately lit up on his mind screen and a deep, sharp pain stabbed his heart. How could he suddenly have gone missing? Or had he been taken? Where was his son at this precise moment? How was he? What was he going through?

Mohnish felt an overpowering urge to let go and scream his heart out. But of course, he couldn't do that in a busload of passengers who had no idea what he was experiencing.

How would they understand? What would they think? Some crazy guy who'd just lost it!

Mohnish alighted from the apron bus and walked towards the aircraft with the other passengers and a few minutes later he was inside, walking down the aisle looking for his row and seat. His mobile began to ring but it took him a minute to reach inside his pocket and take the call amidst the jostling of people and the fact that his hands were tied down by hand baggage.

It was an unknown number and by the time he put it to his ear, the call was disconnected. Wondering who it could be, Mohnish got to his seat, shoved his hand baggage into the overhead locker and sat down. He took a look at the number again. It didn't seem familiar at all but he had called up so many people in the last two hours—contacts of contacts—it might be someone calling back.

He dialled the number but couldn't get beyond static beeps. Connectivity was a problem at airfields sometimes. He tried again once or twice and this time after several beeps the rings to the number began. But no one answered. Mohnish cut the phone, restless. Passengers had more or less settled down and boarding seemed to have been completed. The air hostesses were milling about, assisting passengers who couldn't find an empty hold, running errands for others, passing instructions to one another, clearing the aisles, and getting ready for the safety demos.

"Excuse me," Mohnish said to an air hostess rushing past, "Can you please get me some water?"

He was unbelievably thirsty and his throat felt parched. The air hostess gave a quick nod and moved ahead. She was back surprisingly quickly with a mini plastic bottle.

"Thank you," Mohnish said, just as his phone began ringing. It was the same number.

"Hullo," Mohnish said, pressing the mobile to his ear as he opened the top of the bottle.

"Mohnish Bhatti?" a voice asked.

"Yes, this is Mohnish Bhatti," Mohnish said and took a quick gulp of water.

"Pranjal's father, right?"

Mohnish froze and held the mobile with his hand now. "Yes . . . who's this?"

The phone went dead for several moments.

"Hullo . . . Hullo . . ." Mohnish spoke desperately into the mouthpiece, even as he heard the phone disconnect. His heart was in his mouth. The air hostesses had commenced the safety demo and he could hear the instructions as they mimed.

Mohnish began dialling the number. He had to know who was calling. He just had a few minutes before all the mobile devices would have to be switched off for take-off. All he got was beeps, but no ringing. He cut the call and tried again to no avail.

Then his mobile sprang to life. He took the call on the first ring. "Yes, who's this? I'm Mohnish Bhatti."

"We . . . have your son, Pranjal," the same voice spoke, even as it broke.

"What? Who are you?" Mohnish asked urgently.

"If . . . back, you'll have to . . . ransom . . ." the man at the other end responded, sending a chill down Mohnish's spine.

This wasn't really happening. "Hullo? Hullo? Is Pranjal okay? Is he safe? Please . . . please! Whoever you are . . . please don't harm him!" Mohnish said desperately, hushing his voice as much as he could, leaning forward and resting his head on the seat in front, his mind going crazy.

"Sir, sir, excuse me, please switch off your mobile," an air hostess said, tapping him on his shoulder.

Mohnish waved his hand at her, "Just give me a minute, please," he pleaded with her and spoke into the mouthpiece again, "Hullo! Hullo! Are you there?"

"Pranjal will be safe if you pay the ransom amount of ₹10 lakhs and don't go to the police," the man said in a voice so normal, that it sounded far more menacing and real.

Mohnish's stomach churned. "Yes, yes, we'll pay you the amount—I promise!" he said, almost trembling all over. "Don't do anything to him! Can I . . . Can I speak to Pranjal?"

"Not now," the man replied. "He's sleeping."

To Mohnish, the way it was said, had an ominous ring to it. "Please, please . . . just tell him it's his daddy. He'll wake up . . . please!"

"Sir," the air hostess was back and was sounding impatient, "you need to switch off the phone at once. We are preparing for take-off."

Mohnish looked at her and implored, "Please . . . I have to complete this call . . . my son's been kidnapped. I can't disconnect—just two more minutes."

The air hostess was taken aback. "Sir, please hurry up. No more than a minute, please." She hurried away probably to report to someone senior.

Other passengers threw startled looks at Mohnish as he began talking into the phone again. "Hullo . . . I am rushing back to Pune on a flight that's just taking off from Delhi. I'll call you back as soon as I land! I'll pay you the amount you want, wherever you want . . . just don't harm Pranjal . . . hullo? Hullo!"

There was no response, only blankness. Had the man hung up or was it another call drop? Mohnish was dumbstruck. What was he to do?

He began dialling his wife's number. He had to tell her about the call before the flight took off so that she could inform the police. Or they would never know for the next three hours. The air hostess was back with a senior colleague.

"Sir, please don't make or take any more calls. Please switch off the device."

"Just let me make this one last call to my wife. It's an emergency. Please understand . . ." Mohnish said as Smita's phone began to ring.

"Sorry, sir . . . we have to ask you to immediately switch off or the device will be confiscated," the senior air hostess said sternly.

"But please understand," Mohnish exploded as the other passengers watched, horrified.

"Sir, if you start arguing or shouting, we may have to disembark you and a police complaint will be lodged," the senior air hostess said. "We understand your distress but please stop."

The rings had remained unanswered. Mohnish cut the call. "Okay . . . sorry. Can you just give me a minute to send a message?"

The lady relented. "Okay. Please do it quickly and I am afraid then I'll have to take the device from you temporarily. It'll be returned to you after take-off."

Mohnish swallowed and nodded. He quickly typed in a message.

Smita, a man called and made a ransom demand of Rs 10 lakhs. He says he has Pranjal. My flight is about to take off. Please call this number and tell the man we'll pay. Also inform the police about the call, although the man said we should not go to the cops.

He typed in the number, dispatched the message, switched off the mobile and gave it to the air hostess. Then he slumped onto the back rest, covered his face with his hands and started sobbing.

*****

Chapter 3

"Ten lakhs? That's all the kidnapper asked for?" Saralkar asked with a frown.

"Yes, sir. Why?"

"Sounds a pretty modest figure for kidnappers to demand from an upper middle-class family, if that's what the Bhattis are," Saralkar observed.

"I am not sure of that, sir," Motkar replied. "ASI Tupe of Bavdhan Police Chowky should be able to tell us once he gets here."

"Hmm . . ." Saralkar grunted. "A kidnapper is no different from all of us. He'll always pitch for a much higher amount than he actually expects to get. Normal negotiation tactic."

PSI Motkar nodded. "So, I guess the kidnapper would've expected to get about 5-7 lakhs in Pranjal's case."

"That's peanuts really for all that effort," Saralkar reflected. "Of course people commit all kinds of crimes and kill for far less. Still, it's a point to dwell upon. So, when did the next ransom call come?"

"There was no second call, sir," Motkar replied.

"What? No contact at all in the last three days?"

"No, sir," Motkar shook his head. "Maybe the man panicked or perhaps he suspected the Bhattis had already filed a missing complaint with the Bavdhan Police."

Saralkar sat scowling silently for a minute or two and then asked, "Did they put out a trace on the number from which Mohnish Bhatti received the call?"

"Yes, sir, but there was an unfortunate delay," Motkar said. "The number that Mohnish Bhatti texted to his wife immediately after the ransom call, had two digits transposed. Probably because he was under such stress and since the air hostesses were breathing down his neck to switch off the mobile, Mohnish Bhatti typed '27' instead of '72'."

Saralkar clicked his tongue. "Ah! So, the number his wife passed on to the police was the wrong one and they got the right number only later after Mohnish Bhatti landed in Pune."

"Yes, sir. Real bad. They lost at least three vital hours," Motkar said. "Meanwhile, they traced the wrong number to someone who had nothing to do with the matter. And that kicked up a separate fuss."

"I see. But what about the number from which the ransom call was made? Where has that been traced to?"

Motkar shook his head and just as he was about to answer, ASI Tupe joined them. His face was blanched and flushed and it was clear he'd just taken a look at Pranjal Bhatti's body.

"Good morning, sir," Tupe said in an oddly tremulous voice which contrasted sharply with his wrestler's physique. "We put in our best effort to trace the boy, sir. Poor kid! I wonder how long he's been dead. Can't understand why the kidnapper never called again and directly killed the boy."

Saralkar was gazing at Tupe intently. "You didn't get a trace on the number?"

"The number was switched off after the ransom call, sir. The call was made from the Wakad area. It was a prepaid number, taken from a stolen phone and inserted in another device that was reported stolen by an owner a week ago. The owner had filed a police complaint," ASI Tupe replied. "Neither the number nor the device was switched on again."

"And what about the boy's phone? Did you put that on trace too?" Motkar asked.

"Pranjal's phone had been switched off almost two hours before his mother and sister filed a missing complaint," Tupe replied. "Again that too was never switched on in the last three days."

"And what was his phone's last location?"

"Bavdhan area only, sir. It was switched off at around 3.30 p.m.," Tupe replied.

"And he'd left for class at what time?" Saralkar asked.

"His sister Namita says Pranjal left the house around ten minutes to 3.00 p.m., sir. The class is in Bavdhan itself about fifteen minutes away from home," Tupe replied.

"So, he reached class and shut it off, which explains why the phone was active till then, right?" Saralkar asked.

The first sign of hesitancy appeared on Tupe's face and in his manner. "Yes, sir . . ." he said with a little pause, "it . . . it seems like that."

"Why are you not sure?" Saralkar quizzed. "You couldn't ascertain his presence in class?"

ASI Tupe passed his tongue over his lips. "Sir, Pranjal had joined the coaching class very recently, so many other kids didn't know him that well. He hadn't really made any friends . . . so I couldn't get a positive confirmation from anyone who actually saw him in class that day."

"Not even the teacher?"

"Well, sir . . . she's not sure."

Saralkar scowled. "But surely they must be having an attendance system or a CCTV somewhere on the premises?"

ASI Tupe graduated from licking his lips to chewing at his moustache. "They don't have a CCTV, sir."

"Hmm. So, you—"

"Excuse me, Saralkar saheb," a meek voice interrupted.

Saralkar shot an annoyed glance in the direction of the newcomer.

"I am Dr. Gunjal. I just finished preliminary examination of the body," the young bespectacled man said defensively, probably scorched by Saralkar's look.

"Okay. So, what can you tell us?" Saralkar asked curtly.

Dr. Gunjal cleared his throat. "Cause of death certainly appears to be drowning, although post-mortem . . ."

"Drowning?" Saralkar narrowed his eyes. "You mean the boy was not killed first and then thrown into the river?"

"He died by drowning, sir . . . at least prima facie there doesn't seem to be any other cause," Dr. Gunjal repeated. "Of course only a post-mortem . . ."

"Yes, yes, I know that," Saralkar cut him short, threw quick baffled glances at Motkar and Tupe, then said, "I thought I saw signs of injury marks on his body?"

"Yes, sir, there are injury marks but none look serious enough to have been fatal," Dr. Gunjal replied. "But only after a post-mortem . . ."

"I am not daft, Dr. Gunjal. I understand. You don't have to keep adding the post-mortem disclaimer," Saralkar growled. "Now what else can you tell us that helps the investigation?"

The young doctor looked intimidated. He blinked, as if wondering what Saralkar expected, as he wilted under the latter's gaze.

PSI Motkar who knew Saralkar's ability to render people speechless, came to his rescue.

"Dr. Gunjal, how long has the body been in the water?"

Dr. Gunjal looked at him gratefully. "The body has been in the water for about two days, I think, sir." He seemed to bite his tongue to stop himself from adding the post-mortem disclaimer again.

"Forty-eight hours or more, doctor?" Motkar asked.

Dr. Gunjal shrugged uneasily. "Maybe, sir. The bodies of people who drown generally take two or three days to float to the surface."

The three police officers looked meaningfully at each other. "Even bodies of kids who drown?" Saralkar asked.

Dr. Gunjal's face twitched as if he was on uncertain ground. "I'll check and confirm, sir."

Saralkar nodded as if irritated at the man's timidity. "Anything else that we need to know?"

"Not right now, sir," Dr. Gunjal replied after thinking hard for a moment.

"Then finish the damn post-mortem soon and bring the report to my table," Saralkar gave a parting shot and the doctor hastened away.

There was a minute's silence as Saralkar seemed lost in thought.

PSI Motkar spoke, "If Dr. Gunjal is right, it means the kidnapper disposed of the body the same night or early next morning."

"That's just shortly after the ransom call, sir," Tupe added.

"No, let's not jump to conclusions on that yet," Saralkar remarked. "I am not quite sure if Dr. Gunjal has that level of experience yet. He's too young. But what bothers me is the cause of death—drowning. Which means what? The kidnapper just threw the boy into the river to drown and die? Sounds far-fetched. Wasn't the kidnapper taking a big risk? What if the boy knew swimming? What if he was simply lucky and managed to cling to something and survive?"

PSI Motkar nodded. "You are right, sir. But maybe the kidnapper knocked the boy unconscious or drugged him and then threw him into the river. The boy was then bound to drown in an unconscious state . . . also—there is so much filth and sewage in the river, sir, and that water hyacinth . . . the odds were the boy stood no chance of surviving."

Saralkar grunted, shaking his head slowly. "The one thing I've learned about murderers is that they have a psychological need to make sure their victims are dead. They can't afford to leave things to chance or fate. Because . . . what if the victim survives by fluke? Throwing someone into the river to drown, even assuming he was drugged or knocked unconscious leaves too much to chance. It's unbelievable the kidnapper would have risked that."

Once again, a brooding silence prevailed for some time, then Saralkar looked at ASI Tupe and asked, "Tell us something about the boy and his family, Tupe."

ASI Tupe nodded and referred to the file he had been holding all along. He flipped through the papers, then handed over the file to PSI Motkar indicating the relevant pages.

"Sir, the Bhatti family includes Mohnish Bhatti, age forty-four, who runs an authorised dealership of a sanitaryware company headquartered near Delhi. Earlier he used to work in the same company, then he resigned and started the dealership a few years ago. He's got a set-up on Pashan-Sus Road, with about three or four employees," Tupe said. "His wife Smita Bhatti works as an HR/Admin manager in a small software company. She's forty-two. Her office is located in Hinjewadi Phase II. They have two children——Namita, who's eighteen years old, and Pranjal. The girl is studying BBA in MIT College and she generally comes home between noon and 12.45 p.m., then again leaves for some classes at 5.30 p.m. Till last year she was in Bright Future School, Aundh, where the unfortunate boy Pranjal was also studying in the sixth standard this year.

"Pranjal would usually get home by school bus, just after his sister, around 1.00 p.m. He would then have his lunch and then leave for his coaching class around 2.45 p.m. on his bicycle. He followed the same routine the day he went missing."

"I see. And you've checked out the whereabouts of all family members that day?" Saralkar asked.

"Yes, sir," Tupe replied. "Mohnish Bhatti had travelled to Noida, two days earlier to visit the headquarters of the sanitaryware company. He also visited their plant near Khurja, which is about seventy or eighty kilometres from Delhi. The company has confirmed it. He was throughout with someone and stayed at a hotel in Noida.

"The mother, Smita, was in office all day and she had to stay back a little late that evening. She couldn't contact Pranjal, so she called up her daughter, Namita. The daughter had returned from her college around 12.30 p.m., had lunch with Pranjal, and then dozed off when her brother left around 2.45 p.m. She said she heard the main door open and close, though she didn't actually see Pranjal leave.

"After her mother called, she went out to see if Pranjal was somewhere around, then reported back to her mother.

Her mother then told her to inform Mohnish Bhatti, while she rushed back home from work."

"So Mohnish Bhatti told them to file a missing complaint?"

"No, sir. Namita tried to get in touch with Bhatti but he was not reachable. Once her mother reached home at around 6.45 p.m., the two conferred and decided they must go to the police station," Tupe said. "They lodged the complaint at our Police Chowky around 7.20 p.m. They'd got a photo of Pranjal and his phone details. His mother told me she'd tried the phone numbers of all of Pranjal's friends and he was nowhere to be found."

"And did the mother and sister at all express the fear that Pranjal might've been kidnapped?" Saralkar asked.

"No, sir. Constable Dhanak took the complaint and he said both women didn't talk about possible kidnapping," Tupe said. "In fact, their biggest fear was Pranjal had met with an accident. That some vehicle knocked him down and he was injured or something."

"So when did they finally get in touch with the father?" PSI Motkar elbowed in.

"In fact, he called back after seeing the missed calls and text message from his daughter. Both women were at the police station at that time," Tupe replied. "They told Mohnish Bhatti everything. He was supposed to travel back two days later, but after hearing his son was missing, he frantically made efforts to get a flight back to Pune the same night. And then he got that ransom call just after boarding."

"Hmm . . . so you met the wife the first time when she returned to the Chowky again with her husband's message about the ransom call?" Saralkar asked.

"Yes, sir, the duty constable called around 11.10 p.m. saying Mrs. Bhatti was at the station again and that a ransom call had been received. So, I immediately went," ASI Tupe said. "Both mother and daughter were there and they told me how Mohnish Bhatti had received the ransom call and forwarded the number to Smita Bhatti just before his flight had taken off. We sprang into action to trace the number but . . . that turned out to be a big fiasco."

"Yes, Motkar narrated what happened. But looks like you haven't had much success in tracing the correct number either, Tupe?"

"No, sir," ASI Tupe admitted in a small voice.

"And now the boy is dead . . ." Saralkar said with undue harshness in Motkar's opinion, as if meant as a rebuke to Tupe.

It stung Tupe. "Yes, sir . . . but I swear we did all we could. We put all our efforts and almost all my manpower on the case, sir. We put the number on trace, we circulated the boy's photo and all details. We were fully prepared for the second ransom call, which we thought would come early morning. Unfortunately, it never came . . . Mohnish Bhatti tried calling the number a couple of times. We then made him send a text message . . . but nothing happened. Our constables went around Bavdhan locality and even Wakad, from where the call had been made, with the boy's photos, to check if anyone had seen the boy. We also made the photo viral on social media."

He paused and looked eagerly at Saralkar.

"Hmm. Did you probe the parents whether they suspected anyone of the deed—any enemies, any disputes, any recent incidents of concern?" Saralkar asked in a tone that sounded totally unimpressed by Tupe's efforts.

ASI Tupe shook his head. "We asked the family repeatedly, sir, but they were tight-lipped. Not very forthcoming."

"Did you get the feeling that they were hiding something?" PSI Motkar asked.

"They were scared out of their wits by the ransom call and quite understandably almost dazed and high strung," Tupe replied. "They were just waiting for the kidnapper's call but when it looked like the call wouldn't come, the husband and wife were gripped by terrible misgivings that going to the police had been a big mistake. They just went into a shell thereafter, refusing to say more, pleading with me to leave them alone—saying they should be allowed to deal privately with the kidnapper. They seemed to have gotten around to believing that he would get in touch only when the police were out of the picture and that they'd pay the ransom and get their son back. I tried to reason with the couple but . . . sir, you know how difficult it is to deal with people in such circumstances."

Saralkar nodded, then turned a thoughtful gaze into infinity. Tupe fidgeted as the senior inspector continued to weigh the facts he'd heard so far.

"Well," Saralkar finally spoke, "ASI Tupe, you now have the gut-wrenching task of telling the parents their son is dead, and worse, get them to identify his grotesque remains."

ASI Tupe flinched, his face going pale as if he'd thought that now that Saralkar and PSI Motkar were taking over the case, the task would be theirs. He looked at Motkar, then Saralkar, almost speechless.

"Once you do that, let Motkar know," Saralkar continued, then gestured to PSI Motkar. "Come, Motkar, now that I have thrown up my breakfast, I need to replenish it to get through the rest of the day."

He strode away as Motkar followed with a sympathetic nod to Tupe.

*****

Chapter 4

Three Weeks Ago

"Yes, Mr. and Mrs. Bhatti, what did you want to see me about?" Mrs. Zelam Kaul, principal of Bright Future School asked the couple seated in front of her.

Her tone was polite but her body language was impatient. Parents were tiresome creatures who needed to be tolerated but never indulged. She also gave a quick, stern smile to Pranjal, who of course was expected to continue standing.

"How are you, Pranjal? Preparing hard for the Nationals?" she asked in the most affectionate voice a principal was permitted to use by some unwritten norm. After all, the boy had made the school proud by qualifying from the district to represent the state in national level sub-junior chess championships and could potentially bring the school more glory.

"Yes, ma'am," Pranjal replied with a troubled smile.

"Good," Mrs. Kaul beamed, doling out sage advice, "but don't neglect your studies, okay?"

"Yes, ma'am," Pranjal repeated, knowing well that nothing more was expected or welcome from him.

His heart was beating hard. What was going to happen now, when his parents broached the topic they were here for?

Mrs. Kaul had moved her shrewd, patronising gaze back to his parents now. "Yes?" she prompted and glanced at her watch as if precious seconds were ticking by and she'd just set the stopwatch.

Smita Bhatti took the cue. "Actually, madam, we need some help," she began. "Pranjal . . . Pranjal is being regularly intimidated by an 8th class student and two of his friends . . ."

"Intimidated? Means what?" Mrs. Kaul snapped as if it was she who had been accused.

"The boy has threatened Pranjal several times and beaten him up twice," Smita replied nervously.

Mrs. Kaul's frown deepened. "Beaten up on the school premises? How come I haven't heard about it? We don't tolerate any such nonsense!" Her eyes darted in Pranjal's direction, scanning him intently.

"Not on the school premises, ma'am, just outside," Smita replied.

Mrs. Kaul seemed to relax as if it was suddenly a less serious matter. "I can't see any bruises or injuries on him. Are you sure it's not just a little fight between boys?"

Mohnish Bhatti who had been quiet so far, suddenly spoke, "Pranjal's been kicked and punched on his ribs and private parts, madam. Do you want to see it?"

There was a sharp challenge in his eyes and tone and Mrs. Kaul reacted as if she was the aggrieved party. "Not necessary. You don't have to be rude, Mr. Bhatti."

"I'm sorry, madam, I thought you were making light of it," Bhatti said and slid a paper across to her. "This is a medical certificate from our GP that gives all the details."

He gently looked at his son standing beside him and continued, "Turn around, Pranjal . . ." and as his son did so Bhatti turned to Mrs. Kaul. "And, ma'am, please see this injury on the back of his head. It required two stitches. Pranjal says the boy hit him with a small rock."

"Oh my God," Mrs. Zelam Kaul remarked, her face registering expressions other than haughtiness for the first time. "This is terrible. Who did this to you, Pranjal?"

Pranjal turned around to face her, then looked at his parents as if gathering courage. "Karan Khilare and two of his friends, Alok and Yash. They're all in 8th C, ma'am."

"I see. What happened? Why are they doing it?" the principal asked.

But before Pranjal could reply, Smita spoke, "Ma'am, he's beaten my Pranjal at least twice. In fact, that day he threatened to stab Pranjal in his legs with his compass divider. That boy Karan abuses Pranjal all the time and he's kicked him so hard . . . down there . . . it would've needed surgery the doctor said, had the boy hurt him even a little harder . . ."

Mrs. Kaul nodded. This was much more serious than normal scuffles and complaints. Complicated further by her sudden realization that the boy Karan Khilare was the son of a local corporator. It would need some careful handling.

"Please calm down, Mrs. Bhatti. Please don't worry . . . we'll get to the bottom of this matter," she said, then gestured to Pranjal. "Come here, Pranjal. Now tell me how all this started between you and those boys."

She patted him and put an arm around Pranjal as he moved closer towards her, "Tell me everything!"

Pranjal eyed his parents then spoke almost as if ashamed. "He . . . Karan . . . hates me because Tanya Gosavi is friends with me and is my bench partner in class. Karan says she's his girlfriend . . . and I should not sit with her or talk to her or share my tiffin with her."

"What?" the principal asked, aghast.

"I didn't do anything, ma'am. I told my class teacher, Sharayu ma'am, to change my place, but she didn't," Pranjal said helplessly. "Every time he passes the classroom and sees Tanya sitting next to me, talking to me or borrowing something from me, Karan threatens me during the break or after school. He said he'll kill me . . . if . . . if I sit next to his girlfriend—"

Pranjal suddenly broke down and began sniffling. His mother felt a lump rise in her throat and just managed to stop her own tears from flowing.

"No, no, Pranjal. Don't cry, beta . . ." Mrs. Zelam Kaul said, patting him. "We are going to take care of this problem. Don't cry . . . you are such a champion . . . we'll make sure Karan Khilare and his friends don't trouble you again."

"Ma'am, we've brought this written complaint about the boy to submit to you," Mohnish Bhatti said, gently sliding a printed letter across the table to the principal. "We think the boy needs to be punished for what he's done to Pranjal and the school should deal severely with him . . . rusticate him."

The principal's defence mechanism kicked in immediately. "Now, now, look here Mr. Bhatti. I am fully on your side, but this matter needs careful handling, so let's not make haste—"

"I don't understand, ma'am. My son has been brutally attacked by another student; he's been threatened in school, so . . ."

"I completely understand that, Mr. Bhatti. It's shocking, especially because Pranjal is such a sweet and talented boy. But there's no need to file a written complaint at this stage. You've told me everything so please be assured that strict action will be taken," Mrs. Kaul said, her eyes flashing as she tried to sound both authoritative and compassionate at the same time. "Let me first make enquiries . . . understand the other side—"

"Understand the other side?" Mohnish interjected, "What does that mean, ma'am? Look at the damage the boy and his friends have done to Pranjal. That boy needs to be in a juvenile prison, not in school!"

When cornered, the principal knew very well how to counter-attack and deal with parents. "Mr. Bhatti," she said in a raised voice, "are you going to tell me how to do my job? Believe me I have thirty years of experience as a teacher and school head. I know better than you how to deal with such matters."

"But, ma'am . . ." Mohnish started then fell quiet as his wife Smita's restraining hand clasped his.

"Ma'am," Smita said taking over, "we are worried about Pranjal's safety after this incident, because that boy is a corporator's son. That's why we want to submit a written complaint and put it on record."

"And what if that boy's father, the corporator, files a retaliatory complaint against Pranjal alleging he was the one who started the fights or abused Karan or something like that?" Mrs. Kaul countered. "That's why an official written complaint is a bad idea. It'll only complicate matters. Just have patience. Let me first try and resolve it informally. I am equally concerned about Pranjal's safety. He's a fine boy. He's made the school proud . . . but I have to think of several other aspects—the school's reputation, for example, and that it does not alarm other parents. Also, the other boy's record should not be spoilt."

Mohnish's frustration rose and he almost exploded. "Ma'am, what that boy did is a crime. And you are talking about this not spoiling his life. What about my boy?"

Mrs. Zelam Kaul had had enough. She drew herself up and played her final card. "Mr. Bhatti, if you think it's a crime then why don't you go and file a police complaint? Nobody's stopping you!"

She paused and let it sink in, looked at the parents, then continued, "I am talking to you as a well-wisher and principal—either you trust me or do what you want. Believe me, it's in everyone's interest to settle this amicably. It is not wise to make enemies of such people with political connections. That's certainly not going to protect Pranjal."

She gave the couple the gravest look possible and glanced at her watch again, as if done with them.

*****

"Why do restaurants provide a fork and spoon with paper dosa?" Saralkar observed as he dipped a morsel of his dosa into the chutney and tucked it into his mouth. "It's virtually impossible to eat paper dosa with a fork. Have never seen anyone do it successfully. It's so crunchy and thin . . ."

Motkar sipped his coffee and shook his head slightly, his thoughts still on the crime scene they'd left behind. How could his boss discuss food after what they'd just seen?

"This chutney is fabulous," Saralkar continued with relish. "I sometimes think I consume dosas only for the chutney. What about you, Motkar?"

It would be impolite to not reply, Motkar realized. He pulled his thoughts back and said, "I really like sambar more, sir."

Saralkar made a face. "Really? I am not much of a sambar man. God knows what all they put into it." He gave a little shudder. "And you can never tell how it turns out at different places—either too watery or too sour or too spicy . . . don't you think?"

"Yes, sir," Motkar replied, "but in this restaurant the sambar is usually pretty good."

"Okay, I'll try it," Saralkar conceded, then dipped the next dosa morsel into the sambar bowl and tasted it. "Not bad! You know they say sambar was originally a Maharashtrian dish that migrated to the south with the Marathas and became a hit . . . just like superstar Rajinikanth."

He guffawed at his own joke and it was infectious enough to make Motkar join in with a grudging smile. "Yes, I know, sir, Rajinikanth's ancestors were originally from Maharashtra. His real name is Shivaji Gaikwad, I think."

"Right, although I doubt, he even knows a word of Marathi," Saralkar added and chuckled again.

Motkar said nothing, just sipped his coffee. The sight of the dead boy had stirred something in him and he was really not in a mood for small talk. He was surprised that his usually grumpy and focused boss seemed cheerful though.

"Don't grudge me my paper dosa, Motkar," Saralkar said, as if reading his subordinate's thoughts. "My stomach turned quite literally on seeing the little boy's corpse."

"No, sir, nothing like that. I saw how badly it upset you," Motkar said, trying to dispel the notion that he was judging his boss.

"Hmmm . . . and yet you are wondering why I am yapping away like this, indifferent to the fate of that child," Saralkar asked, putting Motkar in a spot.

Motkar responded with a feeble, awkward, "No, sir . . ."

Saralkar was looking at him like a quiz-master, enjoying the discomfort of a contestant, struggling to answer. "Well, perhaps I am getting old, Motkar! Or I am undergoing a personality change?" Saralkar said reflectively, "So many years of agonising and thinking about crimes and criminals and their bestiality. I've come to the conclusion that brooding constantly does nothing. It's just injurious to health and it certainly isn't any good for my digestion to think about the very thing that just made me throw up while eating."

"I understand, sir," Motkar replied, then said with far more emotion than he ever showed. "Don't you think kidnapping a child and murdering him is the most depraved and foul crime in the world, sir?"

Saralkar finished his last morsel, then took a paper napkin and began wiping his fingers, nodding thoughtfully. "Yes, killing a child in cold blood requires a higher level of despicability than murdering an adult. Also, a total lack of ordinary compassion! The strange paradox is that it is physically easier to kill a child, but morally far more difficult."

Motkar clicked his tongue in agreement. "Would you like some coffee, sir?"

"Sure," Saralkar said. He hailed a waiter and ordered. "Do you know why I threw up today?"

Motkar raised his eyebrows, wondering what the appropriate response would be.

Saralkar continued without waiting for his reply. "I mean I have always been close to throwing up, each time I see a murdered corpse, but I have actually puked only on two occasions—once a long time ago and now today. You know why?"

Motkar was agog . . . eager to know what his boss was going to confide in him. "Tell me, sir . . ."

Saralkar shifted his gaze into some faraway distance.

"It's because when I was ten or eleven years old I was abducted and confined for about a day, and I guess I would have turned up dead like that poor boy Pranjal, if my kidnapper hadn't developed cold feet or if he had been vile enough to go through with it! It's as if I saw my body lying there today in place of Pranjal's."

Motkar gaped at his boss. "My God, sir . . . I had no idea!"

Saralkar gave him a wry, sober smile. "How would you? I haven't told anyone, not even Jyoti."

"Who was it, sir? Were you held for ransom?" Motkar asked, unable to curb his curiosity.

"Details some other time, Motkar!" Saralkar replied. "We have this crime to solve first. Catch the bastard who did this to Pranjal."

As if on cue, the waiter brought him his coffee. "Ah," said Saralkar, taking a sip, "but now that I have your attention, Motkar, let me tell you more about the Marathi origins of sambar. Do you know, there's a possibility it might have been named after Sambhaji, the older son of Shivaji Maharaj? Because it seems it was he who accidently stumbled on the recipe by adding tamarind to ordinary dal . . ."

*****

Chapter 5

Ten Days Ago

Namita's heart raced. Her entire being tingled with a scary, delicious anticipation.

They had kissed on four occasions before—from hesitant pecks to the passionate way they showed in films, clasped in each other's arms—their bodies electrified by that heady sensation, aching and yearning to go further, yet held back by strange inhibitions.

She could feel the restlessness of Rishabh's hands. They wanted to stray to places they had never been before. And she too wanted them to get there, but was it right? Was it too early? She knew many girls, many friends who had let it happen—gone much further—even all the way with their boyfriends.

So there wasn't anything wrong with it, was there? She was eighteen, an adult, and Rishabh wasn't really like any of the many cheap dudes she knew—guys who just wanted one thing.

Rishabh was nice—he made her laugh. He did not smoke or drink or take drugs. He was smart and cocky, pretty good in studies and sports.

"You know, Namita, you have the most luscious lips in the world," Rishabh said, looking at her steadily, his eyes roguish. "Just want to go on kissing you . . ."

"Me too . . ." Namita said, blushing, yet her eyes boldly inviting.

They were in her house, in her room, both parents safely away at work and her brother in school. They locked lips again and that magical sensation coursed through their bodies once more—Rishabh's hands fumbling, trying not to take liberties he desperately wanted to, lest she reproach him. When they ran out of breath, they unlocked their lips and their eyes locked, saying things to each other that they hesitated to put into words.

Then Rishabh's eyes moved down briefly and when he looked back into her eyes, there was a bolder desire in them. "Namita, can I . . . can I touch . . . your . . ." Rishabh said softly, his mouth dry.

Namita's pulse shot through the roof and she gave an imperceptible nod.

Rishabh took a deep breath and his hands reached out towards her soft, heaving mounds and gently squeezed. It was a sublime, heavenly moment in their young lives. He squeezed again, a little more firmly and they were soon kissing again, their hormones in overdrive.

"I . . . can I . . .? Namita, I want to . . . see them . . ." Rishabh suddenly said wistfully.

"No . . . no . . ." she replied, seized by coyness and apprehension.

"Why? Please, Namita . . . I love you . . . please . . . I want to see how beautiful you are. Don't you want to show me . . ." the boy said in a tone that was gentle and persuasive.

Namita looked away, befuddled by how much she herself wanted it to happen—to show herself to him—for him to look at them, touch them and adore her. "I want to . . . Rishabh . . . but . . . but I am scared . . ."

"Scared of what, Namita? Of me? Don't you trust me? I love you, no?" he said, eager and earnest.

He pulled her close and she yielded to his kisses and caresses. "Show me, please," he whispered softly again.

She bit her lips. Her heart and mind and body screamed to do what he was asking. She threw a glance at the wall clock. It was 12.25 p.m.—still half an hour to go before Pranjal came back from school.

"Please . . ." Rishabh said, now nuzzling her neck and fondling her with ardour.

"Okay . . ." she whispered at last, unable to resist his sweet pleadings and her own wish to dazzle him, to please him.

She gently pulled herself away. "Give me a minute," she said and disappeared into the bathroom—to compose herself and take a look before she presented herself to him.

Rishabh grappled with his own elation and excitement— at what he was about to experience. He was no less nervous than Namita. Walking across to the stereo, he selected a track line-up and switched on the music.

Was this really happening? He was as unprepared for it as she was. And then the bathroom door opened and she was standing before him, just looking as if trying to convey to him how much he meant to her—that she was going to do what she was about to. Then slowly, shyly, she slipped out of her top, making him gasp.

"Wow!" he said, soaking in the sight and the indescribable delight running through him.

She rushed towards Rishabh and hugged him, as if she didn't want him to see too much of her at once. Her bra was still on and she'd decided that this was as far as she was prepared to go that day.

He had begun kissing her with a crazed tenderness, then pulling away to feast his eyes on what he'd never seen before in person. The beat of the music added to the mood and he began to mumble, "I love you, Namita!"

And that was when they heard the tap on the door, immediately followed by the sound of the door opening. "Didi, I am back!" said Pranjal as he stepped in and was stunned by the sight in front of him. He froze, his eleven-year-old mind unable to process the situation. Then he sprang back out of the room guiltily as if it was all his fault.

The world came crashing down for Namita and Rishabh and she let out a horrified, little scream of shame and panic and ran inside the bathroom.

How had they not heard the main door open and close? The music—the damned music!

"Shit!" said Rishabh, "Shit, shit, shit!"

They were in big trouble—he and Namita—unless they found some way to make sure Pranjal didn't go off spilling the beans to his parents. "Shit!"

*****

Bavdhan had been a village once—one of the many situated on the outskirts of Pune city. Then as the city grew rapidly in the late 1990s, Bavdhan was merged into the city limits and transformed into a self-contained, attractive locality that was ringed by the Mumbai-Bangalore Expressway on one side and some of the city's most prestigious defence establishments on the other. A hillock running across one flank added to its beauty.

Bavdhan's proximity to the Hinjewadi IT Park made it a preferred residential location for many and the fact that it was in the city, yet away from its mad rush, gave it a certain ambience that differentiated it from the concrete jungles of Aundh and Baner.

The Bhattis lived in a 3BHK apartment on the fifth floor of C Building in a society comprising six such towers of seven floors each. There were 168 dwellings, half of which were 2BHK. The society was about five years old. It had two gardens, a gym, community hall, and a small swimming pool—a gated community like many others, with a name that didn't make much sense—Daffodils Regency—whatever that meant.

When Saralkar and Motkar drove in, ASI Tupe was waiting for them below Building C. Two police vehicles were parked nearby, and the entire society of around 700 residents seemed to have ceased all activity, as if hiding from the police.

"Yes, Tupe?" Saralkar asked the young PSI who appeared hassled and subdued.

"We had taken both parents with us, sir. The mother, Smita Bhatti, identified Pranjal's body but the father . . . Mohnish Bhatti says he's not convinced it's his son."

"Is there a genuine doubt about the identity or is it because he's had too much of a shock?" Motkar asked.

"I think it's just the shock, sir, because the mother is absolutely sure," Tupe replied. "She . . . She actually even identified the underwear Pranjal was wearing, the only piece of clothing he was found with. And she looked for a birthmark on the left side of his neck . . . and showed us a recent injury mark at the back of his head."

"Hmm . . . so it's the same boy, that's been confirmed," Saralkar said. "Did they say anything else? Any suspicions or any other information they'd held back so far?"

Tupe shook his head. "Not really, sir. The man was in no condition to talk and simply kept saying it's not his son . . . then went to pieces. And the woman wasn't in a state of mind to speak because most of her time was spent trying to handle her husband and stabilise him."

Saralkar nodded. "Any update on whether forensics found anything useful with the body? On the body?"

"No, sir. Do you think it would help if divers conducted an underwater search?" ASI Tupe asked tentatively.

"That's not the spot the boy was dropped. Probably the body was carried by the current . . . there's quite a bit of water in the river because of the monsoons," Saralkar observed.

"But it has been a rather dry spell for the whole of last week, sir, so water's not been released from the dams," PSI Motkar remarked. "It won't hurt if the divers take a look."

"Okay," Saralkar conceded, "get it done." Motkar had a point. Maybe the boy's bicycle had been dumped into the river along with his body. "Did you examine the CCTV footages of the roads leading towards or away from the location of Pranjal's coaching class, Tupe? Or for that matter of the main Bavdhan Road?"

"Sir, the team that was examining traffic CCTV footages of all main roads—Bavdhan–Pashan Road, Pashan–Sus Road and Baner–Pashan Road, as well as some of the arterial roads—have reported nothing helpful so far," Tupe said.

"Not even one sighting of Pranjal?" Saralkar asked. "Did you check at private shops, societies, and commercial buildings in the area? Someone's got to have CCTV footage that shows Pranjal stepping out of the class and the direction he took. Even along the way."

"No, sir," Tupe said. "The moment it became a kidnapping case after the ransom call, the focus of our investigation shifted to our informer network, picking up and grilling history sheeters . . . and we were sure the kidnapper would get in touch again, so we geared up for that."

Saralkar grunted. He couldn't really blame Tupe for the course of action he'd chosen. He'd probably consulted and been advised by the zone ACP. Policing was often about making an assessment and choosing where to deploy limited resources at hand, running against time. And very often, even the best of officers and their forces chose what seemed the most promising direction to take, while neglecting policing basics.

"But, Tupe, to trace someone shouldn't you first establish exactly what spot he disappeared from? Where was he last seen? Fortunately, it's possible to do so with technology, even though there is no guarantee you might find what you are looking for. But you've at least got to try and look for it!"

By Saralkar's standards it was a pretty mild rebuke, Motkar thought. It was almost gentle and yet ASI Tupe looked as if he'd been spanked.

"Yes, sir," he replied sheepishly, "I'll get on to it now. Still can't believe the boy was already dead, all the while we were searching for him."

In a surprising gesture, Saralkar gave the young PSI a pat on the shoulder. "It's good it's affected you in this way. A good police officer is one who turns the emotions one feels at a personal level into professional motivation."

The words visibly bucked the young officer up.

"Now, Motkar and I will talk to the parents and you can take down their statements on the basis of that," Saralkar said and gestured for Tupe to lead the way to the Bhatti house.

They took the lift to the fifth floor. The door of the Bhatti flat was half open, as if the family had wanted to shut it but had been requested to leave it open by the cops. The constable who was standing outside, saluted all three officers.

"Sir, the lady, Mrs. Bhatti was asking for you. She wanted to know when they are going to get their son's body for last rites," the constable informed Tupe. "I just told them it might take a day or two."

"Okay," Tupe said. "Anything else? Have some neighbours come to meet the family?" He pointed to two pairs of footwear at the door.

"An old couple, sir. Third floor neighbours. It seems the old man is a retired GP. Mrs. Bhatti called him to examine her husband," the constable replied.

Tupe looked at Saralkar and Motkar, as if for comments or instructions, then gave a soft rap on the half open door, opened it fully, and entered a typically over-decorated middle-class drawing room.

Seated on the sofa was a couple in their mid-sixties, probably the neighbours, and across them sat the Bhatti mother and daughter. The daughter had an arm around her mother, who was bravely trying not to break down, even as her body shuddered with sobs.

All of them looked in the direction of the police officers—a vague apprehension being the common factor in the expressions of all. Saralkar had seen that particular expression on a lot of faces—almost all middle-class folk reacted the same way to the police the first time—wariness and some nameless guilt.

The old couple actually stood up as if remaining seated in front of policemen might be construed an offence. It was almost an auto-reflex that Indians learnt at an early age. But it was fear, not respect, that was behind the reflex and so hardly a compliment.

"Hullo . . . I'm . . . I'm Dr. Nisal," the old man introduced himself. "This is my wife, Madhuri. We live on the third floor."

"Hullo, doctor," Saralkar said, even before Tupe could speak. "The constable outside tells us Mr. Bhatti is not feeling well."

"Yes, Smita called me because Mohnish was dizzy, then he vomited. He has a history of hypertension . . . and when I examined him, I found his BP had shot up to alarming levels. It was 190/130 a little while ago. I have given him a sedative but he may need to be hospitalized if it remains high," Dr. Nisal said. "He needs to be put on IV fluids, if the BP doesn't drop soon. I think the shock has been too much for him to bear."

"I see," Saralkar said, then turned to Smita Bhatti and her daughter with an appraising look.

Mrs. Bhatti was a woman with striking features over which the patina of dignified grief now hung. She had the kind of prettiness that deepened with age, attenuated by her splendid light-coloured eyes. Her whole demeanour was that of a person who knew she had to stay strong, yet wasn't sure how long she could. Saralkar could see a little resemblance to her dead son, mainly the colour of his eyes.

Her daughter Namita had inherited most of her mother's pretty features but her eyes were clearly different—perhaps like her father's. And she had acquired her mother's poise. Her eyes wouldn't meet Saralkar's when he looked at her but he could sense them on him when he wasn't looking. And there was a little more wariness in them than normal, which was odd.

"Mrs. Bhatti, this is Senior Inspector Saralkar and PSI Motkar," ASI Tupe said. "They need to talk to you."

She nodded and then asked, "Have you handled many such cases before, Inspector Saralkar?"

He hadn't expected her to begin the conversation on her own and certainly not with this question.

"Yes," he replied.

"Cases in which a kid is kidnapped and killed?" Smita Bhatti spoke again.

That was a harder question to answer. "Yes, a few cases," Saralkar replied, keeping it brief.

"Do . . . Do all kidnapped children end up dead?" Mrs. Bhatti asked, a lump rising in her throat, "Like . . . my Pranjal?"

"Many do . . . but not all."

"So was my child killed because I filed a police complaint? And the kidnapper . . . panicked?"

"No, approaching the police was the right thing to do, Mrs. Bhatti."

"My son got killed . . . then how was it the right thing to do?" Smita asked sharply, all her grief loaded into anger.

"Mrs. Bhatti, how do you know the kidnapper wouldn't have done it even if you hadn't informed the police?" Saralkar said. "I know of many cases where people paid the ransom and yet the kidnappers didn't spare the child. On the other hand, there are other cases where the kidnappers developed cold feet the moment they knew the police were looking for them and released the child without collecting ransom, without doing any harm."

"You think any of this is of comfort to me, Inspector?" Smita snapped.

"No, Mrs. Bhatti . . . Pranjal has left this world and nothing we say or do is going to bring him back," Saralkar replied without flinching. "But what we can definitely do is to hunt down the persons who committed this crime."

"Can you?"

"Yes, Mrs. Bhatti, we will!"

"How soon?" Mrs. Bhatti continued relentlessly.

Saralkar felt momentarily stumped and he searched for an answer that would be hard to challenge. "I don't have an answer to that question yet, Mrs. Bhatti," he replied cautiously.

Something about the tone and manner of his reply, softened her attitude. She regarded him for a few seconds. "Will you promise to not give up till you find my child's murderer, Inspector Saralkar?"

It was an assurance which no police officer could give. There were so many unsolved cases. Motkar wondered what his boss's reply would be.

"Yes, we will not leave the case unsolved," Saralkar said and Motkar eyed him with concern. He'd never seen his boss allow himself to be put in a position like that by the family of a victim.

Had it got something to do with the fact that the victim was a child and the mother a woman of compelling personality? And she was not done yet.

"And when you catch him, can you shoot him to death on the spot in an encounter?"

All the people in the room, including Smita's daughter, gave her a startled look. All three police officers were thoroughly taken aback.

"No, Mrs. Bhatti," Saralkar replied with bite, "that's not how things are done."

"Why not? He killed my son mercilessly. Why should he be allowed to live?" Mrs. Bhatti demanded. "Didn't the Telangana Police shoot rapists dead two years ago? Don't the UP Police encounter criminals all the time? Then why don't you do it?"

Her eyes flashed at the policemen as if accusing them of being wimps.

Saralkar decided it was time to stop indulging her. "Mrs. Bhatti, I don't specialise in instant justice," he said firmly. "This discussion needs to focus on information that will help us crack the case. So let's do that. I need to talk to your daughter first because she's the last person who was with Pranjal that day before he left the house."

Before her mother could react, Saralkar turned to the daughter and spoke, "Your name is Namita, right?"

The girl was gazing at him wide-eyed as if frightened out of her wits. She blinked nervously, glanced at her mother as if seeking her permission or protection.

Her mother immediately rallied forth. "Why does Namita need to be questioned? She's already narrated everything when we first filed the complaint that evening at the Bavdhan Police Chowky."

PSI Motkar realized now was the right time to step in. "It always helps to go over the same ground again, in case she remembers something which slipped her mind earlier," he interjected softly, then without waiting for any response turned to the girl and said, "Namita, you study in MIT College of Arts & Commerce, don't you?"

Saralkar felt grateful to Motkar as Namita nodded. "Yes," she said, as if it took a big effort for her to open her mouth.

"Which year?" Motkar continued.

"F.Y. BBA."

"Which division?"

"C."

"And what are your usual college timings?"

"8.00 a.m. to 11.30 a.m.," Namita said, finally making

the transition from monosyllabic replies. She looked ill at ease.

"And do you attend lectures regularly?"

"Yes," Namita replied a little too quickly.

She probably didn't go to college to attend lectures, but just to pass the time with friends, Motkar surmised. "How do you commute to and from college?"

"I've got an Activa."

"You have a permanent driving license?" PSI Motkar asked.

"Yes," she again replied extra quickly and glanced at her mother.

"Are you sure or do you have a learner's license still?"

"Learner's," she admitted in a small voice.

"So, what time did you get back home that day?"

"Around 12.30 p.m."

"Had you gone elsewhere after college before returning home?" Motkar asked.

The girl's pupils dilated a little, then she replied sullenly, "Yes, I went to a café with some friends after college."

Another lie, Motkar noted. Harmless lies, but he now had an idea of her expressions and body language when she lied as distinct from when she told the truth. Her mother was watching the exchange hawk-eyed.

"And when did Pranjal return from school?"

"At the usual time—1.00 p.m."

"And how was he? In a normal mood or what?" PSI Motkar probed.

"Yes."

"Does he have a separate key?" Motkar asked.

Something leapt into her eyes, as if she felt suddenly jumpy. "Yes," she replied.

Saralkar, who had been watching quietly, got a feeling that there was an undercurrent of unhappiness in her reply, as if the matter had been a bone of contention.

"Did you have lunch together?"

"Of course." Again, that double-quick reply and an away look, Motkar noticed. The reply was probably for her mother's benefit that she had played the role of the elder sister. "I heated up everything in the microwave and we had lunch."

"Did you talk about anything particular during lunch?"

"No. He was watching TV," Namita replied and even though it sounded perfectly factual and natural, Saralkar again got the feeling she was being economical with the truth. He wasn't sure why yet, but simply because his senses had developed into lie-detectors.

Motkar continued, "What time did he leave for class?"

"Around a quarter to three," Namita said.

"Does he always go to class on his bicycle?" Motkar asked and immediately kicked himself for the use of "does he". He wondered if he should correct himself but desisted, for he noticed the mother and daughter exchange a tense glance.

It was the mother who answered. "Namita was supposed to drop Pranjal and pick him up every day, but it didn't work out," Smita said in a voice that hovered between indicting and protecting her daughter. "All this would never have happened if she had . . ."

She threw a scorching glance at her daughter, who appeared to wilt under the gaze. She hung her head in shame.

Motkar looked at his boss, then let a few beats pass. But before he could carry on, Smita landed a slap across her daughter's face, out of the blue. It wasn't a very hard slap since she was sitting beside her daughter. It was more like a clip, but it was the suddenness of it that caught them unawares.

"Mrs. Bhatti!" Saralkar reacted sharply as Namita looked at her mother, stung and humiliated, then burst into tears.

"My Pranjal would've been alive if my daughter hadn't stubbornly shirked the responsibility of dropping him to class!" Mrs. Bhatti burst out, got up, and strode away into an inside room.

For a second, Saralkar thought the daughter might rush away too, seeking refuge in her room. But she didn't. She remained seated, forlorn but defiant, wiping her tears frequently.

Saralkar glanced in the direction of Dr. Nisal's wife and gestured for help, for the lady to comfort Namita. The doctor's wife obliged, shifting over and sitting beside the girl, gently putting her arm around her.

"Mummy doesn't mean it, okay, beta? She's just beside herself with grief. Don't take it to heart Namita . . ." the old lady consoled.

Namita's face scrunched up again, the tears continuing to flow. "No, Mum hates me. She hates that I was ever born."

"No, no, beta . . . no . . ." the doctor's wife said.

Saralkar signalled to Motkar to continue with his questions. PSI Motkar cleared his throat. "Namita, can we ask you a few more questions? Are you in a frame of mind to answer?"

The girl sniffed but did not reply. More importantly, she had not refused.

"You said Pranjal left for class around 2.45 p.m. Did you see him leave?" Motkar asked.

Namita shook her head. "I heard the door open and shut. I was in my room."

"I see. But then in the description given in the police complaint, you have mentioned the clothes he was wearing. How come?"

A look of sheer panic fleeted across the girl's face as if she'd been caught fudging something. She glanced at the policemen, then down again. It was an odd reaction for a minor detail.

"Perhaps you came out to get something before he left and saw Pranjal in the clothes," Motkar suggested gently.

"Yes . . . I think that's how I knew," she replied, no longer tongue-tied.

"So, after Pranjal left, were you at home all along?" PSI Motkar asked.

"Yes."

"All alone?"

Again, that quiver of panic passed over her face. "Yes, of course," Namita replied, as if unsure she'd be believed.

"What were you doing?" PSI Motkar asked.

There was a pause before she said, "I . . . I slept for some time . . . then did a project we were to submit at college the next day."

There was the lie again. Saralkar knew teenagers were a cagey lot, with many innocent and not so innocent reasons for lying.

"Okay, and what time would Pranjal usually get back from class?" Motkar asked.

"Around 4.45 – 5 p.m."

"Weren't you worried when he got delayed?"

Namita shrugged. "Not really. My mother called around 5.30 p.m. saying his phone was not reachable. I thought he must be down below in the society, chatting with someone. It's only when he didn't show up till 6.00 p.m. that I called my mother again and went out to look for him."

"Then?"

"I searched for him in the society but couldn't find him anywhere, so then my mother told me to call up . . . my . . .

my . . . father . . ." she said. There was something about her tone that Saralkar could not put his finger on, but again he got vibes that suggested there were many undercurrents to this family that needed to be probed.

"But your father's mobile was not reachable?"

"Yes, I tried several times—six to seven times—then sent him a message to call back urgently as Mum had instructed," Namita replied. "And when Mum reached home, both of us went to Bavdhan Police Chowky."

A tap sounded on the front door and two men in white uniforms walked in. "Sir, ambulance—Dr. Nisal had called . . ." one of them said.

Dr. Nisal immediately scrambled to his feet and looked at Saralkar. "I'll just check Mohnish's BP and if it's still high, we'll have to shift him to a nearby nursing home."

Saralkar nodded, then turned to Namita and said, "Thank you, Namita. We'll speak to you again if we have any more questions."

*****

Chapter 6

Seven Months Earlier (January 2022)

"Smita madam, I have admitted it was my mistake . . . it won't happen again I swear . . ." Jayesh Pardeshi pleaded. His hard, swarthy, bearded face showed desperation rather than regret.

He had never been anything but polite to her, ever since Smita Bhatti, as Admin head had retained the services of his two cabs for regular pick-up and drop for company employees. In all, her company had employed thirty cabs for employee transport arrangements, of which Jayesh and his brother Jayant ran one each.

There had been no complaints for almost a year and then suddenly two days earlier a young woman employee informed her about an unpleasant experience with Jayesh.

"The complaint against you is much too serious to be sorted out with an apology and assurances that it won't happen again," she remarked. "You were drunk and offensive, Jayesh . . ."

"I wasn't offensive, Smita Madam, I swear! The girl is lying. I was just slightly drunk . . . and did not like the way she talked to me."

"How do you expect someone to react when they find you are drunk?" Smita Bhatti said. "All she said to you was that you should be ashamed of being drunk on duty."

"It wasn't as if I was driving dangerously or had caused an accident," Jayesh Pardeshi said, scowling, clenching his teeth. "Her tone was really insulting. And then she used that word 'arsehole' twice—once after giving me a tongue-lashing and then when she called you up."

Smita shook her head. "Jayesh, there's no point arguing about this. The company has a zero-tolerance policy for drinking and bad behaviour by hired cab service drivers. I am sorry, we are terminating your services with immediate effect."

Jayesh Pardeshi's face turned totally abject. "Please, Smita madam . . . please don't do that. Times are bad . . . it'll be a big loss for me. And why both cabs? There has been no complaint against my brother . . . please at least let his cab continue, please . . ."

He was almost grovelling and the proud face now had expressions that begged for a little kindness, leniency, and consideration.

Smita didn't want to continue this conversation. She hated having to be the one to deprive people of their livelihoods in this way. It was an inevitable part of her job as an Admin person, to deal with individuals and agencies hired for different types of tasks—housekeeping, transport, maintenance, security—most of which included that class of people for whom dismissal and termination meant an unaffordable loss of employment and income.

"I can't do anything, Jayesh. Both the vehicles are in your name. You have no one to blame but yourself," she said, a little more dismissively than she wanted to.

Jayesh Pardeshi's visage now took on an angry, aggrieved hue. "There was an incident two months ago with another cab driver, Thomas. He was not removed, then why a different rule for my cab?"

"That was a different matter, Jayesh. Don't make wrong comparisons. Thomas was not drunk, like you were."

"But he misbehaved and abused . . ." Jayesh insisted.

"No, he did not abuse. There was a bit of an argument with a male employee for being late," Smita said, now annoyed. "I think you should go now. The decision has been made. It won't change."

"I suppose that cab service owner must have bribed you with something, to let him off with a reprimand," Jayesh Pardeshi said with belligerence. "Tell me how much I should pay you, Smita madam . . . I can do it too."

"How dare you? Get out!" The words were out of Smita's mouth before she knew it. Her light eyes were flashing. The sympathy and guilt she had felt for Jayesh Pardeshi till just a few minutes before, were now replaced by detestation. "You have the temerity to allege I take bribes and offer me money? Leave immediately or I'll have the security throw you out."

Her voice was raised and some of her other colleagues in the department had also turned to look in her direction. Jayesh Pardeshi's face had reddened with anger and his eyes glared at her with fury. He stood up from the chair, his eyes never leaving hers.

"I'll show both you and that girl," he hissed. "You educated folk think you can talk to us and treat us any way you want. You think we cannot hurt you or hit back, right? Just you wait and watch."

His tone and look sent a chill through her, but before she could respond, Jayesh Pardeshi left her cubicle and strode out of the department.

*****

"Do you have any idea who might've wanted to harm Pranjal, Mrs. Bhatti?" Saralkar asked bluntly.

The ambulance had departed, taking Mohnish Bhatti, accompanied by Dr. Nisal. Motkar had gone with them. Saralkar had dissuaded Mrs. Bhatti from going to the nursing home insisting it was more important for her to first answer his questions. Tupe had been dispatched to conduct a thorough search of the society, interrogate the watchmen and other staff, and gather all footage of all CCTV cameras in the premises.

Smita Bhatti appeared to have fallen into a sullen daze. "Your Inspector Tupe had asked me this question earlier too. Do you think the person who took my son was known to us?"

"Yes, that is a strong possibility. If it was a kidnapping motivated only by money, the ransom demand would have been higher. Also, the kidnappers made no attempt to contact you again—to demand or collect ransom, which is strange," Saralkar replied.

She gazed silently at him as if trying to digest what he'd said. "So, you are saying, it wasn't some hardened habitual criminal or gang who kidnapped and killed Pranjal, but some acquaintance of ours . . .?"

"Yes, the likelihood of it not being a stranger is high."

"Because this person bore a grudge against us? He . . . He killed my Pranjal out of spite?" Smita said, her eyes glowing with unshed tears.

"That is exactly what I am asking you. Can you think of anyone who bore you any ill will? Were there any incidents that created some kind of enmity with someone?"

One tear rolled down Smita's cheek. She was silent, her face twitching with emotions and raging thoughts.

"It might be some fallout or conflict . . . even a minor matter that flared up. Recently—or may be even in the last year or two?" Saralkar prompted.

Smita drew in a deep breath and then wept quietly for a minute or two. "There are only two incidents that . . . that come to my mind," she replied finally, composing herself.

And she proceeded to tell him about Jayesh Pardeshi and Karan Khilare. Saralkar listened without interrupting her. When she was done, he said, "Let's start with the Khilare incident at Pranjal's school. You are saying the principal simply called you up a few days later and said Karan Khilare and his friends won't trouble your son any longer. That's it? She didn't inform you what disciplinary action she had taken against the boy or any other details about how the matter had been dealt with?"

"No . . . Mrs. Kaul just said she had done whatever was necessary in the best interests and safety of Pranjal," Smita said. "We asked her to elaborate on what had transpired, to let us come and meet her so that we could be assured. But she refused and kept saying we should trust her word and that the action taken was confidential."

"I see. And did Pranjal tell you if the boys bothered him again?"

"No . . . they didn't touch or hit him again. That I am sure of, but he was fearful," Smita said. "He asked me if we could change his school. I promised him we would do it once the academic year was over."

She stopped and held back the sob that threatened to overpower her. Saralkar let a few moments pass. "Did Pranjal or you ever get any direct or oblique threat, about this matter? Did Corporator Satish Khilare, that boy's father or anyone else, try and get in touch and intimidate any of you?" he asked.

She shook her head. "No . . . but if the corporator has anything to do with Pranjal's fate . . . I swear I'll kill his boy too."

Once again, she had managed to startle Saralkar with her quiet vehemence.

"Mrs. Bhatti, we will investigate this angle and get to the bottom of it, if there is any involvement of the corporator," Saralkar said.

"Will you really? Or will you try and hush up the matter if the corporator is involved? Aren't you cops in bed with these political thugs?" she remarked, her eyes boring into him.

He couldn't blame her. She was only saying aloud what most people thought of the state of affairs—the corrupt cop-politician nexus.

"Fortunately, there are still enough cops around who are not rotten," he replied. "Anyway, do you have a copy of your complaint letter to the school and the doctor's certificate about Pranjal's injury?"

She nodded. "Yes, I'll give them to you."

"Okay. Is there anything else, any observation, any other detail you wish to add, about this matter?"

She thought hard then said, "No . . . I just wonder what would've happened if we'd gone straight to the police instead of to the school. Would they have taken cognisance?"

Saralkar too wondered, knowing the unpredictability of reality. Almost always, unless the crime was too serious to ignore the first reaction of cops was to stop anyone from filing a complaint, especially an FIR.

"They would have to," Saralkar asserted. "Assaulting a minor is a cognisable offence, but the only hitch is Karan Khilare too is a minor, so he would also be treated as a juvenile offender. He wouldn't have been taken into custody or arrested, but he would just be booked."

"In short, nothing much would've happened. The boy would've just got a gentle reprimand, right?"

Saralkar did not react. That was the law of the land—punishments for juveniles, even for heinous offences were mild. "Coming to the driver Jayesh Pardeshi, why didn't you or your company file a police complaint against him for the threats he made?" he asked.

Smita shrugged. "Who wants to get involved in police cases? My company asked the employee who had complained against Jayesh, Abha Das, and me whether we felt it was worth taking all the trouble. Although I was a little uneasy at the way Jayesh had behaved and spoken to me, I thought it had just been in the heat of the moment."

"Hmm, so you first realized Jayesh meant to act on his threats when Abha Das reported a few weeks later that he had stalked her a few times and had made threatening calls?" Saralkar asked.

"Yes . . . the girl had a few really scary experiences when she noticed him watching and following her. And then in one phone call, as I said, Jayesh allegedly threatened to throw acid on her face," Smita paused and gave a little shudder. "It's around the same time that this peon working in my company, Swapnil Shirke, came and told me to be very careful because Jayesh was a dangerous guy with some assault cases against him."

"You said Swapnil had heard Jayesh making threats against you, while he was drunk? What exactly had Swapnil heard?"

"Swapnil lived in the same tenement as Jayesh and a mutual friend told Swapnil that Jayesh said he would teach me a lesson too."

"Did he happen to say how? Was he specific in any way?" Saralkar asked.

"No . . . Swapnil was evasive. He said he didn't want to repeat the kind of things Jayesh had told his friend and the language he had used. He just wanted to warn me to be careful."

Saralkar guessed it probably meant the peon had heard some kind of sexually explicit threats being made against Smita or something equally heinous.

"Still, you and your colleague Abha didn't feel like asking your company to file a formal police complaint?"

Smita sighed. "I forgot to tell you, Abha quit the company and went back to her home town. I don't know if that was due to the stalking or because she got another job. But then I just gave up the idea of filing any police complaint. Unlike Abha, Jayesh had never stalked or called me and threatened since the incident, so on what basis could I complain?"

Saralkar nodded. It was all so relatable. People in this great country had no reason to consider the police as friends, as allies, as protectors. Seventy-five years after independence. Citizens thought they'd be shooed away or ridiculed or not taken seriously—particularly women—let alone helped. Perhaps it wasn't completely true but that was the general perception and lived experience most citizens faced. So, unless the crime was really serious, people avoided going to the police.

"Has anything else happened afterwards that makes you think Jayesh could be involved in some way? Did he know Pranjal or had they met any time?"

"Yes, he knew Pranjal and Pranjal had met him, when Jayesh came to pick up or drop me sometimes. I had also taken Pranjal with me for some Family Day functions at office."

Smita paused, then cleared her throat and said, "And . . . And I also saw Jayesh last week near our house. Pranjal and I were walking back from the market, when I spotted him sitting in a car, looking at us as if watching. When he realized I had seen him, he quickly drove away."

Saralkar's eyes narrowed. Coincidences like these were part of life but when it came to crime, every such coincidence needed to be probed closely, because it was too close for comfort. "Are you sure it was Jayesh?"

"Yes, I am."

"Did you spot his car number or make?"

She gave a wan mile. "It was the same old cab of his, with the same registration number. I have all the details."

She stood up and walked into an inside room.

Saralkar took the opportunity to look around the drawing room. Every house had an atmosphere and a personality. This house emanated an atmosphere of sadness and tension, camouflaged underneath the personality defined by the old-fashioned descriptor—'tip-top'. Or was it just because tragedy had suddenly descended upon the house that he was sensing melancholic interpretations in the ambience that didn't actually exist?

Smita was back in a few minutes and handed over a few papers to Saralkar. "These are the copies of the school complaint and the doctor's certificate for Pranjal's injuries," she said efficiently. "And these are details of Jayesh Pardeshi and his car."

She had neatly scribbled down Pardeshi's mobile number, address, and his vehicle registration number on a sheet of paper.

"Thank you, Mrs. Bhatti," Saralkar said. "And you are sure no one else you know, could have had any reason to hold a grudge against you . . . or seek revenge?"

There was the briefest of pauses before Smita shook her head and looked away. Saralkar wondered if he had imagined her fraction-of-a-second hesitation or had it just been the natural inhibition of a person not given to making unsubstantiated allegations. Of course, she had shown herself to be feisty, so why would she hold back if she had any suspicions of anyone else?

Still Saralkar decided to press on. "It could even be a member of your family or friends circle," he said, trying to provoke a reaction.

Smita didn't glance or frown or even acknowledge what he'd said.

"Who all do you have in your family, both on your side and your husband's?" Saralkar persisted.

A beat passed, then Smita said, "No one's here. When can we perform the last rites on . . . on Pranjal? How long will the post mortem take?"

Saralkar wondered whether she had asked the question because it was on the top of her mind or to deflect discussion on the topic from family. There were many reasons why people felt uncomfortable talking about even the worst conflicts within their family, as if the family was some kind of secret society, sworn to silence. Or maybe because no one was prepared to believe the worst of even the blackest sheep in their families. Or perhaps because they felt it was simply no one else's business.

Saralkar decided now was not the time to press her further, no matter how tempting the prospect of unearthing even a single worm if not a can. As if to signify this round with Smita needed to end, Saralkar's mobile rang. He glanced at the screen and saw it was Motkar calling.

"We won't make you wait any longer than absolutely necessary, Mrs. Bhatti," he answered the question she'd asked and then moved away out of the drawing room into the corridor, to take Motkar's call.

"Yes, Motkar!"

"Sir, Mohnish Bhatti is in a bad shape. He is in no condition to talk and so doctors told me it would be advisable not to question him for another twenty-four hours," Motkar said. "Before that I did ask him a few cursory questions but the man seems shattered. His son's death has hit him very hard."

"I see. Get back here then. I'll be with Tupe downstairs," Saralkar said and cut the call.

He was about to instruct the constable posted outside the flat and head down when he heard Smita address him.

"Inspector . . . they wouldn't tell me how my son died . . . how he met his death. Can you?"

Saralkar knew there was no point in falling back on the cliché of post mortem. Before he could formulate his response, Smita had asked her next question. "I want to know details. You don't have to spare my feelings. Was Pranjal strangled? How much time would it have taken him to die? How much would he have suffered?" she asked him with vehement defiance. "I want to know!"

"No, he wasn't strangled," Saralkar replied. "Look, Mrs. Bhatti, I . . . I don't know the answer to all your questions yet. All I can tell you is that prima facie, it seems Pranjal's death was due to drowning."

"Drowning? But Pranjal knew how to swim. He had learnt swimming . . . he loved swimming! How could he have drowned?"

"Swimming in a pool is different than . . ."

She wasn't really listening and interrupted him again. "Are you saying he was just thrown into the river by the kidnapper and . . . and he drowned?"

That was the problem in giving information that was incomplete. Saralkar grunted inwardly. "We are not sure of that; the post mortem will give us the complete picture of how exactly his death came about."

She stared at him, blinking indignantly, as if trying to work out if he was keeping something from her. "How much time does it take for a child his age to drown and die?"

Saralkar's heart skipped a beat. He hated this. "Between three and five minutes for children . . . very rarely does it take longer."

"So, my child could have suffered for five long minutes . . . 300 seconds . . . 300 counts . . .!"

Saralkar's mouth was too dry to try and console her that Pranjal might already have lost consciousness within two minutes. It almost felt nauseating to split hair like that.

"And the many moments of terror before that . . ." Smita muttered below her breath, then turned around and went inside her house.

Not all his years on the job had helped Saralkar understand what to say in the face of such anger and grief.

*****

Chapter 7

Namita's mobile buzzed as she sat on the bench in the waiting area of the hospital. 'Y r u not taking my call?' read the text from Rishabh. Another one followed. 'Is everything ok?'

She had cut his call thrice since morning—the first time when the police had come home to fetch her parents for identifying Pranjal's body; the second time when she was answering the senior cop Saralkar's terrifying questions; the third time while engaged in getting Mohnish Bhatti admitted to the hospital.

Namita was too disoriented to even text back right now. Ever since the day Pranjal had walked in on her and Rishabh, her life had been thrown into turmoil—her mind fearful and feverish—hating herself, hating Rishabh, hating Pranjal for what had happened. Guilt and shame and rage and self-pity! And beside herself at the thought that Pranjal would tell their mother, riddled by the anxiety that there was no way she could prevent him from doing so.

In her paranoia, she had refused to talk, chat, or meet Rishabh for a few days, even as he kept trying to get in touch. When Namita had finally relented, Rishabh had assured her he knew how exactly to deal with Pranjal and that she shouldn't worry.

`Say something!'` another text from Rishabh pinged on her phone followed by more. `What's happening? Can I call?'`

He'd probably seen the blue ticks of her having read the messages, so her phone began to ring almost immediately. Namita cut the call once again.

`Later.'` She texted cryptically or Rishabh would keep texting and calling. She didn't want to talk to him. She cursed her luck. Why, oh, why had she agreed to take the risk? Why hadn't she told Rishabh to just lay off?

*****

"Sir, it's baffling but there is no footage of Pranjal leaving the society on his bicycle by the front gate that day," ASI Tupe said to Saralkar.

They were in the society office with the manager, Deepak Manjule, a short, balding, fidgety man in his forties with a pinched, alarmed look on his face. He was constantly shifting his weight from one foot to the other, as if that was the only way he could cope up with stress in life.

"I ran through the footage from about 2.00 p.m. onward till 4.00 p.m. on Manjule's society computer here . . ." Tupe continued. "So unless the timing mentioned by the sister is wrong, Pranjal didn't leave that way."

Saralkar cast a glance at Manjule and the man seemed to shrink as if he was somehow personally responsible for Pranjal not being seen in the CCTV footage. "Does the society have a back gate?" Saralkar asked.

"No, sir," Manjule croaked, "but there is a small side-gate, which opens into a small lane . . ."

He stuttered to a halt. Saralkar looked at Tupe questioningly.

"The side-gate is not for vehicles, sir," Tupe explained. "It is mostly used by maid-servants and even by some residents as a shortcut to and from nearby societies."

"Can a bicycle pass through it?"

"Yes, saheb . . ." Manjule replied. "We keep it open till about 5.00 p.m. and then it's locked."

"Have you checked it out, Tupe?"

"Yes, sir . . . it's possible that Pranjal went from that gate, but there's no reason for him to have done that."

"Is there a CCTV camera by that gate?"

Manjule seemed to break out into a sweat and gulped. "It's . . . It's not been functioning, sir . . . I'm sorry."

"Since when?" Saralkar asked.

"Two months, sir."

"So why hasn't the CCTV been repaired or replaced?"

"I had informed Secretary saheb," Manjule replied, "but . . ."

It was all so typically Indian—perhaps apathy, perhaps lethargy, perhaps passing the buck or possibly lack of funds or approval. That was the general attitude everyone lived with.

"I spoke to the watchmen too, sir . . . usually there is one watchman who's also supposed to keep an eye on the side-gate," Tupe said, "but unfortunately he'd left his post for a while between 3.00 and 4.00 p.m. that day, because he'd been summoned by Manjule to do some other task."

"I . . . I had sent him out to fetch some photocopies, saheb . . . and a few bulbs for common areas," Manjule confessed, in a "caught red-handed" tone.

"So, we have no way of knowing for sure whether Pranjal exited from the side-gate too!" Saralkar observed vexedly. "Are you sure there's no section of the front-gate that is not covered by the CCTV, due to the placement or positioning?"

"No, sir. Here, please have a look," Tupe said and clicked on the computer to show Saralkar the view of the front-gate camera.

"Hmm . . . and the watchman on duty is sure he didn't see Pranjal leave with or without his bicycle?" Saralkar asked, as Motkar also entered the society office and joined them.

"Sir, he distinctly remembers Pranjal returning from school that afternoon around 1.00 p.m.," Tupe said. "In fact I have seen the footage too. But the watchman is not confident enough to state with absolute certainty that Pranjal didn't leave on his bicycle at around 3.00 p.m."

"Why?"

"Because he says he was a little unwell that day and might have dozed off for a few minutes a couple of times, that afternoon," Tupe replied.

Again, as Indian as it could get. Poorly paid, ten- or twelve-hour shifts, little leave, sitting or standing in the open or inside a hot, matchbox-size cabin—who could blame watchmen for dozing off? And like all Indians, they too had their share of duty dereliction DNA in their blood.

"I see . . . Tupe, Motkar, we need to solve this puzzle first," Saralkar said then turned to the diminutive manager, "Manjule, I need an updated list of all residents of the society—names, flat numbers, owner or tenant, and their phone numbers. Right away!"

Manjule appeared ready to faint with panic. "Saheb . . . I . . . I . . . don't have a list. We . . . We lost a lot of data when the computer crashed a month ago."

"What? You don't have a back-up?" Saralkar growled wearily.

Manjule did his favourite swallowing act, probably convinced he would be the first person of interest to be jailed in the case. "Secretary saheb . . . is looking into it, sir . . . I don't know much about computers. And because so many other problems were created because we lost data . . . I've still not got around to updating the resident list yet."

The expression on Manjule's face was such that Saralkar half expected him to fall at his feet, any moment. What was the point in blaming the poor wretch?

"I don't know how you do it, but I want a list of residents—owners and tenants - in the next two hours, Manjule," he said nevertheless, then turned to Motkar, "Motkar, speak to the goddamn secretary or chairman of the society and get this done."

Motkar nodded.

"And Tupe, get more men and go door to door to check if anyone saw Pranjal leave by the side-gate that afternoon. Somebody's got to have been around or standing by their windows or in their balconies. Also, talk to all the maid-servants and society staff—sweepers, gardeners—anyone who might have been around and seen the boy exiting . . ." Saralkar ordered then stepped out of the office to take another look at the overall layout of the society.

All the buildings stood on one side, along the main avenue of the society, which was tree-lined and fairly wide. It was dotted with vehicles parked opposite different buildings.

"Where's the side-gate? Behind this row of buildings?" Saralkar asked Tupe who had followed him out and had just finished calling up his Chowky for more men to be sent.

"Yes, sir. There is a narrow strip of avenue behind these buildings and right next to the small society gym, is the side-gate."

Saralkar began walking through the stilt parking of one of the buildings, crossing through to the rear avenue. Tupe pointed to the side-gate in the distance as it came into view. Saralkar could see the gym next to the gate on one side of it and on the other was a kids' playing area with a see-saw, a jungle-gym, and a couple of slides and swings. It was well maintained.

The watchman was seated at the far end and was expected to keep an eye on the side-gate too, which opened into a very narrow lane—a kind of cul-de-sac, on the other side of which stood two other societies.

Two maid-servants happened to stroll out of one of the buildings and used the side-gate to walk into the lane and cross over into the next society, which had a similar side-gate a little down the lane.

Saralkar's eyes scanned the rest of the layout as he kept walking down the rear avenue, past the side-gate. Right next to where the watchman was sitting was a small fenced area.

"What's that? Is that a swimming pool?"

"Yes, sir, but it's not functioning. In fact, since COVID the pool has not been in use and hasn't been restarted because apparently some pending repair work is to be undertaken . . ."

"I see. Have the society thoroughly searched, Tupe," Saralkar said.

"Yes, sir. But is there anything particular you want me to look for?"

Saralkar looked at him grimly. "On the off-chance that Pranjal did not leave the society on his bicycle, we need to check the possibility of whether he was confined by the kidnapper within the society itself and later spirited out by someone in a car or some vehicle."

Tupe's eyes widened. "Sir, you mean the kidnapper and killer could be one of the residents?" He had dropped his voice and the tone had an element of shock in it.

Saralkar grunted. "Why not? But that's a matter of conjecture. What I am saying is we need to see if there is any physical evidence or trace of Pranjal having been held in the society for some time, if there is no certainty that he left it in the first place!"

*****

"Daddy . . ."

"Yes, Pranjal?"

"Can I really become like Viswanathan Anand?"

"Of course, you can, beta . . ."

Pranjal's face was glum as he looked at his father. "But how can I now?"

"Why not? What is there to stop you?"

Again, the boy regarded Mohnish Bhatti, then averted his gaze. "I'm dead, no . . ." he said in a small voice.

And then he was gone. Mohnish's eyes shot open and his body convulsed.

"Pranjal . . . Pranjal . . ." he mumbled hoarsely, as reality crashed back into his consciousness.

He was lying in a hospital bed and his son, Pranjal, was dead. There would be no more chess tournaments, no more swelling of his chest with pride as he watched his son's chess wizardry in action, winning games—immersed in the chequered board, his innocent face set in rapt concentration, his eyes watching his opponent's moves, his brain planning his own, his fingers moving the pieces—and then the quick look in his father's direction every now and then, followed by a half-smile when reassured by Mohnish's presence.

Mohnish Bhatti wondered why he was still alive when his heart had already stopped the moment he had seen his son's mutilated body. Why hadn't he just fallen beside his boy and died there and then? What was there to live for? Instead, his brain had rebelled, refusing to accept that the gory remains were that of his Pranjal. His body had reacted to the shock by going haywire as if it wanted to suffer, not die. Death hadn't wished to claim him yet.

"Hullo, Mohnish Bhatti . . . Where's my 10 lakhs?" the same voice he'd heard on the plane spoke. "Don't you want your Pranjal back?"

"Take all my money . . . just return my Pranjal to me. Where's he? Tell me you didn't kill him! Tell me he's still alive . . . please . . . let me talk to him!"

"I told you he's sleeping . . . he's just sleeping," the man said again as he had said on the plane.

"Please, please . . . let me talk to him once . . . Pranjal . . . Pranjal . . ."

His cries were met with silence and then he heard his son again, "Bye, Daddy . . ."

"Wait, Pranjal . . . don't go . . . Pranjal!"

"Mohnish . . . Mohnish dear . . . calm down . . . calm down . . . it's me, Smita," his wife's voice cut through his sobs as Mohnish floated back to wakefulness.

Through his moist eyes he discerned her face. The devastation he felt was reflected in her eyes too.

"Smita . . . I know he's gone. What are we going to do? How am I going to live without Pranjal?" he said in a voice he couldn't recognise as his own.

Smita was silent. She had no answers. But something in her look and her hands that touched him now, gave him strength, as she always had. A kind of transfusion of spirit that stopped his soul from haemorrhaging completely.

*****

Chapter 8

"Yes, Inspector Saralkar, I did speak to Corporator Satish Khilare about the complaint made by . . . Pranjal's parents," Mrs. Zelam Kaul said, trying hard not to appear rattled.

"Where? Here in your office?" Saralkar asked.

The principal cleared her throat. "Over the phone. One of our school trustees, Mr. Chintan Shah, knows him personally. He set up the call . . . a Zoom call, since Mr. Khilare could not come over . . ."

"Is that a privilege you offer to all parents?" Saralkar said sharply. "I thought parents are generally summoned by school principals to meet them personally for even small matters?"

"No, you are right. But, Inspector, you know how it is with some prominent people, one has to make exceptions," Mrs. Kaul said, apologetically.

"So, what happened in this Zoom call?"

"Well . . . I . . . I told him about his son, Karan's unacceptable behaviour . . . I had called all three boys earlier and got the truth out of them. I told Mr. Khilare it was a very serious matter . . ."

"What was his reaction?" PSI Motkar fired from his end.

The principal cleared her throat once again. "Well, like all parents he became defensive . . . and said maybe Pranjal had started it all. He also said he would talk to his son and tell him to refrain from such behaviour next time."

"I see," Saralkar said. "Has the school issued any official reprimand or warning to the parents of the boys who assaulted Pranjal? Have you put on record in writing the seriousness of this incident?"

Mrs. Zelam Kaul clearly knew she was caught on the wrong foot but tried to brazen it out by assuming the role of a mature educationist. "Well, Inspector, we are dealing with young children . . . we have to be sensitive and careful what we put on record, you see."

It got Saralkar's goat. "You write remarks in the calendars of children for minor mistakes, but didn't feel it necessary to issue a formal written warning to a parent whose son had violently assaulted a smaller boy, enough for him to have injuries that needed stitches on his head?"

Saralkar's voice had suddenly become authoritative, "Why? Because he's a corporator's son?"

The principal had turned pale and sullen. "I . . . we have to be practical, Inspector. These are people with nuisance value and political weight."

Saralkar felt a surge of contempt. "That's precisely how we embolden them. By being deferential."

There was a momentary silence as the principal swallowed the rebuke. When she spoke, it was with resentment. "But surely, Inspector, it can't have had anything to do with Pranjal's disappearance. I mean . . ."

"Pranjal's dead, Mrs. Kaul," Saralkar snapped. "We found his dead body this morning."

He was glad to see shock and fear leap into her hitherto prim and smug demeanour.

"And you might see a lot more of us if our investigation leads us to believe Satish Khilare's involved in this case. For all practical purposes what the corporator's son did to Pranjal on your school premises was a juvenile offence . . . and you played a role in sweeping it under the carpet rather than putting it on record or informing the nearest police station about the incident. All you had to do was call the police and seek their advice."

Mrs. Zelam Kaul seemed to cringe and slump into her chair, no longer looking her imperious, haughty self. "I . . . I did make the boy apologise to poor Pranjal though."

*****

Two Weeks Ago

Satish Khilare twirled the heavy gold ring on his left forefinger. Then it was the turn of the other ring on his right forefinger. He was regarding his son, Karan, with a sour expression.

"Go, don't do it again. You want to beat any one, then your hands and legs are enough. Why use a compass, a brick . . .? Understood?"

Karan Khilare looked at his father's wagging finger and nodded. It was an important life lesson—violence was okay, being a bully was okay, so long as it wasn't serious enough to push the victim to complain.

"Go now and keep away from that boy . . . what's his name?"

"Pranjal . . ." Karan spat out the name.

"Pranjal what? What's his full name?"

"Pranjal Bhatti!"

"You know anything more about him? His family? What does his father do?" Satish Khilare asked.

His son shook his head.

Satish Khilare looked at his Man Friday, Anil Kedari. "Find out, Anil. What's the father's profession, where does the family live—in our area, our ward, or elsewhere?"

Anil Kedari made a mental note and said, "Okay, Satish *bhau.*"

The corporator dismissed his son with a wave of his hand. He had started life in a clan that ran the local country liquor vend and provided muscle where it was needed to settle disputes, mediate, intimidate.

Satish Khilare had once been a rather good kabaddi player, who rose to district level while pursuing his graduation with hopes of playing at the state level too—not a totally rotten fellow like some of the other members of the clan. But the combination of a love affair gone wrong and an abrupt end to his kabaddi career because of a bad injury had raised his bitterness quotient enough to turn back to his roots—money, muscle, local influence, and a hankering to use it all to secure a foothold in city politics.

He had served nearly two terms as a corporator, expanding his ambitions and grip, learning all the tricks of the political trade to further increase his sphere of influence. Satish Khilare had also made the discovery that while a lot of people had money and reach, not many had the stomach or capacity to wield muscle and street power.

And that's what he zeroed in on, as his path to acquire more influence. Of course, he knew it had to be used discreetly and yet showcase it enough to gain a reputation for it.

"That Chintan Shah, arsehole, the trustee of Karan's school told me that the boy's father had talked about going to the police and filing a case," Satish Khilare confided to Anil, with a growl in his voice and a glint in his eye.

"They probably don't know enough about you, Satish bhau . . ." Anil Kedari reasoned, "Otherwise I don't think they would've talked of taking such a step."

"Hmm . . ." Khilare said, "I like to nip things in the bud. Sometimes people need to be taught a lesson before they actually cross your path."

"But Satish bhau . . . if our Karan hit the boy with a brick or a compass, any child's father would've raised a furore . . ."

Satish Khilare scorched him with a glance and Anil stuttered to a halt. "You get on with the task I've given you."

*****

"Call up Satish Khilare, and ask him to report to our office tomorrow morning at 11.00 a.m., Motkar," Saralkar said, as they left the school premises and got into their vehicle.

"He's not going to like it, sir," Motkar said and bit his tongue for having said something his boss wasn't going to like either.

Saralkar clicked his tongue. "What did I just say to the principal, Motkar? The less deferential we are to public representatives and so-called influential people, the better."

"No, sir, I'm saying Khilare might suggest instead we should go and meet him at his residence," Motkar replied.

"If he does, tell him from me, we'll leak the incident involving his son and Pranjal to the media."

Motkar had expected his boss to come up with something like this. Something had raised Saralkar's hackles and he was in a confrontational mood.

"Okay, sir," Motkar replied. He would of course have to convey the message to the corporator in far more tactful language. "But do you really think Khilare would be involved in the kidnapping and killing of Pranjal, sir? Isn't there too much at stake for him as an elected corporator?"

Saralkar gave him a sideways look. "I presume you know his background, Motkar?"

"Yes, sir, I know the Khilare clan is pretty infamous in the Bavdhan-Sus area but most of their crimes are related to shady land deals, extortion and *goondaism* . . . not hardcore spilling of blood or kidnapping and other such heinous crimes."

"Mostly true. But Satish Khilare has a few serious criminal cases against him—including a murder case in Lonavala," Saralkar said. "He was a kabaddi player, you know, and one case he was involved in about ten or twelve years ago was the abduction of a player from a rival team. The victim was released after a week with six fractures to his legs and two to his right hand . . . Khilare was widely suspected to have done it."

"Oh!" Motkar exclaimed. "Were there no convictions, sir?"

"No. The victim withdrew the complaint. There was some settlement . . . and the police had no real evidence, so the case remains unsolved."

"You were on the investigating team, sir?"

"No . . . a senior colleague was. He had told me about it."

"What was the motive, sir?"

"Grudge," Saralkar replied. "During a kabaddi game, the victim had tackled Khilare in a way that resulted in a broken shin bone which put paid to Satish's career. That's the kind of vengeful man he is."

"So you think Khilare took the complaint made by Pranjal's parents as a personal slight and . . .?"

"We need to probe the possibility, don't we, Motkar?"

"Sure, sir, but would a mere complaint against his son amount to a slight?" Motkar reasoned. "And would Khilare take the risk of a kidnapping and killing, given he's a corporator and therefore in the public eye?"

"What's the harm in shaking the tree to see if a few rotten fruits fall off, Motkar?" Saralkar replied. "And as regards slights, don't we see grudges playing out every day? Who might feel aggrieved by what and provoked to what extent is extremely difficult to second guess given the vagaries of human nature."

*****

NINE DAYS AGO

"Baba . . . I have to ask you something," Karan said, picking at his dinner.

"What?" his father asked.

"Can I beat that Pranjal Bhatti again? Only with my hands. As you said . . ." the boy said earnestly.

"What? Why? I told you to keep away from him, no!" Satish Khilare rebuked him.

His son sulked. "I didn't go anywhere near him. Principal madam only called us to her office again and made me and my friends say sorry to that bloody Pranjal . . ." he said.

Satish Khilare scowled. "And you apologised to him?"

"Yes. Principal madam said his parents wanted us to be punished or at least say sorry to him for what we had done," Karan continued. "That's why I feel like thrashing him again. Can I, Baba?"

"No," his father snapped grimly. "Not now. I'll see what to do."

They finished their dinner in silence and Satish Khilare went into his out-house where his staff usually worked.

"Anil, did you find out about that boy's father?"

"About that Mohnish Bhatti, Satish bhau?"

"Yes."

"He's an authorised dealer of a sanitaryware company. His shop is on Sus Road, Nirmala Complex," Anil Kedari said.

"In our area only that means. And where does the family stay?"

"In Bavdhan . . ."

"Good. And what's his background?"

"He used to work in the same company earlier. His wife works in an IT company in Hinjewadi. They've got two children. Older daughter studies in MIT College and the son Pranjal of course is in Karan's school. Apparently, the boy is a gifted chess player and shows promise of being selected at the national championships."

"So just some normal guy . . . no political or police contacts?"

"Doesn't look likely, Satish bhau," Anil Kedari replied.

"Okay. Ask Pawan Gawli to meet me in a day or two."

"But he's *tadipaar, Satish bhau*. His one-year externment is not over yet . . ."

"Hmmm. Then call Sunny Sutar."

"Okay, Satish bhau," Anil Kedari said uneasily. "But what's the need to get someone like Sunny? Let it go no . . . why bother about such a trivial issue? It's not as if that Bhatti will really lodge a police complaint or something."

The corporator gave his aide a cold stare. "Karan was made to apologise to the boy in school. I can't let it go like that, Anil. Get Sunny tomorrow."

*****

Chapter 9

"We searched the entire society thoroughly, sir, and found nothing to indicate Pranjal might've been confined there by any resident," ASI Tupe reported. "We also talked to all families. At least prima facie, no one's involvement can be suspected."

Saralkar grunted. The news of the discovery of Pranjal's body was all over the media by now—splashed on the front pages of newspapers with poignant headlines, running continuously on news channels since the previous evening and of course going viral on social media.

It was going to be another endless day—one of many more to come and Tupe, Motkar, and Saralkar had regrouped to take stock.

"No one recollected seeing Pranjal leave the society through the front- or side-gate at all?" Saralkar asked.

"No, sir. We even asked each and every maid servant who frequently uses the side-gate," Tupe said.

"Then how in the world did the boy leave the society and by which gate and in which direction?" Saralkar said with a touch of exasperation. "Have you looked for CCTV footage in neighbouring societies or on the path to and from his coaching class?"

"We've started the process, sir . . . my team is gathering the footage," Tupe replied.

"Unless the boy turned invisible like Mr. India, Pranjal's got to have been seen somewhere," Saralkar remarked.

"Sir," Motkar broke in, "there might be one other possibility. What if he was kidnapped in the parking area below his building, rendered unconscious, dumped in a vehicle like an SUV and whisked away? Someone who knew his timing and was already stationed below in a vehicle, waiting for him. They also took his bicycle to create the illusion that he had left for class as usual."

Saralkar frowned as he considered Motkar's proposition. "You might have something there, Motkar. The boy is lured into the car or picked up forcibly, gagged and drugged. And yes, an SUV is big enough for a bicycle to fit in . . ." he said meditatively. "Tupe, let's zero in on all the SUVs, bigger vehicles, vans, or tempos that went in and out of the society that day. It should all be available in the CCTV footage."

"Sure, sir . . ." Tupe replied.

"Good thinking, Motkar. Now, have we got that driver chap who'd threatened Mrs. Bhatti?"

"Yes, sir. He's been picked up this morning."

"Good. And what about Satish Khilare?"

"He kicked up a bit of a fuss, sir, but . . . er . . . relented after I conveyed your message," Motkar replied. "The only thing is he'll be here at noon instead of 11.00 a.m."

"Hmm, that's okay. He needed some push-back to show he's not at our beck and call," Saralkar chuckled. "Let's grill the driver, Motkar . . . and Tupe, report back to me as soon as you've made any progress."

"Yes, sir," Tupe said and left while Motkar went to fetch the driver.

Saralkar closed his eyes momentarily. His feeling of world weariness had almost become a permanent condition, ambushing him whenever he had alone time, even if for a few seconds. It was a little over twenty-four hours since Pranjal's body had been found, probably seventy-two hours since he had been killed. What cosmic purpose had been served by his gory death in the grand scheme of things, assuming there was one? Why did things happen—particularly bad things? You looked for meaning to make sense of life, to find purpose in existence, to believe that the fates of all individuals were interconnected in some invisible, mysterious way to the destiny of the universe as a whole. That our lives were just moving pieces in some gigantic, animated jigsaw puzzle, which is why things happened the way they did, because it all somehow made sense.

But did it really? Or was life just a series of random happenings—billions of unrelated occurrences in millions of lives that happened because all humans were just actors in a never-ending soap opera, watched by thirty-three crore gods who needed to be entertained or by some alien civilization in a faraway galaxy, which had designated the Earth as a kind of recreation zone that they tuned into whenever they felt like?

"Sir," Motkar said breaking into his boss's reflections, "this is Jayesh Pardeshi."

Saralkar fixed the young man produced in front of him with his 'laser' look, which he often deployed to make individuals before him feel as though he could look through them and detect all that they hoped to camouflage.

"I'm not Jayesh Pardeshi, sir . . . I'm his brother, Jayant," the man said. "That's what I have been trying to tell your constables. They wouldn't listen."

Saralkar's eyes travelled to Motkar for a second, who seemed equally startled, then they turned to the young man again. "Where's Jayesh?"

"I . . . I really don't know, sir . . . he left on tour with some party three or four days ago."

"To which place? Within the state? Outside the state?"

"I have no idea, sir . . ."

"You live in the same house and you have no idea where your brother's gone?" Saralkar said, raising his voice.

"No, sir. We live in adjacent houses in the same tenement since I got married last year, not under the same roof," Jayant said anxiously. "We just leave keys with each other and I just happened to be in Jayesh's house looking for something, when your cops came."

This time the look Saralkar threw Motkar was a vexed one. This was shoddy policing, no matter who was responsible.

"You mean, even Jayesh's family is not there?" Motkar asked Jayant, a little flustered that he'd not ascertained all this before presenting the man before Saralkar.

"Sir, Jayesh's wife, my sister-in-law, Sushila, had to go to Shrirampur because her uncle passed away. She and her kids should be back in a few days."

"Surely you must've spoken to Jayesh in the last few days or he might've called up?" Saralkar asked.

"He hasn't called, sir. And believe me I've tried but his phone's out of range or switched off," Jayant replied.

Saralkar decided to turn the screw. "You were also working on contract as a driver with Bitcoff IT in Hinjewadi along with your brother, right?"

Jayant's eyes immediately grew wary. "Yes, sir . . . but why are you looking for Jayesh? What has he done?"

"The company terminated the contract because of Jayesh's drunken misbehaviour, right?"

Jayesh licked his lips and replied uneasily, "Yes . . . but I don't know the truth of that incident, sir . . . and it happened over six months ago."

"Is that so? Do you remember who the admin manager of the company was?" Saralkar asked.

"Bhatti madam . . ."

"Your brother Jayesh threatened her with consequences, do you know that, Jayant?"

Jayant grimaced. "Sir . . . I wasn't present, but Jayesh always says stupid things in the heat of the moment. He doesn't mean anything."

"What a good little brother you are, Jayant," Saralkar sneered. "Do you watch TV news or read the papers every day?"

Jayant looked unsure what to make of the question. "Sometimes, sir. Why?"

"Are you aware that a boy named Pranjal Bhatti, who was missing since the last few days, was found dead yesterday?"

A shadow passed over Jayant's face as his brain started making the connection on hearing the name. "Yes," he answered weakly.

"And do you know who Pranjal Bhatti's mother is?"

From Jayant's eyes, Motkar could make out he'd guessed the answer. The driver had gone pale and his voice was tremulous when he spoke, "Sir . . . you are looking for Jayesh . . . because . . . because you think . . ."

Saralkar said nothing, only looked straight at him. Neither did Motkar, when the distressed man darted his eyes towards him.

"But why, sir? Why do you suspect Jayesh?"

Saralkar let the man sweat for a few more beats. "Tell him, Motkar."

Motkar took over. "Just a few days before the boy was kidnapped, his mother Smita Bhatti spotted your brother keeping a watch on her, near her house. Not just that, a few weeks before that someone told Mrs. Bhatti that your brother had talked of taking revenge on her."

The fight seemed to go out of Jayant. Somewhere in his mind, the first doubts had begun to creep in. Saralkar was almost sure Jayesh had some kind of criminal past or had done things that his brother knew made him capable of vengeful deeds.

"Do you know anything about it? Did your brother hint that he was up to something like that?" Motkar nudged again.

Jayant shook his head vigorously. "No, sir."

"Are you still going to say you don't know Jayesh's whereabouts? Or that you've not been in touch?" Saralkar interrupted sternly. "Because then you too will be embroiled in the case. Helping a criminal is a crime too."

"I swear I don't know anything or where Jayesh is, saheb. If you want, I can try and call him right now in front of you," Jayant said.

"Go ahead! Call him and put the phone on speaker."

Jayant promptly reached for his phone, dialled a number, and put it on speaker. The call did not connect and instead the recorded message of the number being out of coverage area played out.

"Call him on WhatsApp. Does he use the same number?" Motkar said, unimpressed.

"Yes, sir," Jayant said and dialled on WhatsApp, with the same result. The screen showed "Calling" which was the equivalent of the call not getting through. It would've shown "Ringing" if the call was connecting but remained unanswered by the receiver.

"Check his WhatsApp messages also, Motkar."

Saralkar knew that he had no authority to force him to do so, if Jayant refused to show them. But rather than detain this man, which was far more illegal, it was better to check if there were any suspicious messages exchanged between the brothers that could provide some vital information on Jayesh's whereabouts or involvement.

But Jayant neither hesitated nor resisted. He quickly complied and handed over his device to Motkar. Motkar scrolled down and began checking. Jayant's body language didn't suggest he was worried that Motkar would find something incriminatory on his phone.

Motkar finished, glanced at Saralkar, and shook his head. "The last messages from Jayesh are from about four days ago—some forwards—videos, jokes, and pornography."

Saralkar nodded and turned his gaze back to Jayant. "Tell me, Jayant, did your brother stalk and harass that girl, Abha Das, who'd complained to the company in the first place?"

For a moment, Jayant Pardeshi seemed to panic and looked set to cave in. Then something changed in his demeanour. "Sir . . . I'm not my brother! You please find him and put these questions to him."

So, it was clear, Jayant wasn't going to rat on his brother and Saralkar was loath to apply any other kind of pressure.

"Alright, you can go, Jayant. But if you get any call or message from your brother, Jayesh, you better let us know immediately, or the next time we'll take you into custody, whether you are involved in the crime or not," Saralkar said in a tone that left no doubt that he meant business, "And don't try to leave town . . ."

Jayant nodded. "I understand, saheb."

*****

FIVE DAYS EARLIER

"He's leaving for his coaching class now . . ." Namita whispered into the phone as she watched Pranjal through the small gap in her room door, which she'd left slightly ajar.

"Okay, I'm waiting for him down below," Rishabh said, sitting inside his Ertiga. He had already removed the air from one of the tyres of Pranjal's bicycle, about ten minutes ago when he drove in.

"But you said you were going to wait in the lane outside the gate," Namita said shrilly.

"Relax, Namita. There was absolutely no place to park in the lane or even wait," Rishabh replied. "That's why . . ."

"He's left," Namita said breathlessly, cutting him short, as Pranjal stepped out of the house and shut the main door.

"Okay, bye. I'll call later, after I'm done," Rishabh said, gearing himself up. He lowered the glass of the passenger seat window a little, looking hawk-eyed towards the parking area, waiting for Pranjal to emerge from the lift.

A minute later he saw the boy, walking to his bicycle and beginning to unlock it. Nervous, Rishabh looked around. There was no one. He quickly opened the car door and trotted towards the stilt parking.

"Pranjal," he called as the boy seemed to realize there was no air in his back tyre.

Pranjal looked up and saw Rishabh. He didn't return the greeting.

"Going to class?" Rishabh asked now a few feet away from him.

Pranjal nodded. "Stay away from *Didi* . . ." *he said unexpectedly. "Don't go up."*

"No, I came to talk to you . . ." Rishabh said, trying hard to stay calm.

"About what? I've to go to class."

"Just two minutes, Pranjal . . ." Rishabh said. "I'll drop you on the way if you want, if you are getting late . . . anyway there's no air in your back tyre . . ."

Pranjal looked at his bicycle tyre in dismay. "No. I don't want to talk to you."

"Look, Pranjal . . . I know you are upset by what you saw that day . . . but . . . but please don't tell your Mum and Dad or you'll get your didi into trouble . . ." Rishabh said, feeling angry and small because he was pleading with an eleven-year-old kid like that. "I . . . I love your didi, Namita . . . if you tell your parents about that day . . . they'll . . . they'll . . . please . . ."

Pranjal was listening with the aloofness only a child is capable of. He said nothing and began walking out of the stilt area with his bicycle.

A flash of despair and frustration shot through Rishabh. This was not going the way he'd hoped it would. What was he to do now?

"Leave my didi alone. Don't come to our house or I'll tell my Mum," Pranjal suddenly said to him.

It wasn't a threat. It wasn't a warning. And yet Rishabh saw red!

*****

"Sir, the corporator, Satish Khilare is here," Motkar said. "Should I get him here now or do you want to keep him waiting a bit?"

"No, I guess he must already be stewing since yesterday," Saralkar said. "In fact, let's start on him before he gets a chance to get over his initial nervousness."

"Okay, sir," Motkar said. "I just got a piece of handy information that we can spring on Khilare."

"What?" Saralkar asked.

Motkar told him.

"Hmm . . . pretend to receive a call or a text in Khilare's presence and come over and whisper something to me," Saralkar said.

"Sure, sir," Motkar replied and went out to fetch the corporator.

Saralkar braced himself for the encounter. He'd dealt with politicians wielding various levels of influence and almost always their focus was on trying to be condescending and in making their displeasure felt at the temerity of being called for questioning.

Satish Khilare was no different, striding in with two of his aides and a lawyer. He eyeballed Saralkar almost immediately and cast a look around the room. "How long is this going to take?" he demanded.

"Can't say!" Saralkar replied tersely. "Please ask the people accompanying you to wait outside."

"Why can't they remain here?" the corporator asked belligerently.

"Because we have only called you, not your entourage," Saralkar replied then turned to the corporator's companions, "All the rest, move outside."

The group began shuffling away, dispersing, looking at the corporator for instructions, if any.

"My lawyer stays," Khilare said.

"Why do you need a lawyer, Mr. Khilare?" Saralkar

asked in a tone that was a combination of puzzlement and a taunt.

The corporator frowned and glanced at his lawyer. "Just in case you try to pull a fast one or try to implicate me in this matter."

It was on the tip of Saralkar's tongue to ask the corporator if he was uneasy or scared to be on his own, but he avoided the temptation.

"We only want to ask you some preliminary questions," he said. "A lawyer's presence is not necessary or permitted at this stage. Let him wait outside and if you think you need to consult him for any particular reply, we will fetch him. Fair enough?"

His tone was deceptively reasonable.

The corporator wavered for a bit but then nodded. A man in his position couldn't let his ego admit he was uneasy to face questions alone. "Okay," he said.

His aides had already left the room. Now the lawyer followed. Saralkar let a few beats pass and waited for the corporator to finish shooting his defiant glances in all directions.

"Can we start? I don't have all day, Inspector!"

"A boy, Pranjal Bhatti, whose parents had recently complained against your son in school, was found brutally murdered yesterday, after going missing for a few days," Saralkar said and paused.

The corporator waited for Saralkar's question that never came. He stared fiercely, then flashed his eyes when Saralkar continued to remain silent. "So?" he finally asked, "What's the connection you are trying to make?"

Saralkar rubbed his thumb and forefinger along his jawline, as if trying to weigh the corporator's response.

"Did you ever meet the parents of the boy or try and get in touch with them over the phone or through someone, after you heard about their complaint and the incident in school?"

"No! Never! Why should I?"

"Well, just to settle the matter or talk to them since it involved a serious charge against your son. After all, you are a corporator from the same ward in which they live," Saralkar said.

Motkar watched the duel warming up between his boss and the corporator.

"I explained whatever I needed to, to the school principal. She had called me. I also asked my son to stay away from that boy. That's all," Satish Khilare said, trying to look unconcerned. "It was a small matter blown out of proportion just because I am a corporator."

"I see. The boy, Pranjal, needed stitches for his head injury. If the parents had filed a police complaint, as they were thinking of doing, your son could've been booked for assault as a juvenile."

Anger suffused the corporator's face and Motkar could see how he struggled to control an outburst—of mouthing a remark that underlined his sway as an elected representative—like "The police wouldn't dare to book my son."

But instead, he snapped, "Who stopped them from filing a case? We had nothing to hide. I would've dealt with it. I don't wish to speak ill of the dead but that boy had said some cheap, insulting things to my son . . . and so the scuffle ensued."

"I see," Inspector Saralkar said. "So this was not a small matter which escalated into something more serious because you were offended and wanted to teach them a lesson?"

"What are you suggesting, Inspector?" the corporator now

exploded. "That I kidnapped the boy and had him killed?" His body language was now aggressive.

Saralkar was unfazed by the show of aggression. "The meaning of investigation is to look at all probabilities . . . motives! Please don't take it personally," he said politely to Satish Khilare, then glanced in Motkar's direction and raised his eyebrows slightly. It was a sign and Motkar immediately responded as planned.

"Sir . . ." he interrupted expertly then walked up to Saralkar and whispered into his boss's ear.

Saralkar listened, nodded, then glanced in the corporator's direction, who was watching with a dark scowl. Motkar withdrew back to his position.

"Would you be able to tell us your detailed whereabouts and schedule for the last five-six days, Mr. Khilare?" Saralkar asked evenly.

"What?" Khilare growled. "Why?"

Saralkar looked at him and answered in a calm, composed voice. "We need it. I'm sure you and your secretary can send it to us."

"I'm not going to give you anything of that sort," the corporator thundered. "Who do you think you are? I'm under no obligation. I don't want to waste any more time on this."

He stood up, ready to walk away.

"Why did you send Sunny Sutar to Mohnish Bhatti's shop then, last week?" Saralkar asked sharply and despite himself, Khilare froze in his tracks, caught off guard.

"I don't know what you are talking about . . ." he replied hoarsely.

"Hmm. . ." Saralkar said, "I am again asking you, Mr. Khilare. Please send me details of your whereabouts and schedule for the last five-six days. And please do not forget, we know something about your background, so it would be best if you can cooperate."

"Okay," the corporator said, stone-faced. "I'll have my secretary send you all the details. But I had nothing to do with the unfortunate fate that befell that boy."

The next moment he had walked off in a huff.

*****

Chapter 10

Ashwini Gholap did not watch television news. She had stopped doing so two years ago. There had been a time when all she'd done was to watch TV news all evening, late into the night, switching channels in the desperate hope that the news she so badly wanted to see and hear would flash any time on the screen.

As days turned into weeks, then months and years, all hope evaporated. The smug anchors and the breathtaking drivel they spouted all day and night long, had become too much to bear—as if it drove home, every living moment, how little it mattered to the world the one thing that meant everything to her.

Every tragedy was an item of media consumption with an amazingly short shelf life—periodically regurgitated sometimes, but mostly done with—like an aerated drink that had already lost its fizz, when first uncorked.

The world had moved on; her husband had moved on; and in a way even she had, except that part of her that had come to a standstill six years ago. That part of her which had been ninety per cent of her being. Would that ever move on? She was no longer sure. Yet it was only that tiny bit of residual hope that made her open the newspaper every day, her wounded soul looking for balm.

Today was no different and yet her heart gave a little leap as her eyes fell on the crime headline on the third page— **'Kidnapped Boy's Body Found in the Mutha River'.**

It was almost as if the sub-editor had copy-pasted a headline from six years ago.

Ashwini began reading the news item and a cold, eerie feeling seemed to sweep over her with every word. If the name 'Pranjal' were to be substituted with 'Atharva', was this newspaper report not uncannily similar to what had happened to her son, six years ago?

*****

PSI Motkar disconnected the call and walked into Saralkar's cabin, still wearing his frown and puckered brow.

Saralkar himself had just got off his call with the commissioner. "It's less than thirty hours since we took over the case, Motkar, why haven't we been able to crack it still?" Saralkar remarked dryly.

"Sir?"

"The new CP, Arundhati Pradhan, wanted to know, Motkar," Saralkar replied. "You got any smart comebacks to that? I couldn't think of any."

Motkar suppressed a grin and experienced a wee bit of schadenfreude. It was always a pleasure to know your boss also had a boss who gave him a tough time. "Sir, the post-mortem has thrown up some new information."

"What? Don't tell me Dr. Gunjal blundered and everything he told us was wrong?"

"No, sir. Most of what Dr. Gunjal said has been confirmed. Death was due to drowning about forty-eight to seventy-two hours before the body was found," Motkar said. "But two more facts have emerged. One is that there are signs of the boy being sexually assaulted—his private parts show marks of injury and his anus was penetrated . . . quite brutal, in fact . . ."

Saralkar gave an involuntary shudder and felt flushed with white-hot anger. "Did they find any traces of semen in his anal area?"

"No, sir . . . I asked. . ."

"But are they sure the injuries are the result of a sexual assault? Because that might change the very complexion of this case."

"Yes, sir . . . I double-checked with Dr. Sule, Dr. Gunjal's senior who actually performed the post-mortem," Motkar said. "He's absolutely certain from the nature of the injuries that it was sexual assault."

"And yet they haven't found any traces of semen," Saralkar said. "So the assault was with what? Penis or fingers . . . or something else?"

"I didn't think of asking him that. Should I call Dr. Sule right now?"

Motkar began dialling Dr. Sule's number, even before Saralkar nodded. As with some unwritten rule of life. Dr. Sule's number was busy.

"Sir, you think paedophilia or some sexual perversion could be the real motive behind the crime?" Motkar asked his boss, who looked lost in thought.

Saralkar pinched the cleft in his chin a couple of times before replying. "Yes, I think we need to probe that angle too now. I had dreaded this possibility and motive the most, because suddenly we will be looking at a huge field of suspects, at random—even total strangers can commit a sexual crime. Shit!"

Motkar nodded. "Should I start with known sexual offenders and paedophiles in our files?"

"Yes, we need to open up that line of inquiry in the light of this evidence, Motkar, but let it not shift our focus totally away from the possibilities we are already pursuing," Saralkar said. "I get a feeling we need to dig deeper into the background of the Bhatti couple. How is it they have no family or relatives here? There's not enough we know about them and something's definitely missing . . ."

"You think they are not telling us everything, sir? Hiding things?"

Saralkar grunted. "Maybe we haven't asked the right questions, Motkar."

He paused, then said, "What do you make of Satish Khilare? Do you think he might have hired this Sunny Sutar to pull off the kidnapping and murder of Pranjal?"

"Sir, I looked up Sunny Sutar's record—he's got several cases of extortion, grievous assault, and rape against him," Motkar replied. "But kidnapping and murder—no! Of course, it's possible he decided to take it a notch higher if Khilare asked him to."

"Hmm . . . now that we've given Khilare a bit of a fright, let's keep a tab on how much of a flutter it causes. Ask your informers to keep their eyes and ears open. Let's see if Sunny or his known associates make a beeline to flee Pune," Saralkar said, "and try Dr. Sule's number again."

Motkar dialled and this time Dr. Sule picked up promptly. Motkar put the phone on speaker. "Dr. Sule, this is Saralkar here. The injuries to the anus of the boy, what were they caused by?"

"Well, I already told Motkar. It was a sexual assault," Dr. Sule replied.

"I know that. But were any instruments or objects used for penetration . . . or what?"

The doctor seemed to pause for a moment before replying. "I can't say for sure . . . but I can't rule it out altogether."

"What do you mean? Surely the nature of the injuries . . ." Saralkar asked sharply.

"It's not as simple as that, Saralkar. I'd say it's a fifty-fifty probability . . ."

"You mean you found no traces of semen in the anus, so you can't conclude with certainty it was penetration by the perpetrator's penis?"

"Yes, it's tricky," Dr. Sule admitted, "but don't forget the body was in the water for seventy-two hours."

"Hmm . . . what else can you tell me, Dr. Sule?"

"That's it, really," the doctor said. "Oh yes, the sexual assault was after death!"

"What?"

"Yes, the injuries to his anus and private parts were inflicted after death," Dr. Sule said.

Saralkar felt like throwing up. The mere thought of what someone could do even to a child's body, was sick and revolting.

*****

Smita Bhatti thought of that last morning with her son. It had been a morning like any other and yet it hadn't. She'd woken at 6.00 a.m. as always, and just as she did every day, she'd first checked if Pranjal was up and about in his room.

Never had she had trouble with waking him up for school in the morning.

He'd flashed his ready smile at her that day as he brushed his teeth. "Good morning, Mamma."

The memory broke her heart now. "Good morning, Pranju. What would you like for breakfast?" she had asked as if it had been any other day.

As his mother why hadn't some sixth sense told her he was in danger of being taken from her. Why?

"Toast and omelette?" she'd continued, before he could reply.

Her Pranjal had wrinkled his nose a little, then quickly said, "Okay, Mamma." As if he preferred something else but didn't want to bother his mother.

Why had she been so lazy? Why hadn't she offered to make his absolute favourite breakfast—Paneer Toasty? Because she had no inkling that it was the deceptively normal morning of what was to be a horrible, twisted day?

Her only thoughts had been focused on getting everything ready on time, so that Pranjal could be off to school, Namita to her college, and she to work. After all, wouldn't they all return in the evening when they had finished doing all that they did on a usual day? How was she to know that Pranjal would return home only to set out again and never return?

Who had taken him from her? Who was the monster? Her heart and mind and body screamed and convulsed with anger and grief, as she sat in the hospital room now, her husband lying on the bed staring up at the ceiling, his eyes bubbling over with tears every now and then and sliding down the side of his face, which he made no attempt to wipe.

They had not exchanged a word for nearly half an hour now; such had been the enormity of their grief—that conversation sounded too shallow and vacuous to fill the desolate silence with.

"Could it have been him, Smita?" Mohnish spoke, breaking the *omerta* they had observed. He turned his face slightly in her direction to see her response.

"Randeep?" she asked, bitter surprise in her voice.

Mohnish nodded. "Who could hate us more than him?"

"After all this time? It's been nearly thirteen years, Mohnish," Smita said, still trying to process the possibility Mohnish had brought up.

"Isn't revenge a dish best served cold?"

A chill began making its way through Smita's body. "You think Randeep is capable of going to this extent? Kidnapping and killing our Pranjal?"

Mohnish was quiet for a few beats. "I've been thinking hard . . . replaying the voice of the man who'd called for ransom in my head . . . and the more I think of it . . . hear the voice—the more it feels like it perhaps sounded, resembled Randeep's voice . . ."

"What? Are you sure, Mohnish? Should we tell the police it might be Randeep?" Smita asked, her tone urgent and anxious.

Mohnish shook his head slightly, closed his eyes with his fingers massaging his shut eyelids, as if trying hard to concentrate and replay the voice in his head yet again. "I can't be sure. Sometimes I feel it's my mind playing tricks on me . . . making it sound like Randeep . . ."

He paused as if overwhelmed, then opened his eyes. "I . . . I think we need to tell the police about our past in any case, Smita . . . about Randeep . . . about us . . . for perspective," Mohnish said. "I don't know if I'm just imagining Randeep's voice . . . but if there's anyone who's most likely to mean us harm and to smash our happiness it has to be Randeep. It's possible that I might be totally wrong in suspecting him but we must tell the police about him."

Smita drew in a deep breath. The idea of dredging up their unpleasant and traumatic past—especially a past that contained a man as loathsome as Randeep Mirdha, set off a storm in her mind. But it was a storm that had to be weathered. Her husband was right. The past cast long shadows, even if one thought one had escaped it.

"Okay, Mohnish . . . perhaps we made the mistake of forgetting Randeep but as they say, the axe forgets but the tree remembers."

She took her husband's hands in hers and squeezed.

*****

"Sir, there were nine SUVs that went in and out of the society between 2.30 and 3.30 p.m. on the day of Pranjal's disappearance," ASI Tupe briefed Saralkar and Motkar. "Besides, there were also three tempos and delivery vehicles."

"So, if Motkar's conjecture is right, any of these could've been used to whisk Pranjal and his bicycle away," Saralkar remarked.

"We've got all the registration numbers," Tupe replied. "In just a few of these the CCTV footage shows people on the front seats as well as back seats, while most others have single drivers. We might need to enlarge and enhance the visuals to see if there appears anything suspicious inside—including Pranjal's bicycle being carried away."

"No taxis or rental vehicles?" Saralkar queried.

"No, sir."

"How many of these are vehicles of society residents?" Motkar asked.

"The watchman could confidently identify five of these

vehicles as belonging to society residents. He was not sure of two, and two other vehicles were clearly recorded as visitor vehicles," Tupe replied.

"And you have already checked out the delivery vehicles and tempo owners?" Motkar asked.

"Yes," Tupe said, "one was a Big Basket grocery delivery van. We've confirmed delivery details and it's all genuine. The van was in and out in about ten minutes. The other vehicle was here for a new refrigerator delivery from a company. Again, we've checked it out. The van was here for a longer time because the flat owner to whom the refrigerator was to be delivered had gone out shopping nearby and had to be contacted. She came back in about twenty minutes and so the vehicle and delivery men were in the premises for about half an hour, because of the delay."

Saralkar drummed his fingers impatiently. "What about the third tempo?"

"Sir, that one needs a little checking out. The driver told the security that he was there to pick up renovation rubble from a flat. But while leaving the society, he said he'd come to the wrong address," Tupe replied. "Now we've got the registration details but we haven't been able to find the owner at the registration address. It's a ten-year-old tempo so we are looking for it."

Saralkar clicked his tongue. "Was it a tempo with a canvas covered body or metal covered small container type?"

"It had a canvas covered body, sir, with a pull-down tarpaulin flap at the rear. It's entirely possible the boy could have been bound and hidden in the back, along with his bicycle. In the CCTV footage, one can see the flap drawn down but unfastened, and a labourer standing on one side, gazing out, parting the flap slightly. There was also one more person sitting next to the driver."

Saralkar drummed his table again. "We have to trace this tempo and its owner immediately. And what about the two visitor vehicles? Which flats did they make entries for?"

"One of them, a brown Ertiga left the flat number blank, sir, and the name scribbled is illegible, as if deliberately done. Ditto with the mobile number—impossible to make out all digits and one digit short," Tupe said. "You know what watchman are like—they don't even see if the entries are made properly. But the watchman on duty said he'd seen the vehicle before, so one of my constables checked for previous entries for the same vehicle in the visitor book. There are two more entries—one about ten days ago and one earlier. In both places the name entered is Rishabh. No surname. In one place the flat number entered is C-502, which is the Bhatti flat."

"Okay, so there is some connection to the Bhattis," Motkar said. "Now we need to find out who this person Rishabh is. Did the watchman recollect what this person looks like?"

"The CCTV footage showed a clean-shaven young man wearing goggles. The watchman said he was about twenty or twenty-one years of age. He was unaccompanied when he entered and later too, one can't make out if anyone or anything is in the back. And yes, the watchman remembers he did not park in the visitor's parking but he doesn't recollect which building he went towards."

"Hmm . . ." Saralkar said, chewing over the facts. "Did your constable make a note of the entry timings of the previous entries of the same visitor?"

ASI Tupe consulted his notes and said, "Fortunately, he noted the time along with the dates, sir. The person came around 11.30 - 11.45 a.m., both times on previous occasions."

"On weekdays?"

"Yes, sir," Tupe said once again, checking his notes.

"Why, sir?" Motkar asked, looking at Saralkar curiously.

"11.30 - 11.45 a.m. —Pranjal's at school, Mum's at office, Dad's at his dealership . . ." Saralkar surmised, "The only one likely to be at the Bhatti home is the daughter, back early from college. So, whoever the young man is, he's probably known to the girl."

"You mean her boyfriend, sir?"

"Could be. Even on that day you said the entry is after 2.30 p.m., right?"

"Yes, sir," Tupe replied.

"And exit?"

"No timing's been recorded in the register, but the CCTV footage shows the car left about thirty-five minutes later."

"Okay . . ." Saralkar said, making a steeple of his fingers. "This Rishabh is certainly a person of interest for us. Find out who he is and trace him."

*****

Chapter 11

One Year Ago (June 2021)

Namita stared in disbelief and awe as a handsome, rakish looking man with a wide grin on his face, appeared on screen. He had long, wavy hair and a stylishly cut French beard, there was a stud in one ear and a leather wristband wrapped around his left wrist. His shirt had one open button and a gold chain peeked out over his chest hair. He looked fit and trim for his age.

"Hi sweetie . . . I'm your papa," he said in a manly, endearing tone.

Namita was speechless—a strange blend of happiness and sadness unleashed in her heart.

"You were just four when I was last allowed to see you! How you've grown into a lovely young woman now, Namita . . ." Randeep Mirdha said to his daughter, his features aglow with a charming smile.

His daughter blushed, thrilled to hear the compliment from her long-lost real father, floored by his personality and manner, compared to the man who had usurped his position—her stepfather, Mohnish Bhatti, whom she resented with all her heart, especially since her real father had got in touch with her suddenly one day, a few weeks ago.

"Thank you, Papa," she replied. "Why . . . Why didn't you ever call or write to me all these years?"

"Well, your mother wanted to have nothing more to do with me . . . and I guess she wanted me erased from your memory too," Randeep Mirdha said with a shrug. "She had forbidden me to visit or call . . . but I did write to you. Didn't Smita ever give you my letters?"

"No . . . Mamma never even told me you had written," Namita said in a small voice, feeling irrationally angry with her mother.

Randeep Mirdha clicked his tongue slyly. "Ah well. She probably thought you would not like your new daddy, if I stayed in touch."

"I don't like him anyhow . . . and I don't call him daddy anymore," the girl replied.

"Oh, forget him! I don't know what your mother saw in that sucker Mohnish," Randeep Mirdha said, pleased to see how the last few weeks had not only brought him close to his daughter but also successfully seeded hostility against Smita and Mohnish. "Tell me, do you remember how much you loved me? You would cling to me all your waking hours – it was always Papa . . . Papa . . . Papa . . .! Do you remember any of it, darling?"

Namita tried hard to think back, trawl her memory for some image, some snippet, some incident that would bring her the comfort and warmth of nostalgia—something that had stuck and not been dislodged by the passage of time. She stayed quiet, unwilling to admit she remembered nothing beyond a fuzzy connection with this man.

"Haven't you seen any of our photos together?" Randeep Mirdha asked, ". . . where I'm playing with you, holding you, tickling you?"

"No, Papa . . ." Namita said, now near tears. Why had her mother deprived her so?

"That's not fair . . . that's cruel of your mother," Randeep said, modulating his tone perfectly. "You were my little doll, you know . . . but never mind. Cheer up, Namita . . . I'll send you some pics, okay . . . of us together . . . you and me!"

"That would be great, Papa . . . did I look cute then?" Namita asked.

"Super-cute, sweetie . . . you were my absolutely adorable princess . . . how I miss you," her father gushed.

Namita was ecstatic to hear his words. Why had her mother separated her from this wonderful man—her real father?

"Why did Mamma divorce you, Papa?" she asked in anguish.

"Ah well . . . What has your mother told you?" Randeep Mirdha replied, side-stepping smartly.

"We . . . We've never really much talked about it," Namita said. "Once or twice she just told me that . . . that . . ."

"What?"

"That . . . That you didn't love her, that you troubled her . . . that you made her very unhappy . . ." Namita paused. "Did you harass her, Papa?"

Randeep Mirdha knew he had to play it right. He scoffed, "How convenient! Look, darling, I don't want to say anything about Smita . . . she's your mother . . . it is all in the past . . . but the truth is, well . . . it was Mohnish who lured her away . . . my own friend . . . she was having an affair with him . . . and that's why she divorced me . . . took you away from me . . ."

It was calculated to create bitterness and anger, and it did. Namita looked at the handsome, crestfallen face of her father and saw the look of injured victimhood, and a bolt of hostility shot through her—towards her selfish mother and her slimy, home-wrecking stepfather.

"But why didn't you stop her? Why did you allow her to take me with her?" she demanded.

Randeep Mirdha sighed and stroked his luxurious mane. "You are still young, Namita . . . you don't know how the laws in this country favour women in marital cases. She also filed all sorts of police complaints against me . . . so . . . so I was helpless, in a way. In court she painted me as a rotten character—smoking, drinking, unfaithful, and such stuff."

He paused, then said, "Anyway, let's not talk about it . . . it was a bad time . . . and I was just . . . helpless. Let's talk about now, Namita. Tell me, what are you doing? How's college? Any boyfriends of my little girl?"

Namita blushed. "No, Papa . . . but I like a guy. Mamma doesn't allow me to go on dates and all yet . . ."

"Oh, come on . . ." Randeep said, "what's the fun of college without dating guys? If I was there . . . I would've allowed you to go wherever you wanted with anyone you like!"

"Really, Papa!"

"Well, I'm super-cool! Anyway, college is still fun, right?"

"Yes . . . I have a wonderful gang of friends and it's great fun."

"And what about home? You happy? Does your mamma have time for you? Does your stepfather treat you well?"

Namita's face had fallen. "It's okay. Mamma's busy with her job and looking after Pranjal . . . and her husband."

"Oh yes, you have a young stepbrother, right?"

"Yes . . . Pranjal."

"How old is he?"

"Ten."

"Okay, so he's the apple of their eye?" Randeep asked deliberately.

Namita didn't reply.

Randeep continued, "I hope they don't give you the feeling they love him more than you . . ."

The answer came quick. "Of course, they love him more. It's always Pranjal this . . . and Pranjal that. And they praise him to the skies . . . good at studies and now that he's winning chess competitions, they are over the moon . . ."

"I see. He's a chess champion, isn't he?"

"Yes . . . he's also undergoing coaching. He's really good . . . like a prodigy . . ." Namita admitted grudgingly.

"Okay, don't let it bother you, sweetie . . . I am there for you, you know."

"Can't I come and stay with you, Papa?" Namita asked wistfully.

"Well, . . . it's not that easy, Namita. Too many complications and your mum might create trouble."

"But I am going to be eighteen early next year. I can decide, can't I, who to stay with . . .?" Namita protested.

"Okay, let me think about it . . . consult a lawyer, okay . . .? Meanwhile I promise I'll come and see you soon," Randeep said.

"Wow! Really, Papa? When?"

"When I am in Pune next, okay? I promise."

*****

"When was the last time you heard his voice?" Saralkar asked Mohnish Bhatti, who was sitting up in his hospital bed now.

Mohnish glanced in the direction of Smita, as he had been doing throughout, as if to draw confidence from her. "At least ten years have passed . . . perhaps more."

"So, how can you be sure it was the voice of Mrs. Bhatti's first husband?" Motkar remarked.

The couple had just told him and Motkar about their past, Smita's first husband, and Mohnish's suspicion that the voice on the ransom call might have been that of Randeep Mirdha.

"He was not just Smita's first husband," Mohnish said sharply, "I had known him much before that as we were trainees in the same company." He paused and glared briefly at Motkar, then looked at Saralkar less belligerently, "They say voices don't change much over a lifetime, isn't it?"

It was one of those lasting, popular notions, probably because between the ages of eighteen and fifty-five, human voices more or less sounded recognisably the same in tone, tenor, volume, and pitch. But the fact was that voices did undergo gradual changes so that it couldn't be said with absolute certainty that one would instantly recognise a voice heard after a long gap.

"Yet, as you said, you didn't recognise it immediately or realize that it sounded like Randeep?" Saralkar said. "Nor are you completely certain now . . ."

"But don't you see that Randeep might've had the strongest motive in harming Pranjal and destroying us?" Smita Bhatti broke in. "If we had a sworn enemy, it was Randeep . . ."

Saralkar nodded. "Given the acrimony of your divorce and all that you told us, we are definitely going to investigate his possible involvement. I am just trying to assess the probability. You both say you haven't set eyes on Randeep for over ten years . . . he has not tried to contact you or threaten you . . . right?"

"That's correct," both husband and wife replied.

"Not a phone call, nor a visit, not a letter, nor email, or message?" Motkar added.

"No . . . we broke off complete contact from everyone," Smita said. "We shifted to Pune from Chandigarh to get away from him . . . and even from both our families, who didn't approve of our illicit affair and our decision to get married after getting divorced from Randeep. We didn't want his shadow looming over us. We had gone through too much already."

"And he's left you alone? There's been no incident, nothing alarming after that?" Saralkar asked.

She was quiet for a few seconds. "No . . . not after we left Chandigarh. Before that, we had two or three tough years, when I first told him about me and Mohnish. Randeep went berserk. He beat me often, threatened me . . . set some goons on Mohnish. Had him hammered within an inch of his life . . . but we fought back. We registered multiple police cases against him. I filed for divorce . . . and then of course Mohnish had some contacts . . . friends who helped keep Randeep in line. Eventually we knew it would be better to leave Chandigarh since our families were also not supportive, which we did."

Mohnish said, "You know, Randeep even threatened to kill Namita once, when she was just three or four . . . I remember it clearly . . . the way he said it. That's why I decided I should reveal my suspicions. A man who can . . ."

". . . threaten to kill his own daughter is quite capable of killing our son . . . my Pranjal," Smita completed his sentence.

Saralkar and Motkar exchanged glances. "Do you have any idea whether Randeep's still in Chandigarh?" Saralkar asked. "Also can you share any details you may have of him— his photo, his last known address, phone number, and yes . . . the police FIRs and cases you have filed against him—to help us trace Randeep?"

Smita nodded. "Yes, I have kept copies of all legal documentation and complaints . . . and some photos of him with my daughter back then. I have his old Chandigarh address and also that of his folks."

"Good, give them to us," Saralkar said. "Is there anything more you can tell us about Randeep? Or any other related matters, incidents, people . . .?"

"No, Inspector," Mohnish said.

Saralkar looked at Smita. "Does your daughter know about your ex-husband—her biological father?"

He saw Smita grimace while Mohnish turned away as if it was some unpalatable, sordid issue.

"I mean . . . Namita knows the story although we've kept all the troublesome details from her," Smita said struggling with distress. "When I won custody of her I'd got clear orders passed from the court that Randeep would have no access rights to her till she reached adulthood."

"I see, but you are sure that her father is not in touch with her?"

A look of alarm spread on Smita's face. "How could she?"

"Okay. We'll start with the information you have given us and see where it leads us," Motkar replied.

"Has there been any progress at all, Inspector?" Mohnish Bhatti suddenly asked. His torment was palpable.

"Well, we have already set up some lines of inquiry—we interrogated the corporator Satish Khilare. He denies involvement . . . but we are checking his movements and for evidence of his involvement. We also interrogated the driver Jayesh's brother, Jayant. Jayesh is not traceable but hopefully we'll find him soon," Saralkar said. "There are several other leads being pursued but it's premature to share them."

A pall of silence hung over the room for a few seconds before Smita spoke. "When will we get Pranjal's . . ." she stuttered to a halt then forced herself to utter the dreadful words, ". . . Pranjal's body?"

Saralkar felt queasiness build inside him. He knew he needed to tell the parents about the evidence of sexual assault on their son's body, but found himself tongue-tied. Would it not be better to spare them?

"The post-mortem's done. Some more forensic tests are being concluded. I think you'll get the body tomorrow," he replied, feeling perfectly justified in being cowardly in not telling them more. Perhaps informing them a day later would help soften the blow.

Motkar glanced at his boss, who avoided his eye. It was good to know even his boss's nerve failed at times.

*****

Jayant Pardeshi's phone buzzed. His heart skipped a beat when he saw it was his brother calling. Ever since the run-in with the cops, he had been wrestling with a dilemma—what was he to do if his brother did get in touch?

Warn him that the police were looking for him or say nothing, just get information from him about his whereabouts and when he was coming back to Pune, as Senior Inspector Saralkar had asked him to?

He was as severely conflicted as anyone in his position would be. Jayesh had always been spiteful and grudge-filled by nature. He was not beyond violence and had often gone too far in harassing those against whom he had an axe to grind. But did that mean he would go as far as to kidnap and murder?

All Jayant's brotherly instincts told him Jayesh wouldn't, but the last six or seven months had been bad for his older brother financially and he had been acting weird for sure.

"Hullo," Jayant said taking the call. "Where have you been, Jayesh?"

"*Arre,* what to tell you, Jayant . . . I lost my phone at a dhaba stop a couple of days ago . . . bloody thieves!" Jayesh said, sounding in a foul mood. "Finally managed to get a second-hand handset today . . . and a replacement SIM card . . . bloody hell . . . it's been a nightmare."

"Oh! Where are you?" Jayant asked.

"Jabalpur," Jayesh said. "First Indore, then some hill-station called Panchmarhi and now in Jabalpur . . . shouldn't have taken this bloody trip! What a horrible party—they keep cribbing—car AC is not cooling enough, upholstery is not comfortable, driving too slowly, suspension not good . . . and the bastards are super stingy."

Jayant listened anxiously. It all sounded genuine with no false note. "So, when are you headed home?"

"I was to get home tomorrow but I guess it's another three days at least. I'm going to charge them a bomb. I am going to say because the trip got extended, I had to cancel another booking," Jayesh grumbled. "And if they don't pay up what I ask for, then I'll teach them a lesson someday."

"Why do you keep talking like that, Jayesh?" Jayant remonstrated. "It'll get you into big trouble someday."

"Big trouble with whom?"

Jayant swallowed. "Cops . . ."

"Cops? Why are you saying that?" Jayesh queried.

"I mean . . . with anyone who gets aggravated if you are always looking for a fight," Jayant said, trying to cover up.

"What the f--k are you saying? You are my younger brother, you bum. Don't try to teach me!" Jayesh yelled at him.

Jayant could make out from his tone that he was drunk.

"Don't get me wrong, Jayesh bhau . . . I'm just telling you for your own good. And come back safely."

"Yes . . . yes. Are Sushila and the children back?" He was referring to his wife and kids.

"No, not yet," Jayant replied. "You haven't spoken to them?"

"No."

"But why?"

"Obviously I didn't have the phone till today. And then before I left that stupid Sushila fought with me," Jayesh said.

That fitted in with his traits. The couple did fight a lot and it had gotten worse over the years.

"I see. Okay . . . so see you back soon, Jayesh," Jayant said, fighting back the urge to tell his brother what awaited him.

"Why? You busy or what? Don't have time to talk to me?" Jayesh asked rudely.

"No . . . nothing like that," Jayant replied, trying hard to sound normal. How could he tell his brother that he was scared of blurting out things he was not supposed to tell him, if the conversation continued.

"Then wait . . . talk to me. I haven't spoken to anyone for two or three days except these stupid passengers," Jayesh mumbled. "What's happening in Pune? Anything interesting last week—this week . . .?"

"Well. Not much that I can think of – the usual . . ." It was then that a thought struck Jayant. He cleared his throat. "The news is full of the kidnapping and murder of a young school boy."

"Is it? Too bad! Tell me about it," Jayesh said.

His tone and voice betrayed nothing untoward to Jayant's ears.

"Actually, you know that Admin manager at Bitcoff IT, Smita Bhatti madam?" Jayant asked gingerly.

"That bitch who removed us? What about her?" Jayesh said with a drunken slur, which was quite pronounced now.

Jayant licked his lips. "It . . . It was her boy, Pranjal, who was kidnapped and killed."

What would be his brother's response? He waited with bated breath—two seconds, five seconds, ten seconds . . .

"Hullo?" he said again.

But there was no reply from Jayesh. The line seemed to have gone blank all of a sudden, as if he was just talking into a void. He hadn't heard Jayesh disconnect the call. Jayant moved the phone away from his ear and looked at the screen. The call still showed as connected, the seconds ticking away.

"Jayesh bhau . . . hullo . . .?" Jayant spoke again.

There, however, seemed no Jayesh at the other end. Was it a call drop? Jayant disconnected and dialled again. No rings passed. What was he to make of it, he wondered, the hair on his hand standing on end. Why had the call gone blank? Had Jayesh disappeared like that because he had something to do with the crime?

Jayant's heart beat hard. What was he to do now? Should he inform the cops about the call? Would that be betraying Jayesh and getting him into trouble? And if he failed to tell the police, wouldn't he be considered an accessory, if indeed Jayesh was involved?

Jayant began to shake, as doubts assailed him. His moment of reckoning had come. He didn't want a police record, when he had done nothing. But was it necessary to call the cops at this time of the night right away? Maybe he could wait till morning and try calling Jayesh again. If he didn't pick up, then perhaps he would be left with no choice but to report to the police.

*****

Chapter 12

"The chocolate-coloured Ertiga is registered in the name of Dr. B.P. Banerjee. He's a cancer specialist attached to three top city hospitals, sir," Tupe said. "He stays in a bungalow in a posh society in Aundh area. It's one of the three cars belonging to the family."

"I see. So, I assume the young man seen driving it must be his son, most likely. Got any information on him?" Saralkar asked.

"We've checked their Facebook accounts, sir. Dr. Banerjee has a son named Rishabh and he's the one we can see in the CCTV footage," Tupe replied. "But we checked out both his and Namita's social media accounts and haven't found any pictures of them together, except one—probably a party, in which both can be seen, but not like a couple. So, we need to establish a closer link."

"Which college does this Rishabh study in?"

"Sir, he's a final year student at Symbiosis Commerce College, not MIT College where Namita studies," Tupe replied.

Saralkar was thoughtful. It was too early to confront the girl and the boy till they had more irrefutable information. "Check the girl's social media accounts and see if you can identify her best friends or those who seem close. Then make inquiries discreetly with one or two of them, whether this Rishabh and she are dating or going steady . . . whatever it is they call it these days," Saralkar said.

"Sure, sir," Tupe replied and was about to leave when Motkar spoke.

"Tupe, when your team first received the missing complaint, did you talk to any of Pranjal's close friends?" he asked.

"Yes, we did speak to four or five friends of Pranjal, but got no really useful leads or hints."

"The children you spoke to were his school and colony friends?" Motkar asked.

"Yes, the ones his mother told us about," Tupe replied. "The only friends we didn't speak to were his chess classmates but that's because he used to go for chess coaching only on weekends."

"Oh, he went for chess coaching too, is it? How about the chess coach? You spoke to him?" Saralkar asked.

"No, sir. I didn't think it was relevant," Tupe said.

"Okay. Perhaps we need to speak to the children again, Motkar. It's always possible with kids that they are holding back on information out of fear or because it's a buddy's secret."

Motkar nodded. "I'll speak to Pranjal's friends."

"And who's the chess coach, Tupe?"

"Sir, she's a former national chess champion, Sunaini Mahajan. She runs a small chess academy in Balewadi area and coaches only a handful of children who are competing at state, national, and international level."

"I see. No harm in speaking to her too, Motkar," Saralkar remarked then turned to Tupe again, "And what's the progress on dredging the river bed near Rajaram Bridge?"

"It's been delayed a bit, sir. There's that crocodile spotting scare reported again, sir, like two years ago," Tupe replied. "A crocodile was sighted last week and on two consecutive occasions this week, . . . after we recovered Pranjal's body."

"But that's usually upriver near Katraj or the reservoir area near Khadakwasla dam, right?" Saralkar asked.

"I am not sure, sir. I'll check. But this is the reason the divers' team gave me," Tupe replied.

"Okay, anything else to report?" Saralkar asked.

Tupe shook his head.

Saralkar grunted. "Carry on, then."

ASI Tupe nodded and left the room. Saralkar turned to Motkar.

"Has Satish Khilare provided details of his schedule and whereabouts for last week, Motkar?"

"Yes, sir. I am having it verified. He claims to have been out of Pune on the day of the kidnapping . . . says he had gone to Bhor and came back next afternoon."

"What's in Bhor?"

"His farmhouse, sir."

"Hmm. Bhor's not more than one and a half hour's distance from here, right?"

"Yes, sir."

"Get someone from Bhor Police to find out how big the farmhouse is and who's usually there. Also how often does Khilare go there. They would know."

"It crossed my mind too that the farmhouse could be the kind of place where the boy was taken," Motkar said.

"We can't make surmises of that kind till we know more, Motkar," Saralkar said. "That's why we should get Bhor Police to feed us some information. And what about this Sunny character?"

"I have checked with my source again, sir. He doesn't have anything more specific," Motkar said. "But Sunny's not skipped Pune so far. Shall we bring him in for questioning?"

"Serves no purpose unless we have some sort of concrete evidence to connect either Khilare or Sunny to the kidnapping," Saralkar said.

The rings of Motkar's mobile interrupted their discussion. "Sir, it's Jayant Pardeshi, that driver's brother," Motkar said, before he took the call.

"Jabalpur?" Motkar asked, as he listened intently to Jayant. "And when did he say he's going to be back? Okay, keep me informed if you get any more calls from Jayesh."

He disconnected and briefed Saralkar. "Let's put the number on tracking, Motkar, now that it's active again," Saralkar observed. "We can never be sure whether the brother didn't pass on a warning to Jayesh that we're looking for him."

"Yes, sir. And how do we proceed with tracking down the elusive first husband, Randeep Mirdha?"

"Let's see if we can get any convictions or prison time for Randeep Mirdha on the NCRB database or chargesheets filed by Chandigarh Police," Saralkar said. "Smita Bhatti said she'd filed domestic violence and dowry harassment cases against him, which are non-bailable. The Chandigarh Police might have a record."

A knock on the cabin door interrupted their conversation. It was a constable. "Sir, there's a lady here to see you. Said her name is Ashwini Gholap."

"What does she want?"

"Sir, she said she has some information about a case, which she'd like to share only with you," the constable replied.

"Okay, fetch her," Saralkar said to the constable then turned to Motkar, "Get in touch with Chandigarh Police and hopefully we might be able to locate Mrs. Bhatti's ex-husband."

A second, softer knock sounded on his cabin door. "Sir, may I come in?" the woman standing outside Saralkar's cabin asked. "I'm Ashwini Gholap."

Pushing forty-five, Ashwini Gholap sported a bob cut over a gaunt face on which an expression of anxious determination had permanently settled in. She wore a working woman's attire of a neat, sober saree and held a file in one hand while a large faux leather handbag hung from her shoulder.

Saralkar's face turned politely dour as he waved her in and offered her a seat next to Motkar. "Yes, Mrs. Gholap, you said you wanted to see me about some case?"

Ashwini nodded.

"A murder case?"

"Yes. Ashwini Gholap is my maiden name actually. I am divorced now," she clarified, without the usual irritation that women showed when addressed by the wrong salutation. "I am Atharva Jambhekar's mother . . . whose murder remains unsolved till date. It's six years ago that he disappeared."

She paused, as if waiting for Saralkar to grasp the preamble. Her tone was soft and matter-of-fact, without emotional charge, but there was a slight slur in her voice like a form of speech disorder.

"I see," Saralkar said, casting a glance at Motkar to check for any signs that he knew about the case, but his assistant's face showed no flicker of awareness.

"Have you heard about Atharva's case, sir?" Ashwini asked evenly.

"No, I haven't," Saralkar said, thankful for the remarkable composure of the woman.

There were cases that never came to Homicide for various reasons, possibly because they were investigated by other squads—Crime Branch, CID, Narcotics, Organized Crime or even special teams, created by erstwhile police chiefs, based on their priorities and prevailing challenges.

Then the penny dropped as to why Ashwini Gholap was here, when she spoke again. "I read about the kidnap and murder of that poor child, Pranjal Bhatti . . . I believe you are investigating the case."

"That's right," Saralkar replied his interest quickening. "Do you have some information that might help us?"

"Just like Pranjal Bhatti, my Atharva went missing one day . . . kidnapped by someone . . . and his body was found five days later in the Mutha river, near Mhatre Bridge," Ashwini resumed in the same tone, without flinching. "I think there are such striking similarities in both crimes, that maybe you . . . the Pune Police can reopen and reinvestigate my son's case too. I have a file on it for you to take a look, since you don't know about the case."

She held out the file she had been carrying. Saralkar took a moment to reach out and take it from her, as he processed what she had just said. Scepticism was second nature to him as a person, doubly so as a police officer. He wasn't about to jump into a cold case because the woman before him claimed there were similarities to the current case.

"Atharva would have been seventeen now. I don't know why the murderer was never caught. I am sure the police tried hard," she said, emotion creeping into her voice, just a little. "Every time I approached someone I thought could help—top policemen, politicians, legal luminaries, journalists—anyone who had any influence, I've been given assurances . . . but nothing's happened."

She paused as if searching for something in Saralkar's eyes. It wasn't the first time Saralkar had dealt with the haunting, hopeful fortitude of this particular kind—of a close family member of a murder victim, whose case had remained unsolved for long. It was a stoicism hard to deal with, because of the immense sense of guilt and helplessness it invoked in police officers confronted with it.

"It might not be any different this time too, Ms. Gholap. Breakthroughs are rare in cases that have remained unsolved that long," Saralkar said with a gentle bluntness few people are capable of getting right.

"You mean to say . . . you are making no headway in Pranjal Bhatti's case too?"

"No, I am not at liberty to talk about that investigation . . . but just because prima facie the two crimes are similar, does not mean there is a connection, so please don't get your hopes up," Saralkar said.

Ashwini blinked rapidly, the stoic expression wavering momentarily. "But . . . I've got to know before I die . . ." she said, her voice low and urgent and the slur more evident. "I've already suffered one stroke last year . . . I was lucky to survive . . . and the doctors tell me if I am not careful, a second one could be fatal. So don't you see I've got to know what happened to my boy . . . who killed him, and why. Surely there's got to be a link?"

The poignant sadness in her tone rendered the two conscientious cops in the room speechless. What could be an appropriate response? Inadequate commiserations? Or bland, empty reassurance?

"Let me have a look at the file first," Saralkar finally said, opening the file to glance at the contents more as a cursory look through.

Inside lay six years of a thick paper trail of the case—copies of official investigation documents and reports, newspaper clippings, appeals and correspondence with various authorities over the years as the case lost traction, and intermittent summaries of the lack of progress. All the papers were full of underlined content, annotated scrawls in the margins, comments, questions, references to other pages. Atharva's mother had clearly pored over each page again and again, picking up contradictions, inconsistencies, missing information and other observations, hypothesis and doubts.

Saralkar closed the file and met her expectant eyes. She spoke before he could.

"I know you'll need time to go through it, sir. You can keep it—it's your copy," she said. "So may I come back to see you next week?"

"Ms. Gholap, we will also need to thumb through our police records, besides this file, maybe talk to the erstwhile investigating officers who worked on this case earlier, before I can tell you if we are taking it up," Saralkar said. "My colleague PSI Motkar will get in touch with you once we have reviewed the case status."

Ashwini gave a quick sideways glance to Motkar sitting next to her and a slight nod, before turning back to Saralkar. She was silent for a few seconds, staring searchingly at Saralkar's face—a gaze which wordlessly expressed its unfathomable grief.

"I had just returned home late from work that evening. Hardly met Atharva for ten minutes, before he bolted out with his beloved skateboard . . . he was an under-fourteen state medallist, you know," she spoke finally. "No premonition, no unexplained uneasiness . . . that I would never see him alive again. So ordinary our parting was . . ."

Her eyes suddenly welled up and with almost superhuman effort she seemed to be able to halt them from spilling down her face. "I stopped believing in God. I don't believe in heaven or somewhere above where I might be united with him again. That's why I need to know before I suffer another stroke . . . before I die, who snatched him from me and why. I'll be very grateful, sir . . ."

A brief, awkward silence fell over the room, Ashwini looking for a commitment that Saralkar did not honestly feel capable of making.

PSI Motkar cleared his throat. "Please leave your mobile number with me, madam."

She gave him her number, then got up from her chair and left with a softly murmured "Thank you".

Silence reigned for a few moments, as if she'd left behind her grief in the room that weighed both the men down. Then Saralkar exhaled heavily, as if he'd held his breath all the while. "Will you be able to plough through this and pull out the case papers from Records?"

"Yes, sir," Motkar said without hesitation. He took the thick file from his boss. "You don't look enthused about this, sir."

"Worth taking a look at, Motkar, but too early to be enthused," Saralkar observed. "Nothing blindsides cops more than leads that fall into their laps."

Motkar nodded. "Life's incredibly cruel isn't it, sir? To not know for six long years who killed your child and why, must be sheer agony."

Saralkar gave him a long stare but as if he wasn't really looking at Motkar. "Yes. As if one grieving mother was not bad enough, we now have another on our hands, whose grief is even older . . ."

*****

Chapter 13

Saralkar hated cremations. There was nothing solemn about them. The rituals nauseated him. Whatever symbolic and deeper meanings they signified were lost to most people. Families did not know what they were doing except that it was usually done this way to ensure their loved one's soul was put to rest.

Nor did attendees know any better, except for marking their presence and paying clichéd condolences to those bereaved.

Saralkar particularly detested the loud, raucous grieving that accompanied many funerals, which seemed forever poised to turn the occasion into a staged public spectacle to showcase loss. And then of course, there was the other type of cremation that felt like everyone was just going through the motions—as if nobody was really sad or interested in the person who'd just passed away, except for getting it all over with.

Most of all he hated the paraphernalia—the squelched flowers and the ghee and other prayer material that transformed the last rites into a messy, revolting event rather than a dignified one.

He had no intention of being present at Pranjal Bhatti's cremation but he was ethically obliged to tell the Bhattis about the post-mortem results. He braced himself for the task the moment Motkar informed him Pranjal's body was ready for release.

"Have they made sure the body is presentable?' he asked Motkar. "I don't want any distressing scenes brought on by some shoddy neglect."

"They've done the best they could, sir."

"Have you seen it for yourself?"

Motkar nodded. "Yes, sir. Would you like to make sure for yourself?"

Saralkar curled his lip in distaste and looked at Motkar. "Are you trying to be cheeky, Motkar?"

"Absolutely not, sir," Motkar said with raised eyebrows, mildly satisfied he'd managed to needle his boss for needlessly doubting him.

"Well, intimate the family that we are coming over to hand over the body."

"Okay, sir."

For a moment Saralkar was tempted to delegate the unpleasant task to Motkar but dismissed the thought.

Four hours later, he finally mouthed the words that had been sticking in his throat for long. The tempest of emotion that the sight of their son's body had evoked in the Bhattis had made Saralkar pause. Was it really necessary to add to their acute sorrow before the last rites were done, he'd wondered. He'd decided to postpone telling them till after the cremation. Discretion was not just the better part of valour, but also of truth-telling sometimes.

"Mr. and Mrs. Bhatti," he finally said when the couple sat desolately at home, back from the crematorium and all the visitors—mostly neighbours and acquaintances—had left. "There's one new fact that has emerged . . . which . . . which you need to be told about."

The couple looked at him with wary eyes; Mohnish, as if unsure of surviving another blow and his wife, Smita, as if defiantly drawing on all her powers of resilience to face the fresh curveball that life was going to throw at them. "What is it, Inspector?"

Saralkar felt Motkar's gaze on him too, watching how his boss was going to acquit himself in breaking something this sensitive to an already devastated couple.

"It appears unfortunately that Pranjal was sexually assaulted," Saralkar said, not mincing words, yet using his intonation to the utmost to break this decidedly unpalatable fact to the parents, as gently as humanly possible.

His remark was greeted with a few seconds of stunned silence. Both Mohnish and Smita were staring at him as if he'd spoken in a language that they simply didn't understand a word of.

Finally, a strangled sound escaped Mohnish's lips, as if somebody had snapped his spinal cord, leaving his vocal cords only to make guttural sounds.

"What do you mean sexually assaulted?" Smita Bhatti found her voice. "What was done to Pranjal?"

This was the exact question Saralkar had been hoping to avoid. But she had asked him upfront now and he would have to answer it in all its gruesomeness, unless she backed off.

"I can tell you, Mrs. Bhatti, but are you sure you want to hear it?"

"Of course. He was my son and I want to know what he suffered," Smita replied savagely.

Her eyes were blazing and Saralkar glanced momentarily at her husband to see his reaction. Mohnish had gone blank, zombie-like, as if his faculties were not prepared to handle the overload.

"Very well," Saralkar said, talking with deliberate slowness as if calibrating the information. "There was anal penetration."

He saw Mohnish cringe and raise his hands to cover his face first and then his ears. Smita's face was hard as if ready for more details.

". . . however, the assault was after his death . . ." Saralkar continued.

All the hardness of her face disintegrated and fell away in a moment and tears sprang from her eyes—tears of incredible fury. "After he died? Pranjal's body was violated after he died . . .?" she spluttered with rage. "Are you trying to say my boy was kidnapped and killed by some pervert . . . some sick paedophile? Oh God! Oh God! What did my Pranjal even do to deserve this?"

She turned to her husband and flung herself into his arms.

Saralkar did not reply immediately, waiting for the squall of emotions to pass. He glanced at Motkar instead and was taken aback to see something akin to angry sadness, darken his face.

"Answer me, Inspector!" Smita asked.

"It's a possibility that a paedophile took him, given this new information," Saralkar admitted. "Although we are not sure how the motive fits in, with what we know so far. Tell me, was Pranjal close to any older man or a youngster—an older friend—somebody well known to you, whom Pranjal would easily trust?"

Mohnish Bhatti shook his head. "I can't think of anyone like that . . . we . . . we . . . don't have any close relatives or friends to speak of. Nor have I seen him hang out with older boys or adults in the society. It's got to be some stranger."

"How about someone in his chess class . . . someone he looked up to, or met?" Saralkar asked.

Both husband and wife looked at him, bewildered, as if they had trouble entertaining the very possibility.

"Someone from his chess coaching? Pranjal looked up to his coach, Sunaini Bhagwat. And some older players there but . . . but they would hardly be capable of such ghastly acts," Mohnish said.

"I see," Saralkar said. "Do alert me if you can think of anyone later. I'm afraid I'll have to take your leave now."

Saralkar glanced at Motkar and both cops began walking out of the house.

"Inspector Saralkar!" Mohnish suddenly called out.

"Yes?"

"I hate to say this but I have just remembered there is one person who . . . who . . ." Mohnish stuttered to a halt and looked at his wife, who was regarding him quizzically.

"Karan . . . Karan Jerajani . . ." he said to her.

The look in her eyes instantly became angry and hostile.

"Who's Karan Jerajani?" Saralkar asked.

"Someone we once thought of as our friend," Smita said. "He turned out to be a slimy, sleazy man."

"Does he live in Pune?"

"No . . . he's working in Navi Mumbai now, but when he was in Pune, he frequented our place," Mohnish said.

"Tell us what made you think of him just now?" Saralkar asked.

"Well, we've not been in touch for almost three or four years now," Mohnish said. "Karan and I were hostel mates. In fact, he also knew Randeep. When Smita and I moved to Pune,

I bumped into Karan after several years. He'd worked abroad for some time and had moved back to India for a job again . . . in Pune. He was good company and would often drop in at our place, because he was single and we also liked meeting him."

Mohnish paused then asked Saralkar hesitantly, "Are you aware that I was one of the winners of KBC?"

"Kaun Banega Crorepati? No . . . tell me about it."

"Well, about four years ago I won ₹40 lakhs as prize money on KBC! It made a big difference in our lives . . . to our financial condition," Mohnish said. "Karan had excellent GK and so I'd arranged with him that I'd use my 'Phone a friend' option to call him if I got stuck with some question. He agreed and jokingly said I'd have to part with 10% of my total winnings if the answer he helped me with turned out to be correct. At least I thought it was a joke.

"Well, when the time came, I called him and he gave me the correct answer, which helped me greatly. A couple of weeks after the euphoria had died down, Karan first demanded 10% from me. I was perturbed since I hadn't really expected him to ask for the money. Soon his demand became more frequent and serious. Smita and I discussed it and I was really very grateful to Karan and valued his friendship; so I decided to gift him a check of ₹1 lakh as a gesture of gratitude. His refused to accept it and insisted he wanted what was originally agreed upon—10%. It led to an argument because I said I had made no such promise. Two days later he again dropped by and we had a massive showdown in which he abused Smita and me . . . and made all kinds of sick comments. I lost my temper and told him to get out of my house. From then on, he's made all kinds of defamatory posts about me on social media and in our college WhatsApp groups. He also keeps sending me offensive messages now and then . . ."

Saralkar had been listening carefully. "I see, but how does all this connect with the sexual assault possibility we were discussing?"

Mohnish seemed to hesitate then spoke, "As I said, Karan was always welcome to our home. He seemed to be very fond of Pranjal . . . always playing and tickling and horsing around. We never thought anything about it . . . but then suddenly one day about two years ago, long after Karan was out of our lives, Pranjal told us that he sometimes found Karan's touching, kissing, and fondling excessive . . . he did not like it."

"He was hardly six or seven years old when we fell out with Karan," Smita took over, ". . . and he must've been just two or three when Karan first started visiting our house regularly. Pranjal also seemed fond of Karan and I don't remember him ever telling me anything that sounded problematic . . . but it's true that he became less enthusiastic about being or playing with Karan after he turned five. He'd wriggle free if Karan picked him up or hugged him . . . he'd push him away if Karan tried to be affectionate or do physical *masti*—again none of it seemed alarming or unnatural. We just thought that like any boy growing up to school-going age, Pranjal didn't like being treated like a baby any more.

"And so, suddenly when he told us after Karan had stopped coming home that he didn't like Karan's touching and horsing around—the thought did cross my mind if Karan had tried something inappropriate."

"Did you try to draw Pranjal out about the matter?"

"Yes, I did ask Pranjal if there had been any particular incident," Smita said, "but he didn't reveal anything and just said, even his own father Mohnish didn't insist on constantly hugging or kissing him or being physically affectionate as much as Karan tried to. That it had annoyed and irritated him. It was a telling remark and for a while I wondered if Karan had tried something funny. But Pranjal didn't look disturbed and didn't mention it again, so I also dismissed it from my mind."

"Okay, so Karan Jerajani nursed a grudge against you and there is a possibility that his overt affection for Pranjal might be open to sordid interpretations," Saralkar summed up. "Has he sent you messages or called you recently in the last two or three months, Mr. Bhatti?"

"No. I blocked him about a year ago after a very abusive, drunken late-night call from him," Mohnish said. "I hadn't done it earlier because after all he had helped me win at KBC . . . so I thought someday he might come to his senses or need my help in some matter . . . but in that last call he said such obnoxious things about Smita and me and cursed the family in the foulest terms. I decided enough was enough."

"Did he mention or make any remark about Pranjal at all, during this call?" Motkar chimed in.

"He didn't . . ." Smita replied before Mohnish could reply, "but I took the phone and told Karan what Pranjal had said to me . . . and that he was a filthy, perverted man to make a child feel like that."

"Oh, how did he react then?" Motkar asked.

"He started screaming that I had a dirty mind . . . but I think it knocked the wind out of him, because he disconnected the call then," Smita said.

"I see, and there's been no further attempt at contact from him after that?" Saralkar asked.

"No," Mohnish said.

"Okay, that's about it for now, Mr. and Mrs. Bhatti. I don't want to make your day more agonising than it has already been so far," Saralkar said and gave the couple an awkward nod.

"You are no closer to finding my son's murderer than you were the day his body was found, are you, Inspector?" Smita asked, but not in her usual, combative way. There was more dejection than aggression.

Saralkar was quiet for a few seconds. "No, there is progress but yes, everything about justice is awfully slow."

He stopped, for it sounded incredibly trite even to his own ears, as Ashwini's face flashed through his mind. No, justice was as unpredictable and elusive as everything else in the world—fast for some, excruciatingly slow for others and perhaps never ever to be had for many unfortunate souls.

Any talk of justice was like a mere lollypop given to infants so that they wouldn't howl, sucking on to the drool of hope, while they waited interminably.

*****

Tupe was waiting for them when Saralkar and Motkar got back. Saralkar could make out that he was itching to share information.

"You look like a cat on a hot tin roof, Tupe. Tell me what has got you so excited."

"Sir, I spoke to Mitali Bhandari, who happens to be a good friend of Namita. She confirmed Rishabh and Namita had started dating a while ago . . . her parents have been kept in the dark and a few times the couple has met in each other's houses and sometimes even in friends' houses when their folks have been away," Tupe said, then arrived at the crux of the matter, "About fifteen days ago, Mitali said, Namita called her up in sheer panic and confided that her brother Pranjal had walked in on her and Rishabh . . . while they were . . . er . . . getting intimate . . ."

"Getting intimate? How intimate?" Saralkar asked.

"The girl Mitali wouldn't say, sir . . . but she told me Namita was terrified that Pranjal would tell her parents . . . and that it was so shameful that both she and Rishabh would be humiliated."

"Did she tell you the date this happened?" Motkar asked.

"Yes . . . and I checked that it matches with the day Rishabh made an entry in the society register last time," Tupe replied.

"What else did Mitali say?"

"Sir, she said, over the next few days Namita spoke to her again and said Pranjal hadn't told anything to her parents yet, but she lived in constant fear that he would. He had stopped talking to her normally and she was too ashamed to speak to him."

"Hmm . . . and what about Rishabh's reaction? Did Mitali know anything about that?" Saralkar asked.

"Yes, sir, I'm coming to that," Tupe said. "Apparently, Namita had stopped taking Rishabh's calls after the incident and refused to meet him. He in turn got in touch with Mitali and begged her to convince Namita to meet him once. Mitali spoke to Namita and arranged the meeting. Later, Namita told Mitali that Rishabh had promised he knew how to handle Pranjal and would make sure he didn't tell Namita's parents. Mitali asked Namita what exactly Rishabh was going to do, but Namita didn't confide in her."

"And we know from the CCTV footage that he was present in the society on the day Pranjal went missing, around the time he left for class . . ." Motkar added.

"Exactly!" Tupe said.

Saralkar chewed over the information for a few seconds, then said, "Okay, so it's time to confront the youngsters. Let's start with Rishabh, see how he reacts and then bring in Namita."

*****

Chapter 14

Six Years Ago (December 2016)

Ashwini Jambhekar woke up to a familiar headache. Like every night since her Atharva had been taken from her, she had cried herself to sleep in the wee hours of the morning. Had it been 2.00 a.m. or 3.00 a.m. when sleep had finally overcome her?

Why had she woken up again? Why hadn't she died in her sleep? What was there to wake up to and face a new day, when her Atharva was no more?

She could hear her husband Neeraj's peaceful breathing, punctuated by mild snores, beside her on the other side of the bed. How could he sleep through the night normally like that? Did he dream of Atharva? He never even talked about Atharva, as if the son they had raised together and doted upon for eleven years had just been a visitor in their lives—who had now left and therefore out of sight and out of mind.

When had Neeraj stopped caring and grieving? When had he returned to his routine—to his job and back to living his life? As if Atharva had been a brief interlude to the long melody of life that would continue uninterrupted.

Ashwini looked at the wall clock. It was 6.30 a.m. Sleep, which had been hard to come by, had abandoned her in just a few hours. And although she felt zero motivation to get out of bed, like every single morning in the past eight months, lying in bed made it even worse—tossing, turning, crying in despair—while her husband slumbered and no comfort was forthcoming from him.

Over the last few months, he had ceased even to attempt consoling her. He would just go silent, sitting or standing wherever he was, whenever Ashwini was overcome by grief and started sobbing or talking about their son—and the tragedy that had befallen them.

Except for a small wrinkle on his forehead, Neeraj would freeze, refusing to respond either by word or gesture. His eyes would be staring at the floor, his face empty of expression, his body language suggesting he was pinned to the spot, forced to be there because he couldn't be elsewhere—as if he'd run out of things to say to her about the matter or his feelings had reached some saturation point.

Ashwini sat up now. The sooner she started with chores the better, before futility and despair overpowered her. Ten minutes later, she had dragged herself into the drawing room and to the front door to check if the milk had arrived. She opened the door and picked up the cloth bag they hung outside, in which the delivery boy put the milk pouches.

It was then that she noticed another larger cloth bag, its neck tied up with a piece of string, lying next to the milk bag. It was not theirs, so what was it doing here?

Perhaps it belonged to the neighbours across the corridor and had somehow been placed next to her door by the milkman. Her gaze shifted to the neighbour's door, but their milk bag was hanging in the place it usually did. So, whose bag was this, lying at her door?

She stared at it, then gingerly bent down to touch it. It appeared stuffed with something, but she could not make out what it was. She then lifted it off the ground and realized it was quite heavy. Ashwini's puzzlement increased and her first instinct was to call out for her husband and ask him what was to be done about it. "Neeraj . . ." she called out feebly, then again, louder, "Neeraj . . ."

There was no answer. Either he was still fast asleep or had chosen not to respond, as he sometimes did. She couldn't just stand there indecisively, so she dragged the other bag in and shut the door. It was too early to start checking with neighbours if it belonged to any of them and if it did, sooner or later they would come looking for it.

She went into the kitchen, washed the milk pouches, poured the milk into a vessel and put it to boil. Her mind went back to the other bag. Would it not be better to open and see what was in it, so that she might get some indication of who it belonged to? All she needed to do was untie the string, look inside, and tie it back after ascertaining the contents.

She had been particularly intrigued by the string tied around the neck of the bag, either used to ensure the contents didn't spill out or to make sure no one could casually see what was inside. Ashwini untied the double knot of the thick jute string and opened the bag. Inside were plastic carry-bags, taped up with scotch tape.

She frowned and hesitated, for through the thin plastic layer of the carry-bags, she could feel what seemed like something wrapped in newspaper. What could've been wrapped up so carefully and what was it doing outside her door? Now that she had begun the process of finding out, she undid the scotch tape and pulled out the paper packet, which was taped with brown tape. And then she gasped, because taped to the newspaper packet was a small note with a felt-pen scrawl that read— "Sorry for Pintu!".

It suddenly felt as if a python had coiled itself around her and began crushing her bones, her organs, her entire being into pulp. Her vision blurred as the words hit her again—"Sorry for Pintu". Pintu—her life, the nickname of her son, Atharva—kidnapped and murdered eight months ago. Why had someone sent such a message and what was in the packet?

Ashwini began shaking all over as she tore away the paper. Out fell wads of currency!

For a few seconds she couldn't comprehend what she was holding—bundles of cash—one thousand and five-hundred-rupee notes, demonetised in one stroke, barely a month ago on 8 November 2016, that had unleashed pandemonium in the country.

Her brain tried its best to make sense of the surreal situation. Was this someone's idea of a sick, sadistic joke—dumping wads of demonetised currency at her doorstep as compensation for the death of her child? A cold fury gripped Ashwini. She wanted to scream. She threw the cash she was holding down on the floor.

"Neeraj!" she called out and rushed to the bedroom. "Neeraj!" she said hysterically as she began shaking her husband awake.

Neeraj's eyes opened with the usual glint of defensive moroseness. "What? What's wrong?"

"Come out," she said, unable to articulate further.

"But . . . what is it, Ashwini?" Neeraj said, frowning at her abruptness.

"Come out and see . . ." she said, turning around and walking out.

Neeraj got up and followed her out, still chafing mentally. The first thing his eyes fell on as he entered the drawing room was the boiling milk spilling all over the stove in the adjacent kitchen. He clicked his tongue, threw an angry glance at his wife who seemed to be oblivious, then walked over and quickly turned off the stove.

"The milk boiled over. Why weren't you watching?"

The comment didn't seem to register with his wife. "Look at this! Look at what someone sent . . ." she said, pointing at the floor near the door.

He saw the weird expression on her face, her whole body swaying and twitching with emotion. Neeraj turned his gaze to the object she was pointing to and saw the cash peeping out of the torn newspaper packet. It was his turn to be taken aback.

"What's all this, Ashwini? Where did this come from?"

"That cloth bag was lying outside our door, next to the milk bag," Ashwini replied in a burst of coherence. "When I opened it, I found these bundles of cash, wrapped in newspaper in plastic carry bags, with this note . . ."

She thrust the note at her husband, who was staring at her aghast. There was a few seconds of silence as she continued to look at him wildly and Neeraj tried to come to grips with the situation.

"My God . . . who do you think left this?" Neeraj managed to say as he read the note.

"Who else? This is blood money . . . the man who kidnapped our Atharva and murdered him . . . is the man who sent these packets of money as some sort of sadistic compensation."

"What? Why would he do that? It doesn't make sense," Neeraj said, ". . . This . . . This demonetised currency . . . somebody's played some mischief. Let me check with the watchman first if he saw any stranger come into the building with this bag."

He scrambled away to throw something on and went down to talk to the watchman.

*****

Rishabh Mukherjee had gone through the stages of shock, fear, denial, and breakdown within thirty minutes. Morose defiance had set in now.

"I . . . I haven't done anything!" he said, "I . . . had just gone there to meet Namita."

"So why were you denying your presence a few minutes ago?" PSI Motkar asked.

Rishabh was quiet for a beat, trying to bring coherence into the chaos that was his mind now. "Namita and I . . . thought it better not to mention my visit in the middle of this crisis."

"So, you entered the society around 2.40 p.m., parked the car, and went up?"

Rishabh hesitated again. "Yes . . ."

"I see. Who opened the door? Namita or Pranjal?"

Rishabh's face twitched and the lie followed, "Only . . . Only Namita was at home."

"Pranjal had left?"

"Yes."

"Namita told you that?"

"Yes."

"Sure?"

This time Rishabh only nodded; his mouth probably too dry to repeat a lie.

Saralkar's voice boomed from behind Motkar, "You are lying, Rishabh."

Rishabh shook his head vigorously. "No, sir . . . no, sir . . ." he croaked. "Why would I do that? You can ask Namita."

Neither Motkar nor Saralkar responded, letting the silence do the work for them as Rishabh sweated away with guilt.

"I . . . I have nothing to do with Pranjal's disappearance, sir," Rishabh pleaded, his voice shrill.

"We know Namita and you had a problem with Pranjal," Motkar said carefully.

"What problem, sir?" Rishabh said, attempting to look unfazed.

"A couple of weeks ago, Pranjal saw something he shouldn't have, didn't he?"

Rishabh looked as if he'd come into contact with a live wire, but tried putting up a brave front. "I don't know what you are talking about, sir."

"You are still lying, Rishabh," Saralkar hollered again, but this time got up and walked closer to the young man. "The more you lie, the longer you remain here."

"You . . . you can't just hold me like that, sir . . . I know that," Rishabh said, not to dare the senior inspector but more to show he was not totally unaware of what the police couldn't do.

"I see, you know all that," Saralkar said. "Well, here's what we *can* do. Let's head to your father's hospital now and with his permission, search your brown Ertiga and subject it to forensic analysis."

"What? Search the car? Why?"

"Because we suspect it was used to kidnap Pranjal that afternoon and dump his bicycle in the dicky," Saralkar said.

"That's totally false, sir . . . I did nothing of the kind!" Rishabh bleated. "How can you accuse me of kidnapping Pranjal? On what basis?"

"If you are innocent, Rishabh, there's nothing to worry," Saralkar said. "The car search will reveal the truth. If we find no DNA or fingerprints of Pranjal . . ."

He knew how sweeping the claim was, but this was a generation brought up on television and OTT shows. It would ring true to Rishabh's ears.

Rishabh wavered, his whole body agitated.

Motkar spoke now. "Or instead of going through all this trouble, just tell us the truth because we are sure Pranjal hadn't left the house and you met him that day."

Rishabh buried his face in his palms and when he raised it again, Saralkar almost felt sorry for him.

"Sir . . . I didn't do anything to Pranjal. I was just waiting for him below their building, to talk to him . . . to tell him not to rat on us to his parents about what he'd seen! But he simply shooed me away . . . he didn't want to talk."

"Narrate to us the exact conversation you had with him," Saralkar said.

Rishabh sniffed and told them how he had tried to reason with Pranjal.

"Then what happened? Pranjal rode away on his bicycle?" Motkar asked in a scoffing tone.

Rishabh half swallowed and blinked. "Yes, sir, Pranjal rode away to class! That's all that happened."

"Another lie, Rishabh," Saralkar's voice boomed. "I think at this point, you got so angry that Pranjal wouldn't listen that you grabbed him, put a hand on his nose and mouth, gagging him, or may be knocked him unconscious, put him in your car, loaded his bicycle in the dicky so that no one would realize he had not left and then drove away with him."

"No, sir! No, sir . . . that's totally wrong . . . I didn't even touch Pranjal, let alone kidnap him. Believe me!" Rishabh said vehemently. "He rode away, sir . . ."

"No, he most certainly didn't because he was not seen leaving the society by the CCTV at the gate. Only your car was seen leaving the premises so where did he vanish between you confronting him below the building and the gate?" PSI Motkar said. "You are lying that you saw him ride away!"

A shameful look settled on Rishabh's face. "Sir, I didn't mean to lie," he said abjectly now. "The fact is I was afraid that Pranjal would just take his bicycle and ride away without giving me a chance to talk to him . . . so . . . so . . . I just deflated the back tyre of his bicycle when I reached there."

"What? Go on."

"My plan was to deflate his tyre then use that pretext to offer him a ride to his class so that I could talk to him persuasively," Rishabh said, sounding utterly wretched. "Believe me, sir, I had thought I would even offer him some money or promise to buy him anything he wanted. All this, I thought, would be difficult to talk about in the open so I wanted to offer him a ride and sort of cajole him."

"I see," Saralkar said, fascinated by how pathetic and sordid life was in some ways that a young man felt the need to do all this to stop a natural, intimate act from becoming a source of humiliation to him and his girlfriend. "So, what did Pranjal do when he noticed the deflated tyre?"

"He just walked away with the bicycle in hand, though he didn't turn towards the gate. He turned the other way."

"Sure?"

"Yes, sir . . . I swear I didn't do anything to Pranjal. That's the last I saw of him."

Motkar and Saralkar looked at each other. So that was almost a confirmation that Pranjal had gone out of the society by the small side-gate and not the main-gate. And the most likely explanation, Saralkar thought, was that the side-gate probably led to some cycle or auto repair shop, where Pranjal usually got air filled.

"Get a statement from him. This needs to be double-checked. Meanwhile, I'll ask Tupe to find out if there is a cycle repair shop in the lane leading out from the side-gate."

*****

SIX YEARS AGO (DECEMBER 2016)

The click of the latch lock broke the trance Ashwini had fallen into, staring at the bagful of money.

Neeraj, back from his enquires with the watchman, entered the house and quickly shut the door behind him. "The watchman says there were no visitors to the building after midnight . . . and this morning only the usual milk and paper delivery boys came," he said. "Of course, he is not totally sure since he began washing cars after 5.30 a.m. and also used the toilet."

Ashwini gave him a pre-occupied look. "He came right up to our door—Atharva's killer. He was less than twenty-five or thirty feet from us . . ." she said in a strange tone, ". . . to mock us . . . to fling at us the ransom amount he had demanded for Atharva's life . . . ₹5 lakhs . . ."

"What? You counted the money?" Neeraj asked.

Ashwini shook her head. "No . . . but I am sure that's how much it is."

Neeraj walked over to the bag, removed all the packets wrapped up in separate plastic carry-bags and newspaper. He stared at the wads of five-hundred- and thousand-rupee notes. "You are right," he said and looked at Ashwini, who was again staring at the money lying on the floor.

She extended her hand which held the note. "Here's the note!"

Neeraj took it from her and looked at the scrawl again. Anger coursed through his body and he beat back the urge to crumple the note and throw it away.

"Let's call the police!" Ashwini said.

"The police? Why?" Neeraj asked.

She looked at him quizzically. "Because it's a fresh clue. They can trace him . . ."

"How?"

"Perhaps the killer got his fingerprints on the bag . . . the serial number of the notes could lead to him . . . maybe they can do handwriting analysis of the note," Ashwini replied.

Neeraj scoffed. "A fat lot they've done so far . . . the cops are useless . . . they don't care. It's just another case for them."

"You don't want to call the police and hand over all this cash and note to them?"

"No," Neeraj replied, "it won't do us any good."

Ashwini frowned. "What do you mean it won't do us any good? It's foolish to think like that. Even the smallest of clues can possibly lead to nailing Atharva's killer."

Neeraj flushed with rage. "They got a little body full of clues when they found Atharva. What did they do? They couldn't zero in on even one suspect . . . and you think they'll be able to trace him from clues in this bag? No, they'll just nod at us, tell us to give them a few weeks to come back with results, gobble up the money amongst themselves and forget about it."

"What rubbish are you talking, Neeraj?"

"It's not rubbish. That's what will happen," Neeraj retorted. "It's you who is mad to follow up and repose your faith in the police!"

"Then what do you want to do, Neeraj?" Ashwini said, her hackles raised. "Throw away the bag and burn the money?"

"No, burn the bag and keep the money," Neeraj said.

A shocked breathlessness descended upon Ashwini; her ears red with the words she'd just heard. "You want to keep the filthy blood money which our son's killer has dumped at our doorstep?" she asked unsteadily.

"Yes . . . because it's futile and much more dangerous to take it to the police! Don't you read reports every day of how cops are recovering hauls of demonetised currency. All this money is now not legal tender and cash needs to be explained. The moment we take it to the police they are not going to believe some wild story that the killer left it. They'll assume it's our black money stash and start grilling us, harass us, or as I said, simply gobble it up," Neeraj said. "So it's better to get it converted into the new currency—some of it by depositing it into our bank accounts and the rest I'll get it done through a person I know."

"What kind of a father are you, Neeraj," Ashwini shouted, sick and repelled to the core by the man she had been married to for thirteen years. "All that your son's memory means is five lakhs . . .? That too from the man who killed him?"

"You know nothing about what Atharva meant to me, Ashwini!" Neeraj countered. "Like you, I can't turn my son's tragic death into an excuse to wallow in never-ending self-pity and behave like I am dead myself."

He glared at her like a person who had finally been provoked to retaliate after restraining himself for long. "I am a practical person. It's idiotic and pointless to go to the police with this claim, which is going to be disbelieved," Neeraj continued. "I neither trust them nor have any hope, so I'd much rather dispose off the bag and the money privately, without drawing attention. No one with unaccounted, demonetised cash is safe, so whatever happens I am not going to do something that we'll come to regret."

"Shame on you!" his wife said. "I am taking the bag to the police station this evening. You can stay home like a coward!"

She walked away into the bedroom. Her husband had other plans.

*****

Chapter 15

One Week Ago. 3.00 p.m.

As he walked in the direction of the side-gate, his bicycle in hand, Pranjal stole a quick glance over his shoulder. Rishabh Mukherjee was still standing by his chocolate brown Ertiga, staring angrily in his direction, his hand on his hip.

Pranjal wondered if he would still go up to meet Namita, although he'd told him not to. Not that Pranjal could do anything about it if he went up to their flat. What he'd seen ten days ago hadn't stopped bothering Pranjal. He could barely look at his sister since then. He didn't want to embarrass her; he didn't want to see the look of shame and fear in her eyes. It was as if a big wall had suddenly been erected between them.

Namita too couldn't bring herself to talk to him or even be in his presence. Several times the burden of what he'd seen brought Pranjal close to telling his mother—if not about what he'd seen but at least the fact that Rishabh had come home in their absence. But he was scared that once he said something to his mother, he would end up telling her everything. And that, he instinctively knew, would mean a lot of trouble for his Namita didi.

So, Pranjal kept it to himself. And yet, how was he to protect his sister from Rishabh? He hoped his sister would look after herself.

Pranjal opened the side-gate and stepped out into the lane. He hoped the cycle shop was open so that he'd get air filled and not be late for class. He didn't like the class but then there really was no choice.

The cycle shop was open, but Raghu, the boy who usually worked there, wasn't around. Instead, a middle-aged man was lounging on a plastic chair. He glanced at Pranjal.

"If it's a puncture, you'll have to wait," he said.

"Where is Raghu?" Pranjal asked. "I need to fill air in the back tyre . . ."

"Raghu will be back in twenty or thirty minutes. I am just watching the shop for him while he's gone," the man replied.

Pranjal was crestfallen. "Can I fill air in the tyre, Uncle?" he asked the man.

"Help yourself," the man said, "I can switch on the pump."

Pranjal had not done it before but he had watched Raghu fill air in the tyres, several times. He had no choice but to try now.

"Okay," he said, "please put the pump on."

The man scrambled to his feet. "You've got money, right? Raghu said five rupees for both tyres."

"He takes two rupees from me, Uncle," Pranjal replied.

The man had switched on the pump now. "Is that so? Okay then . . . fill it up."

Pranjal picked up the air tube, squatted on the ground

and applied it to his tyre valve. There was a hiss of escaping air as he struggled to clamp the tube to the valve properly. He finally managed and the air began filling up.

The man stood watching. "Don't overfill . . . the tube might burst," he instructed.

Two minutes later, Pranjal was done, paid for the air and began riding away on his bicycle. Shit, he was late by at least ten minutes. He pedalled swiftly and was soon on the Bavdhan-Pashan main road. There wasn't a lot of traffic but he still wasn't sure he'd make it in time. This tuition teacher was in the habit of turning away latecomers or subjecting them to a little bit of tongue-lashing, depending on her mood, even though it was a private coaching class.

"Pranjal . . ."

He suddenly heard a familiar voice call out.

"Pranjal . . ." the voice called out again and Pranjal looked in the direction it was coming from.

A familiar face was waving out to him frantically to stop. Pranjal stopped his bicycle.

*****

"Sir, I've retrieved details of Randeep Mirdha's crime record from the NCRB database. He was convicted for domestic violence and harassment and served a three-year sentence," PSI Motkar said. "He had cases filed against him for attempt to murder and threats against Smita and Mohnish Bhatti . . . but I think they were really not pursued by the couple and are still awaiting disposal."

"Did Chandigarh Police revert with any information?" Saralkar asked.

"I haven't got much more from them, sir, except that Randeep probably left Chandigarh a few years ago and that there are no complaints filed against him thereafter. He's still got relatives there, although he sold his parent's property after he got out of jail," Motkar replied. "No idea where he's moved to."

"Can't you find him on any social media sites—Facebook, Instagram, LinkedIn, and stuff?" Saralkar asked.

"Tried it, sir. Nothing. I have also asked Chandigarh Police to check if he was issued a passport and driving licence in Chandigarh."

"So, how about a quick trip to Chandigarh?" Saralkar suggested.

"I was thinking on the same lines, sir, but there's a lot to do here too," Motkar replied.

"Hmm . . . true, but if he has relatives or friends in Chandigarh, you probably won't have too much trouble tracing Randeep Mirdha's current whereabouts. And if you can't that means there's something fishy and we need to ferret him out, using other means," Saralkar said.

Motkar nodded. "You want me to leave for Chandigarh right away, sir—tonight or tomorrow morning?"

"No, it can wait another day or two. I need you around," Saralkar said. "What's the development with the driver and the corporator?"

Motkar didn't have encouraging news on either front, but there was no bush to beat around, even if he had wanted to. "The driver Jayesh Pardeshi has just gone off the radar, sir. He's not returned to Pune and his phone is not reachable."

"What? He's done a skip after that phone call with his brother?"

"Not sure, sir, because the brother said they spoke briefly once more the next day, but thereafter there's been no contact. The brother himself is panic-stricken and we've warned him we'll take him into custody if his brother does not show up in two days."

"But hadn't you put the driver's phone on tracker?" Saralkar said. "What was his last location?"

"About seventy kilometres from Jabalpur, sir, on the Jabalpur-Nagpur highway."

"So, he was returning to Maharashtra. What about the family he was ferrying?"

"He hadn't given any details to his brother," Motkar replied. "I am already in touch with Madhya Pradesh Police and have forwarded them the details of the car, along with Jayesh Pardeshi's photo and description."

"What the hell is happening, Motkar? We are left looking like incompetent buffoons," Saralkar remarked. "Are criminals getting smarter or are we getting stupider? And what about Khilare, the corporator?"

"Sir, we spoke to Mohnish Bhatti's employees at his dealership. The two who were present when Sunny Sutar visited the showroom said that two more toughies accompanied him. They asked where Mohnish Bhatti was and left when they learnt he was out of station. They also asked when he was likely to return," Motkar said. "They made no threats. We also managed to get CCTV footage and it appears they were in and out of the showroom in about ten minutes. My informer also found out that if Bhatti had been present, the plan was for Sunny to warn him not to take the school matter further or he would regret it. But since Bhatti was not in Pune, nothing happened and Sunny was going to go back and meet him the following week."

"That's all?" Saralkar asked sceptically.

"No, it seems that if Mohnish Bhatti were to not heed the warning or talked back, then Sunny was to arrange to damage his showroom at a later date, to get Bhatti to back off. That's what my informer told me."

"Are you sure?"

"Yes, sir. In fact, I have got a confirmation from another source too," Motkar asserted.

"Another source? Who?"

Motkar savoured the moment. "Khilare's personal assistant, sir. Anil Kedari."

Saralkar grunted. "Why would Kedari reveal this information to you and why would you believe him, Motkar?"

Motkar couldn't help but smile. "I know Anil Kedari a little, sir. We went to the same school as kids for a year or two. When I had called him to pick up Khilare's schedule, I leaned on him a little. Told him that he too would get into trouble. He swore Khilare had nothing to do with the kidnapping but spilled the beans about what Sunny Sutar had been instructed to do."

Saralkar was still frowning. "You are sure he wasn't playing you? Why would he risk breaching Khilare's trust?"

"I wouldn't have relied on Kedari's word alone, sir, but it's been confirmed separately by my informer, as I said."

Saralkar still wasn't ready to let it go. "Maybe that's the story they are floating around to reach our ears, so that we give Khilare the benefit of the doubt. What about Khilare's Bhor farmhouse? Any inputs from Bhor Police?"

"Yes, sir. Bhor Police told us, Khilare visits the farmhouse once in a month or two. Usually, there is no one else there except a caretaker. Some years ago, Bhor Police had raided the place, because a few rave parties had been held there. The matter was brushed under the carpet because Khilare claimed he had no clue about these parties being organised. The organisers confessed to keeping Khilare in the dark and as for the boys and girls who were detained, all their families bribed their way out."

"I see. So, no more rave parties?"

"No, sir. Apparently, Khilare now uses the farmhouse only as a getaway or to entertain people he needs to keep in good humour—politicians, government officers, industrialists, actors, spiritual gurus, and other worthies."

Saralkar tapped his table, dissatisfied. "Didn't you ask your friend Kedari what Khilare was doing at the Bhor farmhouse on the day of Pranjal's disappearance?"

"Kedari said he hadn't accompanied Khilare that day," Motkar replied.

"Hmm," Saralkar clicked his tongue. "We need to find out what Khilare was up to, so that we know whether to waste any more time and effort on him at all."

"I'll see what I can do, sir," Motkar said.

Just then ASI Tupe entered.

"Yes, Tupe?" Saralkar asked.

"Sir, your conjecture of there being a cycle repair shop, accessible from the lane on which the side-gate opens, was correct. It's more a puncture repair shack, located about 150 metres away, on the corner of the main arterial road. A young man called Raghu runs it. We showed him Pranjal's photo and he instantly recognised him. He told us Pranjal came regularly to his shack to fill air or for oiling his bicycle."

"Did he know Pranjal was kidnapped and killed?" Saralkar asked.

"Yes, sir, he was aware of it, but he doesn't recall whether Pranjal came to his shop that afternoon," ASI Tupe said. "He says he is at the shop most of the time but sometimes he's got to go out for some work or with a customer to fix a puncture elsewhere. When he leaves the shop, a neighbouring shack owner or some acquaintance who's around minds it. Raghu says this happens almost every other day. He is not sure, but he thinks he'd asked a knife-sharpener, who is in the vicinity sometimes, to mind his shop for fifteen-twenty minutes that afternoon. He doesn't have the man's mobile number nor any idea where he lives. They just have a nodding acquaintance."

"Damn it!" Saralkar snarled and thumped the table. "When the hell are we going to get to know for sure how Pranjal left the society and by which gate?"

He simmered for a couple of minutes, deep in thought, darkness on his brow, then turned to Tupe and Motkar, his face hard. "We are left with no choice but to search Rishabh Mukherjee's car. Talk to his father about it. We also need to question Namita Bhatti, so just call the Bhatti couple and the girl and say they are required to come to our office urgently. Don't tell them why or mention Rishabh . . . just say it is in relation to the case."

Motkar and Tupe nodded.

"It's really going to be traumatic for them, sir," Motkar observed. "Can't we wait till we've searched Rishabh's car. Then if forensics finds anything, we can question the girl."

Saralkar was quiet, turning it over in his head. He finally grunted. "No, let's get it over with. We can't afford more sluggishness on this case. We ought to have gotten somewhere by now!"

*****

Karan Jerajani had long ceased to analyse himself or decipher his impulses. He hadn't made peace with existentialist questions like "Who am I?" or "What am I?" or "Why am I like that?".

He had simply stopped seeking answers to them, for he was what he was and life had to be lived like all other human beings around him lived it, without beating oneself up too much, gaining whatever pleasure and happiness one could, avoiding pain and camouflaging traits that the world would frown upon, to the best extent possible.

He had found online resources to indulge his appetites and they did work to a certain extent. But it was nowhere like the real thing and so he got up session after session, even more frustrated.

There was no substitute for gratification—the kind of gratification that almost everyone else in the world had established a moral and legal right to—but people with his predilections would never be able to do so, for some things were too abnormal and vile for even the most tolerant, liberal, and compassionate human hearts to abide or give the benefit of the doubt to.

Why, Karan himself often felt disgusted at his own depraved longings and fantasies—whenever they became too beastly to control or manage. As if he had no right to exist as a person because something deeply filthy inside him craved for a hideous, forbidden pleasure, which was abominably harmful to some innocent, defenceless victims.

And all this thwarted carnality had disproportionately bedevilled his life, spilling out in the form of venomous, long-standing grudges and hostility towards someone or the other he knew, over minor slights of petty friction.

Karan got up and walked to the closet now—something he always kept locked. He unlocked it and looked at the life-like soft toys now. He picked one that seemed to provide the comfort he fancied right now and locked the closet again. He went to bed with the one he'd chosen. It was nowhere like the real thing but it was better than nothing.

*****

Two Years Ago (February 2020)

"I sense hesitation, Mr. Jerajani," the psychiatrist, Dr. Gargi Naidu remarked. "For these sessions to be effective, there are two imperatives—firstly, you need to trust me, and secondly, you need to talk freely what it is you are undergoing."

Karan Jerajani broke into a smile. "Well, it's difficult for a normal man to realize there is something a little bit abnormal within him . . ."

"You'll be surprised how many feel a little bit abnormal, as you put it," the psychiatrist said.

"You mean it's normal to be abnormal?" Karan asked with a chuckle.

Dr. Gargi smiled back. "Go on, tell me . . . I'm listening."

Karan cleared his throat and the smile gave way to a taut seriousness, "I . . . I have a problem . . ." he managed to say.

"What kind of a problem?"

Karan's eyes looked away, his Adam's apple bobbed up and down. "Sexual . . ." he murmured, with a sharp intake of breath.

"I see. Can you please elaborate?"

There was a long beat as Karan continued to look away, as if too scared to put what he felt like into words. He finally looked up. "Will all that I say remain completely confidential?" he asked, his voice dry.

"Yes, Mr. Jerajani," the psychiatrist said simply, without hesitation.

Karan nodded, sighed, then spoke. "I . . . I am attracted to . . . children."

He let fall the last word in a near whisper, as if horrified and ashamed of himself.

Dr. Gargi stirred in her chair. She hadn't expected this.

She had been expecting more common conditions. "Hmm . . . by children what age-group do you mean?" she managed to ask.

Karan appeared to have sunk into himself, as if some descent into a private doom. "Very . . . young children . . . between five and ten years old . . ." he whispered again.

"I see. Boys or girls?"

"Boys."

The psychiatrist was still trying to reorient her approach to this unexpected case. She couldn't also escape her own first response, of being filled with revulsion. Was she sitting in front of a paedophile? Someone who had molested children? She struggled to frame her next question.

"Are you married, Mr. Jerajani?" she asked.

"I was, but not anymore."

"You are divorced?"

"Yes, about six years ago."

"And . . . er . . . did you have a normal sex life before you separated?" Dr. Gargi asked, slowly finding her bearings.

"At first . . . yes, but not for long," Karan replied, now feeling just a little less nervous.

"Do you have children, Mr. Jerajani?"

"No . . .! Do you think it's because I don't have kids of my own that . . . that I . . ." he spluttered to a halt as if unable to put in words again, what he'd already confessed to.

The psychiatrist did not reply. Instead, she asked another question. "Since when have you experienced attraction towards little children?"

Karan blinked and looked away as if he'd turned on some inner searchlight to look deep inside for answers. "I . . . I have always been fond of children . . . I like to play with them . . . hold them . . . kiss them . . . tickle them affectionately, cleanly . . ." he said. "That's quite natural, isn't it?"

Dr. Gargi nodded. "Yes, it mostly is, but in your case, you think it turned unnatural at some point, is it?"

Her own heartbeat was up, for this was an area she didn't have a lot of experience in.

Karan Jerajani was quiet again, staring this time at the carpet. His voice was shaky when he spoke. "A few years ago, I began to notice . . . experience . . ."

He stopped as if too ashamed to bring the words to his lips.

"Experience what?" the psychiatrist asked, holding her own breath, fighting her own instincts as a human being, of passing negative judgement.

Karan licked his lips and said just one word. "Arousal . . ."

Despite her professional training, Dr. Gargi Naidu felt sickened. She struggled to bite back her personal feelings. "I see. Does it happen with all children you might come into contact with or only someone in particular?"

Karan Jerajani closed his eyes. "It . . . It started with . . . one child in particular—the son of a close friend. I was shocked . . . I was disgusted . . . I didn't know what was happening. I hated myself most because . . . because it felt so pleasurable."

He looked at her, his eyes seeking understanding, which she was not equipped to provide.

"Mr. Jerajani, have you actually indulged in . . . in sexual activity with that child or any other . . ." Dr. Gargi asked, now unable to keep the loathing from her voice. "Have you molested kids?"

Karan Jerajani seemed to turn speechless, then burst into tears.

*****

Chapter 16

Saralkar did not really like using the phrase "compromising position" to suggest someone, especially women, found in a vulnerable state, since it seemed to imply it was somehow their fault to let themselves be put in a potentially exploitative situation. But he had to admit: it was a useful euphemism, avoiding much mutual embarrassment, while talking to complainants or victims.

"Lies . . . all lies! Nothing like that ever happened," Namita Bhatti said, the pitch of her voice becoming shriller with every word.

Her eyes flashed defiantly at the policemen. Saralkar could see glimpses of Smita Bhatti in Namita's response and demeanour. She now turned to look at her mother. "They are lying, Mamma!"

Her mother's eyes had clouded over with the competing emotions of grief and fury.

"I am sorry to have to confront you with this, Namita, but Rishabh has given us this account . . ."

Saralkar began saying and was immediately interrupted by Namita's loud protestations.

"It's a lie . . . he's lying! You've all got dirty minds . . . let me go! Mamma, why are you letting him do this to me?"

Saralkar glanced at the lady officer, ASI Sanika Zirpe, whose presence was necessary since they were questioning Namita.

ASI Zirpe took the cue and admonished Namita. "Don't shout and scream! Answer the questions. Say what you wish to calmly."

Namita glared at her, then looked away.

Smita now spoke with barely suppressed incredulity. "You really think my daughter and . . . and that boy conspired to . . . to kidnap and kill my Pranjal?"

"Mrs. Bhatti, your son was last seen alive by someone when he came back from school. Your daughter says he left for class at 2.45 p.m. but he was neither seen leaving from the front-gate, nor is it confirmed yet that he left by the side-gate. The young man Rishabh drove his car into the society around 2.40 p.m. and was seen leaving at 3.10 p.m.," Saralkar said. "He has confessed that he had come to meet Pranjal, deflated his bicycle tyre because he wanted to coax or threaten your son, to ask him not to reveal what he saw transpired between Rishabh and your daughter about two weeks ago.

"Thereafter, there is no trace of Pranjal. In these circumstances, we have to establish whether your daughter Namita and Rishabh had anything to do with your son's disappearance."

"But Inspector, Namita is Pranjal's sister," Mohnish Bhatti spoke before Smita could. "How can you even imagine she would've had a hand in this . . . and what proof do you have that she and Rishabh were . . . seen in a . . . in a compromising position by Pranjal . . . I mean . . ."

Saralkar knew he had to be gentle but stern. "We haven't come to this decision of questioning Namita without some proof. Also with due respect, Namita is Pranjal's stepsister, so it is not out of the realm of possibilities that she could be involved. Desperation makes people do unbelievable things, which we as police officers see every day. So, much as this is painful to you as parents, please let us do our jobs."

He looked at both Smita and Mohnish Bhatti authoritatively, then turned to Namita. "Look, Namita, even as we speak Rishabh's car has been taken for forensic examination. It's clear he was in the society between 2.40 and 3.10 p.m. Now you tell us what happened."

"How would I know what happened?" Namita replied defiantly. "I didn't even know Rishabh was there."

"That's a lie, Namita. We know from your call records that you and Rishabh spoke to each other twice between the time he entered and left the society," PSI Motkar intervened.

She jerked her neck up at him, angry and haughty, then looked away.

"There's no point lying," Saralkar said. "Just tell us the truth. Had you and Rishabh planned this?"

"Planned what?" she said. "I don't know what you are talking about."

"Planned to talk to Pranjal and try and persuade him not to tell your parents about what he'd seen earlier?" Saralkar asked, trying to balance gentleness with firmness.

Namita's gaze wavered, her lips quivered. She looked at her parents, then away, choosing to be quiet.

"Namita, beta . . . tell them the truth. We won't get angry," Smita spoke. "What happened that day? Did . . . did that Rishabh and you by any chance . . . do anything to Pranjal?"

Namita turned all her fury on her mother. "Mamma, how can you think like that about me? You think I am a murderer? That I planned to kill Pranjal? That's what you think of me? Your own daughter?"

"No, no, beta . . . just tell them what happened. Why hide it? Tell them the truth," Mohnish said.

Namita gave him a scorching glance, dripping with contempt. "You are not my father . . . you shut up and don't tell me what to do."

ASI Zirpe did not require a cue from Saralkar to speak this time. She was an experienced enough police officer.

"Stop this melodrama at once," she warned Namita tersely. "Stop it. Just answer Saralkar sir's question. You are an adult. If you continue this stupidity, I'll ask your parents to leave and you will be questioned all alone."

Even Saralkar was impressed by the way she'd pressed the right button and delivered the message, for Namita seemed to shuffle nervously in her seat and calm down.

"Quickly tell us what happened," Saralkar said in the same vein.

Namita nodded. "Yes . . . I was scared Pranjal would squeal to Mamma about . . . about that day. So Rishabh said he would speak to Pranjal alone, cajole him, coax him, and make sure he'd understand. That's when we decided the best way would be to run into Pranjal when he was on his way to class and then talk to him. That's all that Rishabh did that day . . . but Pranjal walked away."

Saralkar hoped she was telling the truth. It matched with what Rishabh had told them, but it could well be they had agreed upon a story they would stick to. It was, of course, entirely possible that Rishabh and Namita had actually tackled the hapless Pranjal inside the Bhatti home that afternoon, tried to threaten or persuade him then knocked him unconscious, put him in the car along with his bicycle and Rishabh had driven away.

But it was unlikely, Saralkar thought, and he hoped the forensic work in Rishabh's car found no evidence to suggest the contrary.

"Is there anything you have left out? Are you hiding any information, any details?" Saralkar asked the girl. "Because if we find more contradictions, then the next meeting with us will be much more difficult."

Namita sniffed and shook her head.

"And you are not trying to protect Rishabh by not fully revealing something you know? Maybe he harmed Pranjal by mistake . . . in panic? I hope you are not trying to cover up for him?" Saralkar asked.

Namita gave him an angry scowl. "No . . . Rishabh hasn't done anything . . . don't try to frame him."

"Mind what you are saying, young lady," ASI Zirpe snapped and wagged a finger at Namita.

"That's all for now," Saralkar said. "You may go. But we may have to call you again, if need be."

Namita stood up instantly and began walking off. Her parents hastened after her.

Saralkar felt sorry for the couple. No parent deserved to suffer so much. He hoped he could make amends by solving the case.

*****

SIX MONTHS AGO

"Why haven't you remarried?" Randeep Mirdha asked.

They had been drinking for over an hour now and catching up. Karan Jerajani had just finished telling him how his marriage had ended up in divorce.

Karan took a swig of his whisky as he considered the question from his one-time college mate. An honest answer was hardly an option. Macho frivolity was.

He shrugged and winked mischievously at Randeep, "Cramps my style, buddy. Why pick up one when one can have many?"

Randeep grinned back. "Ah! The pleasures of being a player."

Both of them roared with laughter at each other's wit, like any two men who had drunk too much.

"How about you, Randeep?"

Randeep shook his handsome head. "Who'd marry a jail-bird?"

Karan nodded soberly. "Hmmm . . . but it's remarkable you've bounced back so well after you got out. I half expected you to have turned into a hardened criminal or a junkie or something like that."

"Who's to say I haven't, Karan," Randeep quipped, then pointed to Karan's nearly empty glass. "You want a repeat?"

"No . . . no, I'm good. I'm done."

"How about one for the road?" Randeep insisted.

"If I have one more, you'll have to drive me home, buddy," Karan replied. "Can't hold my drink the way I once used to. Growing older, I guess . . ."

"Okay, I'll get one for myself, then," Randeep said. He signalled to the waiter and ordered.

Karan Jerajani downed his last sip then regarded Randeep. "They've done rather well for themselves, haven't they? Smita and Mohnish."

Randeep's face darkened but he said nothing.

Karan continued, "He's got a sanitaryware distributorship. Smita's working at an IT company as admin manager. They've got a son, Pranjal . . . nice boy, some sort of chess prodigy . . . good flat . . . and of course, do you know Mohnish won a lot of money at KBC a few years ago?"

Randeep nodded. "Yes, I heard. They've prospered."

Nothing was spoken for a few seconds as the waiter came and served Randeep's drink.

"You in touch with your daughter?" Karan asked.

Randeep took a sip, wondering whether to reveal the truth. "Once in a while," he said eventually.

"Ah! Don't you ever feel angry at what they did to you?"

"What do you think?" Randeep said meeting Karan's eyes.

"Of course, you do," Karan said and let a few beats pass before speaking again. "You know they cheated me too . . .?"

"Cheated you? What do you mean?" Randeep asked, his eyes narrowing.

"In a different way than they cheated you, of course. Money!"

"How?"

Karan clenched his jaws and drew in his lips with anger, as if the wound was still raw. "You know I helped Mohnish in the 'Phone a friend' round, right? I bloody well paved the way for him to win big," he said.

"Ah yes, I know. I had watched the programme. It's only then I came to know you were in touch with him," Randeep said.

"Yes . . . and what did that ungrateful bastard and that bitch do?" Karan hissed. "They refused to part with the share which we'd agreed to in advance. The arseholes!"

"Oh! They did that? How much had they promised you?"

"Ten per cent of the winnings . . . and do you know what that prick Mohnish did? He offered me a token sum of ₹1 lakh and said he had promised me nothing and thought I was joking when I had said ten per cent to help him with the 'Phone a friend' question. One lakh? What does he think . . . I'm a beggar? It's not even the bloody money . . . it's the ungratefulness . . . .and that slut . . . your ex-wife Smita, she said her son was uncomfortable with the way I played with him . . . that I was a filthy man . . . as if I am some bloody paedophile! After all the affection I showered on the boy . . ."

"That's bloody shocking and a cheap shot!" Randeep said, feeling his own flash of anger. "Typical of those two—a thoroughly rotten couple—first she cheats on me multiple times then accuses me of being a serial adulterer and wife beater! And that bastard Mohnish . . . whom I loved and trusted as a friend . . . he betrays me and steals my wife! What kind of a friend does that?"

He paused, his eyes bloodshot now, "And they took my daughter from me, leaving me to rot in jail."

He gulped down his drink and leaned back. Karan leaned forward and asked conspiratorially, "Don't you ever think of taking revenge, Randeep?"

Randeep Mirdha was quiet for a while, then looked steadily at Karan, "All the time! They don't deserve to be happy and prosperous after what they've done to me."

Karan Jerajani nodded and added, "You are right. Wish we could find a way of really hurting them . . . badly."

Both men gazed at each other—the same bitter flame burning in their minds.

*****

The ride back home from the Homicide office was made in silence. Neither Mohnish nor Smita spoke and Namita sat in the back, sullen, frigid, and resentful, clacking away at her mobile. A couple of times, Smita threw a glance behind only to be totally ignored by her daughter.

"Who are you texting?' she asked finally as they neared their home.

Namita did not reply.

An obvious suspicion arose in Smita's mind. "Is it that boy Rishabh?" she asked, seething.

"It's none of your business, Mamma. I am an adult now and can do whatever the hell I want!" Namita retorted as the car came to a halt below their building. She alighted, slammed the car door, and headed for the lift without waiting for her mother and stepfather.

Smita was quick to follow, even as her husband tried to counsel restraint.

"How dare you talk to me like that?" Smita said, as soon as they were inside their house.

Namita ignored the question and began walking into her room.

"How dare you speak to a person who might've harmed Pranjal?" Smita shouted, enraged even more.

"Mamma, don't talk rubbish. Neither Rishabh nor I have murdered your dear son! We are not crazy!" Namita replied nastily.

The front door opened again and Mohnish walked in to see mother and daughter in the midst of a confrontation.

"*Your dear son?* That's how you talk about your little brother? Was he nothing to you?" Smita asked, anguished and angry.

"He was my stepbrother, not my real brother . . . your son with this man . . ." Namita said, pointing at Mohnish, ". . . not with my real father, who you betrayed shamelessly!"

"Namita . . ." her mother said with a groan, "Don't say things like that . . . it's hurtful, beta . . . you don't know many things. That's not the truth . . . my Pranjal is gone . . . please don't do this to me just now."

"Do what to you, Mamma? I am not doing anything. I am just stating the truth," Namita replied. "You've been trying to pretend we are one family but we are not. You are my mother, but only the three of you were a family, to which I have never belonged!"

She glared at Mohnish, then said, "You might have married him, Mamma, but that does not make him my father! My father is such a handsome, grand, big-hearted man . . . and I am proud to be his daughter!"

The shock hit them like shrapnel, from a bomb.

"Namita . . ." Smita's eyes were suddenly anxious and yet steely. "Has Randeep contacted you? Have you been in touch with that man?"

Namita looked at her defiantly. "No. But so what if I had? You cannot stop me!"

"Namita," her mother quickly grabbed her by the arm, "tell me the truth. Are you in touch with Randeep? The man is a crooked manipulator!"

"I've already told you I am not in touch," Namita lied, "but you have no right to say bad things about my real father . . . you cheated on him . . . you left him . . . you sent him to jail . . . you took me away from him!"

"Namita . . . Randeep is not your father," Smita said.

"What do you mean he is not my father? Then who is? You are lying, Mamma!"

"I am not lying, Namita. Randeep is not your father."

"Are you saying you had an affair with someone else too, while still married to him and I am someone else's child altogether?" Namita demanded, flaring up.

"Watch your mouth, Namita," Mohnish suddenly intervened. "You are talking about your mother!"

Namita's eyes flashed. "This is between me and my

mother. You mind your own business. You are no one to me!"

"Stop it, Namita," Mohnish said, trembling. "You are my child, as much as Pranjal was! I am your father, not Randeep!"

Namita stared at him wildly. "No, you are not!" She turned to face her mother.

Smita had slumped onto a sofa. Her proud spirit had taken a battering beyond endurance. She nodded weakly. "Mohnish is your real father too, not Randeep."

"How can that be? It's a lie!"

"No . . . it's just complicated, beta. We were going to tell you some day when you'd be able to take it," Smita said. "Mohnish is anyway your father for all practical and legal purposes, so we didn't want to upset you by telling you how it all came about."

"I . . . I don't believe you! You divorced my papa, got my custody, put him in jail . . . you got married to this man when I was nearly four years old. You were married to my papa when I was born . . . his name is on my birth certificate."

Namita suddenly came to a halt and looked at both. "You mean . . ." The unspoken words trembled on her lips as she struggled to make sense of it.

"Yes," Mohnish said, looking at her, "we . . . your mother and I were in love much before she finally gathered the courage to leave Randeep and marry me. Even I didn't know you were mine, till almost a year after your birth. Smita told me only then. As it is we were both filled with guilt that we were not doing the right thing by Randeep, who was her first husband and my good friend . . . but Smita and I realized we could not live without each other and knowing you were ours, made it impossible to continue . . ."

"Lies . . . lies . . . lies! Whenever I asked Mamma about my real father, why did she never tell me this? Why didn't she ever say before that Randeep wasn't my father? My birth certificate has his name . . . the court documents granting you my custody also records his name as my father. Nowhere is there any proof I am not his daughter! Why?"

She stomped away to her room, leaving the couple drained and anguished.

"Oh my God, why are we being punished like this? Our own daughter does not believe us. Are we going to lose her as well, Mohnish, now that Pranjal has already gone . . ." Smita Bhatti broke down.

"No . . . no . . . don't think like that, darling . . . don't!" Mohnish said holding her close. "We'll prove it to her. She's our daughter! Don't worry."

"I have a horrible feeling Randeep has somehow gotten in touch with Namita. Her behaviour towards you has changed since almost a year. I have observed that. What should we do? And what I am really scared of is that through her, Randeep is taking revenge on us. Maybe he extracted all information about Pranjal from Namita and got him kidnapped and killed?"

Mohnish and she looked at each other with alarm.

"Do you think we need to tell the police Randeep might be in touch with Namita?"

"No . . . no . . . we have to protect Namita too. Let's play this more cautiously. We've already voiced our suspicion about Randeep's grudge against us, so the police might be already looking for him. In the meanwhile, let's first find out on our own if Randeep is in contact with Namita," Smita said, resolutely.

*****

Chapter 17

"We've been barking up the wrong tree," Saralkar said, as he got off the phone. "The forensic team's conclusions on Rishabh Bannerjee's car more or less rule out the possibility that Pranjal might've been in it at some point in time."

"Cars can be cleaned thoroughly at car washes, sir," Motkar said doggedly.

"But he's got an alibi too, Motkar," Saralkar said. "Tupe's been checking."

"What alibi?" Motkar asked, turning to Tupe.

"We checked out Rishabh's whereabouts for the rest of the day after he left the society and almost all of it's confirmed, till around 9.30 p.m., when he returned home," Tupe replied.

"I see. So, it would've been impossible for him to have been at all these different places with Pranjal confined in his car," Motkar worked it out.

"Yes. If he'd kidnapped Pranjal, he wouldn't be carrying him around hidden in the car, for all those hours," Saralkar said. "He would've needed to dump him in a hideout of some kind and required some accomplice, say Namita, but their call locations show they were never together or at the same location for the rest of the day."

"So, should we knock both Rishabh and Namita off our list of suspects, sir?" Tupe asked.

Saralkar nodded grumpily. "Yes, unless something new comes up."

A collective, brooding silence followed, which Motkar broke a minute later.

"There's one more suspect we can eliminate, sir."

"Who?"

"The driver, Jayesh Pardeshi," Motkar replied. "Madhya Pradesh Police informed me this morning that Jayesh Pardeshi's car was involved in a highway accident on the Jabalpur–Nagpur Highway. He's critical and so are two of his passengers. Two other passengers are dead."

"Has Jayesh's identity been confirmed? They are sure it's him, not some impersonator?" Saralkar asked, looking desperately for something awry.

"It's definitely him, sir. Plus, his car and the identities of his passengers are also confirmed. The MP Police has sent me all the details and pics too," Motkar said. "I've also called up his brother, Jayant, who knew nothing about it. He's leaving right away for MP. Should we send a constable to accompany him to reconfirm identity and the facts, sir?"

"Do that!" Saralkar replied. "Let's not leave any loose ends."

"Okay, sir. I'll send Constable Bidkar."

Saralkar grunted. "Great, now all that's left is to exonerate Satish Khilare. When are you doing that, Motkar?"

He looked at Motkar almost accusingly, then brooded

silently for a few minutes, turning away from Motkar and Tupe to look outside his window for inspiration.

None was forthcoming. "This is bloody ridiculous," he finally said. "Let's get on with tracking Mrs. Bhatti's ex-husband, Randeep Mirdha, and that spiteful friend of theirs . . . what's his name?"

"Karan Jerajani, sir," Motkar replied.

"Right! Motkar, you better start for Chandigarh to smoke out Randeep Mirdha, and Tupe, we'll add ASI Sanika Zirpe to our team. Both of you divide the pending inquiries and follow-ups between you plus all the investigations Motkar was pursuing. I'll go after Karan Jerajani. He's working in Navi Mumbai, right?"

"Yes, sir," Motkar said. "I'll brief Tupe and Sanika Zirpe on my lines of inquiry, which they can take over."

"Good, it's high time we doubled down on cracking this case," Saralkar said, wondering how many times in his career he had been at this juncture, when promising leads had fizzled out and no fresh breakthroughs were in sight.

Frequently, he realized with surprise, for one of the most dangerous phases in crime investigation was exactly this kind of trough—clues turning into duds—for it was at this stage police officers would first start losing interest in cases, getting demotivated and demoralised—a natural enough process for most human beings.

Well, he couldn't let his shoulders droop, could he? For the much heavier burden of an unsolved case would be upon them, once he let them droop.

*****

FORTY-ONE YEARS AGO (1981)

The boy had, by now, sensed something was not quite right. He had regained consciousness just a few minutes ago and realized they were still in the strange, bleak shed. Only it seemed darker now, as if evening had fallen. The last thing he remembered was munching the orange candy he had been offered.

Why had he been brought here, where there was no one around? Where was his friend, Eknath, this uncle's son, with whom he was to go to the circus? Why was Mahadik Uncle—who would usually always smile at him playfully—looking so grave and stern, his eyes constantly shifting and blinking? Why did he keep opening the only window slightly and glancing out, then quickly shutting it?

The boy felt tongue-tied, but the words finally came. "Mahadik *Kaka,* where is Eknath?"

The man darted a look at him, then said, "He's coming."

"But why didn't we go to your house to pick him up?" the boy asked.

The man stared at him long and hard, then repeated, "He's coming."

He then dug into his pocket and produced another hard-boiled orange candy. "Here, have this."

The boy looked at the outstretched hand and the man's face. He felt scared but took the candy, because somehow, he felt that if he refused, the man would get angry.

"Go on. Eat it . . . you must be hungry," the man urged.

The boy didn't unwrap the candy and put it in his mouth.

"I want to go to the toilet, Mahadik Kaka . . ."

A look of utmost restlessness passed over the man's face. "What? To piss or to shit?" he asked angrily.

"To piss," the boy said, suddenly feeling as if he might do it in his pants itself.

The man looked around the room, as if searching for

a toilet that had gone missing. He then once again stepped towards the window and glanced outside.

"Come . . ." he gestured to the boy, clasped him by the shoulder, and opened the door slightly.

The man again threw a look around. There was no one in sight. The boy could see the sun setting on the horizon and hear the noise of passing vehicles on the road some distance away. But he could hear no other hustle-bustle. The shed stood on an isolated patch of farmland.

"Quick, you can pee here," the man said.

"Here?" the boy asked, uneasy at the idea of being asked to do so just outside the creaky door of the shed that the man was holding open.

"Yes. Quick!" the man said urgently.

"But . . ."

"Shut up and get it over with!" the man snarled.

The boy did as he was told, scared to look at the man. He wanted to scream but was too terrified to do so. As soon as he was done, the man shoved him back inside the room and quickly bolted the door.

They sat in silence for a few minutes. Then the boy plucked up courage and said, "I want to go home, Mahadik Kaka . . ."

"Not now," the man said.

"Then when?"

"Later . . ."

"But you said you were taking me and Eknath to the circus . . . where is Eknath? It's already evening!" the boy said, aggrieved now.

The man looked at him, then reached into his bag, and brought out a knife.

It filled the boy with fright, his heart thudding like a hammer.

"You are going nowhere anytime soon . . . and if you ask me another question or don't listen to what I say, you'll go home in hundreds of pieces! Do you understand?"

The boy had only just relieved himself, but he still wet his pants.

After all these years, Saralkar could still remember the sheer terror of that moment and the frisson of fear that had enveloped his body then, more than forty years ago.

*****

Karan Jerajani's office was located in one of those swanky corporate parks that adorned Navi Mumbai—impressive, glittering high-rises that made you feel you were abroad, just like people did when they stepped into malls, cocooned away from the sub-par experience of the average Indian's quality of existence.

"I'm here to meet Karan Jerajani," Saralkar said to the receptionist, who looked the senior inspector, attired in plain clothes, up and down.

"Mr. Jerajani sees people only by appointment."

"I assure you he'll promptly see me without one," Saralkar replied amiably.

"And you are?" the receptionist asked a little more cautiously, flummoxed by Saralkar's confidence.

"Police," Saralkar replied, keeping it cryptic. "Do you wish to see my I-card?"

The receptionist was by now worried. "No need. Can I just have your name, sir, so that I can inform Mr. Jerajani?"

"Tell him, it's Senior Inspector Saralkar."

She nodded, quickly put a call through, and whispered something into the mouthpiece, presumably to Karan Jerajani or his flunky. She kept the phone and looked at

Saralkar. "Can you just wait a few minutes, sir? Mr. Jerajani's assistant will be here to take you to his office."

"Sure. What is Mr. Jerajani's post here?"

"He's senior vice president, sir."

"Ah!"

Barely a minute or two later, a young man stumbled out into the lobby, conversed with the receptionist, and skipped over to Saralkar. "Good morning, sir . . . I am here to accompany you to Mr. Jerajani's cabin."

Saralkar nodded and followed the young man, the receptionist watching him in awe as he went, as if she half expected him to return soon with Karan Jerajani in cuffs. The office interiors were even more plush as Saralkar walked past people in cabins, cubicles, and meeting rooms, furnished with a lively décor and strategically placed murals, flanked by wood-panelling.

Karan Jerajani's cabin was a creation of wood and glass, about double the size of Saralkar's own modest cabin at Pune Homicide. Karan's name and designation were displayed outside, as if to underline how distinguished and important he was in the company.

As he first entered the cabin, through the door held open by the assistant, Saralkar caught a glimpse of a nervous face trying desperately not to appear pale and anxious. Karan sprang up from his seat instantly and his taut face gave a little twitch, which seemed like an attempt to smile. He held out his hand like a peace offering to an enemy.

"Hullo . . . I am Karan Jerajani."

Saralkar shook his hand and settled into a seat, across the table. Karan glanced at his assistant. "Can you just send us some tea, Arush?" He then looked at Saralkar, "Is tea okay with you, Senior Inspector, or would you like something cold?"

"Beer," Saralkar quipped, leaving Karan Jerajani gaping at him.

"Beer?" he said and looked at his assistant helplessly.

Saralkar watched his discomfiture for a couple more seconds then spoke again, "Tea is fine! Beer was just a slip of the tongue, although I've always believed it would be so much more convivial to interrogate someone over beer."

Karan blinked at him, now visibly taken aback and thrown off balance. "Tea," he said to his assistant and dismissed him, then took his seat.

"Interrogation?" he asked Saralkar, loosening his tie slightly. "I don't understand, Inspector . . ."

"Oh, pardon my choice of words, Mr. Jerajani, I have come all the way from Pune just to ask a few questions."

"I see. In regard to what . . . I am not able to figure out," Karan said.

"I'll come to that in a minute, Mr. Jerajani," Saralkar said and paused deliberately. "First, can you tell me where you were the whole of last week?"

"I was here, in Navi Mumbai. Why?" Karan said, biting his lips.

"I see. You attended office every day?" Saralkar asked.

"Yes . . . yes . . . why?"

"I presume you have an electronic attendance system? Do you swipe in and out every day?"

"Yes . . . but why are you asking me these questions like I am some kind of accused?" Karan asked, looking more than a little flustered and annoyed.

Saralkar gave him an offended, cold look. "Do you have a problem answering these questions?"

"No, absolutely not . . . but . . . but don't I need to at least know what this is all about?" Karan protested, trying and failing to look haughty.

"Would that change your reply or your whereabouts last week?"

Karan frowned. "Of course not. As I said . . . I was very much here."

"So, can you get someone from your HR to provide me your swipe in and swipe out details or attendance record, to confirm you were indeed here on all days last week?" Saralkar said.

Karan shrugged defensively. "I can . . . but why do I need to show any proof that I was here, Inspector?"

"Because then it might eliminate the need to ask you any further questions, if it's confirmed you were here and nowhere else," Saralkar replied, watching him closely. "I won't need to take more of your time perhaps."

Karan looked cagier and more uncomfortable every minute. "Let me see," he said reaching out to his intercom phone, then glanced at Saralkar without really meeting his eyes. "I . . . I just remembered in fact . . . that I was unwell for two days and hadn't come in . . ."

Saralkar looked at him sharply. "I see. When was that?"

Karan gave him the dates.

"Hmmm . . . were you at home then?"

"Yes, yes . . . just a little fever."

"Who else is at home?"

"No one . . . I'm on my own."

"I see. Your family—wife and kids—live elsewhere?" Saralkar asked.

"No . . . no, I'm divorced and have no kids," Karan replied reluctantly.

"Ah! Did you go to see a doctor?"

"No . . . not really. I just took some paracetamol and slept. Rest was all I needed."

Saralkar nodded. "Okay. So, anyone at all who can confirm you were confined to home? Maid-servant, cook, society watchman, neighbours, friends . . . any acquaintance or colleague who happened to call on you on those two days?"

Lines of panic seemed to crisscross Karan's face as if his muscles were undergoing some kind of minor earthquake. "This . . . This really is too much, Inspector! There is no reason I need to get someone to vouch for me . . . it's preposterous!" he said, fidgeting with a stapler on his table, as if he'd like to lunge at Saralkar and staple some fleshy part of his body or face.

"There is a reason, Mr. Jerajani. Believe me."

"What reason?" He was glaring at Saralkar now, fear camouflaged as anger.

Saralkar let a few nerve-wracking beats pass, then said, "Pranjal Bhatti, the son of your one-time friend, Mohnish, was kidnapped and killed on the days you claim to have been sick."

Karan Jerajani flinched, as if struck hard, but it was difficult to interpret if this was genuine shock or his nerves going haywire with guilt. "What? Oh my God! I . . . I had no idea!"

"Really? You don't read newspapers, watch news, or get online updates on social media?" Saralkar asked.

Karan dodged the question, instead asking his own. "How did this happen? Have they caught the culprit?"

"If we had, I wouldn't be here today," Saralkar replied curtly.

Karan's face turned red and he looked as if he was about to have an epileptic fit. Just then there was a knock on the cabin door and an office boy entered with tea. Several moments of fidgety, uncomfortable silence followed in which Saralkar never took his eyes off Karan, who appeared to be incredibly restless.

As soon as the office boy left, Karan Jerajani burst out, "What the hell's that supposed to mean, Inspector? What have I got to do with it?"

Saralkar let the question hang in the air as he took a sip of the tea. As was wont these days, less than a teaspoon of sugar had been put in the tea. Saralkar glanced at the agitated face of Karan, reached out for a sugar sachet, and emptied one into his cup. He stirred it as he said, "I understand that the Bhatti couple and you parted ways on a bitter note, a few years ago?"

Karan pursed and un-pursed his lips, then replied in a voice that had suddenly gone hoarse. "We . . . We had some differences."

"That sounds like an understatement from what I've heard," Saralkar remarked. "Tell me about it."

"You said you know about it already."

"Yes, but I'd like to hear your version, Mr. Jerajani."

Karan loosened his tie a little more and said, "I helped Mohnish win the 'Phone a friend' round on KBC. He was supposed to pay me a certain share of the winnings, but instead offered me a small token amount . . . that's what soured the friendship."

"Ah, but I believe you were quite infuriated and you had a rather volatile falling out. They say you made threats of teaching them a lesson and you hold a grudge against them for not paying you the money you demanded," Saralkar said.

"That's . . . That's just spiteful of them to allege!" Karan Jerajani spluttered with anger, "It was never about the money . . . I don't need it . . . I earn many times more in this corporate job! It was the shabby way Mohnish went back on his word . . . and you think I would go so far as to kidnap Pranjal and kill him? Because of that?"

Saralkar nodded. "I would hardly expect you to say you did it, if you have indeed committed this foul deed, Mr. Jerajani."

"Why do you keep saying I have, Inspector? On what basis? I tell you I haven't," Karan's voice rose.

"Well, in order for me to eliminate you from the inquiry, I need you to get someone to confirm you were ill at home and were nowhere near Pune," Saralkar said equably.

"But why is the onus on me? Do you have any proof I was in Pune that day, Inspector, and that I committed this ghastly crime?" Karan asked.

It was a question Saralkar himself would've asked if he were in Karan's position. Saralkar lowered the tea cup. "Mr. Jerajani, I came here to Navi Mumbai instead of summoning you to my office at the Pune Homicide Squad. If you are going to take this hostile position then I am afraid our next round of questioning won't be in your office but in mine, which you will not find to your liking."

"What is this? Police intimidation?"

Saralkar pushed his chair back. "Apart from the facts relating to this grudge, the Bhattis have also indicated that Pranjal had expressed that you touched and played with him in a physically inappropriate way. He told them about it after you stopped visiting."

The colour had drained from Karan's face, as if he'd suddenly seen a ghost. "That's . . . That's untrue . . ." is all he could mutter. The fight seemed to have suddenly gone out of him.

It intrigued Saralkar and he had to stop himself from jumping to conclusions. "This information about you assumes particular significance in the light of the fact that Pranjal's body showed signs of sexual assault, Mr. Jerajani."

Karan's body language was as if he'd received an excruciatingly painful blow in his gut. "No . . . no . . . please! I . . . I was very fond of Pranjal . . . I could never have done something so utterly horrible to him!"

Saralkar stood up. "There are two ways of clearing this shadow of doubt. Either we need witnesses to confirm you didn't leave your Navi Mumbai flat on those two days—someone who can establish your presence here or wherever you were. Or you would need to submit a DNA sample so that we can match it against the semen found on Pranjal's body."

Saralkar had slipped in the subterfuge about semen found on the body to watch Karan's reaction and he saw the man grimace. "You have seventy-two hours to call me and come over for the next round of questioning at my Pune office."

Karan's eyes were glazed and sullen now. "I've really done nothing. This is harassment!"

It got Saralkar's goat. "I've seen some of the hateful and obscene messages you sent to Mohnish Bhatti in the last few years, before he blocked you. That was harassment, not this."

Karan Jerajani cringed but said nothing. Saralkar shot him a final look and left the cabin.

It was only when he was back on the highway that the senior inspector realized he'd forgotten to probe Karan about his links to Randeep Mirdha. He cursed himself. How could he be so absent-minded? He was definitely slipping, perhaps a symptom of growing old.

*****

Chapter 18

"My brother pretty much spoiled his own life," Mahek Naqvi said to PSI Motkar, who was seated on a sofa in front of her. She glanced at her husband, Zafar, sitting next to her. "Zafar and I tried to help stabilise Randeep, to knock some sense into him but prison had bent him in ways no one could ever straighten, except he himself."

Motkar nodded. Chandigarh Police had been as helpful as they could, providing him with Randeep Mirdha's updated crime record, other information and also put him in touch with Randeep's married, younger sister, Mahek Naqvi, née Mirdha.

Inter-faith marriages, especially Hindu-Muslim ones, never failed to surprise Motkar, as with most Indians—as if it were some kind of freak phenomenon of nature—particularly in the current atmosphere, which presented a mortal threat to such couples. Would these two have imagined when they got married sixteen or seventeen years ago that their union would one day be derogatorily referred to as 'love jihad' in the so-called New India?

"After his jail term, we put him up for about six months to help him find his feet," Zafar Naqvi added. He was a forty-five-year-old, well-to-do businessman, who dealt in sports goods and equipment. "I asked Randeep if he would like to join me, since I knew he would find it difficult to get a job under the circumstances."

"So did he?" Motkar asked.

"Yes, briefly, for less than a year," Zafar said, "but after he shifted out to his own place, he told me one day that he was not interested in continuing to work with me."

"How did he get the money to shift to his own place? I believe he was quite broke because of the divorce and legal fees for other cases," Motkar asked.

"Well, my father had left him some money when he passed away just before Randeep got out of jail. Randeep also sold the Chandigarh house my parents used to live in," Mahek replied. "He then rented a flat and was soon up to no good—drinking, drugs, women, racing, betting . . . he was a complete mess."

"Oh, but what did he do for a living?"

"Nothing," Mahek said, then hesitated before continuing. "He got into real estate . . . shady deals, began lending money to people at high interest rates. All we know is that within a year or two the money dwindled and he was in urgent need of rehabilitation because of drugs. Zafar and I got him admitted to a rehabilitation centre near Shimla."

"Can you tell me the name of the centre?"

Zafar Naqvi told him and took over the narrative. "He came back sober three months later. He told us he'd turned over a new leaf and learnt his lesson. I told him he could join me again to handle corporate sales, since he had done his MBA and had worked in a corporate job before his marriage troubles, divorce, and jail . . . but he declined saying he'd already been a burden on us. He talked about starting a small restaurant . . . but said he knew a restauranteur friend with whom he would work first and then start his own."

Zafar paused and looked at his wife, as if he wanted her to take the baton and tell what came next.

"Then about a year later he came to us and said he needed about ten lakhs urgently. He said he owed the sum to someone with underworld connections and that he would really be in trouble if he didn't pay up . . . Zafar asked him who the party was and how he'd come to incur the debt, but Randeep wouldn't say. Although Zafar was reluctant, I persuaded him to give my brother the money in cash."

Motkar raised his eyebrows. "You gave him the entire amount in cash?"

"Yes . . . it was a mistake . . . but you know Zafar and I have always felt indebted to Randeep, because he stood firmly by me . . . by us when Zafar and I were getting married, in the face of strong opposition from both families. Without him, it wouldn't have been possible," Mahek said. "Sometimes I wonder where that wonderful brother of mine lost his way and became something totally different."

There was genuine affection and love in that voice.

"You said it was a mistake? Why? What happened?" Motkar probed.

Mahek and Zafar looked at each other. "That's the last we saw of him. Randeep just took the money and disappeared. And till date he's not been in touch again," Mahek answered in a tone that still held bewilderment. "He spoke to me a couple of times after he took the money . . . his phone number was reachable and he was very much in Chandigarh . . . and then suddenly one fine day he was gone.

"All that we received was a letter he sent by courier saying we should trust him and that he'd return the money but needed to leave Chandigarh because things had really gotten hot for him."

"He didn't mention where he was fleeing to or who was after him?"

"No . . ." Mahek replied, "Randeep wrote he didn't want to put us in danger . . . that I should preserve the letter and in case someone came looking for him, we should show it as evidence that we had no idea about his whereabouts and had also been victims of his deceit."

"I see," Motkar said. "Have you still kept the letter?"

"Yes. Would you like to see it?"

"Sure, but before that please tell me how long ago was this?"

"About six or seven years ago," Zafar said.

"And he's not returned the money or tried to get in touch?"

"No . . . not a whisper out of him," Zafar asserted.

"During all these years, did you never feel the need to approach the police to report Randeep was missing with your money?" Motkar asked the couple.

A beat and a glance passed between Mahek and Zafar, then Zafar spoke. "Mahek and I did discuss it . . . but then we thought—what would be the point? By God's grace, we don't need the money . . . so it's okay if Randeep's taken it. We consider it repaying our debt to him. Also, if he was fleeing gangsters, maybe he does not want to be found, we reckoned. Or he's found a place to hide and live in peace."

Motkar nodded. In a sense it was impeccable logic and

yet he wondered if the couple was hiding something. "Mr. and Mrs. Naqvi, I hope you do realize that I am here because the Pune Police is looking for Randeep and investigating his possible involvement in a serious crime. If it is discovered at some stage that you knew his whereabouts but kept it from us, it would amount to abetment," Motkar said in the most official tone he could muster.

The couple frowned at him with almost exactly similar expressions on their face, as if the adage that a couple begin to resemble each other after long years of marriage were uncannily true.

"What do you take us for, Inspector Motkar? We have no idea where Randeep is," Zafar spoke disapprovingly and turned to his wife, "Get that letter and show him."

Mahek nodded, got up, and walked into an inside room. As soon as she was gone, Zafar spoke in an undertone. "What crime, Inspector? What is Randeep suspected of doing? I'd rather you tell me in Mahek's absence. She'll worry unnecessarily."

"The kidnapping and murder of his ex-wife Smita Bhatti's son," Motkar said, watching closely as Zafar seemed to recoil with what appeared like genuine horror.

"Oh my God!" he said after moments of speechlessness. "Are you sure?" He glanced anxiously in the direction he expected his wife to reappear.

Motkar didn't answer his question. Instead, he said, "Did your brother-in-law speak of taking revenge on his ex-wife? Did he harbour deep anger and hatred against her?"

Zafar Naqvi shrugged, still coming to terms with what Motkar had said. "Well, naturally he was angry with her. Who wouldn't be? I mean from Randeep's point of view she had cheated on him, divorced him, and married his friend . . . and to add insult to injury she filed a case of domestic violence, which led to his imprisonment. She, sort of, ruined his life."

He suddenly stopped short, as he heard his wife slam a cupboard in the inside room and begin walking back to the drawing room.

"Here's the letter," Mahek said, as she came and sat next to her husband and handed over the envelope and letter to Motkar.

Motkar pulled out a handkerchief from his pocket and took the envelope containing the letter. He noticed the handwritten address on the envelope and assumed the letter inside it would also be handwritten. "Thank you. Can I take custody of it to get some forensic analysis done?"

Mahek looked at her husband, then asked, "But what has this letter got to do with your investigation? It's been lying with us for several years . . . and as Randeep said, if anyone comes asking for the money, it shows we know nothing about him. If you take it away then . . ."

"Mrs. Naqvi, if no one has come for so many years, chances of anyone arriving at your doorstep now demanding money are minimal," Motkar reasoned. "And I'll make sure to return the letter to you once tests are run on it."

Her husband nodded at her as if to reassure her that he agreed with Motkar.

"What crime do you claim my brother might be involved in?" Mahek asked, looking a little disturbed.

Zafar barged in before Motkar had a chance to reply. "I already asked Inspector Motkar about it. He says he's not in a position to reveal that at this stage."

He looked pleadingly at Motkar as if to do him a favour and leave it at that.

"It's a very serious crime, Mrs. Naqvi, and I can't talk about it," Motkar said. "But we are looking for him and he needs to turn himself in, if he knows what's good for him. Because one way or the other, eventually we'll find him."

It was meant as a warning and Motkar scanned both husband and wife's faces for a reaction. Both of them looked as if they were hiding some information prima facie.

"I'm his only next of kin. I'm his sister. Don't I have a right to know?" Mahek asked.

Motkar shook his head and changed the topic. "By any chance, are you aware if Randeep was in touch with his wife and daughter, after he got out of jail?"

"Not that I know of," Mahek said, "but why would he? That woman was nothing but trouble for him. My brother was no saint. He cheated on Smita and mistreated her but she really managed to screw up his life! He should've just let her divorce him and let her go, instead of letting his ego get in the way. In the end it singed him. She got off scot-free and lived happily ever after with her new husband, I guess."

"Didn't your brother ever express a wish to meet his daughter?"

Mahek frowned. "It was all so long ago. Randeep had been very fond of Namita, so he did talk about her once in a while, but I don't think he even thought of taking the risk of contacting her. By then, he was wary of what Smita would do again—turn the law on him. So he steered clear . . ."

PSI Motkar nodded. There wasn't much more to be extracted from the Naqvi couple at this stage. He got up. "Thank you for this information. One more request—do you have any other letter or something that has Randeep's handwriting—something he wrote to you from prison?"

Mahek shook her head promptly.

Motkar looked at Zafar. "How about you, Mr. Naqvi? He worked for your firm. Do you think you can find some office note or anything in Randeep's handwriting?"

Zafar shook his head doubtfully, "I'll really have to check. After all this time, I doubt it."

"How about some birthday or anniversary card he might've presented to you?" Motkar persisted.

"That I might be able to find," Zafar said and a few moments later, he'd produced a marriage anniversary card from a closet.

Motkar got a sense his wife didn't seem happy about it but didn't intercede or voice her displeasure. He thanked the couple and left the house.

Mahek watched Motkar leave and turned to her husband. "Why did you let him take the letter and the card?"

Zafar looked at his wife. "It'll show we cooperated with the police, Mahek. I know Randeep calls you up sometimes, even if you haven't told me."

He eyed her sharply and knew at once he'd hit bull's eye.

"What are you talking about, Zafar?"

"Look, Mahek, this is serious if he is indeed involved in a crime. Police will find out one way or the other if you are in touch. We might all get into trouble. Think about us and our children now . . . not just your brother."

His wife hesitated. "Believe me, Zafar . . ."

Zafar loved his wife but that was different from believing everything she said.

*****

Two Months Ago

"You come to Pune often, Papa?" Namita asked breathlessly, still unable to believe she was sitting across from her father, in flesh and blood.

It had come as a massive surprise when Randeep Mirdha's message had popped out of the blue, that morning. `I'm in Pune today, sweetheart. Can you meet me between noon and 1.00 p.m.?'

`Of course, Papa. Where?' she had responded as soon as she saw it.

He had texted back with the name of the café for their rendezvous and told her not to be late, since he had to leave at 1.00 p.m. sharp. And here she was now, feasting her eyes on him. Randeep had swept her off her feet, by presenting her with a lovely pair of earrings.

"Happy birthday, sweetheart. I know it's still fifteen days away, but I won't be here, will I?" Randeep Mirdha had said and kissed her on her forehead.

It had felt so good. Her father, her real father! How she had yearned for this moment.

They'd ordered some coffee and snacks, while she adored the earrings he'd gifted her. He'd gushed over how pretty she looked and how proud he was of her. And then she'd asked about his Pune visit.

"Well, I do come to Pune sometimes—maybe once or twice a year," he'd replied casually.

"You come here on business, Papa?"

Randeep hesitated. "Yes . . . on business."

"What business are you in, Papa?" Namita asked.

Randeep cleared his throat. "I offer some very exclusive, premium services," he replied. "But first, tell me, are you happy to see me or am I a disappointment in real life?"

Namita burst into tears—tears of joy of finally having met her long-lost father and quiet sobs of pent-up emotions of having missed him all these years. And then she'd talked and talked as Randeep listened and comforted her.

"You never told me where you live now, Papa."

"Didn't I?" Randeep said evasively.

"No, you just said, not in Chandigarh any longer."

"Right. I left Chandigarh. Too many bad memories," Randeep replied.

"Then where?"

Randeep flashed his dazzling, disarming smile. "I travel so much that I call myself homeless."

He let out a gregarious chuckle, only to see a wrinkle appear on his daughter's brow.

"I don't understand, Papa . . . you mean you don't have a . . ." she paused, wondering how to frame her doubt.

"No . . . no, I have a flat in Ahmedabad . . . but it's a small bachelor pad," Randeep replied carefully.

"Ahmedabad!" Namita said, her face brightening. "It's a nice city, no, Papa?"

"Yes . . . yes but not as nice as Pune," Randeep said hastily. "Very hot throughout the year."

"Oh, but I heard it's a fun and happening place!"

Randeep shrugged. "Well, for someone like you who's lived in Pune, Ahmedabad would be a trifle dull," he lied smoothly.

Namita nodded wistfully, then said, "Can't I come and live with you, Papa?"

Randeep sniffed, looked at the eager face of his daughter regarding him and gave her a pat on the cheek. "Sweetheart, you know how much I want that to happen!"

"Then can I . . .?"

He sighed and gave her a sad, little smile, "I wish it were that easy. I've spoken to some lawyer friends and . . . they all say there might be some legal complications involved."

"What legal complications, Papa?" I . . . I am going to

turn eighteen this birthday. Surely no one can stop me from choosing to be with you, then?" the girl said defiantly.

"I know . . . but . . . but you see, when your Mum took you away from me, she imposed a lot of conditions as part of the custody agreement," Randeep said, patting Namita's curly, black hair. "That's why I have consulted lawyers to find some way out . . . I . . . I don't want to take any chances, you know. Trust me, Namita, I have to tread carefully . . . but I am working on it."

The girl looked away in disappointment and her eyes filled up with tears again.

"Hey . . . hey, Namita . . . don't cry, please. Tell me, are you unhappy there? Do Mum and her husband trouble you?"

Namita shook her head silently and wiped her tears. "I miss you, Papa . . . all the years you were not there."

Randeep took his daughter's hand in his and kissed it tenderly, "I know, my princess . . . I know. I need some time. Let me think of a way to make sure your mum does not object and play spoilsport, okay?"

Namita nodded, touched by her father's reassurances.

Randeep smiled back at her. "But I would need your help."

"What help, Papa?" Namita asked.

"Well . . . I need you to give me as much information about your household as you can. About your mum, your stepfather, Mohnish, and their son . . . what's his name? Prajwal."

"Pranjal."

"Yes, Pranjal," Randeep continued, "I want to know everything you know about the family. About Mohnish's business, Mum's job, your stepbrother's school, and other things within the family—disputes, secrets, property, money, daily routines . . ."

Namita frowned, taken a little aback. "Why, Papa?"

Randeep realized he had stepped on her scruples. He gave her a warm smile. "Your mother will hate the idea of you wanting to live with me. She'll do anything to prevent it. That's why we need a bargaining chip. That's where this information will help. Understood?"

Namita looked at him, confused. She wanted to ask "How?" but the affectionate look on her father's face was such that she just nodded and smiled back. "Yes, Papa!"

*****

Chapter 19

"Pranjal had a lot of potential, but he was no prodigy," Sunaini Bhagwat said.

She looked almost too normal to be a chess champion, ASI Sanika Zirpe thought. Not that she had met any chess champions before, but police officers were as prone to stereotyping people as common folk.

"He came for your coaching sessions on the weekends, is it?"

"Yes, he started about two years ago and was developing quite well," Sunaini said. "Poor boy . . ."

"You heard about his kidnapping and murder on the news?" ASI Zirpe asked.

"Yes," Sunaini said, adjusting her saree and flicking back a strand of her hair that had strayed onto her forehead.

"Have you talked to Pranjal's parents or met them afterwards?"

Sunaini looked at her, startled, as if the thought had simply not struck her. "No . . . I haven't," she replied, "I . . . I am bad at such things. I know it's awful of me. Makes it look as if I don't care."

ASI Zirpe nodded without saying anything.

Sunaini Bhagwat looked at her searchingly. She appeared like a woman who'd grappled with much sadness. For a moment ASI Zirpe wondered if the chess coach suffered from depression—that malady seemed to be here, there, everywhere.

"Have you caught the kidnappers . . . the killers yet, officer?"

"No," ASI Zirpe kept it brief.

"Oh! May . . . May I ask why you have come to see me exactly?" Sunaini asked. There was a little bubble of anxiety in her demeanour.

"To see if there is anything you can tell us that might help," ASI Zirpe replied.

"Me? How? Pranjal just came here for chess training on the weekends. Beyond that I knew nothing about him or his family . . ."

"Well, children of that age usually develop an affinity, a bond with a teacher and sometimes confide in them," ASI Zirpe said. "Did Pranjal ever say anything to you that was cause for alarm or that you felt was odd?"

Sunaini frowned. "Honestly, I don't encourage my students or their families to get close . . . I just focus on chess and improving their game, their thinking, the various techniques and gambits . . . I . . . I am not the bonding kind . . . it's the same with all my students, not just Pranjal."

ASI Zirpe regarded the awkward, flushed expression on her face and was tempted to ask her why, but desisted. "Okay, well, how did Pranjal seem when he came for your class last? That must be the weekend before last."

The chess coach's eyes narrowed, as if trying to recollect.

"I . . . I think he was his usual self . . . oh yes . . . except I noticed some injury to his head! Or was that on the previous weekend, before that?"

She suddenly looked scatter-brained, as if unsure. "I . . . I am not really sure. I think he'd been beaten by some boy in school. That's what I remember him telling me."

"That was about three or four weeks ago, Mrs. Bhagwat," ASI Zirpe remarked.

Sunaini shrugged. "Perhaps . . . whatever it was, he seemed listless and out of sorts then. I was a little worried, because he'd topped at the district level and just qualified at the state level. He needed to perform well but was not playing up to his mark."

"Was it a very prestigious championship he had been selected for?"

Sunaini looked at ASI Zirpe, shocked. "Of course . . . it paved the way to his being selected to participate at national level sub-junior championships," she said. "I suppose like most people you have no idea about how chess tournaments are structured in India and the world."

ASI Zirpe could sense some kind of righteous bitterness and contempt in her tone. "How much do you know about volleyball, Mrs. Bhagwat? Or volleyball tournaments in India, especially women's volleyball?"

Sunaini was clearly taken aback. She blinked as if the question had confused her. "Nothing. Why?"

"Well, chess is not the only game people know little about, madam. At least everyone knows your name and association with chess. I have played volleyball nationals and no one would ever recognise me," ASI Zirpe said.

Sunaini gave her a sour, graceless look. "Hmmm. Do you have any more questions, Inspector?"

"Yes, just wanted to know why is it you prefer to keep students and families at a distance?"

A troubled sadness spread over Sunaini's face. "How is this question relevant to Pranjal's case?"

"Maybe not, but I am a volleyball coach myself. I am just curious to know your viewpoint as an eminent coach of a brainy game," ASI Zirpe replied.

Sunaini seemed to soften. "I don't know about other games but when coaches and mentors get too emotionally invested in their wards or students, it can really wreak havoc. I know from personal experience. My own coach—"

She suddenly stopped and after a beat continued, "Anyway . . . but it's not just the students, it can be a big problem with parents who are passionate about their child too. Fathers and mothers can really make life hell for a coach with their demands and expectations. In fact, I have had to discontinue some very promising students when their parents got aggressive or overbearing in a bid to push their children's chess careers."

"Oh, really? I do know about pushy and passionate parents, but luckily in volleyball it just does not seem glamourous or interesting enough for people to push," ASI Zirpe said.

Sunaini didn't seem to be listening or getting the irony. She just gave a vague nod. "Not long ago, I had had to file a complaint against a parent too, who was so obsessed with his son's chess that he kept harassing and haranguing me."

"Oh, is it? What happened then?"

"Thankfully, he stopped bothering me and only then did I withdraw the complaint," Sunaini said with a little shudder.

"No such trouble with Pranjal's parents, I hope?" ASI Zirpe asked.

"No, no . . . they never bothered me and neither did they put pressure on Pranjal, because that can be quite bad too," Sunaini said and glanced at her watch. "If you don't mind, Inspector, I need to get ready to go to a local chess tournament I promised to inaugurate."

"Thank you, Mrs. Bhagwat," ASI Zirpe said and stood up.

Sunaini got up too. "You know, it was really awful of me not to even call Pranjal's parents . . . I'll do that this evening."

Sanika Zirpe once again got the feeling that the chess coach had been battling depression for long. Did every boon come with an inbuilt curse, she wondered.

*****

"So, you think Randeep Mirdha has assumed a new identity and has relocated elsewhere? And neither the authorities nor his family or anyone else knows where he is?" Saralkar asked, summing up Motkar's long, detailed telephonic briefing.

"Yes, sir. I've gathered and verified all the information about him available here in Chandigarh. Apart from the police, his sister, and brother-in-law, I met his restauranteur friend, a former drug addict Randeep was in rehab with, an ex-jail-mate, and some of the women he had dalliances with," Motkar said. "No one's heard from Randeep for years now and all of them say he just dropped out of sight. I'm fairly sure they know nothing."

"Is there any truth about him fleeing from gangsters, because he owed them money?" Saralkar asked.

"That's what he told his sister, Mahek, but no one else has really confirmed who this gangster might be or if it's even true," Motkar replied.

"I see. You think there's a possibility Randeep might be dead?"

"Nothing points to that, sir," Motkar said. "My hunch is that his sister knows his whereabouts but unless we have some clear indication that she's hiding information, we can't grill her about that."

"Hmm . . ." Saralkar said. "Okay, I think your job's done there, so get back to Pune, Motkar."

"Yes, sir," Motkar replied, then continued with some hesitation, "Sir . . . may I take a day off and go to Shimla? It's just about three hours away from here."

Saralkar grunted. "What's the fun of going to Shimla all alone, Motkar? That too when there's no snow? Sorry, you are needed here, pronto."

He cut the call before Motkar could argue further, then turned to Tupe and Zirpe who had just trooped into his office. "Either of you getting anywhere?" Saralkar asked the duo.

"Sir, I think we've finally found CCTV footage of Pranjal cycling along a section of Bavdhan main road," Tupe replied. "We are enhancing the image to be absolutely sure, but it certainly looks like Pranjal from the attire and the bicycle. He seems to be headed in the direction of his class."

"So that confirms beyond doubt that he definitely left the society alive and on his own," Saralkar said.

"Yes, sir. This should remove all doubt. I'll show you the footage as soon as it is enlarged and enhanced."

"Good. But if we have got the CCTV footage now, why did we miss it so far?"

"Sir, this is footage from the CCTV camera of a bank's branch. We had put in requests to a few establishments but they required internal permissions and formalities before handing it over to us. So, we got the bank's footage only yesterday," Tupe explained.

"Good. Now collate footage from other CCTV cameras too, from that spot onwards, till we can zero in on the patch or spot after which Pranjal isn't seen again," Saralkar said. "If the kidnapper whisked Pranjal and his bicycle away from the road, his vehicle must've followed the boy for some distance or laid in wait for him somewhere. Either way, it's got to be among the vehicles that passed by in either direction, wherever Pranjal is last seen in any CCTV footage, within the time frame of just a few minutes of that last sighting."

"So, sir, you want us to get the numbers of all four wheelers that can be seen passing by within a few minutes, before or after Pranjal is last sighted on CCTV?"

"Correct. I know it's not going to be easy because most vehicles rush by, footage is often hazy, other vehicles are in the way. But it's worth trying," Saralkar said. "And like earlier, you can leave out smaller cars."

"Sure, sir," Tupe replied, then said, "One more thing, sir . . . the dredging of the river where Pranjal's body was found has yielded nothing. No sign of the bicycle either."

Saralkar grunted and shook his head. He turned to ASI Zirpe. "What've you got, Zirpe?"

ASI Zirpe quickly briefed him about her visit to Sunaini Bhagwat.

"Did you ask her where she was on the day of Pranjal's kidnapping?" Saralkar asked, once Zirpe had finished briefing.

"Sir?" ASI Zirpe said, taken aback. "I didn't think we considered Sunaini Bhagwat a suspect . . ."

Saralkar nodded. "We don't, but it's a good question to put and observe reactions—assess how truthful a person is being. Anyway, have her background checked—just routine.

And did you get the names of other students in Pranjal's batch for chess coaching?"

ASI Zirpe bit her lip. "No, sir . . . I didn't think it might be relevant . . ."

"It might not be. All the same, do it," Saralkar remarked. "Anything else to report?"

"Yes, sir," Tupe said. "Constable Bidkar who'd gone to Jabalpur to probe the driver Jayesh Pardeshi's accident, returned this morning. He's verified all the facts and the driver's identity. Jayesh Pardeshi continues to be critical but it's clear he could not have played any role in Pranjal's kidnapping."

"Okay, another one gets ticked off our suspect list. What about that Corporator Satish Khilare's visit to his Bhor farmhouse? Any more clarity on it?"

"It seems Khilare is planning to usurp some tract of forest land bordering a plot he had purchased earlier to build a resort. He was in Bhor basically to bribe some government officials. That's what the Bhor Police surmise, since a middleman's assistant also happens to be a police informer. The informer tipped them off about the officials Khilare met," ASI Zirpe said.

"Hmm, so committing a crime, but not the one we are investigating," Saralkar observed, almost sounding disappointed.

He was quiet for a while, tapping his left shoe on the floor, a faraway look in his eyes. His gaze finally turned to ASI Tupe.

"Tupe, call up Karan Jerajani. Remind him, he's supposed to be here for questioning tomorrow."

"But, sir, I thought you had given him seventy-two hours . . . that is until day after tomorrow?" ASI Tupe asked.

"Yes, if he says that, tell him I have preponed the questioning in view of the circumstances," Saralkar said. "He has to be here tomorrow."

*****

An unknown number flashed on Mahek Naqvi's mobile screen. The calls always came from unknown numbers—mostly landlines from different cities, a day or two after she had given a missed call on the number Randeep had instructed her to call on. He had told Mahek, he would never take a call from her, so that no one would ever be able to connect her to him. He would instead call back from some unknown number and destination a day or two later during the day time when she was usually alone at home, after her husband had left for work or between 6.00 p.m. and 7.00 p.m. in the evening when she was out for her walk, which Randeep knew she took regularly. In case she wasn't alone, she just had to disconnect the call or pick it up and say "wrong number".

Then she would again call the number Randeep had given at her own convenience and the same process would be repeated. No texts or WhatsApp messages were to be exchanged.

Today, the call was again from a landline. It showed the code 0832. Mahek wondered where Randeep was calling from. Earlier she would take the trouble to check the STD code, but now she rarely did. Her brother seemed to be always on the move.

"Hullo, *Bhaiyya . . ."* she said breathlessly.

"Hi, Mahek. How are you, sister dear?"

"Are you okay? You taking care of your health, or no?"

"How about Zafar and the kids and you?"

"All good! Look, bhaiyya, I called for something urgent," Mahek said, unable to continue with the pleasantries, anxiety gnawing at her.

"What happened? What is it?"

"A police officer from Pune Police came looking for you two days ago," Mahek said.

She suddenly felt a tense, eerie silence at the other end of the line as if her brother had stopped breathing.

"Okay," he finally responded. "Tell me what he said."

Mahek began telling him all.

*****

"I know someone who can hack phones," Mohnish Bhatti said to his wife, as they lay sleepless beside each other in the dark.

It was 2.00 a.m. An hour ago, they had run out of pain and tears for the day—as if there was a daily quota beyond which no human being could grieve even if they had lost their own child. That they would have to wait till the tap of that emotion opened again the following day.

"Are you saying we should hack Namita's phone?" his wife responded, quick to catch the drift.

"Yes, if she's in touch with Randeep, we will get to know. And we'll also know if he's behind Pranjal's . . ." The words choked back in his throat.

"You are right, Mohnish! I will have to get her phone when she's either sleeping or showering," Smita said.

"But Namita bolts the room from inside," Mohnish said.

"Not in the night. She's scared. She opens it just before going to sleep."

"She'll know as soon as she wakes up. She'll know we've taken her phone."

"Let her. What's she going to do? Make a scene? Hate us for a few days? She already does! But at least we'll know if . . . if . . . she's in touch with Randeep and if he's involved," Smita said. "Let her hate us . . . maybe we can at least save her. We might get some hints about Randeep's whereabouts and inform the police."

Mohnish turned on his side to face his wife. "There is also an alternative way . . . because even though I suggested it, I am not sure hacking our own daughter's phone is right."

"What alternative way?" Smita asked.

"DNA test! Let's prove it to her I'm her father," Mohnish said. "When the evidence is in front of her eyes, she'll know what the truth is . . . and . . . and . . . then she'll herself tell us if she's in touch with Randeep and if he had any hand in Pranjal's fate."

"But that will take time, Mohnish. We need to know now . . . immediately. Let's hack Namita's phone first. The DNA test can be done later to convince her," Smita said, sitting up in her bed. "Should I get the phone now? Will you be able to get it to the hacker early morning?"

"No, no, Smita, I need to talk and fix it up with the guy," Mohnish said. "We'll take the phone tomorrow night. Let's plan this properly without haste."

"That would be another twenty-four hours, Mohnish. We don't have all the time in the world!"

"Yes, I know, Smita. But if we want this to work, we have to be patient. I don't want to leave the phone with the hacker . . . I want to be there when he does it," Mohnish said. "After all, we have to protect Namita and whatever stuff is on her phone too."

Smita fell silent reluctantly. Mohnish was right. "Okay," she said and fell back on her pillow, her mind still working furiously.

Fifteen minutes later, she sensed her troubled husband had fallen asleep, from his gentle breathing. But sleep hadn't come to her. For somewhere, from the corner of her mind she had remembered, with a start, a casual conversation with Namita more than a year ago. Namita had just stepped into her bath, when her phone had started ringing. She had called out to her mother to take the call. By the time Smita had got to Namita's phone, the rings had stopped. Smita had told her the call was from one of her professors and something had been so urgent that her daughter had told her to text back the caller immediately with a short message she had dictated from the bathroom itself. And obviously, in the process, Namita had told Smita her password, with the strict caveat that she was not to take the opportunity to look at anything else on her phone.

By some miracle, Smita had managed to recollect the password now. Could it be that her daughter hadn't changed her password since? Most unlikely, Smita's rational mind told her. On the other hand, even if there was miniscule possibility that Namita hadn't, wasn't it worth a try? It was a tantalisingly tempting thought.

Should she make an attempt to get into her daughter's phone, Smita wondered. Tonight? And if that didn't work, then they could get it done by the hacker as they had just discussed. Smita Bhatti sat up in bed, getting ready to tiptoe into her daughter's room.

*****

Chapter 20

Karan Jerajani was four pegs down and yet the sense of panic refused to subside. The 240 ml of whisky he'd imbibed offered no escape from the reality of his predicament. It diluted nothing—in fact made it starker. He faced ruin—imprisonment, loss of job, total humiliation. There was no getting away from it.

Ever since the cop had given him seventy-two hours to furnish proof or witnesses of his whereabouts, it had felt like a dreaded countdown that could only end badly. He couldn't bear to think what would follow if he confessed. Once they knew he was a paedophile, he could expect no mercy. And now the call in the evening from the cop's assistant, asking to present himself tomorrow, not day after, had left Karan in total despair.

It was then that the thought had germinated—the only way out of the inevitable indignity and wretchedness to follow. Yes, that was it—it was time to end his depraved life!

He stood up now and strode to the balcony of his tenth-floor flat. He stood holding the railing, swaying and looking at the darkness of the night. It was time to let go. There was really nothing to hold on to. He had nobody who would really miss him; nobody who would really care if he was humiliated. His parents had passed away, so no one even to mourn.

He took a deep breath. All it required was one little act of courage, though the world would condemn it as cowardice. Karan mounted the railing and jumped.

A short, handwritten note fluttered under his empty whisky glass.

I didn't kill Pranjal Bhatti, but I am a paedophile. If possible, I request this fact not be made public and my death be declared an unfortunate accident.—Karan Jerajani

*****

Smita Bhatti opened her bedroom door and stepped out into the passage. Everything was quiet. She moved silently towards her daughter's room. No light showed from underneath the door. She stood listening for sounds—her daughter's voice, low volume music—anything to suggest Namita was not yet asleep.

Inevitably, her eyes fell on the door of the third bedroom opposite Namita's – Pranjal's room which would forever remain empty, even though full of memories of her deceased son. She gagged as a lump rose in her throat. Her legs almost gave way under her, so debilitating was the sudden clamour of grief in the still of the night.

It took Smita a few minutes to regain her composure. She put her hand on Namita's door and pressed down the handle gently, hoping the click was muffled and the door wouldn't creak. It was unlocked, as she'd expected and Smita stood blinking, peering into the room. The dim night light was on and she could make out the form of her daughter, sprawled on the bed, sleeping on her stomach as was her habit.

Smita stepped forward trying to make absolutely sure her daughter was asleep. In the soft glow of the night light, she could see Namita's face, half buried into her pillow. She didn't have to look far for Namita's phone. It lay right next to her on the side table, hooked to the charger, where Namita must've put it down when overcome by sleep.

Smita looked at her daughter carefully. Despite her conviction that she was doing no wrong, she hesitated momentarily. She had to protect her child from Randeep, even if it meant snooping. She would take the phone, slip out of the room and try the password she had remembered, so that she could gain access to her daughter's messages, contacts, and other stuff on her phone. And if she wasn't successful, she'd just return and plug back the phone so that Namita would never know. And tomorrow night she would take it again and give it to Mohnish so that the hacker would be able to do the needful instead.

Smita gently unplugged the phone from the charger and began tiptoeing from the room. Suddenly, the device erupted into an alarm and began flashing too. It had been so unexpected that Smita dropped the mobile, then quickly picked it up and looked at her daughter. Namita still seemed to be undisturbed.

Smita began retracing her steps to get out of the room, desperately trying to switch the phone off, casting a glance over her shoulder. She shut the door as she rushed out and went into the drawing room, but the alarm wouldn't go off. She saw a screen prompt for entering a pin to shut off the alarm. Smita's thoughts raced, trying to think of a way to stop the sound. She was sure it would wake both Namita and Mohnish up, if the alarm continued for some more time.

An idea struck her. Maybe if she went out of the house and tried to remove the battery or waited till the alarm died own, it would solve the problem. It had to stop in a while. It couldn't go on for more than ten or fifteen minutes, could it? Then she realized it was pouring outside. She couldn't wait in the lobby of the building. It would disturb people. Perhaps she could wait inside her car. Yes, that was the solution! She scrambled to pick up the car keys and open the main door.

But just as she was about to step out, Namita strode into the drawing room, her face suffused with anger. "Why have you taken my mobile, Mamma? Give it back to me at once!" she screamed. "I never thought you would stoop to this level!"

*****

If there was one thing that was at the top of Saralkar's hate list, it was being woken up at unearthly hours. His definition of unearthly stretched from midnight onwards to about 7.00 a.m. in the morning. Not that it mattered, for being a cop, keeping unearthly hours was a part of the deal and he'd been woken from his slumber or dragged out of bed on far too many occasions than he could remember.

The call from Navi Mumbai Crime Branch came at 6.00 a.m., almost as if the caller had dialled the moment the clock struck six.

"Hullo . . ." Saralkar said, in a dangerous tone, ready to bite the caller's head off.

"Good morning, Saralkar sir. Inspector Deokar calling from Navi Mumbai Crime Branch . . ."

"What's it, Deokar?" Saralkar asked, making no attempt to camouflage his rudeness.

"Sir, were you investigating a man called Karan Jerajani in connection with a case?" Deokar asked without preamble.

"Yes. Why?"

"Sir, he seems to have jumped to his death from the balcony of his apartment, late last night," Deokar replied.

Saralkar grunted and sat up, all vestiges of sleep now having deserted him. "Has he left behind a suicide note or something?"

"Yes, sir," Deokar replied and read out the lines Karan Jerajani had scribbled.

"Shit," Saralkar cursed, using a word he generally avoided using. "Are you sure it's suicide?"

"Nothing so far to contradict the fact, sir," Deokar replied. "Would it be possible for you to brief me on the dead man's suspected involvement in the case you are investigating? Since we found ASI Tupe's incoming call on Jerajani's mobile, we called him up. He gave us to understand that you had summoned Karan Jerajani to Pune for questioning today?"

"Yes," Saralkar said. "Look, Deokar, I'll need to come over and take a look at his stuff and any information about Jerajani that you find. It's important."

"Okay, sir. When can we expect you?"

"By mid-day. It's pouring so depends on the expressway traffic," Saralkar replied.

"Sure, sir. Was he . . . er . . . a murder suspect?"

"Kidnapping and murder, Deokar," Saralkar said. "And while we are talking crime, it's also a heinous crime to wake up a senior officer at 6.00 a.m., you know, especially when it would have made no difference if you'd called an hour later."

"Sir?" Inspector Deokar asked, unsure whether to laugh or apologise. He'd been up all night, and in his assessment, had called up Saralkar at an hour which wasn't unearthly. "I am sorry if I called too early, sir," he nevertheless mumbled for Saralkar did outrank him and was not a name unfamiliar to those in Maharashtra Police.

"Ah well, see you later," Saralkar said, assuaged, but still a little annoyed. He cut the phone and lay back. An uneasy thought had struck him. Had he, by any chance, been responsible for pushing the unfortunate Karan Jerajani over the brink? Even for a hardened police officer like him, it was a disconcerting thought. Had the man killed himself because he was guilty or because he wasn't?

Saralkar decided the quicker he got started for Navi Mumbai the better. He wondered if Motkar had got back from Chandigarh and began dialling his number. The rings passed and just as he was about to cut the call, Motkar's groggy voice answered, "Good morning, sir . . ."

"You in Shimla, Motkar, or back in Pune?"

"Yes, sir," Motkar replied, ignoring the Shimla barb. "Reached past midnight."

"Ah well, I would've let you catch up on your beauty sleep, Motkar, but I have to head to Navi Mumbai right away. Karan Jerajani seems to have committed suicide. And left a note admitting to being a paedophile but claiming not to have kidnapped or killed Pranjal," Saralkar said.

"My God, sir! Did our summons lead him to take his own life?" Motkar blurted out, fearing the worst.

"Either that or foul play, because it sure can't be a coincidence."

"You want me to come along, sir?"

"Your company is always enthralling, Motkar, but no, you file your report on Randeep Mirdha and Chandigarh, but also I want you to go through the Atharva Jambhekar file by tomorrow."

"Sure, sir . . . I should've done it earlier, before leaving for Chandigarh."

"Never mind. Just do it urgently," Saralkar replied and called off.

As he got ready to leave, he cursed his absent-mindedness for having forgotten to ask Karan Jerajani about Randeep Mirdha, when he'd questioned the former at his office. And now the man had gone beyond all interrogation, except by the Almighty, if there was one!

*****

Smita Bhatti woke up to a splitting headache. Her husband had persuaded her to take sleeping pills after the flare-up with Namita in the wee hours of the night. The alarm, the blasted alarm, had ruined everything, not to mention her own impetuousness.

She hadn't even known that there existed easily downloadable, anti-theft alarm apps for mobile phones. She had never come across anyone who used one. Why would anyone do it? When and why had Namita decided to use it? Was it because she had anticipated her mother trying to snoop on her mobile? It hurt to know her child knew exactly what she was capable of.

Their argument had been an ugly one. Her daughter had gone ballistic, demanding back her phone, shouting and screaming at the top of her voice, accusingly.

"You are not a mother—you are a monster!" Namita had shrieked as they grappled physically over the phone. "Give it to me . . . give it to me at once! Shame on you, Mamma . . . shame on you!"

Smita had been as shocked by Namita's rage as by her own brazen fierceness against her own daughter. Their raised voices and duel had finally awoken Mohnish and he'd rushed out into the drawing room. He had made Smita return the phone to Namita, who promptly rushed inside her room with it and slammed the door on them.

Smita had broken down in tears of fury and Mohnish had comforted and rebuked her by turns, then made her take the sleeping pills. She had finally slipped into slumber, exhausted, angry, and ashamed.

Smita looked at the clock now. It showed 10.00 a.m. Mohnish wasn't beside her. He had probably left her to sleep it off. Apart from the headache, Smita felt beset by a strange mixture of nausea and ennui. What was there to wake up to? She had lost her son. Had she also burnt the bridge with her daughter last night?

She pulled herself up and trudged out of the bedroom. The house seemed strangely silent. Neither Mohnish nor Namita were anywhere to be seen or heard. Where were they? Had Namita left for college and Mohnish for work? The empty house suddenly seemed too much to bear. She slumped on the drawing room sofa as a lump rose in her throat. Just a week ago this house had been a dwelling and now it felt like a morgue.

She picked up her phone and just as she dialled Mohnish's number, she heard the key being inserted into the front door lock. Mohnish opened the door and walked in looking flustered and agitated.

"Where were you, Mohnish? And where's Namita?"

Mohnish's distressed expression became more acute. "I . . . I don't know . . . the CCTV footage at the front gate shows she walked out with a trolley bag around 6.30 a.m. this morning."

"What? What do you mean?"

Mohnish walked up and sat next to Smita. "When I woke up at 9.00 a.m. this morning, she was gone, Smita . . . no message . . . nothing! I tried calling on her mobile but it was switched off. I then went downstairs. Her two-wheeler was in the parking area, in its place. So, I asked the watchman at the front gate. He told me he had come for his shift at 8.00 a.m. and hadn't seen Namita leave. So, I ran through the security footage and saw her walking out with the trolley bag."

He held up his mobile and showed her the screen grab from the CCTV footage, showing Namita walking out with the bag.

Smita's heart was beating hard. "You mean she . . . she . . . left because of last night? But . . . But where could she have gone?"

"I have no idea, Smita! I spoke to the night watchman who had been on duty. He had casually asked Namita whether she was going out of town and she just nodded," Mohnish replied. "We need to check with all her friends. It's possible she's just furious with us and went to some friend's place to cool off."

But Smita thought she knew her daughter better. "No . . . Mohnish . . . she's gone to him . . . Randeep. He's taken her . . . he's taken her away from us . . . first he took our son and now our daughter! He's had his revenge. We've got to go to the police . . ."

Mohnish looked stunned. He felt palpitations begin in his chest. He looked at his wife and nodded, then scrambled to call the police. Had another nightmare begun, even before the first had ended?

*****

Saralkar knew exactly what happened to a human body when it fell from the tenth storey. He didn't need imagination for he'd seen his share of suicide, murder, and accident victims who'd met that gruesome fate.

Karan Jerajani's splattered remains were not very different—the skull cracked open, every bone in the body broken, a hand almost ripped away, all the organs burst open, oozing out their contents. Saralkar had declined the invitation to see the body and had just skimmed through the photographs Inspector Deokar had shown.

Deokar had also taken him to Karan's apartment and shown him the immense amount of paedophiliac material they'd retrieved—photographs, magazines, sex tools, the mind-boggling gallery of digital child pornography, including graphic images, videos, and games. Above all the life size soft sex dolls that were clearly meant for pleasuring by their now deceased owner.

"As you can see, sir, plenty of evidence that Karan Jerajani was a hardcore paedophile. Looks like he was your man, sir—whatever he claims in his suicide note," Deokar remarked.

Saralkar was too preoccupied with his thoughts to respond. "You've got his phone, right?" he asked instead. "I'll need it."

"Sure, sir, but let my team finish with it, and we'll share all the contents and material retrieved from it," Inspector Deokar replied.

"Look, Deokar, he's dead. You have all the evidence of suicide. You don't need the phone but we do urgently, to crack open my case . . . if there really is a connection," Saralkar said. "What I particularly need to find out is what Karan Jerajani was up to on the day of Pranjal Bhatti's kidnapping and in the days leading to it and later."

"But, Saralkar sir . . . that's highly irregular! How can I just hand over such a vital piece of electronic evidence before I . . ." Deokar protested.

"I understand that, damn it. I am asking you a favour, Deokar," Saralkar said. "Look, do you have anyone in your team who's good with retrieving stuff from mobiles—chats, messages, data, calls, files, downloads, etc.?"

Deokar looked at him doubtfully. "Yes, sir, I have a constable who is handy with it."

"So, lend him to me for a couple of hours to let me ascertain if there is any incriminating stuff on Karan's mobile that ties in to my case," Saralkar said. "I can at least get started on the basis of the material or leads, if any."

Inspector Deokar seemed to think over it, as if looking for some hidden, dodgy loophole, then finally relented. "Okay, sir . . . but please let only my team member handle and process the device."

This time Saralkar gave him an offended look. "Deokar, I don't need lessons in what might contaminate evidence or compromise your investigation," he said with an acerbic edge to his voice that made Deokar want to swallow back his words.

Saralkar's glare brought forth a fumbling apology. "I didn't mean that, sir . . . I'll just send Constable Kazi to you with the device."

*****

Chapter 21

Karan Jerajani's phone had yielded its secrets, courtesy Constable Kazi's skills and two hours later, Saralkar was seated in front of Karan Jerajani's psychiatrist, Dr. Gargi Naidu. She'd just confirmed that Karan had consulted her a few times, but hadn't visited for almost three months.

"Did he stop coming on his own or how come?" Saralkar asked.

"Quite honestly, Inspector . . . I recommended to him that he consult a senior psychiatrist—a colleague of mine, Dr. Pradeep Mhatre, who has more experienced in er . . . handling patients with his condition," Dr. Naidu said.

"Paedophilia?"

"Yes . . . I . . . I just thought I wasn't equipped to . . . to . . . really help him beyond a point. So, I also gave him a reference."

"I see. So, did he consult the psychiatrist you had referred him to?"

Dr. Gargi Naidu shrugged. "I don't think so. Every now and then Karan would call up or WhatsApp me . . . but I urged him to go and visit Dr. Mhatre. I would've known if he had."

She stopped and gave a shudder. "I feel so horrible . . . to know he's done this. Maybe I should've tried to help him instead of sending him to someone else. Are you sure, Inspector, he killed himself . . . that he didn't accidentally fall over because he had too much to drink?"

"The alcohol may have impaired his judgement, but it's quite clearly a case of suicide. In fact, there is also a witness who saw him jump," Saralkar replied.

"Oh my God! Did Karan leave a suicide note?" Dr. Gargi asked, clearly distressed.

Saralkar nodded. "Yes. Did he ever talk about taking his life?"

"No . . . no. He didn't display any suicidal tendencies or express such thoughts, but you can never say with patients suffering from acute psychiatric disorders," the psychiatrist said. "Did he mention a specific reason in the note?"

It was a tricky question and Saralkar decided to calibrate what he revealed. "He feared being exposed as a paedophile. Could that be the trigger?"

"Yes . . . yes. I can very well believe it in his case. You see, unlike many sexual offenders, Karan Jerajani was guilt-ridden and utterly ashamed of his paedophilic predilections . . . terribly frustrated because the urges were beyond his control and could not be easily satiated. Worse, it involved committing an unforgivable transgression against a child, which only added to his guilt and shame."

"May I ask if Karan ever confessed to child abuse? To having sexually molested a child or having engaged in sexual acts with children?" Saralkar probed.

Dr. Gargi Naidu shook her head forcefully. "No . . . no. He . . . he was aware it was a crime and that I would have to report it if he had told me of an instance . . . but all the same I'm sure Karan did engage in . . . er . . . sexual acts with children infrequently . . . but I doubt he would've molested or abused a child."

"Isn't it one and the same thing? It's abuse."

"Yes, Inspector you are right . . . what I meant is the element of overt aggression or coercion," the psychiatrist said. "I . . . I guess like everything else in this world, there must be paid services for . . . er . . . even a depraved thing such as this and I think Karan Jerajani did avail of them."

"Is paedophilia clinically treatable?" Saralkar asked.

Dr. Gargi Naidu frowned. "There are certain medications but the efficacy is not very high. Most of the focus by psychiatrists also is therefore on counselling and therapy for this particular disorder. But as I said, I have very little experience with it."

"Did you ever feel your counselling helped make any difference to Karan in managing his impulses?"

Dr. Gargi gave a sad smile. "I think it only helped to the extent that he . . . he could at least speak to me about it . . . express the worst kind of thoughts that went on in his mind about this taboo subject. You know, unlike other sexual conditions like homosexuality and LGBTQ issues, which are now slowly gaining societal understanding, acceptance, or sympathy and are decriminalised . . . paedophilia will forever remain stigmatised and criminalised, because the victims are children. No one, including psychiatrists, can ever see paedophilia as an illness but rather a horrifying depravity and perversion . . . a terrible crime because even psychiatrists are human beings. So, I have my doubts if counselling is really the answer."

"I guess one has to draw the line between mental disorder and depravity somewhere, Dr. Gargi . . . or psychopaths and serial killers can claim they couldn't help what they were doing," Saralkar remarked.

"Which in a way is true but you are right, Inspector. There has to be a line and paedophiles cannot escape responsibility for their actions," Dr. Gargi Naidu asserted.

"One last question, do you think Karan Jerajani could have been capable of kidnapping, molesting, and killing a child?" Saralkar asked.

Dr. Gargi looked as if someone had knocked her breath away. "What?" A look of utter disgust passed over her face. "Is . . . Is that what you suspect him of? And you think that's why he committed suicide?"

She looked at Saralkar searchingly.

"We have to look at all possibilities Dr. Gargi."

"I . . . I can't really answer your question! Not until I know the facts, Inspector."

Saralkar nodded. "Okay, fair enough. Well, then, can you tell me if he ever talked about a boy called Pranjal Bhatti?"

Dr. Gargi made a gesture as if the name rang a bell and stood up, went to a cabinet and found a file. She walked back to her table and began perusing the contents of the file. Shuffling through the papers, she stopped at a page. Then flipped back a few more pages.

"There's no surname but he mentioned the name Pranjal during two sessions," Dr. Gargi said, looking up at Saralkar. "He refers to the boy as the child of a couple, who were once his friends."

"That's right. Can I see your notes?"

"Not unless it's a legal necessity, Inspector, if you don't mind," Dr. Gargi replied. "I . . . I can give you a gist of what

Karan said, but it would not be ethically right to show you my notes."

"I understand. So please tell me, what did Karan say about Pranjal?"

"Is Pranjal the boy Karan is suspected of kidnapping and killing?" Dr. Gargi asked.

"Yes, it's the case I am investigating."

"Then please give me ten or fifteen minutes to read through my notes and I might be in a better position to brief you," Dr. Gargi replied.

"Sure. I'll just step outside into your reception area and make a few calls while I am waiting," Saralkar said and got up.

The reception area had been empty when Saralkar had reached Dr. Gargi Naidu's clinic, as her morning consulting hours were just coming to an end. He took out his mobile. He had felt it buzzing several times in the last half an hour while he'd been talking to the psychiatrist. Most of the calls had been from Motkar; there was one from Inspector Deokar and a few others.

Motkar had also sent a text message beseeching him to call immediately.

"Yes, Motkar?" Saralkar said as soon as Motkar took his return call.

"Sir, Namita Bhatti has gone missing," Motkar said, coming straight to the point. "She left the house around 6.30 a.m. in the morning with a trolley bag."

He quickly narrated the sequence of events at the Bhatti household the previous night leading up to Namita's flight from home. "Her mobile has been switched off since 6.40 a.m., just after she made a cash withdrawal of ₹40,000 from her account, from a nearby ATM," Motkar continued. "She probably took an auto from the main road but we haven't traced the auto-driver as yet. We have flashed her photo across Pune police stations and also on Auto Rickshaw Union WhatsApp groups, but there's no response so far."

"What about the airport, railway station, and luxury bus stands?"

"She has not taken a flight for certain, but she could very well have taken a train or a bus," Motkar said. "The parents think she's headed for wherever Randeep Mirdha is, who Namita believes is her real father."

"Hmm . . . okay. I'm texting you Randeep Mirdha's two contact numbers which I just found on Karan Jerajani's contact list," Saralkar said.

"That's great news, sir. Just what we have been looking for."

"I know—piece of luck that fell into our lap just at the right time. Now look, get details on both numbers and put them on tracking. Get someone to call him posing as a tele-caller or something to confirm Randeep's identity. We have to ascertain where he is and then put together a team to nab him," Saralkar instructed. "And if the girl has run to him then it needs very, very careful handling."

"Yes, sir."

"Give me a call once you have confirmed it's Randeep Mirdha and the numbers belong to him," Saralkar said. "Then we'll discuss and chalk out the plan to nab him."

"Okay, sir."

Saralkar cut the call and dialled Inspector Deokar's mobile, who picked it up after a few rings.

"Sir, your hunch seems to be right. The WhatsApp calls Karan Jerajani made to one of the numbers on the day he claimed to be ill and indisposed seem to suggest some sort of a pimp, who caters to people with paedophilic appetites," Deokar said. "But rather than nab only that individual, we think it would be better to bust the racket, which will require setting up a more elaborate plan."

Saralkar groaned inwardly, but he knew Deokar was right from the policing point of view. Arresting one individual would be short-sighted. They needed to round up the gang, if any good was to be achieved including rescuing the children who were being victimised and abused.

"Okay," he conceded. "I understand, Deokar, but whenever you decide to move in, I would need to interrogate the witnesses to ascertain Karan Jerajani's whereabouts on those two days and who he was with."

"You have my word, sir," Deokar replied.

"Good."

Saralkar switched off the phone, knocked on the door of Dr. Gargi's consulting room and re-entered.

"Yes, Inspector, Karan Jerajani made several direct and indirect references to Pranjal," Dr. Gargi said. "In fact, in our very first session, I believe he was referring to Pranjal when he shamefacedly confessed to having experienced arousal. Later too, whenever he spoke about Pranjal by name, he opened up about how he fantasised about the boy . . . and said he would often visualise and think of him and immediately feel unnatural stirrings. He also expressed a lot of hostility and aggression towards the boy's parents on occasion. In my notes, I have also jotted down that Karan told me he had visited Pune just to have a glimpse of the boy once or twice."

Saralkar felt his flesh crawl. "Is that so? When was this? Recently?"

Dr. Gargi looked at the file and said, "This was about a year ago. In another session, five or six months ago, Karan actually said he'd thought of kidnapping the boy."

"What?"

"Yes, he said a friend had suggested it," Dr. Gargi said, then hastened to add, "You must understand though, Inspector, that these are fantasies, however despicable . . . and does not mean Karan would actually go and act upon them."

Saralkar nodded, battling a sudden feeling of nausea and anger. How could anyone think of a child in this manner? What sick mind would have such fantasies? And yet, this sick mind—was it to be pitied or detested—for the man with that mind had been sufficiently ashamed of himself to have committed suicide? The question was, had Karan Jerajani been part of the ghastly deed or just run it in his head?

"Okay, Dr. Gargi, but if he talked of his fantasies about Pranjal and of kidnapping him so explicitly, then I might require copies of your notes, as supporting evidence. And perhaps your testimony too," he said. "Thank you for providing me this perspective."

*****

"Something bothering you?" the woman straddling Randeep Mirdha said, falling back on to her side of the hotel bed with a sigh of disappointment.

In his profession, Randeep Mirdha knew the importance of strategic candidness, with a dash of charm. "I'm so sorry. I admit I have been a little off colour," he replied, taking the woman's hand in his and kissing her fingers.

The woman looked at him and smirked. "I am going to give that a two-star rating . . ."

"Oh, come on, darling . . . I wasn't that bad!"

"Considering what you charge, that qualifies as a dud," the woman replied, then got up to go into the shower.

She was a well-preserved stunner of around forty-five. Why wouldn't she expect the best, Randeep thought.

"Okay, I promise the next one is going to be a five-star premium ride," he said, bragging mischievously.

She glanced over her shoulder and said, "Take me to some super place tonight for dinner, okay?" and disappeared into the bathroom.

Randeep nodded at the closed door, then admonished himself. He couldn't let that disturbing phone call with his sister yesterday affect his game, could he! He couldn't afford to. This woman was one of his best regular clients—someone who booked him almost every alternate month—different cities, different hotels. Someday, he hoped, she'd invite him to go with her to a foreign destination too. And she was actually fun company and a tigress in bed.

No, he had to get his act together. He had to stop worrying and steel his nerves. His eyes strayed towards his mobile. He scrolled the messages and noticed one from Namita. He tapped on it and went into a tizzy when he read it.

Papa, I've left home for good. Coming to Ahmedabad. Will reach late tonight. Please text your address or pick me up at Paldi Bus Station. I am switching off my phone. Will check later. Luv, Namita

The unexpected had happened. Randeep cursed himself for not having anticipated it. He began dialling Namita's number frantically, but it was switched off, exactly as she had said in her message. He swore with frustration and typed a text.

Namita, what have you done? I'm not in Ahmedabad right now. Call me as soon as you get this message. Don't go to Ahmedabad. How

are you travelling? Get down wherever you are
and return home. Call me asap.

He sent the message and stared at the screen, as if willing the device to perform telepathy and magically activate Namita's mobile at the other end.

"I was thinking of taking you up on your promise right away," the woman said, appearing fresh and wet from the bathroom. "You up to it, lover boy?"

Randeep looked up at her, startled, and gave a weak smile. No, he was not up to it in his present state of mind. But uber class gigolos like him could hardly furnish excuses of inner turmoil to clients—especially someone as rich, regular, and ravishing as the one in front of him.

"Let the foreplay begin, darling," he said bravely, pulling her towards him.

*****

Chapter 22

Saralkar disliked talking on the mobile while driving. And here on the Mumbai-Pune expressway it was like tempting fate to stage an accident. "Yes, Motkar," he said taking the call and putting the mobile on speaker.

"Sir, both numbers belong to a person called Ronny Mehra, with an Ahmedabad address in the Satellite area. We've asked for photo ids from the mobile company and put the numbers on tracking. Currently, the location of both phones appears to be in Jaipur."

"Ronny Mehra . . . that sounds close enough to Randeep Mirdha, but we can't be sure it's him yet," Saralkar remarked.

"Should we get in touch with Ahmedabad Police, sir, to scan for information on Ronny Mehra?" Motkar asked.

"No, no. Have we got his call details?"

"Not yet, sir."

"And has Namita's phone been switched on?"

"No, sir. We'll be alerted the moment it does," Motkar replied. "I have put on hold making the call to Ronny Mehra's phone as a tele-caller, because the phone was not registered in Randeep's name."

Saralkar felt the impact of a car overtake him from the lane on his left, at a speed that could only be called irresponsible. These guys endangered their own lives and that of others.

"Look, it has to be Randeep Mirdha. Why else would Karan Jerajani have saved the numbers in that name?" Saralkar said. "Moreover, I have seen some of their chats on Karan's phone. They were in touch. So, here's what you do, Motkar . . . make the tele-caller call and record his voice. Then play it back to Namita's parents and see if they recognise the voice as Randeep's. Keep in mind confirmation bias, so play them three or four different voices and see if they recognise this one spontaneously."

"Sure, sir," Motkar said. "By when would you be reaching Pune, sir?"

"Another two hours, I guess, unless there is a jam at Lonavala. It's just started pouring again."

"Okay, sir, I'll call you if there's anything urgent to report."

Saralkar cut the phone and switched on the windshield wipers. He loved the rains but not when he was driving on the expressway, with maniacs overtaking him at record speeds.

*****

"What's with you, tusker? I thought I turn you on?" the woman asked, feigning disapproval. "Or having an off day?"

Randeep was proud of his skills to please his clients and didn't remember when he had last let someone down. He felt thoroughly embarrassed. "I . . . I am so bloody sorry . . . I . . . I don't know what to say . . ." He looked at her, then away.

She studied him. She liked this man—good-looking, well-mannered, good sense of humour, spoke well, and could talk on a variety of topics. And of course, he was an excellent lover. He came highly recommended and she had grown fond of him—Ronny Mehra.

"What's up? Want to tell me?" she asked.

Randeep looked at her and decided to be honest. "I've got a little personal problem."

"What kind of problem?"

Randeep wondered if he should tell her. "Actually . . . I learnt this morning that my . . . my . . ." he hesitated.

"What?"

". . . that my daughter has run away from home."

"You have a daughter?" the woman said, astonished, then squeezed his arm. "Oh my poor baby! No wonder you were so dull. Why didn't you tell me?"

"Well, I didn't think there was any point . . ." Randeep mumbled. "Listen . . . can I ask you a favour? Can I leave? I . . . I know it's going to spoil your trip and I am so sorry. I'll ensure you'll get a full refund but please . . ."

The woman frowned and gazed at him, annoyed. For a moment it looked as if she was going to throw a tantrum. She was well within her rights to do so. She had paid top dollar for his services, this hotel, this luxury trip. Even if it might be a drop in the ocean for her.

He could of course just walk off, and there'd be nothing she could do to stop him. But Randeep knew he would lose business, because she would talk and word would spread about how he left her stranded. Being a male escort was no cakewalk. It depended totally on goodwill and reliability, as much as delivering total customer satisfaction.

"Please, Anu . . ." he said again.

She finally sighed. "Okay. I guess you won't be much fun anyway otherwise, not to mention totally below par. Go, Ronny."

"Thank you so much . . . you are a gem, Anu," Randeep said, kissing her smack on the lips. "You won't regret it . . . I promise you an unforgettable experience the next time—truly!"

"Hmm . . . we'll see," Anu said as he jumped out of bed and rushed to the bathroom to shower and change.

He was back in ten minutes. Anu was still lounging in bed. "There were two calls for you on your mobile . . . perhaps news of your daughter," she told him.

Randeep buttoned up his shirt and picked up his mobile. He could see two missed calls from the same number. Could it be Namita calling from someone else's mobile—fellow passenger maybe—to avoid using her own phone? Should he call back? As a rule, he never took such risks. Just as Randeep hesitated, the mobile sprang to life again. It was probably Namita. Who else could be calling again and again?

"Hullo," he said, taking the call.

"Hullo, sir, am I talking to Mr. Ronny Mehra?" ASI Zirpe spoke in her best imitation of a tele-caller.

"Who's this?" Randeep responded warily.

"Sir, there is a delivery for you. We need to confirm your address, please," ASI Zirpe said, trying to sound as girlish as she could.

"What delivery?" Randeep asked, his suspicions uncannily aroused.

ASI Zirpe ground her teeth. Why could the man not speak more than two words at a time? "It's a courier, sir. Please confirm your address—13, Krystal Tower . . ."

Randeep instinctively felt something wrong. "I'm not in town," he said and cut the call. For a few seconds he stood frowning and anxious. He was sure he had ordered nothing and no courier was expected.

"Not about your daughter?" Anu asked, checking herself out in the mirror as she got dressed.

"No . . . no," he said distractedly and suddenly his heart skipped a beat as his mind began joining some indiscernible dots. Mahek's phone call that Pune Police had come looking for him. Namita's message that she had fled home and was coming to Ahmedabad, and now the phone call about some courier delivery! Was some plan afoot to entrap him? By setting up his daughter as bait, so that he would be a sitting duck for the police to swoop down upon? Because it couldn't be a coincidence that all of this was happening at the same time, could it?

Or was he over-reacting and joining dots which weren't really connected? Because, would Namita allow herself to be used to trap him? Perhaps they had convinced her that he was behind the kidnapping and killing of her stepbrother? Randeep wavered. He was leaving Jaipur and returning to Ahmedabad on the assumption that Namita had genuinely run away and was coming to him. But if that wasn't the case and she was just being used to lure him to Ahmedabad, it would be downright foolish to go. Yet, what if Namita really had fled home? He couldn't let down his daughter, could he?

His phone began ringing again. He froze. It was Namita calling. He took the call, stepped out into the hotel room balcony, and shut the glass door behind him. "Namita?" he said cautiously.

"Papa, why are you telling me to return to Pune?" Namita's agitated voice came through. "I want to be with you. When are you reaching Ahmedabad? I'll stay in a hotel till then. I have money."

"But . . . But you should've called me before taking such a step, beta!"

"No . . . Papa . . . you don't know what Mamma did last night. It was impossible to stay there for a minute longer."

"Okay . . . okay, Namita, calm down. Where are you right now?"

"I'm in Surat . . . that's just four hours from Ahmedabad, no?"

"Yes. How are you coming? By road or train?"

"By road, Papa . . . Volvo. I'm so happy, Papa. I am going to see you!"

"Me too. Look, Namita . . . I'll just call you back on WhatsApp video call, okay?" he said and cut the call abruptly.

He needed to be certain she was really travelling in a bus and not being used to trap him. He had to make a decision on whether he believed her or not. He punched the buttons to make the WhatsApp video call. The screen flickered to life and he saw Namita's face, although there was pixellation and disturbance, suggesting the network was patchy.

"Hullo, Papa!" she said and flashed a smile at him. She certainly looked as if she was riding in a bus. He could see the upholstery and the bus window and even the landscape flitting past.

"Hi, beta . . . just let me glimpse your fellow passengers—turn the screen to show me what's around you?"

"Why, Papa?" Namita asked, puzzled.

"Just do it, beta."

Namita did as she was told. There was no one in the seat next to her, but he could see the passengers across the aisle and in the rows behind. Namita certainly seemed to be alone with no sign of policemen or anyone else who looked suspicious to Randeep's eyes. Of course, there could still be policemen in civilian clothes, but it didn't appear to be so.

"Okay," Randeep made a quick decision, "I am going to take some time to reach Ahmedabad so here's what you do . . ."

He quickly gave her instructions, where to go and what to do once she reached Ahmedabad. ". . . understood? I'll also message you on WhatsApp but switch off the phone immediately now and only switch it on for a couple of minutes to check for my messages. Otherwise, I'll directly meet you, as soon as I reach."

"Where are you, Papa?"

"I'll tell you when I come," Randeep replied. "Look, your mum must've already lodged a missing complaint and they'll try to find you by tracking your phone location . . . so . . . so use it minimally."

"But I am committing no crime in coming to be with you, Papa. I am an adult now. They can't make me go back!"

"I know, but we'll talk more when we meet, okay? Your mother might say I kidnapped you and that'll definitely create trouble."

"But I'll tell the police you haven't, Papa! Mamma can say anything she wants . . . she even thinks you kidnapped and killed Pranjal . . . and that I helped you . . . but that's not true, is it, Papa?"

The words sent a chill down Randeep's spine. "Hush, Namita. Somebody will overhear. I'm cutting the call now . . . and you switch off the phone . . . okay?"

The call ended. And then Randeep Mirdha alias Ronny Mehra began shaking uncontrollably.

*****

"Sir, Namita Bhatti's phone turned briefly active for about fifteen minutes," Motkar said, barely able to hide the excitement in his voice, ". . . and the only number she dialled was one of Ronny Mehra's. The call was connected for a few minutes, so they definitely seem to be in touch."

Saralkar felt a micro-moment of elation. So, they had finally traced the elusive Randeep Mirdha and if things went well Namita would lead them to him. "Where is she?"

"She was near Surat, sir, so probably on course to Ahmedabad."

"And is Randeep still in Jaipur?"

"That's right, sir," Motkar replied. "ASI Zirpe spoke to him posing as a tele-caller."

"What new information could she get?" Saralkar asked.

He was on the home stretch, near Talegaon, having mercifully not encountered a jam, despite the rain and peak hour evening traffic on the expressway.

"He was terse and dismissive, sir, but we managed to get his voice recorded. Not sure if the clip might be enough for the Bhatti couple to recognise, but better than nothing," Motkar informed him.

"Okay, get the voice sample checked and also we'll need a team ready to leave for Ahmedabad to nab Randeep," Saralkar instructed. "I think I should reach office in about an hour's time."

"Right, sir . . . but what is he doing in Jaipur if he knew Namita was headed to Ahmedabad?"

"Hmm . . . good question. Have you got his call records yet for the last few weeks?"

"Not yet, sir."

"That's going to be crucial to establish his involvement," Saralkar said. "Okay, see you in a while."

He cut the call and brooded. His mind flew back to the messages between Karan Jerajani and Randeep Mirdha that he'd found on the former's mobile. Karan's call records had also shown calls exchanged in the previous week, including on the day of Pranjal's kidnapping as well as a few times prior to that. Could any of it be conclusive? Only a thorough investigation would help get to the bottom of it all.

*****

"So, you off?" Anu asked as Randeep hauled his bag and prepared to leave the room.

"Yes . . . how can I thank you, sweetie? Are you . . . are you staying back?" Randeep asked apologetically.

"Of course. You can do me a favour, Ronny . . . can you recommend anyone locally from Jaipur who can keep me company?" Anu asked. "Of course, someone classy . . . like you."

Randeep looked at her, perplexed, then gave an awkward smile. "I . . . I can't do that, sweetheart. You are asking me to recommend a competitor."

"Well, why not, Ronny? Haven't I glowingly recommended you to my friends?"

"Yes, but that's different, Anu."

"I know, but now that you are scooting away, it's only fair you help me have some fun," Anu said.

Randeep turned on a charming smile. "Frankly, I hate the idea of you with some competitor."

Anu burst out laughing. "Looks like you are falling for me, Ronny boy. Wouldn't that be devastating for you professionally to be a one-woman man?"

He nodded and gave her a sly look.

"Okay . . . I understand," she said finally. "Never mind . . . by the way, last week were you with the friend I recommended you to?"

"Yes. How do you know that, Anu?"

"Ah well! She gave me rave reviews. Couldn't stop talking about your skills. Seems like you guys went to Pune, right?"

Randeep's face fell. For the first time he wished his clients didn't talk among themselves. "Yes. Look, sweetie, I got to go now. Bye . . . thanks again and sorry. Take care . . ."

He gave Anu a quick kiss and opened the door.

"Bye . . . Ronny. Hope you find your daughter safe and sound. And remember, you owe me a great one, next time . . ."

She winked at him and waved.

*****

Chapter 23

"That's him . . . that's Randeep's voice," Smita Bhatti asserted, the moment she heard the call recording.

"Are you absolutely sure, Mrs. Bhatti?" Motkar asked. They had played four recordings for her in different male voices and she'd picked up the right one without hesitation.

"Yes . . . where is he? Arrest him immediately," Smita said fiercely.

Motkar nodded. "Let's see what your husband's response is," he said and walked out of the room into the next room where ASI Tupe was waiting with Mohnish.

"Play the recordings, Tupe. Mr. Bhatti, tell us which one you recognise as Randeep's voice."

ASI Tupe played the four short audio clips to Mohnish who listened with rapt attention. "I . . . I think it's the third clip. Can you please play it again?"

Motkar noted, he too had recognised the right clip, but probably was more cautious by nature. ASI

Tupe played the audio clip again as Mohnish listened to it, this time with his eyes closed.

"Yes . . . that's Randeep," he declared.

"And after hearing it, how sure are you that the man who made the ransom call to you, was also Randeep?" PSI Motkar asked.

Mohnish Bhatti frowned a little. "I . . . I badly want to believe it was . . . that's what I thought when I replayed it in my mind later . . . but I can't say for sure. There was too much noise around me and . . . and the call was breaking."

"I see . . ."

"But about this recording, I'm absolutely certain it's Randeep. Please nab him before he harms my daughter . . . please!"

*****

"Hi, sweetheart, one of your three husbands calling," Randeep said in his usual roguish, flirtish voice as soon as the phone was picked up.

"Come off it, Ronny honey! At least I have just three husbands. God knows how many women you have been with," the woman responded, with a little squeal of laughter. "Tell me, what's up? Is this your fortnight-after call?"

"In need of help, sweetheart. This is an SOS and you are the only one I can count on," Randeep said to the lovely forty-three-year-old widow he was talking to—another of his regulars, who had grown fond of him.

"What trouble, Ronny? I bet it's something sordid."

"No, no, . . . listen . . . you have that gorgeous flat in Ahmedabad, right, where we er . . . spent that great weekend a few months ago?"

"Yes. What about it?"

"I need it to accommodate someone tonight," Randeep said.

"Someone? You think I am going to allow you to use my flat for one of your rendezvous, Ronny?" the woman said petulantly. "You have some cheek!"

"No, no, sweetheart. It's not like that at all. It's for my niece," Randeep said quickly.

"Your niece?"

"Yes . . . yes . . . my sister's daughter. She's just eighteen and is reaching Ahmedabad in a while. She's alone . . . just for tonight, darling, I promise, it's all above board. I'll be eternally grateful to you . . . please," Ronny said earnestly.

"But why can't she stay in a hotel or something?" the woman said reluctantly.

"That's the thing, sweetie. My niece got robbed during the journey, and has very little cash with her. No credit card . . ." Randeep said, having already thought it through. "She's shaken. That's why I need this huge favour, please . . . I'll make it up to you, I promise!"

"Oh, I see," the woman considered thoughtfully. "Okay, I'll inform the neighbour who has the keys to the flat. Give me your niece's details."

"You are an absolute angel," Randeep said and gave her Namita's first name only and her mobile number, saying she would call and collect the keys from the neighbour. "Thanks a ton! We are going to have an absolute ball next time, sweetheart."

"Well, I certainly hope for something special, Ronny! Anyway, where are you now?"

"Jaipur . . .er . . ."

"On one of your joy-rides?" the woman asked wistfully.

"Well, it's my job, sweetheart, mostly dull and boring except when someone like you comes along."

"Liar!"

"Not lying at all. You don't know how delightful you are, sweetie," Randeep said on autopilot, itching to get off the phone.

The woman blushed despite herself. Randeep was one man who had not made her feel cheap, when she'd dared to find guilty pleasures. He'd not treated her like a rich slut, like one or two other escorts she'd engaged before. He'd actually behaved like a gentleman.

"Bye and thank you," he said and ended the call.

He began furiously typing in the address and other instructions to Namita in a WhatsApp message, as he heard the Jaipur-Ahmedabad flight boarding announcement. It was a big relief that he'd managed to arrange this accommodation for Namita. He could hardly take her to his flat, which was a small one BHK unit, with several tell-tale signs of his profession. He needed to clean up and for that he needed tonight.

`I'll be returning to Ahmedabad only tomorrow, so make yourself comfortable at my friend's flat. I'll see you tomorrow.`

He signed off the message to Namita and made his way to join the queue of passengers.

*****

Saralkar stifled a yawn. He would've liked nothing better than to call it a day, or rather, a night. The drive to Navi Mumbai and back had left him more fatigued than he cared to admit. He was long past the age when he could sustain on a hurried breakfast, just a dosa to make do as a meal and several cups of tea. His stomach was growling with hunger, waiting for the *pav-bhaji* he had ordered from the canteen. Where the hell was it? He needed to eat quickly.

There was a movement outside his cabin door and he looked expectantly, only to see Motkar walk in, rather than a canteen boy with his pav-bhaji.

"Sir, from his mobile records, it's confirmed that Randeep Mirdha was in Pune on the day of Pranjal's kidnapping, the day prior to that, and the day after," Motkar said, waving the papers in his hand and thrusting them towards Saralkar for perusal.

For a moment, Saralkar forgot his hunger. "That's it then . . . call the team," he said, "and ask the blasted canteen guy if he plans to starve me to death!"

Motkar nodded and walked out to summon Tupe and Zirpe. Much to Saralkar's relief, the canteen boy walked in a few seconds later with his steaming pav-bhaji.

"Where's the extra pav?" Saralkar asked him straight away.

"Saheb, I . . . I didn't know you had ordered extra pav . . . I'll get it right away," the boy said deferentially.

"And why are you guys so stingy with Amul butter, damn it?" Saralkar fumed.

The canteen boy looked at him timidly, swallowed, and said, "I . . . I'll get a dollop of butter too, saheb."

"Get back here in no time, okay!"

The canteen boy nodded and bolted. Saralkar tucked into the pav-bhaji with gusto. It didn't taste half as good as it looked, but who cared when one was hungry. He only hoped the boy would return with the extra pav and butter before Motkar and the team gathered. But that was not to be. He had just about finished the first pav-jodi, when Tupe and Zirpe sauntered in behind Motkar, who stopped short.

"Should we let you finish your food, sir?"

"No . . . no. Who knows when the guy will be back with the extra pav," Saralkar said grudgingly as he wiped his hands with the single tissue provided. It always seemed woefully inadequate to him. He waved his team to grab seats. "Okay, what are the last known locations of Randeep and the girl, Namita?"

"The last time she switched on her mobile thirty minutes ago, Namita's location was at Anand, sir, about an hour away from Ahmedabad," Motkar replied.

Saralkar looked at his watch. "So, she should be reaching Ahmedabad city any time now?"

"But, sir, Randeep was still in Jaipur about an hour ago," Zirpe added. "His phone's switched off now."

"Have you run through the numbers he called from Jaipur after his call with Namita?" Saralkar asked.

"I think he's making WhatsApp calls, sir," Zirpe replied.

Saralkar considered, then quickly came to a decision. "Okay, we'll go for him. Here's what we are going to do . . ."

He briefed the team succinctly. They discussed the nitty-gritties along with a backup plan.

"Any other doubts?" Saralkar asked, looking at the team.

The only response came from behind. "Can I serve you the extra pav and butter, sir?"

*****

Namita Bhatti had never spent a night all alone, in her entire life. The sprawling flat with all its luxury furnishings, could not alleviate her nervousness or her fear. How was she going to get through the night? She would keep the lights on, of course, but she was doubtful if she'd be able to grab even a wink of sleep.

When her father had messaged her about the arrangements he'd made for her at a friend's flat and the address, she'd felt dismayed and vulnerable. For she'd never anticipated the possibility that her father might actually not be waiting to receive her in Ahmedabad. That he himself would be elsewhere and not present in the city she had run away to.

It was her fault, of course, that she'd not first checked with him before leaving home. But after what her mom had tried to do the previous night, Namita had found it intolerable to stay on. It had been her tipping point.

The twelve-hour bus journey from Pune to Ahmedabad had given her time to think and reflect, but she had felt no regret. Her mother had acted unforgivably. First of all, how could she have even believed for a minute that she had been involved in Pranjal's kidnapping with Rishabh? Then the pathetic attempt to deny Randeep was her biological father and that it was actually Mohnish. And then . . . stealing her mobile to invade her privacy and check if she was somehow hand-in-glove with Randeep in plotting Pranjal's gruesome fate!

To stay in that house had become unthinkable. When she'd switched on her phone intermittently during the journey, she'd seen the dozens of missed calls her mother had made as well as the grovelling messages, begging her to return home. But none of it had moved Namita. Her mother deserved all the distress she was causing her! Namita had blocked her number.

There had been pleading messages from Mohnish too—the man she'd been brought up to believe as her stepfather and now trying to pass off as her real father. No, no, Randeep Mirdha was her real father—otherwise wouldn't they have told her the truth much earlier? Why would they have hidden it from her all these years? It was true that Mohnish had always been loving and affectionate towards her but somehow, she had never got vibes of a real father from him. There was something missing! Something lacking! But with Randeep she'd connected instantly. That could only be because he was her biological father. But what if he wasn't? Namita hastily dismissed the momentary doubt from her mind.

There had been many more messages from different friends. Probably the word had got around that she had left home. Most of all, there was a flurry of missed calls and messages from Rishabh—wistful, crazed messages asking her to contact him, to tell him she was safe. He would not tell anyone; he would come and be with her; he loved her; he loved her like crazy—over and over again.

Rishabh's messages soothed her like nothing else did. After what they'd gone through together at the hands of the police, she had fallen for him even more. He was the one for her. He had come through in the ordeal. He'd tried to protect her. She decided she would reply or better still call him now. It would make everything a little more bearable if she spoke to Rishabh. She didn't care if the police traced her call. What could they do? They couldn't force her to return home. She was an adult, wasn't she?

*****

"Why do even super-express trains have such unclean toilets?" Saralkar grumbled as he returned and sat on his berth.

While Tupe, Zirpe, and four constables had left by road, Saralkar and Motkar had managed to get two berths on the Duronto Express, the fully AC overnight train from Pune to Ahmedabad, from the quota usually kept for VIPs, high government officials, police officers etc., which if unutilised would go to normal waitlisted passengers otherwise.

Motkar ignored the rhetorical question. He had an important update to impart, having just checked his messages.

"Sir, both Randeep and Namita switched on their phones. Namita's is still on . . . both are in Ahmedabad, but not at the same location. Ahmedabad Police should be able to help us find the exact locations."

"Hmm! What time does this train reach Ahmedabad, Motkar?"

"6.30 a.m., sir."

"Good, Team Two should also be reaching by then I guess. So, we stick to Plan A. You and Zirpe go for the girl and Tupe and I after Randeep," Saralkar said, as he lay down on his berth. "Now, do you snore, Motkar?"

"Not much, sir."

"Well, I do, so muffle your ears if you can," Saralkar quipped, switched off the light and closed his eyes, letting himself be rocked to sleep by the gentle rhythmic motion of the train.

*****

Randeep Mirdha aka Ronny Mehra crashed onto the sofa, lit a cigarette, and poured himself a drink. He'd finished tidying up his bachelor pad and as far as it was feasible; it was now fit to bring home his daughter to, the next day.

The question really was, what next? What was he going to do if Namita insisted on staying with him? But even before that, what was going to be the fallout of her act of running away from home and coming to him? How was he going to handle the suspicions of having been involved in the kidnap and murder of his ex-wife's son, Pranjal, as well as instigating his daughter thereafter to flee from home?

Randeep took a few deep puffs but no answer blew out with the smoke. The liquor soothed but had no suggestions to offer either.

His eyes began to shut. It was almost 2.00 a.m. No point in thinking about it. The only thing he could do tonight was to switch on his phone briefly and message his daughter that he would meet her in the morning around 10.00 a.m., so that she would not panic.

*****

Namita had finally fallen asleep after 2.30 a.m. The phone call with Rishabh had comforted her. He had begged her to return to Pune, asking how they were to date and love each other if she decided to live with her father in a different city, here onward. He had rebuked her for not confiding in him earlier and to have just gone away like that. He had told her how much he loved her and made her blush.

She had told him she just wanted to meet her father and get away from her mother for some time till she could think straight and sort the matter out in her head. She'd narrated to him all that had occurred. They had talked for an hour, cheering her up considerably and then she had received her father's message, which was so reassuring that she had finally been able to doze off, although still scared of being all alone in that big house.

Her eyes suddenly shot open now and she woke up with a start, scared and unsure where she was. It felt as if she'd just shut her eyes only moments before. Namita blinked, trying to figure out what had woken her up. The lights were still on. But she could make out that it was already morning.

Suddenly the peal of the doorbell pierced her senses and she almost screamed with fright, as the bell continued to ring, jangling her nerves further. Who could it be, her terrified mind wondered. What was she to do? Could it be the neighbour from whom she'd collected the keys or the caretaker of the flat or someone like that? Or could it be her mother along with the police, somehow having tracked her down?

Just as Namita tried to compose herself and steady her nerves to go and take a look, her phone sprang to life. She had forgotten to switch it off. She glanced at the screen and heaved a sigh of relief. It was her father. "Hullo, Papa!"

"Thank God! You gave me a scare, darling. Open the door, sweetie, I'm outside."

*****

"Sir . . ."

Motkar's voice woke Saralkar up and his assistant's face swam into focus. Saralkar could sense daylight and hear murmurs all around. The train seemed to be stationary.

"Have we already arrived?" Saralkar asked and glanced at his wristwatch. It showed 6.30 a.m.

"No, sir. We have a problem. There's been a derailment on the track ahead, so we are going to be stranded here at Vadodara station for some time, although it's not a scheduled halt," Motkar replied. "The train's probably going to be about ninety minutes late."

Saralkar scowled. He had been banking upon landing up at both locations—Randeep's and Namita's—as early as possible in the morning, when both would have been less alert or prepared. That advantage would now be lost.

"Have you checked where Team Two and the constables are?" he asked.

"They are already on the outskirts of Ahmedabad, sir," Motkar replied.

"Okay, so we fall back on Plan B. Tell Tupe and Zirpe to stake out the girl's location," Saralkar said. "Have we got the exact address from Ahmedabad Police?"

"Yes, sir . . . we have the society name but not the flat number."

"Okay, so ask them to take a lady constable from Ahmedabad Police with them. She can make inquiries with the society security or check the CCTV footage to identify which flat Namita is in."

"Okay, sir. And what about Randeep's house?"

Saralkar chewed his upper lip for a few seconds then said, "Let me speak to Ahmedabad Crime Unit Chief Dinesh Parmar and see if I can persuade him to raid Randeep's house on the pretext of a bootleg alcohol tip-off. Remember Gujarat is a dry state."

"Nice thinking, sir," Motkar said and earned a rare smile from Saralkar, as his boss began dialling the number of Dinesh Parmar.

Motkar himself got busy in communicating with Team Two.

*****

"But why, Papa? Why do you have to leave Ahmedabad? Why do we have to lie low?" Namita asked the man she believed was her father.

"I told you I needed to straighten a few things," Randeep said. "We have to take steps to protect both you and me legally from Smita and Mohnish."

"What's illegal in your eighteen-year-old daughter wanting to live with you, Papa?"

Randeep felt vexed. "Namita, did you consult me before you left home in haste? Now that you are here, you must let me take what I think is the best course of action in the circumstances."

How could he tell his daughter he had woken up early morning with a terrible foreboding—a kind of sixth sense that the police would swoop down upon him anytime? That alarming uneasiness over and over, that he needed to flee Ahmedabad before he landed into the clutches of the cops.

"So where do you want to take me?" Namita asked him.

"Leave that to me," he replied. His feverish mind had already worked out a plan. He had a client who owned a farmhouse near Udaipur—a lovely place far away from prying eyes. He knew the client—a smart, kind-hearted woman whose husband was a self-confessed gay—would help.

But the key was to leave Ahmedabad before anyone picked up their scent.

"Okay, Papa, but can I at least bathe and get something for breakfast," Namita asked.

"Of course, beta," Randeep said, trying to downplay his impatience, ". . . but be quick. We'll get something to eat on the way."

*****

Chapter 24

Saralkar fretted. "When is this damn train going to move?"

Motkar shrugged then glanced at his watch. Before he could reply, the train gave a little jerk and the horn sounded. "Thank God!" Motkar mumbled.

The delay had been slightly shorter than expected. As the train began to chug out of the station, Motkar's phone rang. It was ASI Zirpe.

"Motkar sir, we have taken our positions. We've confirmed from the security as well as the entry in the society register that Namita is in Flat 805, which is at the far end of the society. The flat belongs to a lady called Pamela Virani, so Namita is staying there as a guest because the apartment is usually empty," Zirpe said. "The Ahmedabad lady constable with us, Jharnaben, will now be going to the flat disguised as a garbage collection lady to confirm it is indeed Namita. Should we go ahead as planned and any fresh instructions, sir?"

"Just a minute, Zirpe . . ." Motkar said and quickly briefed Saralkar. Saralkar listened then gestured at Motkar to hand over his phone. "Zirpe, cover all exits. Once the girl's identity is confirmed, don't waste time, confront her, but tactfully," Saralkar said. "Tell Namita that you are there only to get a statement from her that she is safe and had left home for Ahmedabad on her own volition. That will ensure there is no unnecessary fracas or resistance from her."

"Yes, sir . . . I understand. And has Randeep been picked up or is someone keeping a watch on him?"

"The Ahmedabad Crime Unit will update me any time now and Motkar will let Tupe know," Saralkar replied and returned the phone to Motkar.

The train had now picked up speed. Saralkar dialled the Ahmedabad Crime Unit chief's number. The call went unanswered. DCP Dinesh Parmar had sounded reluctant when Saralkar had spoken to him about forty-five minutes earlier, but had agreed to carry out a raid on Ronny Mehra's house. Still, Saralkar knew, it was difficult to infuse the same urgency and priority to the task of another officer from another force. A man like Dinesh Parmar would already have his hands full with his own work, so little wonder that he had been unenthusiastic.

Saralkar clicked his tongue and hoped Randeep Mirdha wouldn't slip out of their hands. Damn the delayed train!

*****

"Papa," Namita said, emerging from the bedroom, having finished her bath and packing.

"Ready? Let's get going," Randeep said, giving her a tense smile and thrusting his hand out to take Namita's trolley bag.

"I just wanted to talk to you about one thing before we leave . . ."

"What? Let's talk in the car. We are getting late, Namita . . ." Randeep said impatiently.

"It's important, Papa . . ."

Randeep, who was about to open the front door of the flat paused restlessly and took a couple of steps back towards his daughter. "What is it, Namita?"

Namita looked at him awkwardly. "Mamma claimed something very . . . very strange the other day."

"About me? Don't believe everything Smita says about me!"

Namita shook her head. "No . . ."

"Then what? That I kidnapped your stepbrother?" Randeep asked, eyeing her apprehensively.

"She even thinks that I helped you, Papa . . ."

"That's the reason I want to protect both of us against such accusations," Randeep said.

"But I am not talking about that, Papa . . . Mamma said something else . . ."

"Out with it, beta . . . quick!"

Namita coughed. "She said that . . . that I too am really her second husband's daughter, not yours . . ."

"What? That's pure nonsense!" Randeep said vehemently. "You are my daughter! You were born almost three years before Smita started her . . . her affair with Mohnish. Why else will your birth certificate . . . all other documents, show me as your father?"

"I know, Papa . . . but she said that a DNA test can prove he is my biological father . . . because she and Mohnish Bhatti had been together since much earlier, before she admitted it," Namita said hesitantly. "Do you think, it could be . . . true?"

Randeep's face had gone red with anger, as if doubt had suddenly and insidiously opened up a hitherto unsuspected possibility in his mind. "How dare she? How dare she . . ."

His eyes and expressions suddenly frightened Namita. There was a dangerous glint of fury in them.

*****

"Look, Tupe, let's decide for ourselves instead of bothering Saralkar sir again," ASI Sanika Zirpe said. "I'll also accompany Constable Jharnaben and stay out of sight till the door is opened. I'll hover in the background . . . and the moment it's a positive identification I will directly confront Namita. Why wait for Jharnaben to return and then for me to go for a second time?"

ASI Tupe nodded. "I agree it makes sense but why not at least inform PSI Motkar that we are changing the plan slightly?"

"Because we are wasting time, that's why," Zirpe replied. "We are the officers on the spot."

"Careful! I am just worried something might go wrong . . ."

"Come on . . . Namita's just a girl," Zirpe said, then nudged the Gujarat Police Constable Jharnaben, a stout, smiling woman of about her own age, to move.

Jharnaben was dressed in a Gujarati saree and was armed with a plastic dustbin meant for dumping waste collected from different flats, while Zirpe had put on gloves and the shiny jacket over her T-shirt and trousers to try and appear like the housekeeping staff of the society, holding a perfunctory mop in one hand. Both took the elevator to the eighth floor, Jharnaben giggling intermittently, making Zirpe a little nervous she'd muff her lines or role.

"Jharnaben, take a good look at the photo of the girl again," Zirpe said, holding up the photograph.

Jharnaben nodded. "Don't worry," she said in Gujarati and then repeated it in Hindi.

"I'll wait here," Zirpe said, as they exited the elevator

on the eighth-floor landing. She stood by the staircase, from where she could see the apartment, without being noticed. There was only one other flat on the floor at the other end of the corridor.

Jharnaben nodded, then proceeded to ring the bell of the apartment, which displayed the name plate Pamela Virani.

*****

"Saralkar, my team had gone to this Ronny Mehra's house," DCP Dinesh Parmar of Ahmedabad Crime Unit spoke into the phone. "He's not there. The watchman of the building told them he left about forty or forty-five minutes earlier in his car."

"Shit," Saralkar hissed to himself, then said, "What's the make and car number, Parmar?"

Parmar told him.

"Can you flash the number across Ahmedabad and get the car intercepted under the pretext of a traffic offence?" Saralkar asked him.

DCP Parmar hummed and hawed. "I'll flash it across and relay instructions for interception, but . . . I can't promise anything for sure."

"Okay, thanks for the help," Saralkar replied, cursing under his breath.

"What's happened, sir?" Motkar asked.

"Randeep is not at home . . . left home early morning it seems, probably to pick up the girl, I reckon, which means he already might be with Namita, inside the flat. Warn Tupe and Zirpe urgently," Saralkar said, his face grim and worried.

*****

Jharnaben heard someone shuffling inside the apartment, just as she was about to ring the doorbell again. She sensed someone was looking at her through the eye-hole, after which she heard more shuffling and the door half opened. A young girl's face peeped out defensively and Jharnaben's practiced eye immediately made positive identification with the pic she had just seen.

Zirpe too glanced furtively down the corridor and recognised Namita.

"What is it? Namita asked.

"I'm the garbage collection lady . . . where's your garbage?" Jharnaben said, speaking rapidly in Gujarati.

Namita looked blank. "Speak in Hindi, please," she replied.

Just as Jharnaben started speaking, ASI Zirpe decided it was time to take matters into her hands. "Namita . . ." She called out and began striding down the corridor, just as her phone began ringing at that very moment.

Namita recognised her instantly and instinctively began shutting the door, but Jharnaben had already thrust her body in the way, pushing back, keeping the door from closing as ASI Zirpe joined her too.

"Namita, wait . . . I have only come to talk to you and take your statement . . . please listen . . ." Zirpe said to the girl. She had no time to attend to the phone now.

Both Jharnaben and she were surprised at how much force Namita seemed to be putting into closing the door.

"Namita, I am not here to catch you . . ." Zirpe repeated, pushing hard.

And then suddenly the resistance on the door seemed to give way, as if Namita had let go. Jharnaben and Sanika Zirpe fell forward as the door opened. As she slipped, Zirpe's eyes fell on the man standing beside Namita with a revolver in his hands.

She blanched with fear as she recognised him. It was Randeep Mirdha—a tense, taut look on his face.

*****

"What?" Saralkar asked, incredulous. "Randeep surrendered without any attempt to resist or escape?"

The team was huddled in a small room provided by the Ahmedabad Crime Unit at its office, about an hour later. Saralkar and Motkar had reached Ahmedabad and driven straight there.

"Yes, sir," ASI Zirpe replied. "He just said Namita was here of her own will and that he had not enticed or abducted her. He promptly offered to give a statement and cooperate in any way we required. I was surprised how calm and composed he was despite being extremely nervous."

"But you said he had a firearm in his hand?" Motkar said.

"Yes, sir. It really gave me a jolt and sent a shiver down my spine to see him standing there with a revolver in his hand . . ." Zirpe explained. "But he put it on the table as soon as he had ascertained who I was. Then he said he had a license for the firearm and showed that to me. He told me he kept it for self-protection. When I told him he was under suspicion for kidnapping Pranjal he said he had nothing to do with the crime and was willing to be interrogated."

Tupe nodded in agreement. "Sir, when I reached the flat, Randeep was standing unthreateningly and willingly agreed to be taken into custody, saying he was innocent."

Saralkar and Motkar exchanged glances.

"In fact, the girl caused much more trouble, sir," ASI Zirpe said. "Namita started screaming hysterically at us . . . and refused to accompany us. She even pushed Constable

Jharnaben when she tried to stop her from walking off in a huff. I had to then . . . er . . . subdue her, sir."

"By twisting her arm . . .!" Saralkar observed.

"Better than a slap, sir . . . best I could do to restrain Namita."

"Hmm . . . still it could be termed as police brutality," Saralkar replied wryly. "Anyway, get that transit remand paperwork for Randeep expedited. Motkar and I will have a word with him now. And have Namita's parents been told she is refusing to go back to Pune so we can't force her to accompany us back?"

"Sir, her mother's reaching Ahmedabad in about an hour's time," Tupe said. "She luckily got a ticket on the 10.30 a.m. flight from Pune. We can hand over the girl to her mother and by then we should have got the transit remand for Randeep so we can leave by road."

"Okay, let's have our little pow-wow with Randeep now, Motkar," Saralkar said and began walking towards one of the interrogation cells that DCP Dinesh Parmar had allotted them. Motkar followed.

When they entered the cell, Randeep Mirdha was sitting sombrely on a chair, staring at the floor. He looked up apprehensively at the two officers and stood up. Saralkar gestured to him to sit, but Randeep waited till both Saralkar and Motkar were seated, before settling down again.

He was tall and slim, with a luxurious mane of hair, which surprisingly he didn't touch self-consciously. Dressed in a plain white shirt, blue jeans and sport shoes, the man betrayed a certain flamboyance without looking dandy.

"Randeep Mirdha alias Ronny Mehra," Saralkar said.

Randeep nodded slightly and smiled tensely.

"Unlike you, I have only one name. I am Senior Inspector Saralkar from Pune Homicide and this is PSI Motkar."

Randeep nodded again and his eyes strayed to Motkar, perhaps reminded that this was the officer who had met his sister, Mahek Naqvi.

"Sir, I have nothing to do with the crime you are investigating," Randeep began. His voice was deep and strong.

"What case am I investigating?" Saralkar cut him short.

"I . . . I have not lured Namita here, nor have I kidnapped and killed my ex-wife's son, Prajwal."

"Pranjal," Motkar corrected him.

"I am sorry, Pranjal . . ." Randeep said.

"Who told you that you are a suspect in Pranjal's kidnapping and murder?" Saralkar asked.

"Namita . . . she said my ex-wife suspects that . . . and the police think so too."

"And?"

"And . . . and your lady colleague Zirpe madam also said I am a person of interest . . ."

"Who else told you?" Saralkar prompted again.

Randeep stole a glance at Motkar and shrugged, shaking his head.

"How about your sister, Mahek Naqvi?" Motkar asked.

"Absolutely not . . . I broke contact with her many years ago," Randeep asserted quickly.

"I see," Saralkar said. "Maybe you learnt it from your friend Karan Jerajani then?"

A wary look crept on to Randeep's face. "No . . . why would I hear it from him?"

Saralkar did not reply, just stared silently at him then switched to another question. "Why do you have a new name—Ronny Mehra?"

Randeep sighed. "I needed a new identity. Randeep Mirdha has a prison record. I wanted to start a new life."

"So, you changed your name legally?"

Randeep shook his head sullenly.

"That means all this—Aadhar, PAN card—in your wallet is illegally obtained?" Saralkar asked.

Randeep brushed back his hair for the first time and gave an ingratiating half-smile, "Sir, you would know more than anybody how easily one can obtain such documents."

Saralkar's expressions became harsh. "But you have also got an arms license issued on your new identity. That's an even more serious crime, Ronny. Why did you need a firearm, Randeep? For kidnapping and murder?"

Anxiety had leapt into Randeep's face. "No, sir . . . no . . . I am not a criminal. I have not kidnapped or killed anyone. Please, sir . . . I just needed the firearm for self-defence, protection . . ."

"Self-defence? Protection? From whom?" Motkar turned on the heat.

"Sir . . . I fled Chandigarh. I had made some acquaintances in jail . . . gangsters! They are after me. I made some wrong decisions . . ." Randeep answered unconvincingly.

"Gangsters? What gangsters? You are bluffing. Chandigarh Police has no such information of any gangsters seriously swearing vengeance against you," Motkar said. "You fed the story to your sister and brother-in-law to explain your sudden disappearance with their money."

Randeep glanced at Motkar, looking non-plussed. Then he sighed again. "Yes . . . I needed the money to start a new life in a new city," he admitted.

"So, we come back to the question—why do you need a firearm?"

Randeep replied, "Sir, I do need it for self-defence and protection. There are risks involved in my profession."

"What's your profession?" Saralkar asked. "What kind of work do you do that creates enemies who might get so violent that you require protection?"

Randeep Mirdha looked away, now totally uneasy. "Sir, must I tell you that? It's got nothing to do with me being suspected in this case."

"Why do you need to hide your profession, unless it's illegal or criminal?"

"I'm not a criminal, sir . . . that's why I immediately agreed to be interrogated . . . even taken into custody . . . because I haven't done anything. Wouldn't I have tried to run away if I was involved with the kidnapping and murder?" Randeep pleaded, then turned a little belligerent, "And anyway, sir . . . what proof do you have against me?"

Saralkar stood up from his chair and moved closer to Randeep, who immediately looked uneasy as if he anticipated third degree.

"Sir . . ." he said defensively, "I am cooperating fully. If . . . If there is one thing I swore to myself when I got out of jail, it was that I would never ever do anything that would put me back in there. Please, sir . . . I did not kidnap my ex-wife's son or murder him. Why would I do that?"

"Revenge! Your ex-wife cheated on you, put you in jail, ruined your life. Plenty of motive," Motkar said. "So you kidnapped and killed her son."

"No, sir. It's not like that. I . . . I don't believe in revenge," Randeep replied, flustered.

"And yet isn't revenge what you discussed with your friend Karan Jerajani just a few months ago?" Saralkar said sharply. "In Mumbai, at a bar? About how you two could join hands to wreak revenge on the Bhatti couple, against whom both of you nursed a grudge?"

For the first time Randeep Mirdha looked perturbed. "Sir, I admit I met Karan. I . . . I don't know what he's told you. He was drunk and blabbering a lot of stupid things. But I was just listening, that's all!"

"But we have learnt you discussed the idea of getting even with Mohnish and Smita Bhatti by kidnapping Pranjal. We've seen WhatsApp messages between Karan and you about a plan."

"Sir, sir . . . I totally refute all this. I can't be blamed for what Karan messages me," Randeep said, now breaking into a sweat. "Do you have him in custody? You please bring us face to face and I'll confront him on the lies he seems to have told you!"

Saralkar nodded. "So, you admit the idea of kidnapping Pranjal was discussed?"

"He talked; I listened, sir . . . I thought he was completely sozzled," Randeep said.

"Then how do you account for the messages mentioning a plan and the fact that so many calls have been exchanged between you for the past few months?" Saralkar said. "What did you and Karan talk about so much?"

"Sir . . . we had met by chance after a long time on one of my trips to Mumbai. Karan then got into the habit of calling me quite often usually when he was drunk. And that's it, sir . . ."

Saralkar raised his eyebrows. "We also have a witness who confirmed that Karan mentioned the plan to kidnap Pranjal was suggested to him by a friend," he said, citing what Dr. Gargi Naidu had told him.

Randeep Mirdha shook his head vociferously. "I don't know who your witness is or what Karan told someone, but believe me, sir, I didn't hatch any plan to kidnap Smita's son, with Karan or anyone else."

"Then what were you doing in Pune on the day Pranjal was kidnapped?" Saralkar slipped in the question suddenly.

Randeep Mirdha looked bushwhacked and stared speechless at both police officers for a few seconds.

"Don't try to deny it. We have your mobile phone records," PSI Motkar added.

Randeep turned away, then again looked at Saralkar. "Sir . . . I . . . I had come for some professional work. I . . . I absolutely have nothing to do with the kidnapping, sir."

"What work?"

"The nature of my work is such, sir . . . I . . . I can't talk about it," Randeep whined.

"Why? What's so secretive about it? Are you some spook or a nuclear scientist or something?" Saralkar asked sarcastically.

Randeep shifted in his seat and replied, "Sir . . . total confidentiality is very important for . . . er . . . my clients."

"I'm beginning to lose my patience with all the secretiveness, Randeep. If you don't tell us what you were doing in Pune within two minutes, then this interrogation will turn a lot less pleasant the moment we reach Pune, later today," Saralkar said in a voice that was meant to chill the man in front of him, which it did.

Randeep Mirdha grappled with his thoughts and professional ethics, such as they were . . . and finally spoke. "Sir . . . I . . . I work as a premium grade male escort. That's . . . been my profession for the last several years as Ronny Mehra," Randeep said, with a disarming awkwardness.

There were still things in the world that took even Saralkar and Motkar by surprise. Motkar gaped. Saralkar looked disbelievingly amused.

"You are a gigolo?" Saralkar asked.

Randeep nodded. There was an odd kind of vanity in his manner along with acute embarrassment. "Yes, sir . . .

that's the reason I was in Pune then. I have a very upmarket clientele . . . whose identities I . . . I cannot compromise."

"I see . . ." Saralkar said. "Who were you with?"

"I just told you, sir . . . I can't reveal that."

"Man or woman?"

"A woman, sir, I . . . I work as a male escort but my services are only for women. All the more reason I cannot disclose their identities," Randeep said earnestly.

"That won't do, Randeep. We can't take your word for it. Sounds too much of a coincidence that you happened to be in Pune on the very day Pranjal was kidnapped and the day after, too," Saralkar said. "Unless you get the person you were with to testify."

"Sir, I can give you details of the hotel we stayed in—one of the best five-star hotels in Pune," Randeep said.

"That's still not enough, Randeep. You might have stayed in the hotel but that doesn't rule out your involvement in the crime, which was committed outside."

"But, sir . . ."

"Look, you have to tell us who you were with so we can confirm and take the concerned lady's statement," Saralkar said bluntly. "Till then you are our chief suspect. Think about it on our way to Pune . . . and decide. There are also a couple of calls you exchanged with Karan Jerajani on both days while you were in Pune. He too doesn't have an alibi for both days so it is our contention that you and Karan conspired to kidnap and kill Pranjal."

"No . . . no, sir!" Randeep said, looking unnerved. "That's totally false. Yes . . . Karan and I spoke a few times that day, because he wanted a contact. You can ask him about it . . . he'll tell you why."

Saralkar gazed at him for a few beats. "Karan's dead. He committed suicide two days ago."

The expressions that crowded Randeep's face were too natural to be faked. His jaw had fallen open and he stared at Saralkar and Motkar aghast. "What?"

"You didn't know your partner-in-crime was dead?"

"He was not . . . not my partner, sir, and I haven't committed any crime," Randeep croaked.

"Well . . . the point is, you are on your own. So tell me about the phone calls that day between you and Karan. He's dead, so you can't plead confidentiality, can you?" Saralkar said.

Randeep Mirdha shut his eyes as if ashamed, then opened them. "Sir . . . sir, I . . . I am ashamed to say this but . . . but Karan wanted me to put him in touch with . . . with someone who could arrange for . . ." He stopped and gesticulated as if wondering how to say it. "Karan . . . you know, was kind of a paedophile . . ."

The penny dropped for Saralkar. So that was the reason for the flurry of phone calls. "Go on."

"I . . . gave him the number of a person who might help him although I was very reluctant . . . but Karan had kept pestering me," Randeep said.

"You filthy wretch . . . and I had almost started feeling sorry for you!" Saralkar snapped.

Just then there was a slight knock on the cell door. "Yes?" Saralkar called out.

It was Tupe. "Sir, we've got the transit remand paperwork. We will have to present him to the magistrate in a bit. Also, Mrs. Smita Bhatti is here."

Saralkar turned around to watch Randeep's expressions, but he didn't look any more or less alarmed than he already was by the news of his ex-wife's arrival.

"Okay. Let's get ready to leave," Saralkar said to Tupe. "Are the vehicles here?"

"Yes, sir."

Saralkar stood up and said to Motkar. "I'll just thank Dinesh Parmar and come back. Will you double check if the remand paperwork is in order and if any more formalities are pending from our end?"

"Sure, sir."

Saralkar strode out of the interrogation room. Tupe, Zirpe, and the constables all seemed to be on their feet. At the far end of the corridor, in a small partitioned enclosure, he could see Smita Bhatti remonstrating with her daughter, Namita, as he walked over to Dinesh Parmar's cabin across the open yard, knocked and entered.

They had hardly exchanged pleasantries and discussed things for a few minutes when they heard a loud scream and then a commotion outside. Both officers rushed out and crossed the small yard in the direction of the commotion. Saralkar was not prepared for the scene he saw. Lying dead on the floor of the corridor leading to the interrogation cells, was the bloodied body of Randeep Mirdha, writhing in the throes of death. Two constables and ASI Tupe were kneeling over him, along with a few Gujarat Police constables.

A few feet away, held in the grip of ASI Zirpe and two other constables, stood Smita Bhatt, a ferocious, wild look in her eyes. Her hands were bloody and a knife lay at her feet. She was staring at her ex-husband with hate-filled expressions. Her eyes turned to Saralkar as he came into view.

"I decided to encounter him myself . . . since you said you wouldn't!" she said.

It was one of those rare occasions in Saralkar's life that he stared totally dumbstruck!

*****

Chapter 25

One Month Later

"Let this be a lesson to you, Saralkar," CP Arundhati Pradhan remarked at the end of her long harangue. Saralkar had maintained a polite, uncharacteristically deferential demeanour during the meeting, as the CP had held forth on the findings and conclusions of the departmental inquiry report which had probed the incident in Ahmedabad. While the report hadn't been unduly harsh on Saralkar, Pune Homicide Squad and most members of the police team excepting ASI Sanika Zirpe, CP Arundhati Pradhan had been scathing.

How could Saralkar's team have been so utterly incompetent and negligent? What could be more shameful than a suspect being stabbed to death in their custody, right in the midst of a posse of cops? How could Smita Bhatti have come anywhere close to striking distance of Randeep Mirdha?

The facts had been too damning for Saralkar to convincingly deny ASI Zirpe's obvious lapse in permitting Smita Bhatti to get a glimpse of her ex-husband on the pretext of confirming it was definitely him. Zirpe had confessed to Saralkar that she had given in to Smita Bhatti's repeated requests to just rage and rant a little at the man whom she suspected of killing her son and who had estranged her daughter from her.

It had been an incredibly foolish and misguided act of sympathy towards an overwrought mother by a police officer that had taken the life of Randeep Mirdha, who for all his faults had been no kidnapper and killer, as subsequent investigation had established. Randeep had been telling the truth about his presence in Pune. He had just been a male escort, no more. In fact, Smita now stood charged with murder of her innocent ex-husband, Randeep Mirdha aka Ronny Mehra.

"Am I still in charge of investigating the case, ma'am?" Saralkar asked, now that the CP seemed to be done blowing off steam.

Arundhati Pradhan eyed him with a scowl. "Yes, for now, Saralkar. Unless you want me to transfer it to a different team?" she snapped.

"Why would I want that, ma'am?" Saralkar retorted.

"Perhaps you've hit a dead end and the investigation is going nowhere," the CP said, fully aware she was touching a raw nerve.

"No, ma'am," Saralkar bristled. "We haven't been sitting idle, despite the distraction of the departmental inquiry."

"Are you saying you have new leads, Saralkar?" Arundhati Pradhan asked.

"Yes, we are pursuing a particular line of inquiry that had been overlooked," Saralkar said, keeping it vague.

"How long do you need to come up with something concrete?"

"About a week, ma'am."

The CP cracked her knuckles. Not many women did that, Saralkar thought. It was a habit that was mostly restricted to men. Why? He didn't know.

"I hope it's not merely a hunch or conjecture, Saralkar."

It got Saralkar's goat. "I cannot have cracked all my cases through just hunch and conjecture, ma'am," he replied icily.

Arundhati Pradhan was shrewd enough to tread on someone's toes and yet step back as if nothing had happened. "I mean, do you have a theory or do you have a suspect?"

"Both," Saralkar said cryptically.

"Hmm. Well, at least two of your suspects have ended up dead so far. Let's hope the latest one has better luck."

Saralkar felt affronted, despite knowing the CP was implying nothing scandalous. But before he could mouth any kind of verbal protest, Arundhati Pradhan spoke again. "Brief me in a week's time or I'll have to transfer the case to another team. All the best, Saralkar!"

"If I fail, I'll put in my papers on my own, ma'am," Saralkar let fly, stood up, and left.

*****

TEN DAYS EARLIER

Saralkar groaned as he entered his cabin. The Pune Homicide Squad office lay eerily deserted, as if exhaustion and fatigue had driven the team away. Even Motkar was not in yet.

Saralkar had had his share of crises in his career. But this was a mess like no other. This case felt like his nemesis—he had been floundering from the beginning. One after the other the leads had turned out to be damp squibs and the suspects unlikely to be culprits. The conjectures and motives had collapsed. It was as if Pranjal's kidnapper had left behind no trail that could lead up to him or her.

For the last three weeks, he and the team had been consumed by fire-fighting—dealing with the terrible fallout of Smita Bhatti's grisly knife attack on her ex-husband. Randeep Mirdha had died two days later, followed by the setting up of a departmental inquiry into the matter.

When his team of officers and constables were not deposing before the inquiry officer, there was the tedious task of verifying Randeep Mirdha's claim of innocence— reconstructing his movements in Pune and ascertaining that he had been in the city on those two days only as an escort. Simultaneously, further investigations had to be conducted into Karan Jerajani's activities on those two days to rule out his involvement in the crime too.

The psychological toll on the morale of his team had been telling. There had been an air of shock and disbelief, which had quickly given way to a mood of collective failure in preventing what had occurred in Ahmedabad. ASI Sanika Zirpe had faced the brunt of the ire, but the team had quickly rallied behind her to ensure she wouldn't be made the lone scapegoat by the departmental inquiry. However, it was one thing defending Zirpe before the inquiry officer, quite another to deny or downplay the facts within the team.

Saralkar had advised her to go on leave, while stoutly opposing the suspension recommendation being considered by the inquiry. All said and done, he himself had felt a strain like never before, compounded by the realization that the case still remained unsolved and that two innocent people had become additional victims during the investigation. Yes, Karan Jerajani had been a paedophile and Randeep Mirdha an ex-convict with an unsavoury past and perhaps present, but both of them had had the misfortune of being suspects in the case and met terrible fates as a direct result.

Worse, the real perpetrator was out there scot-free. Somewhere in the maze of information, there had to be a lead that had fallen through the cracks, which would indicate and point in the direction of the culprit. Saralkar was damned if he wasn't going to catch the kid killer.

He had to reapply himself to the task at hand and pull his team members out of their stupor, too. And that meant having to start again, going through the material with a fine-tooth comb, looking into lines of inquiries that had not been pursued or pursued only thinly.

There was a light tap on his cabin door. "Come in . . ." Saralkar said.

He was surprised to see Mohnish Bhatti walk in. The man seemed to have turned frail beyond recognition in the past few weeks. If losing his son Pranjal hadn't been enough of a debilitating blow, his wife, Smita's deed seemed to have knocked out whatever remaining spirit that had been left in him. Saralkar wondered how he was dealing with Namita, now that only the two of them remained of what was once a family.

"Hullo, Inspector, sorry I . . . I have not come to pester you . . ." Mohnish said, apologetically.

"No, no . . . Mr. Bhatti, please sit," Saralkar said.

A week after the Ahmedabad incident, Saralkar had sat this bewildered, broken man down and given him a complete overview of the investigation, the departmental inquiry, and how it would take some time before he and his team could make any further progress on his son's case.

Mohnish had sobbed like a child, pleading with Saralkar to help get his wife released on bail and to request authorities to take a compassionate view of her horrifying crime. Of course, none of it was feasible or even practical, but Saralkar had tried his best to comfort Mohnish with empty words and phrases that human beings always fell back on.

Saralkar wondered what the purpose of his visit today was. Mohnish cleared his throat, then opened the small bag he had brought. He took out a smart phone with a handkerchief and put it on Saralkar's table. "This phone was received at my showroom yesterday with a note that said 'Sorry about Guddu'—that was Pranjal's nickname. The note further said 'Check the Bitcoin wallet' . . ."

Mohnish took out a chit of paper the size of one's palm and placed it on the table and continued, "In the Bitcoin wallet set up in my name on this mobile phone, is one Bitcoin transferred to me . . . by someone anonymous. The value of this Bitcoin is currently around ₹18 lakhs . . . I understand . . ."

Mohnish's voice was tremulous now. Saralkar's mind boggled as he tried to digest the information. What did it all mean? Did it mean what he was thinking? "You mean, you feel this was sent by . . . by Pranjal's kidnapper?" Saralkar asked, trying to bend his mind around the possibility.

"Who else could do such a sick, creepy thing, Inspector?" Mohnish said, rage and grief twisting his face. "It's him . . . it's him . . . that bastard! He killed my son . . . destroyed my family . . . and now he has the gall to send me this as if to mockingly compensate for my loss. You must catch him, Inspector! He's out there . . . the cruel monster . . ."

Saralkar felt his stomach turn. How devilish could a man be to kidnap and kill a man's child and then send him money?

*****

There was an odd, startled reaction on PSI Motkar's face when Saralkar briefed him later, after Mohnish Bhatti had left.

"What is the matter?" Saralkar asked.

"Sir, this is one more eerie, uncanny similarity with the 2016 Atharva Jambhekar case!"

"What do you mean?"

"Sir, a few months after Atharva's death, his parents received a bag of cash full of demonetised currency, just after demonetisation had been announced, with a note saying 'Sorry for Pintu'" Motkar replied.

A chill ran down Saralkar's spine. "Tell me what happened exactly."

"Atharva's mother, Ashwini Gholap, who met us a few days ago, was the one who had found the bag with ₹5 lakhs of demonetised currency next to her milk bag. Somebody had either placed them in the night or early morning," Motkar explained. "She woke her husband, Neeraj, and showed him the bag. He rushed down to make inquiries with the watchman of the building. But the watchman didn't report any suspicious person or stranger having visited the society, since the previous night. Neither had any of the neighbours who went out for early morning walks seen anyone . . ."

"So did the couple immediately report the incident to the police?"

Motkar shook his head. "The husband and wife disagreed on what to do, although both believed it was the cruel handiwork of the killer. Neeraj felt it would serve no purpose going to the police with the bag and might instead get them into trouble in the prevailing situation, because it was unexplained, demonetised currency."

"Yes, who can forget that dumb, pointless ordeal of demonetisation? What did they do then?"

"The couple had a big argument and Ashwini left for office, emphatically telling her husband she was determined to hand the bag over to the police later that evening. But when she came home, the bag was missing," Motkar said. "Neeraj had disposed it off in some way and refused to tell her what he'd done with it. The couple had another row, following which Ashwini anyway went to the Crime Branch to report what had happened. The investigating officer was intrigued and thought she was telling the truth but when he questioned Neeraj, he flatly denied the entire incident. He said his wife was under great psychological stress because of the tragedy of their son and was probably hallucinating. His wife kept insisting and he kept refuting. Frustrated, Ashwini filed an affidavit and forced the authorities to put her statement on record . . . but of course, since there was no evidence nor any witness whatsoever, nothing came of it."

Saralkar sat lost in thought. "Hmm . . . you are right. Sending the Bhattis a Bitcoin as compensation is uncannily similar to leaving a bagful of demonetised currency for the Jambhekar couple," he said finally. "It's too much of a coincidence—this similarity of modus operandi. Moreover, this pattern of mocking the family of the victims by sending them compensation for their loss . . . disturbingly feels like having emerged from the same evil mind."

"In fact, sir, I've gone through the entire file and jotted down all the similarities between the two crimes," Motkar said. "Do you want me to get the list?"

"Yes, Motkar. It certainly merits a closer look than I thought. Perhaps Ashwini Gholap was right . . . and I, with all my experience, was wrong," Saralkar replied.

Motkar noticed a twinge of remorse in his voice, an emotion which his boss might have felt earlier, but never expressed in all the years he had known him. He got up to fetch the Atharva Jambhekar file from his own desk. Tupe walked in just as Motkar stepped out.

"Sir, we've got the list of vehicles along with registration details and owner's names," Tupe began.

"What vehicles?" Saralkar asked absent-mindedly.

"Sir, you had asked me to prepare a list of four-wheelers passing to and fro, by the spot where Pranjal was last seen on CCTV, just a few minutes later and before," Tupe said.

"Right. Because one of those vehicles might well have been following Pranjal or waiting for him," Saralkar recollected.

"Yes, sir," Tupe replied. "So I carefully ran through the footage and made a list of vehicles that passed in either direction, five minutes before and after Pranjal was seen at the spot . . ."

"Why five minutes?"

"Because, sir, the next CCTV where Pranjal should've been spotted if he continued on the same road going towards his class, is about three minutes away on bicycle. So, we figured it had to be one of the vehicles that passed by to or fro, within a window of about three minutes before or after and added two minutes as buffer either way," Tupe explained.

"Not exactly accurate if someone was waiting for him already in that patch between the two CCTVs . . . but okay, we have to narrow it down somewhere," Saralkar said. "So you have confirmed all owner and registration details but not verified for discrepancies in the records?"

"Not yet, sir."

"Okay, let me have a look at the list and I'll call you in a bit so that we can watch the footage together and assess which vehicles appear most likely to be involved depending on suspicious or odd movement," Saralkar said.

He took the list from Tupe and ran through the names and registration details, including car makes. Tupe exited and Motkar walked in with the Atharva Jambhekar file.

"Here it is, sir," Motkar said, laying it in front of Saralkar.

"Before we start, get in touch with the Cyber Cell and find out if they can trace the Bitcoin transaction to its source," Saralkar instructed. "If there is any possibility of tracing the account and identity of the person who purchased and transferred this Bitcoin into the wallet account set up for Mohnish Bhatti, without his knowledge."

"Sure, sir. I'll also check if it's possible to trace the purchase of the smartphone sent to Bhatti, from its IMEI number," Motkar replied.

Saralkar nodded grimly, clenching his teeth, "I have a feeling the person who did this knows exactly how to ensure none of this can be traced back to him. But we are going to nail him good and proper, whatever it takes!"

*****

ELSEWHERE . . . FIFTEEN NIGHTS EARLIER

"Have you slept?"

"No . . ."

"I want to tell you something."

"What?"

"You know Pranjal's mother killed someone and went to jail!"

There was a pause in the whispers.

"Yes . . . she thought her first husband had kidnapped and killed Pranjal."

A long silence followed in the dark.

"Will she kill us when she knows the truth?"

"We . . . We didn't kill Pranjal. He did . . ."

"But we watched . . ."

"That's not the same. We didn't do it. He's done it earlier, too . . ."

"I know . . . but I don't remember anything."

"I do . . . as if it happened yesterday. His name was . . . Atharva."

"Just like Pranjal?"

"Yes . . . the same way."

"Why?"

"Same reason!"

"But . . ."

"Shhh! Go to sleep. I don't want to talk about it."

Silence reigned again, but both whisperers lay awake, remembering what they had witnessed, never to 'ever forget'.

*****

Chapter 26

Saralkar gazed at the whiteboard listing the similarities between the cases of Pranjal Bhatti and Atharva Jambhekar. Motkar and he had spent the last two hours doing that. Pranjal had been eleven years old and Atharva had been a few months short of twelve in 2016, when he was kidnapped and killed.

Both had gone missing, having left the house for an activity that was part of their daily routine—Pranjal on his way to coaching class, Atharva when he went out to play. Both families received only a single ransom call, after which there was no contact from the kidnapper.

Both boys were found in the Mutha River, flowing through Pune—Pranjal's body near the Rajaram Bridge and Atharva's near Mhatre Bridge. Both bodies had no clothes on, except their underwear. Post-mortem reports of both bodies suggested death by drowning and evidence of sexual assaults that were certainly similar and with no sign of semen discharge.

Most importantly, both bodies had received a terse apology message with creepy forms of monetary compensation for the loss of their children.

And as the two cops discussed all the aspects threadbare, something suddenly struck Saralkar—another eerie similarity. Just like in Pranjal's report, the doctor who had conducted the post-mortem on Atharva's body had noted that the sexual assault injuries on the boy had been inflicted after death—not before. The discovery had set Saralkar's pulse racing.

They had immediately contacted Dr. Sule and mailed him both reports to get a confirmation on this fact for it showed a similarity that was too identical to deny as the handiwork of the same man. And as they waited for Dr. Sule to revert on the matter, another puzzling fact hit Saralkar that had simply not registered on him earlier.

"Motkar, how in the world could both the boys have been sexually assaulted after drowning, if they had already been thrown into the river?" Saralkar had suddenly said, thumping the table.

Motkar blinked, but before he could respond, Saralkar's phone rang. "Hullo . . . yes, Dr. Sule, tell me . . ." Saralkar said, putting the phone on speaker mode.

Dr. Sule spoke in his usual, ponderous way. "Saralkar, you asked me to revert on a specific point—my opinion on the nature of the wounds resulting from sexual assault on both children, as mentioned in the two reports . . . but I took the trouble of going through both reports in their entirety, because I avoid piecemeal opinions."

Saralkar wished he would avoid the preamble and get to the point. "That's very thorough of you, Dr. Sule."

"Well, I can confirm from the conclusions drawn in both

reports that the wounds were indeed inflicted after death in both cases—there is no doubt about that," Dr. Sule continued unhurriedly. "As to why exactly it was done, I cannot say, but your hypothesis that it might be just to mislead us into believing that the murders were committed by a sexual offender might be right, Saralkar . . ."

Saralkar grunted. "Thank you, Doctor. I know you are a busy man and I really appreciate that you reverted today itself."

"I . . . I am not yet done Saralkar," Dr. Sule spoke again as if offended, just like a man whose speech is being cut short by the host. "There is one more similarity in the two deaths that I noticed, which I think is very important . . ."

"What is that, Dr. Sule?" Saralkar asked, feeling a tingling sensation, his ears pricking up.

"Both bodies were found in the Mutha River, right?" Dr. Sule asked.

"Yes."

"Well, yet their organs, lungs were filled up with chlorinated water . . . not normal river water, with all its pollutants, organic matter, and micro elements," Dr. Sule said.

This was the goosebump moment that Saralkar hadn't experienced in this case so far. It had arrived now. "I see. So, Doctor, are you saying the boys did not drown in the river but in some swimming pool . . .?" Saralkar asked, his excitement rising.

"Correct, they cannot have died by drowning in river water," Dr. Sule asserted.

"Which means, even though their bodies were found in the river, they were drowned in some swimming pool and then thrown into the river to make it appear they died by drowning in the river . . ." Saralkar said slowly, as if the path in front of him had suddenly begun to light up.

"I wouldn't hazard a guess on that. You are the detective . . . I am merely saying the water in their organs is not consistent with drowning in a river. Rather it indicates death in a chlorinated pool," Dr. Sule replied.

"Dr. Sule, I really can't thank you enough . . . this turns the investigation on its head. Thank you!" Saralkar said, elated and feeling energised after a long time.

He cut the call and turned to Motkar, who too was looking alive, instead of looking droopy-shouldered which had become much too frequent recently. "You got that, Motkar? It answers the very question that intrigued me just before the phone call—how could the boys have been sexually assaulted after drowning. The answer is we now have to find the murderer who drowned two kids in a swimming pool six years apart, then inflicted wounds on their private parts to feign sexual assault and threw their bodies into the river to make it appear they drowned in the river."

"Yes, sir . . . to camouflage that they were actually killed in a swimming pool. I think we might need to re-evaluate all our lines of inquiry, in this light."

Saralkar nodded, his face now hard. "I can't wait to get my hands on this kid killer!"

*****

The bald, clean-shaven, tall, slim man finished his session on the stationary bicycle and stood up. Sweat glistened on his face and body. He picked up his towel and wiped himself. He didn't like to go to gyms and so he had converted one room on the ground floor of his bungalow into a well-equipped mini gym.

He stepped out of the mini gym now and strolled towards his small private swimming pool. Its dimensions were 15 mtr.

X 5 mtr. with a depth of 4 feet of shimmering blue water. He checked his watch and realized he had time for a quick dip. The man quickly went up to his bedroom, changed into his trunks. Back by the pool, he checked out the temperature of the water with his foot. It was just right.

He took the plunge and swam four laps, then paused for breath. Every day he wondered if some day he might see the ghosts of one of the two boys he'd drowned in there. One, long ago. The other, just recently. It had been so easy. Both had been too trusting, allowing him to hold up their legs above water, as he promised to teach them how to do a handstand underwater.

He had first explained the technique to them, then demonstrated it—dipping underwater, placing his palms on the pool floor and lifting his legs out of the pool vertically and holding steady for a minute. And once the kids were suitably impressed by the feat and ready to try it out for themselves, he had said, "Take a deep breath, beta . . . dip you head under and put your palms on the floor as I showed you. Go on . . . I'll be holding your legs."

And once they did that, he'd help them raise their legs— five seconds, ten seconds, fifteen seconds, twenty seconds . . . and then the boys had started wriggling, trying to emerge out of the water; fifteen more seconds and they'd started thrashing about, as Uncle didn't seem to realize they wanted to break through the water surface and gasp for breath; twenty more seconds and the thrashing had become more desperate but he had held their legs tightly so that it was now practically impossible for the boys to save themselves, their upper bodies unable to lift themselves above the water, try as they did.

Twenty more seconds and their arms had started flailing as water flooded their mouths and noses and filled up their passageways, their lungs; the air supply to their brain cut and they started slipping out of consciousness.

Thirty seconds more and all struggle had ceased; another twenty seconds and they were beyond help, totally limp. Add thirty seconds for safety to ensure their souls left their bodies and life was extinct.

Atharva Jambhekar—six years ago, and Pranjal Bhatti—just a few weeks ago. He'd felt no pleasure in what he'd done to them. But it had to be done. It was so much better than injuring them and leaving them handicapped or maimed.

Of course, the world thought killing was wrong, but human beings had always been killing others since the creation of the world. Killing was very much part of human nature—just another human response to cope with life. There was nothing right or wrong about it as such. Rules only applied to losers!

*****

"Okay, so we can narrow our focus down to these six vehicles," Saralkar said as they finished watching the CCTV footages for the third time. Tupe had done a good job, comparing and juxtaposing clips from the two cameras, along with timing the movements of various four wheelers.

"All the six are big cars, the intervals after which they have re-appeared between the two CCTV cameras is long enough for us to consider they might've picked Pranjal up and at least two of the vehicles might have been waiting for him in that patch between the two cameras."

"Yes, sir, that patch of the road is like a black hole, where there are absolutely no private or public CCTVs," Tupe said, ". . . although in any case the whole road has very few working CCTVs."

"Hmm . . . I am particularly interested in that blue Fortuner, which came from the opposite side, stayed in that black hole for nearly thirty-five minutes and then passed the second camera in the same direction," Saralkar remarked. "Also do one thing, Tupe . . . just run the car details and owner names through Mohnish Bhatti and also Ashwini Gholap. Check if any of the owner names are known or sound familiar to them or otherwise ring a bell . . ."

"Yes, sir," Tupe replied. "I am also dispatching our constables to check out the addresses. At least three vehicles have some pending traffic challans, so it would be a pretext to gain access. The other vehicles we'll check out with some other excuse."

"Good. Most importantly, make sure our constables check if any of the owners live in a bungalow with a swimming pool or in one of those societies with one," Saralkar said.

"Swimming pool? Why, sir?" Tupe asked, since he still wasn't privy to the information.

"Because Pranjal was drowned in chlorinated water, found in swimming pools. And then thrown into the river," Saralkar replied and explained what Dr. Sule had brought to their notice.

"Tell the constables, they are not to do anything that might alert or arouse suspicions in the people they visit," Saralkar warned emphatically.

His phone began ringing just as Tupe left. It was ASI Sanika Zirpe calling and for a few seconds Saralkar wondered whether to take her call. He had firmly stood by her, but there was no convincing way to explain away to the inquiry commission why Zirpe had been lackadaisical and had casually permitted Smita Bhatti within close proximity of the suspect, Randeep Mirdha, in their custody.

He took the call. "Hullo, Zirpe, how are you?" Saralkar said gruffly. It was a question he almost never asked anyone normally.

"Sir, can I join back? I'm totally fed up at home," Zirpe said.

"Zirpe, didn't I tell you I will let you know when the time is right?" Saralkar said, toning down his natural terseness.

"But, sir, I want to make myself useful till the inquiry gives its verdict," ASI Zirpe said. "I heard we have new leads . . ."

"Zirpe, there's no question of you working on this case any longer," Saralkar said quickly. "You should know that."

"But, sir . . . I've admitted my mistake . . . that doesn't mean I had any hand in what occurred. How would I know Smita Bhatti would do something like that?"

"Zirpe, don't let's discuss that. The Inquiry Officer is looking into it," Saralkar replied. "Listen to me and stay put."

He wished he could say something positive, but he knew she was precariously poised. The senior officer conducting the departmental inquiry was a stickler about fixing accountability and known not to mince words.

"It's looking bad for me, isn't it, sir?" Zirpe asked in a low voice.

"I've faced two inquiries myself, Zirpe. It's very hard, I know, but most departmental inquiries take into account an officer's previous record and mitigating circumstances," Saralkar replied.

There was momentary silence and then ASI Zirpe said, "Sir, there were other officers present too as well as the constables. Why must I be the only one held responsible?"

In normal circumstances, Saralkar would probably have snapped at her like at any other officer trying to shift the blame, but he replied in a far more measured tone, "Zirpe, all your colleagues and even the constables have tried their best to ringfence you from blame, but I don't think you should forget what actually happened," Saralkar said. "After Namita and Smita Bhatti had a showdown, Smita kept pestering you to let her confront Randeep for a few minutes in the interrogation cell, which you rightly refused. Then when she noticed Randeep being taken to the toilet by a constable, after I left to meet Dinesh Parmar, Smita begged you to let her stand in the corridor, so that she could at least be able to eyeball him as he passed by on the way back from the toilet. And you agreed to it on the pretext of Smita making a positive identification of Randeep, possibly imagining it would be harmless. So, it was totally your decision to be persuaded to do something irregular and inadvisable on compassionate grounds."

Saralkar paused, waiting for Zirpe to say something but there was only silence from the other end. He continued, "What happened then was clearly a result of this lapse— Smita lunged at him and stabbed Randeep and you failed to stop her. By the time you and the others managed to rip her away, Randeep was bleeding to death. Yes, all other team members including me can't absolve ourselves of the blame, but in all fairness, I can't ask other officers or constables to admit to a much larger share of the onus than they are actually responsible for."

Again, there was silence for a while and then ASI Zirpe spoke, "I am sorry, sir . . . I didn't mean to . . . you are right! I . . . I just don't want to lose my job . . . I am so proud to be a policewoman. It is my life!"

Saralkar felt a knot in his stomach. He hoped it wouldn't come to that. "You are a good officer, Sanika . . ." That was all he could say, hesitating to give her any reassurances. He would fight tooth and nail if they even tried to suspend her, but in life you could only fight battles and never be sure which ones you could win.

Zirpe called off and Saralkar sat back thoughtfully. He had been with the Ahmedabad Crime Unit Chief Dinesh Parmar, when the incident had occurred and had first been briefed by Motkar about exactly what had happened. He had cross-verified the sequence of events, speaking to all members of his team as well as the Ahmedabad cops who had witnessed it.

ASI Zirpe had been shaken and cagey, but even she had more or less admitted the facts. Saralkar had realized immediately that an inquiry would be set up. He had agonised over whether he ought to brief his team to come up with a consistent account that downplayed Zirpe's lapse and make it appear more like a collective failure. But besides being untruthful, that would be unfair to the other team members.

Finally, he had decided to simply take the stand that he bore full responsibility for the lapse. But the inquiry officer was too experienced and senior to get side-tracked and went ahead meticulously to fix responsibility. However, Saralkar's stand at least sent a message to his team that their depositions before the inquiry were to be such that it did not lead to the solitary indictment of Zirpe. And his team members had tried their best.

There was a knock on the door and Motkar entered. "Yes, Motkar? Any breakthrough on the Bitcoin wallet? Is the Cyber Cell anywhere close to establishing the transaction trail?"

Motkar shook his head. "No, sir. It's going to take time. As you might know, cryptocurrency is literally private currency and it's bought and sold on private international exchanges. It's almost like a parallel financial universe that is not dependent on conventional monetary or banking systems."

"But isn't it now being regulated and brought under the scanner for government control?" Saralkar asked.

"From what the Cyber Cell officers told me, it's a long way before cryptocurrency can be fully regulated," Motkar replied. "Who transacts with whom is quite opaque, because Bitcoin is simply not legal tender, issued by any government in the world, so the controls are in the hands of cryptocurrency platforms, which have their own confidentiality and business rules. Just like the Swiss Banking system does not part with customer information, for example."

"Hmm . . . I see . . . bloody ingenious. Well, I guess, there's no substitute to old-fashioned police leg-work then. If there's one thing I dread, it is that someday I'll leave a case unsolved because I simply was not up to it."

Motkar didn't know what to say. "We'll get there, sir."

"You heard that cricketing saying, Motkar—a batsman is only as good as his last innings. Well, I suppose it's applicable to cops, too. A good cop is only as good as his last case," Saralkar said wryly and grunted.

*****

Chapter 27

Constable Dhanak drove up the winding road uphill. Bungalows were lined up on both sides of the road. He had also passed the entrance to a trendy restaurant. Pune city never ceased to amaze him. He had been posted in Pune for over ten years, yet had had no idea of this locality at all, hardly a few minutes away from Bavdhan, on a little hillock off what was known as the Bhugaon-Paud Road.

When had this hillock, just on the edge of Pune city, been populated with bungalows and cottages, belonging to those who could only be described as well-off people, with money to invest and spare? Dhanak was almost halfway up the hill when he found the address he was looking for—a two-storey bungalow, tucked a little off the curving road. It was guarded by a big gate that was padlocked. There was no sign of a watchman.

Dhanak stopped his motorcycle and took out a paper from his shirt pocket. He glanced at the third and last address on his list— 'Ashwathama' was the name of the bungalow he had been looking for. Yes, this was it. The city survey number also matched with the one displayed on the side of the gate.

Dhanak tried to swing open the gate, despite the padlock, just to check. The owners were clearly not at home. The constable wondered what to do. It was almost 4.00 p.m. He came to a decision. He would wait for an hour for the owners to turn up or then contact ASI Tupe for further instructions. Maybe he'd have to return the next day, early morning.

He wished he could grab a cup of tea but realized there were no shops or shacks along the road he had driven up. The restaurant he'd passed had been too upscale for him to afford tea and perhaps they didn't serve any in the first place. Maybe he could drive down to Bhugaon Main Road again, where there would be plenty of shacks. But that was too much trouble so he decided against it. He parked his motorcycle and sat on top of it, and flicked out his mobile to entertain himself.

Forty-five minutes later he got restive and was wondering whether to call Tupe right away rather than wait any longer, when he saw the blue Fortuner turn the corner and stop right in front of the bungalow gate. A tall, bald, middle-aged man alighted from the driver's seat, went up to the gate, and opened the padlock. He seemed to notice Dhanak as he walked back to the car to drive in.

The man was wearing goggles and seemed to give him a hard stare, without saying a word.

Constable Dhanak got down from his perch on the motorcycle and said, "Is this Fortuner yours, saheb?"

"Yes," the man said slowly, "why?"

"So, you are Mr. Ranjit Sapatnekar?" Dhanak asked the next question.

The man did not reply for a few seconds, then answered with a counter question. "Who are you?"

"I'm Constable Dhanak from Traffic Branch, saheb . . . there are some pending traffic fines logged against your Fortuner, which I am here to collect . . ."

The man continued staring at him with his goggles on and Constable Dhanak felt a little uneasy. "I didn't know the Traffic Branch sends constables to people's homes to collect traffic fines," the man said.

Dhanak shrugged and improvised, "It's a new initiative for pending fines, beyond a certain amount and period."

"I see. How much is the pending fine amount?" the man asked.

"Three challans . . . I think totalling ₹4,500," Constable Dhanak replied, exaggerating. Actually, there was only one challan which had showed up against the car number.

"For what offences? I don't think I violate traffic rules," the man said.

"Well, there is one for stopping on a zebra crossing, one for wrong parking, and one for speaking on the mobile while driving," Dhanak said, getting creative.

The man continued staring at the constable through his dark goggles. On that isolated hill road, Constable Dhanak felt inexplicable stirrings of fear.

"I have received no intimations of these violations," the man remarked finally, in the same flat, controlled voice.

"I don't know about that," Dhanak said. "Why don't we go inside your house and I'll show you the violation details and the CCTV screen-grabs online, so that you can ascertain it's your car, pay up or choose to challenge the challans issued?"

The man put his hands on his hips and was quiet for a few beats, still staring at Dhanak like some alien, sending chills down the constable's spine. Then he took out his wallet from his back pocket and counted out nine crisp five-hundred-rupee notes. "Issue me the receipts against the amount," he said.

*****

Mohnish Bhatti regarded the list ASI Tupe had placed before him. None of the names on it really seemed familiar. He shook his head. "I . . . I don't recognise any name here that I might have come across in connection with Pranjal," he said.

"Are you absolutely sure, Mr. Bhatti? It could be anyone you might have come in contact with . . . even several years earlier," ASI Tupe said. "Please look at the addresses or even the car models carefully."

Mohnish looked at the names again—Palekar, Mulla, Sapatnekar, Bhojwani . . .

"No," he said again. "Has Saralkar saheb been able to trace who transferred that Bitcoin?"

It was Tupe's turn to say no.

*****

"I didn't get a chance to go inside, sir," Constable Dhanak said. "He paid the challan amount I mentioned in cash, then and there at the gate. So, there was no opportunity to ascertain if there was a swimming pool on the premises."

"You waited outside for nearly an hour. You couldn't try and look inside through the bars of the gate or something?" Saralkar grumbled.

"Sir, the gate had no bars . . . it was totally shuttered. And I really didn't expect he would pay up just like that. I thought I would get a chance to go inside . . ." Dhanak tried to explain.

"Hmm. So he owns the blue Fortuner, stays about ten or fifteen minutes away from Bavdhan in an isolated bungalow scheme on the hillock off Bhugaon Road, and you say . . . his overall manner and demeanour aroused suspicion in your mind," Saralkar summarised.

"Yes, sir . . . his way of staring was very disconcerting and . . . and sir, who pays a traffic challan even without having a look at the CCTV grabs or date of violation and other details?" Dhanak reasoned.

Saralkar nodded and turned to Tupe. "Have you got this Ranjit Sapatnekar's license details and pic?"

"Yes, sir," Tupe said and handed him a printout.

Saralkar scanned it—Ranjit Sapatnekar—the license had been renewed three years earlier and was valid for another two years. The man seemed to be around forty-eight years old, going by the date of birth mentioned. The pic showed a man with an unsmiling face, sharp features, staring at the camera as if it were an enemy.

"Was it the same man?" Saralkar asked, turning to Constable Dhanak.

"It's him, sir, except that he's bald now and does not sport the moustache that we see in the pic."

"And he was wearing goggles, you said?" Motkar added.

"Yes . . . he didn't remove them even for a second," Dhanak replied.

"But then can you be sure it's him?" Saralkar asked sceptically. He knew all policemen developed the ability to spot resemblances between photos and real faces even through disguises, but there were limits.

"Yes, sir . . . it was definitely him!" Dhanak said.

"Okay then, Tupe, show this pic to Mohnish Bhatti. He may not have recognised the name . . . but the face . . ."

"Sir, Mohnish Bhatti's left for Ahmedabad," Tupe interrupted, ". . . because his wife has a court appearance tomorrow for a decision on further custody with the Ahmedabad Police."

"Well then, WhatsApp Sapatnekar's pic to him," Saralkar said, "and Motkar, when are you meeting Ashwini Gholap to show her the list of car and owner details? You can show her Sapatnekar's pic also now."

"Sir, when I called her up, she insisted on coming here to take a look at the list. She said she wanted to meet you," Motkar replied.

Saralkar clicked his tongue then said, "Alright, I suppose we owe it to her. Ask her if she can get her ex-husband along."

"Sure, sir."

"And Tupe, gather as much information as you can about Ranjit Sapatnekar—what's his profession, family, background, any police record, everything we can get," Saralkar said, gesturing simultaneously that the meeting was over.

"Right, sir," Tupe replied. He and Dhanak left the cabin.

Saralkar noticed that Motkar had hung back. "Something on your mind, Motkar?"

Motkar hesitated. "Not about the case, sir . . ."

"What, then?"

"The day Pranjal's body was found, you mentioned that you had also been kidnapped as a child . . ." Motkar said, treading cautiously.

Saralkar nodded. "Yes . . ."

"You said you'd tell me about it later . . . I am just curious to know what had happened. That is, if you don't mind, sir . . .?"

Saralkar looked away, quiet for a few seconds, as if preparing to relive a difficult memory and casting aside his inhibitions. "Well, . . . I had a friend . . . a classmate in school at Miraj, Eknath Mahadik. Then my father got posted to Sangli, which was hardly twenty kms away, but since we shifted, my school also changed. About three or four months later, Eknath's father . . . I called him Mahadik Kaka . . . lured me away on the pretext of taking Eknath and me to the circus. He said he'd already taken my father's permission, which I had no reason to doubt since the families knew each other in Miraj. Mahadik Kaka took me to a sort of make-shift shack on a farm on the outskirts of Sangli town . . ."

"Oh! Was it for money, sir?" Motkar asked.

Saralkar shook his head. "He didn't want money. Mahadik Kaka told me that my classmate, Eknath, his son would soon join us and then we'd go to the circus, but I soon realized something was wrong," Saralkar said. "He offered me sweets, which were laced with something that knocked me unconscious. When I came to, it was evening. That's when Mahadik Kaka threatened me after I started asking him questions. By that time, I was scared to death. You know, Motkar, I still remember that fear . . . the fear that something horrible was going to be done to me . . . that my life was at someone's mercy . . ."

Saralkar stopped, and Motkar could make out how deeply it had affected him.

"How long did your ordeal last, sir?"

"Till about dawn the next morning," Saralkar said. "Less than twenty-four hours, but as they say, every minute was harrowing once I realized he'd kidnapped me. By the time darkness fell, I was sure he was going to kill me that night!"

"My God, sir! So, was it the police who rescued you or did you manage to escape from his clutches?" Motkar asked.

"Neither," Saralkar replied. "He let me go. He dropped me about a kilometre away from my house at around 5.00 a.m. . . . warned me he would come back and kill me and my parents if I told anyone he had kidnapped me. That's the last thing I remember, because I fainted. An hour later someone spotted me. I was delirious, had high fever . . . and I think I was in that unconscious state for almost three days. The next thing I remember is waking up screaming and realizing I was in my own house, safe and sound."

"But what did he want, sir? Why did he do it?" Motkar asked. "Or was it some grudge against your father?"

Saralkar shook his head. "No, nothing like that. For a long, long time I didn't know the motive. My father told me much later what he'd learnt from the police after they arrested Mahadik six or seven months later, when I finally blurted out who had kidnapped me."

A soft knock on the door interrupted the conversation. "Come in," Saralkar said, halting his narration. Motkar looked fretfully at the door.

Ashwini Gholap entered, followed by a bespectacled, well-dressed man, who appeared trim and grim. "Hullo, sir," Ashwini said, then gestured in the direction of the man. "This is my ex-husband, Neeraj, Atharva's father."

Neeraj Jambhekar nodded quietly at both policemen.

"Please come in," Saralkar said, "Sit . . ."

The couple took their seats. "Inspector Motkar told me there has been some progress in the investigation and that he wanted to show me something," Ashwini said.

"Ashwini insisted I come along, that's why . . ." Neeraj Jambhekar added, awkward and reluctant.

Saralkar studied him for a beat, then said, "You don't have much faith in the police, Mr. Jambhekar, unlike your wife?"

A slight wrinkle appeared on Neeraj's forehead. "It's six years since my son's murder . . . and going by the fiasco in the case of this child's investigation also, can you blame me for feeling as I do?"

He had obviously read in the newspaper or news channels about Smita Bhatti's murder of her ex-husband in police custody and the setting up of an inquiry.

"And yet you are here, Mr. Jambhekar," Saralkar replied gently.

Neeraj Jambhekar smiled with cynical bitterness, displaying a twisted humour, with his next utterance. "I didn't want Ashwini to do to me what Smita Bhatti did to her ex-husband."

Ashwini cast a withering glare at him. "Stop talking nonsense, Neeraj. I know you want Atharva's killer caught, as much as I do!"

She turned her sour look towards Saralkar and said bluntly, "Sir, when I approached you citing similarities between my son's disappearance and murder and Pranjal's, you were dismissive, even though you didn't say so. So, what am I to understand from PSI Motkar's call? Does it mean you've found some concrete link now? Or are you just going through the motions of checking out a possibility, just because you are facing the heat?"

Saralkar was surprised by the perceptiveness and forthrightness of the woman in front of him. He glanced at Motkar, then back again at the couple. "You are right, Ms. Gholap. I did not think at first the cases had any common link, even though the circumstances in which both your son and Pranjal were kidnapped and killed were similar. But there are two things that have come to light recently, which have forced me to change my mind," Saralkar said, looking at the couple.

Both were listening carefully but appeared sceptical in different ways. "What are the two things that have influenced your outlook?" Ashwini asked sharply.

"I understand from the case papers that a few months after Atharva's death, you discovered a bag of demonetised cash at your door one morning, along with a note," Saralkar said, then paused. He noted the change of expressions on both faces, regarding him. He continued, "I believe you reported it to the investigating officer, even filed an affidavit, but your husband denied anything like this had actually happened. He claimed it was a figment of your imagination, due to your disturbed, psychological state of mind. May I know what the truth is?"

Ashwini cleared her throat. "Of course, we received that bag with demonetised currency and that sick note. Neeraj and I argued on the course of action to take. He thought it futile to take it to the police, while I felt we must report it and hand it over for clues. But by the time I returned from office to take it to the police, Neeraj had already disposed it off."

"You reported the incident to the police all the same?" Motkar said.

"Yes, because that's what had really happened . . . but of course they didn't believe me, because I neither had the bag nor the note and Neeraj flatly denied it. The investigating officer, PSI Shirsat, had anyway started thinking of me as a nuisance and a psycho," Ashwini said, but quite oddly without any rancour.

"And what do you have to say to that, Mr. Jambhekar?" Saralkar asked.

"I stick to what I had said earlier. Nothing like that happened," Neeraj replied with an impassive face. "Anyway, what is its relevance to your change of mind?"

Saralkar had not expected him to change his stance. There was no motivation to. "Well, the reason I am raking it up is that something similar happened in the case of Pranjal's family," he said, watching the couple carefully.

"What? You mean . . . this boy's family also received a bag of cash?" Ashwini asked in a breathless voice.

"Not cash but something that could be called an unconventional form of monetary compensation for the loss of the child, along with an apology note, just like the one you said you received—a one-liner."

"Oh, my God!" Ashwini gasped and turned to her ex-husband who was now looking disturbed. "Neeraj . . . Neeraj . . . it has to be the same man!"

Saralkar let a beat pass, then asked Neeraj, "I need to know whether there really is a pattern—the same devilish mind at work. Whether it's true you received a bag of demonetised cash. Because if it is just Madam's imagination as you claim then what Pranjal's family has received does not point to a definite link to your child's murderer. Then it is just an isolated instance and we cannot consider it a pattern."

Neeraj did not look at him. He was staring fixedly at the floor, his mind feverishly processing the information he'd just received.

"Neeraj, Neeraj . . ." Ashwini nudged him, "for God's sake at least confirm it to them now! Tell them it really happened. That I was telling the truth."

Neeraj frowned at Saralkar. "I . . . I'd like to hear what's the other reason for your change of mind first."

Saralkar sensed here was a cynical, shrewd man who would only put his cards on the table if he was convinced it would lead somewhere. His antagonism towards the police would continue till he saw reason to think otherwise.

"Okay, I'll tell you that, too," Saralkar conceded. "When we compared the two post mortem reports—of Atharva and Pranjal, our expert discerned two striking anomalies. One, both boys had been mutilated in a manner as to suggest sexual assault, but in both cases the injuries to the anus were inflicted after death, which means after the boys had drowned. Now how could that have been possible if the boys had been thrown into the river and drowned?

"None of us had noticed this oddity, although it had puzzled me a bit when I first saw Pranjal's report. But now we realized it was ditto in Atharva's case, too. And the answer was again in the post-mortem reports, which the expert brought to our notice—a detail that too had been missed completely before. The fact was, the water found in the lungs and internal organs of both boys was chlorinated water, not river water, with its pollutants and different organic elements."

"What? Chlorinated water?" Neeraj Jambhekar said, a big scowl on his face. "How is that possible if they drowned in the river?" he broke off, staring aghast at Saralkar.

"Exactly! So the only logical conclusion that can explain these anomalies is that both boys were drowned in a swimming pool, then mutilated for it to appear they had been sexually assaulted so as to suggest the perpetrator was a paedophile or sexual pervert, and then they were thrown into the river to make it appear Atharva and Pranjal were killed by drowning in the Mutha," Saralkar said.

Ashwini suddenly broke down into sobs and dissolved into inconsolable tears. Neeraj's hands involuntarily went out to pat, comfort, and hold her. His eyes held a faraway, dazed expression. Saralkar felt sorry for the couple. To live for six long years without any closure was complete hell.

"I am sorry, I know how distressing these details must be for you," he murmured. "But I hope you now see why I need to know for sure whether we are on the right track at least now—that indeed the two cases are connected and whether the evidence adds up in leading us to the killer."

Neeraj's eyes were watery when he glanced at Saralkar. "Yes . . . Ashwini is right. A bag full of demonetised currency amounting to ₹5 lakhs . . . was left at our door. Ashwini found it when she opened the door to take the milk pouches," he said and went on to describe in detail what happened that morning, six years ago.

As Saralkar listened, he couldn't help empathising with Neeraj's thought process at that time. The weeks and months after demonetisation had been a crazy period of chaos and disruption. The claim of so much cash being left at their door would not have been accepted easily. Instead, they could well have faced harassment from authorities hunting black money. And Neeraj was right to have nursed serious apprehensions. A lot of crooked people, including policemen, had used all kinds of means to convert demonetised currency into new notes.

"So, may I ask what you did with the money? Did you retain the bag, or the apology note or any evidence of having received the cash?" Motkar asked.

Neeraj was quiet again and looked at his wife as if seeking her concurrence. But in fact, it was she who replied. "I . . . I was mad at him. I hated Neeraj when I returned home to find the bag missing. He wouldn't tell me anything except that he had disposed it off," Ashwini said. "I went to the police and when they checked with him, he scoffed at the idea. Our simmering differences came out into the open and I could not stand a life with him any longer. I told him I wanted a divorce. So, we filed for a mutual consent divorce. He remarried and we went our separate ways. Then, about three years ago on Atharva's birthday, Neeraj came to my house and told me what he'd done with the money."

She paused and looked at him, as if asking him to continue. Neeraj Jambhekar spoke. "I got the cash converted into new currency. I knew someone who got it done for a percentage and then I established a corpus in my son's name to award a scholarship every year to a deserving student in the twelve to fifteen age group to fund their year-long coaching in skateboarding . . . since Atharva loved the sport and was so good at it."

Neeraj choked and paused. "The killer had sent us money, perhaps to mock us . . . but my thought was, why allow him to get away with it? He would've expected us to hand it over to the police or throw it away in disgust—and thus dictate our reaction. I was determined not to do either. Initially I decided I'd use the money to announce a reward for anyone who could give us information on Atharva's kidnapper. It would be the perfect way to use his own money to entrap him. But the more I reflected on it, I realized my son had gone and establishing a scholarship in his name was a much better way to keep his memory alive . . ."

Saralkar felt a great respect for the man. "I see. I think you chose a very dignified option, Mr. Jambhekar. Not many people could've managed that," he said.

"Thank you. And yes, I have kept the bag and the note safely. I also retained two random bundles of cash in case it might be useful for forensics someday. You can have it all," Neeraj said.

For whatever it was worth, Saralkar thought it was a piece of luck that Neeraj Jambhekar was a meticulous man.

"So, Inspector, what list was Inspector Motkar talking about? Please tell me how we can help and whether you have a clear suspect in sight?" Ashwini asked.

Saralkar glanced at Motkar who had the list ready in his hand.

"We want you to have a look at this list and tell us if any of these names are familiar or remind you of any person connected to you, especially with regard to your son, Atharva," Motkar said. "As of now we cannot tell you how near or far we are from closing in on a suspect, but we are working on some crucial circumstantial evidence and if you find any of the names on this list familiar, then it would help us determine if our investigation is on track."

The couple nodded and Motkar placed the list before them on the table. Both Ashwini and Neeraj looked at the names carefully, more than once as if trying to squeeze their memories. Neeraj was the first to respond. "I can't say any of the names remind me of anyone we knew in Atharva's context . . ."

He looked at the two officers and then at Ashwini, who was still reading and frowning.

"What about you, Ms. Gholap?" Motkar asked.

Ashwini sighed, put her forefinger on a name and said, "I seem to remember that after Atharva's death, a boy called Gaurav Sapatnekar replaced him to represent the state at the Zonal Skateboarding Championship. I wonder if this R.V. Sapatnekar is related to him . . ."

A shudder passed through Saralkar as a startling new possibility began to form in his brain—like a switch in his mind had been suddenly activated.

*****

Chapter 28

"Y ou didn't do well again today. Why?"
The question was answered with silence.

"Come on, what's wrong?"

"I . . . I can't concentrate."

"Is it because you are still thinking of . . . that day?"

"Yes," came the agonised reply.

"You can't let that happen!"

"I can't help it. It didn't happen to you when Atharva was . . ."

There was a longish beat. "It did. It still does . . . but I have learnt to live with it."

"How?"

"I pray . . . every single day . . ."

"To God?"

"To God and Atharva . . . to forgive me."

"Does it help?"

"Yes, most of the time . . . but sometimes it doesn't."

"Show me how to pray."

A prayer was recited then emulated. More silence followed.

"I wouldn't have called out to Pranjal that day, if I knew . . ."

"Just pray. You can't change what's done."

"Did you know he was going to . . .?"

The silence was thick with anguish and guilt.

"I guessed when he began talking about swimming . . ."

"Then why didn't you try to stop Pranjal from coming with us?"

There was no reply for some time. "It was too late . . . I didn't know how to stop it . . . what to do . . . I was scared."

Both whisperers sank back into the oppressive silence.

"I feel like telling someone or I'll . . . burst."

"Hush . . . pray . . . pray just like I told you . . . then you'll feel better . . . shhh."

*****

"Has Mohnish Bhatti reverted with his wife's response on the list and Sapatnekar's photo, Tupe?"

"No, sir, I have tried his number a few times, but he didn't take the call," Tupe replied. "A little while ago he texted saying he still hasn't had a chance to meet his wife long enough to discuss anything . . . that once her court appearance is over, he might get to see her for some time."

Saralkar clicked his tongue impatiently. "What about the background check on Ranjit Sapatnekar and if he has any police record?"

"We are still working on the background check, sir . . . but at least prima facie he doesn't have a police record of any kind. However, there seems to be an NC lodged against him at Baner Police Station a few months ago," Tupe said. NC, in police parlance, referred to non-cognisable complaints for minor offences like abuse, altercations, bad behaviour between people, in which the police had no powers of arrest or investigation unless directed by a magistrate. Most such NCs were handled by local cops, playing informal mediators or counselling both parties. However, it was also true, many times cops persuaded complainants to lodge an NC instead of an FIR for matters which were slightly more serious, simply to reduce their workload.

"An NC at Baner? Have you got the details?" Saralkar asked.

"Not yet, sir. We got to know about the NC by sheer accident. One of the Baner constables had come here for some other work. He and Dhanak got talking and the Baner constable caught a glimpse of Sapatnekar's photo and name," Tupe explained. "He then said some lady had lodged an NC against Sapatnekar a few months ago. Dhanak has now gone with him to Baner Police Station to verify and get a copy of the NC if possible."

The rings of Tupe's mobile caused him to look at the screen. "Sir, it's Dhanak. May I take the call?"

"Go ahead."

Tupe took the call. "Yes, Dhanak." He listened for a few seconds. "Okay, so the NC is definitely against Ranjit Sapatnekar . . . I see . . . okay . . . and who is the complainant? Sunaini Bhagwat? Okay . . . yes bring a copy of the NC . . . or just take a pic of it on your camera mobile . . . okay."

Saralkar's ears had pricked up at the name of the complainant—Sunaini Bhagwat. Hadn't he heard it recently? Memory eluded him. Sometimes he wondered if he was suffering from early Alzheimer's.

"Sir," Tupe started briefing him, "a lady named Sunaini Bhagwat had . . ."

And then it suddenly came back to Saralkar. Of course, Sunaini Bhagwat—Pranjal's chess coach, whom ASI Sanika Zirpe had interviewed. And hadn't she reported about the chess coach having had to lodge a complaint against some pesky parent?

"Call up Zirpe," he said, interrupting Tupe. "Right away!"

*****

SIX WEEKS AGO, 3.10 P.M.

Pranjal waved back at the familiar face, calling out to him from the back seat of the big blue SUV, waiting on the opposite side of the road. "Hi, Rohan!" he hollered back.

"Come here . . ." Rohan gestured from across the road.

"I'm already late for class, Rohan," Pranjal replied, getting ready to cycle away.

"My father wants to congratulate you," Rohan said, pointing towards the driver's seat. The window of the front seat had zoomed down and a bald man wearing goggles turned and smiled at Pranjal.

Pranjal had met Rohan's father a few times at chess competitions and also when he came to pick or drop Rohan at their chess coach Sunaini Bhagwat's house. But Rohan had stopped coming there a few months ago. He didn't know why. All Pranjal knew was that Rohan was a very good chess player and had narrowly missed being selected in the state team because Pranjal beat him by a few points. He reluctantly crossed the road with his bicycle now. He was really going to be late and receive a firing.

"Hullo, Pranjal," Rohan's father said as he came alongside the car. "Congratulations on your selection."

He put out his hand and Pranjal shyly shook it. "Thank you, Uncle . . ."

• 328 •

"Did Rohan tell you we have a chess board and set, which was once used by Viswanathan Anand?" Rohan's father asked.

"Really!" Pranjal said with awe.

"Yes," Rohan said excitedly. "My dad bought it for me . . . you want to see it?"

"I would love to!" Pranjal replied.

"Come with us, then. We are going home only," Rohan's father said.

Pranjal hesitated, "No, Uncle, I'm already going to be ten-fifteen minutes late for class . . ."

Rohan's father shrugged. "Rohan says you like swimming. We've got a swimming pool also . . ."

"Yes . . . yes, Pranjal! You can see the chess set and then we can swim in our pool also!" Rohan joined in.

The two temptations together were a bit too much to resist for the eleven-year-old. Pranjal hadn't swum for a long time. The society pool had been under repair for ages now. "But I don't have my trunks," he said.

"I've got a spare one," Rohan said quickly.

Pranjal hesitated some more. "But my parents will scold me if I bunk class."

"Look, don't worry about that. I'll come to drop you back. I'll speak to your mum and dad then, okay?" Rohan's father said.

"But, Uncle, my bicycle . . ."

Suddenly a voice spoke from the passenger seat next to the driver. "Papa, why are you forcing him? If he doesn't want to come, let it be, no . . ."

Pranjal was startled and peered inside. Rohan's father had also turned to look at the person in the passenger seat.

"Who's that?" Pranjal asked Rohan.

"That's my older brother, Gaurav."

But Rohan's father was already talking to Pranjal again. "Your bicycle will easily fit in behind in the dicky. Come, hop on, Pranjal."

"Yes, come no, Pranjal," Rohan coaxed him. He didn't have any real friends.

Pranjal gave in. No sixth sense whispered to the boy that he was making the same mistake that another boy named Atharva had made six years ago!

*****

"That's him! Ranjit Sapatnekar!" Sunaini Bhagwat asserted, without a moment's hesitation, as soon as ASI Sanika Zirpe showed her the photo.

"And you confirm that you filed an NC against him at Baner Police Station about six months ago?" Zirpe asked, thrilled to be back to doing her job.

"Yes . . . I was fed up with his persistent harassment. He'd keep initiating arguments with me on the subject of his son Rohan's coaching—pestering me about why I was not teaching him this tactic or that gambit and about why I was not paying more attention to his son," Sunaini said. "He had a very obnoxious, intimidating manner and it became very unpleasant since he'd paid fees for a year in advance. He would also call or text any time. Then when Rohan didn't perform well in a few tournaments, he said all kinds of things about my dedication and that he would post on social media how poor a chess coach I was . . . it was too much so I put my foot down and refused to coach Rohan further. Ranjit Sapatnekar became furious and made all sorts of threats, which really disturbed me. That's when I decided the matter had gone too far and went to lodge a police complaint. Baner Police told me that they could register an NC, not an FIR, given the nature of the offences."

"Okay. Did Baner Police tell you what action they took?" ASI Zirpe asked.

"Yes, they called me one day and said they had contacted Ranjit Sapatnekar and he was there with them. They said he'd accepted it was his fault and that he'd said things in a fit of temper because I refused to refund coaching fees," Sunaini Bhagwat said. "The officer asked me if I could come to the station since Sapatnekar was prepared to apologise in front of them. I was reluctant. I told them I had no wish to meet him for any compromise or redressal meeting and that they should take a written apology from him and book him according to law. The officer said that generally in NC cases they usually called the parties together to settle the matter, but could do nothing more. There was a provision of a written bond only in case of repeated harassment or if a lot of people complained against someone being a nuisance, but not otherwise. So, I just left it at that."

"I see. But did you face any trouble from Ranjit Sapatnekar again?" Zirpe asked her.

"No . . . thank God . . . because he was a weird, creepy man . . . although his son Rohan was not a bad chess player. In fact, he's replaced Pranjal in the state team now that . . ."

Sunaini Bhagwat stopped mid-sentence and her face turned pale. "Is . . . Is that why you are inquiring about Ranjit Sapatnekar?"

She stared horrified as the thought grew on her.

*****

PRESENT DAY

The team was waiting for Saralkar when he returned from the CP's office. "We've got a week," Saralkar said. "If we don't snare our man with enough evidence to convince the CP, the case will be handed over to a new squad."

There were a few seconds of hushed silence. "Why don't we bring Ranjit Sapatnekar in for questioning, sir? We know now it's him . . ." ASI Tupe said.

"Somehow he doesn't look like the kind who'll confess during interrogation, Tupe," Motkar countered. "It would be premature to bring him in without concrete evidence."

Saralkar listened and nodded. "Motkar's right."

"But, sir, everything points in Sapatnekar's direction . . ." ASI Zirpe said.

"What's everything?" Saralkar asked. He looked at Tupe and Zirpe.

Tupe said, "Sir . . . Atharva Jambhekar's parents have identified Ranjit Sapatnekar as the father of Gaurav who replaced him to represent the state after Atharva's death. We have now also received confirmation from Mohnish Bhatti that his wife recognised Sapatnekar's name and photo. Pranjal's coach, Sunaini Bhagwat, confirmed Ranjit's son Rohan replaced Pranjal and that his behaviour towards her was aggressive and threatening . . ."

"Then of course the biggest evidence is the presence of his car at the spot, around the time Pranjal disappeared, sir . . ." Zirpe added.

"It's strong circumstantial evidence, sir . . . plus the motive is also so powerful," Tupe said. "He killed Atharva six years ago and now Pranjal, so that his sons could take their places, since they were standby candidates. You yourself brilliantly worked out the motive, sir."

Saralkar smirked. "Working out motives is much easier than proving them beyond reasonable doubt. Ask Motkar. The fact is we still don't have evidence to connect Ranjit Sapatnekar to the Bitcoin transfer and no material evidence that he committed the crime. And we can't rely on confession, because we simply don't have irrefutable evidence to pin him down yet . . ."

A grim silence reigned again. Then Motkar spoke. "Sir, I have a slightly delicate idea . . ."

"Delicate? What?"

"Sir, can we try and talk to his sons? If even one of them spills the beans, we would have made headway and got something substantial to confront Ranjit with," Motkar said.

"Hmm . . . not a bad idea, Motkar, but one fraught with risk, because it's legally dodgy even if the children tell us all. On the other hand, it can backfire on us badly, if they reveal nothing . . ." Saralkar said thoughtfully.

He was silent for a few minutes, then said, "Still it's worth trying because it's more likely to work than questioning Ranjit Sapatnekar directly. So, let's do this, but we have to plan with precision."

The team suddenly looked energised. "We have all details of their daily routines—Ranjit and his sons—right, Tupe?"

"Yes, sir."

"Good! We need to first identify the best place and time to catch the younger child, Rohan, alone, so that Zirpe can seek him out and get him talking. Simultaneously, we close in on the older son, Gaurav, who's in college and open a conversation with him. Depending on what the outcomes are, we then confront their father," Saralkar said.

An hour later, the action plan and coordination required was finalised.

*****

ASI Sanika Zirpe saw the two-wheeler approach and stop a little distance from the gate of the Karate Academy, which was actually a part of a larger sports complex, with a different gate.

For the last twenty minutes, Zirpe had seen many parents drop their children off, who then promptly rushed inside the gate. She hoped Rohan Sapatnekar would not scoot inside the academy at the same speed, as soon as his brother dropped him off.

The task she faced was to wait for Gaurav to drive away, before she could stop Rohan from disappearing inside for his karate class. As luck would have it, Rohan got down from the back seat of the scooter and waved as his brother moved away. Then he began trundling inside with another kid, who'd just been dropped by her parent.

"Rohan . . . Rohan . . ." ASI Zirpe called out. The kid wheeled around. Sanika Zirpe gave him a big smile and gestured at him to come towards her.

Rohan gave a half smile but looked unsure who the unknown lady was and why she was speaking to him. ASI Zirpe walked up to him. "Do you recognise me? My, how big you have grown!"

A few minutes into the conversation with the unsuspecting boy, ASI Zirpe gently introduced the name of Pranjal Bhatti.

*****

"You are Gaurav Sapatnekar, right?"

The lanky, good-looking youngster, seated in a corner of the Crossword bookstore, paging through the latest paperback of an Indian author, looked up at the girl, his age, who had just asked the question. "Yes, I am Gaurav . . . sorry . . . have we met before?" he asked surprised and confused.

"I am Namita, Pranjal Bhatti's sister," the girl said evenly.

PSI Motkar and ASI Tupe, who stood separately a little

distance away, dressed in plain-clothes posing as casually browsing readers, watched for the youngster's reactions.

Gaurav looked visibly disconcerted. Motkar wondered if he'd just turn away and run out of the bookstore.

"Can I talk to you for a few minutes?" Namita asked gently.

It had been a Saralkar brainwave to seek the help of Namita Bhatti for breaking the ice with Gaurav. He had been worried that if any police officer approached the older Sapatnekar sibling, he would just clamp up or be so scared so as to make him panic.

Sanika Zirpe couldn't be in two places at the same time, since she had been tasked with approaching the younger sibling, Rohan. That's when Saralkar had wondered aloud if it wouldn't be a smart move to get Namita to help. The people in Saralkar's team had looked at one another, flabbergasted.

"She's around Gaurav's age, she's a girl, she's not a cop, and she's the victim's sister—a rather effective combination," Saralkar had reasoned.

But given what the team had seen of Namita's attitude and behaviour so far, why would she help, Motkar had raised a valid doubt.

"She will," Saralkar had asserted, "given all that's happened."

His keen psychological insight had proved correct. Namita had almost jumped at the opportunity to help, as if she had been waiting for a chance to redeem herself. It had helped that she now knew for sure, Mohnish Bhatti was her real farther and, hence, Pranjal her real brother. The guilt of somehow having played a hand in her mother's action also seemed to be on her mind.

Saralkar and Sanika Zirpe had briefed Namita, sworn her to secrecy, and told her exactly what to do. The only thing remaining to be seen was whether Saralkar's unorthodox gambit would work on Gaurav and get him to talk.

"I don't understand," Gaurav fumbled. "Talk to me about what . . .?"

"Gaurav, your younger brother, Rohan, already confessed the truth," Namita said, "just a little while ago."

Gaurav stared wildly, as if struck by a thunderbolt. He backed away slightly, then spoke, "Confessed to whom? Where is Rohan? You mean . . . he . . . he came and told you . . . something?"

Namita just nodded. Motkar was impressed how well she was handling this.

"What do you know? Is Rohan okay? What has he told you?" Gaurav asked with rising panic. His brother's words a few days ago were fresh in his mind— *"I think I will burst if I don't tell someone."* Had Rohan just done that?

"About your father . . . and what he did to my brother, Pranjal," Namita said calmly, her eyes not leaving Gaurav.

Gaurav seemed to shrink. The book he was holding fell to the floor and he began shaking.

Namita glanced at Motkar as if looking for a cue about what to do. Before Motkar could react or step in, Gaurav suddenly said, "I knew this day would come . . . I knew Rohan would tell someone, someday!"

*****

Saralkar listened as first Zirpe and then Motkar briefed him. It had all gone according to plan so far.

"Well done," he said, trying hard not to feel prematurely vindicated. There was still a long way to go. The testimony of the two boys was of little value as evidence, to arrest their father. All Ranjit Sapatnekar would have to do was cry foul, allege coercion and illegal means to obtain statements from his children, and all the effort would go up in smoke. But yes, at least they had glimpsed the truth.

"Sir, Ranjit Sapatnekar usually picks up Rohan in about

half an hour from now, from outside the karate class," Zirpe said. "Do we take him into custody once he arrives there?"

Saralkar shook his head. "No, that might not go smoothly. Therefore, I have thought of a little twist in our plan to get Sapatnekar to cooperate."

Motkar sighed inwardly. Trust his boss to make things complicated. "What would that be, sir?"

"Well, you and I will meet Ranjit Sapatnekar outside the karate class, Motkar," Saralkar said, "and tell him we've received a ransom note addressed to him, stating his kids have been kidnapped and they would be released only if he confesses to having kidnapped and killed two boys—Atharva Jambhekar and Pranjal Bhatti."

Motkar's jaw dropped. "But, sir . . . aren't we going a bit too far? I mean . . ."

"Yes, I know what you mean, Motkar . . . and yes we are going too far," Saralkar admitted. "But how else do we get him to self-incriminate in a way that will help us find evidence against him? Besides we haven't harmed the children or forced them in any way to tell us the truth."

"No, sir . . . we tricked them into telling us the truth and isn't that already a tad unethical?" Motkar found himself retorting.

Saralkar glared at him. "Yes, both *tricked* and *unethical* are the right words, Motkar. . . lest you forget, you suggested it!"

Motkar reddened. "Yes, sir, I did . . . but there's a big difference in what you are proposing to do now."

Saralkar snapped, "I know you take your role as my conscience-keeper quite seriously . . . but do you think a ruthless kid killer like Ranjit Sapatnekar is going to give up his secrets or confess to his crimes, unless he has something precious to lose?"

Tension crackled in the room in the silence that followed.

Motkar fidgeted. "Still, sir, to use this ruse of his kids' lives being in danger to entrap a killer? Do the ends justify the means?"

Saralkar gave his assistant a hard stare. "Motkar, this man used his own children to entice two unsuspecting boys to their deaths! And nothing can compare to the trauma he's inflicted on his own kids by making them . . . in a sense . . . accomplices in murder!"

"I know that, sir . . ."

Saralkar looked at his watch and held up his palm. "We don't have the time to debate this. I'll do this on my own so that none of you can be held officially responsible for the subterfuge, nor will it violate your ethics, Motkar."

"No, sir . . . I'll come with you. That's not what I meant at all. Please, sir."

Saralkar looked at him for a few seconds then nodded. "There's something to be said for a man's conviction, Motkar . . . and I don't want to ask you to carry out something you don't agree with. But it would add authenticity if you came along. Just don't say a word that might compromise your convictions. Let me do the talking."

"Okay, sir," Motkar replied.

Saralkar turned to Tupe and Zirpe. "Make sure the boys don't get anxious or scared. We'll let you know if any assistance is required."

*****

"He's here, sir," Motkar said as the blue Fortuner came into sight and stopped by the roadside, outside the karate academy.

Ranjit Sapatnekar lowered the driver-side window and looked at his watch. His son Rohan would generally be waiting for him on the pavement.

Saralkar watched him as the man drummed the steering wheel impatiently. "Let's go, Motkar," Saralkar said and stepped out of their vehicle. Motkar joined him and both crossed over to the other side of the road.

"Are you Mr. Ranjit Sapatnekar?" Saralkar asked as they came alongside the car window.

Ranjit Sapatnekar turned his goggles in their direction as if to study Saralkar and Motkar, "And you are?"

"Are you waiting for your son Rohan?" Saralkar asked, staring hard at the goggles. He noticed a quick flicker or a blink behind the shades.

"Why is it any of your business?" the reply came sharp and hard.

"It seems to have become our business now," Saralkar replied calmly. "I'm Senior Inspector Saralkar. A little more than an hour ago we received a note claiming that Gaurav and Rohan Sapatnekar, children of Ranjit Sapatnekar, have been kidnapped."

In a flash, Ranjit Sapatnekar was out of the car and stood towering over them, glaring through his goggles. "What the hell are you talking about?"

A feeling of trepidation crept over Motkar, but he noticed his boss as usual looking unfazed.

"The note we received claims your younger son, Rohan, was picked up from here and your older son near the Crossword store in Aundh about fifteen or twenty minutes apart," Saralkar said. "It also mentioned that you pick Rohan up from here around this time and that you drive a blue Fortuner . . . that's why we were waiting for you to check this out."

Ranjit had still not removed his goggles and was staring at them with baffled anger. "I don't get it . . . who are these kidnappers? And why would they send a note to the police?"

"Exactly! We were baffled too and that's why we are here to verify if this is a genuine kidnapping and not some prank," Saralkar replied smoothly. "If your children carry mobiles, why don't you try and call them to check if they are safe."

Ranjit was breathing heavily now. "I'll check inside the karate academy if Rohan's inside first."

"Sure . . . I'll come with you," Saralkar said.

Ten minutes later they were back outside, Ranjit Sapatnekar more anxious than angry now. He had also tried the numbers of both his sons and found the phones switched off. He shot questions at Saralkar. "But why have the kidnappers taken my sons? What does the note say? What do they want?"

Saralkar looked at him gravely. "Now that it seems to be confirmed your sons have gone missing, I suggest you come with us to the Bavdhan Police Station and let's discuss the matter threadbare."

"But why don't you tell me what's in the note?" Ranjit demanded aggressively.

"Mr. Sapatnekar, the police follow certain procedures while dealing with such crimes. I suggest you stop asking questions and accompany us, so that we can put things in motion to quickly trace and get your children back safely," Saralkar replied. "Let's go!"

Without giving Ranjit a chance to argue further, Saralkar turned to Motkar and said, "Motkar, let's get back to Bavdhan Police Chowky. I'll come with Mr. Sapatnekar in his car."

He then proceeded to get into the passenger seat of Ranjit Sapatnekar's car, who was left with no choice in the matter.

Motkar couldn't help admire the way his boss had handled it so far. He got into the car and began following Sapatnekar's blue Fortuner.

*****

Chapter 29

"**D**o you have any enemies, Mr. Sapatnekar? Someone who hates you?" Saralkar asked Ranjit, now seated across the table from him at Bavdhan Police Station.

Motkar hovered in the background with Tupe.

"Enemies? No! Why would I have enemies? Why do you ask?" Ranjit responded with a scowl.

"Because the letter we received appears to be written by someone with a deep grudge and strangely no ransom money has been demanded."

"Can I have a look at the letter, Inspector?" Ranjit said tersely.

"No, it's been sent for forensic analysis."

"But surely you must have a copy?"

Saralkar shook his head. "I'm afraid I can't show it to you before we confirm certain facts mentioned in the letter."

"What facts?" Ranjit said through clenched teeth.

Saralkar deliberately paused, opened the table drawer, feigned a search then brought out two pages stapled together. He pretended to read as Ranjit Sapatnekar fumed.

"Can you please hurry up, Inspector? Will you tell me what facts you wish to confirm and what the bloody hell do the kidnappers say they want?"

Saralkar looked up at him, wooden-faced. "We are equally concerned, Mr. Sapatnekar. This note alleges that you, Ranjit Sapatnekar, kidnapped and killed two children—a boy named Atharva Jambhekar, about six years ago, and just recently, another child named Pranjal Bhatti, whose case is currently being investigated by us."

He was watching Ranjit's reactions, as were Motkar and Tupe. The jaw muscles of their quarry had suddenly tightened and his forehead had wrinkled into angry folds. But since the goggles were still on, the expressions in Ranjit's eyes remained hidden.

"Utter bullshit!" Ranjit growled. "I have done no such thing!"

"I see," Saralkar said. "Then why would these kidnappers make such allegations against you?"

"How would I know, Inspector, why some psychopathic nutcase got this into his head and kidnapped my boys?" Ranjit exploded.

PSI Motkar sensed this was the perfect juncture to step in with a question. "But even a nutcase won't just randomly make such a wild charge against you specifically, unless there is some connection, Mr. Sapatnekar. This nutcase would have to know you, right? Or the boys he says you kidnapped? So, do you know any such nutcase with an irrational grudge against you? Or did you or your children know these unfortunate victims, Atharva and Pranjal, by any chance?"

The intervention by Motkar seemed to have caught Ranjit off guard. He paused, as if trying to adjust his senses to the tone and flurry of questions. "Of course . . . I . . . we don't know any of these children."

"Not even Pranjal Bhatti, whose case has been all over the media?" Motkar nudged.

"Well, only to that extent . . . as news! Why would I know the boy personally?"

"Are you absolutely sure of that?" Saralkar took over the baton of questioning again.

Ranjit turned on him with something akin to fury. "Yes . . . I am sure, damn it. Now why don't you stop wasting time, Inspector, and get off your fat arse to find my boys!"

Saralkar showed no signs of temper or offence. "For that, you first need to stop lying, Ranjit."

"What the fuck do you mean? I'm not lying!" Ranjit snarled.

Saralkar let a beat pass then stood up from his chair, looking down at Ranjit. "You are lying that you don't know Pranjal personally. Your son Rohan and Pranjal both played competitive chess and went to the same coach, Sunaini Bhagwat, till a few months ago. Your son has now replaced Pranjal from the district to represent the state at the national level championship, after Pranjal's death."

Ranjit Sapatnekar, pushed on the back foot, reacted as if he believed attack was the best form of defence. "That doesn't prove anything . . . that doesn't prove I knew the boy. What kind of useless policemen are you? Why aren't you doing anything to get my children back?"

Saralkar smirked. "Well, we can definitely do something to get Gaurav and Rohan back, if you agree to the kidnapper's demands in the letter."

"What are those demands? Tell me, damn it," Ranjit said aggressively.

"That's what I was coming to, Ranjit," Saralkar replied, his voice calm but face hard as stone. "But before that you need to do three things—stop ranting, mind your language, and remove your stupid goggles."

"You can't . . ." Ranjit started saying but was suddenly cut short by Saralkar in a tone that was harsh and authoritative.

"Shut up and do it immediately!"

Ranjit Sapatnekar looked as if he had received a cracking slap across his face and had suddenly woken up to the full force of Saralkar's authority. He hesitated for a few seconds, then removed his goggles, folding them and putting them in his shirt pocket. His face suddenly became human and whole. It was a bitter, hard face with eyes that looked out with dull malice, as if something irretrievably twisted lurked behind them.

"Good," remarked Saralkar. "Now here's what the kidnappers have demanded—that your boys will be safely released only when you make a full confession about having kidnapped and killed Atharva Jambhekar and Pranjal Bhatti. Secondly, we, the police, have to confirm that we have arrested you on the basis of your confession and key evidence that you hand over to us."

Not a muscle moved on Ranjit Sapatnekar's face as he listened silently, his eyes lowered, breathing heavily.

"Did you hear what I said and are you willing to meet the demands?" Saralkar asked a minute later.

"Have my children been held hostage by the family members of those two boys?" Ranjit asked in a hoarse but expressionless tone.

"All we know is that the families of both boys are untraceable . . . so it is possible they are the ones behind your sons' kidnapping or perhaps they hired professional gangsters,"

Saralkar replied in a matter-of-fact tone that Motkar wondered how he managed to bluff with.

"Does the letter say why they believe I've committed the crimes they allege?"

"Yes. And we are making our own inquiries to verify the reasons given," Saralkar said, studying Ranjit carefully. "In fact the letter lists many similarities between the cases of both boys—not the least being the manner of death and the strange fact that even in the case of Atharva, it was your older son, Gaurav, who replaced him to represent the state at the zonal and national skateboarding championship, after the boy was kidnapped and killed. It certainly sounds too curious to be a mere coincidence."

Ranjit gazed at him with a chilling, trapped expression. "How do I know they won't harm my boys, if I do as they say, instead of releasing them?"

"You mean will the kidnappers kill your boys as revenge once you confess you killed Atharva and Pranjal?" Saralkar asked sharply.

Ranjit flinched. He licked his lips. "Yes, wouldn't I be endangering the lives of my kids, if I give in to the demand?"

"Then wouldn't they simply have killed your sons instead of taking them hostage and demanding your confessions and arrest?" PSI Motkar butted in. "It's you who is wasting time now!"

The rebuke by the diminutive-looking, quiet officer, seemed to singe Ranjit. "Why are you assuming that the allegations in the note are correct?"

"Well, you haven't denied them so far, Ranjit Sapatnekar," PSI Motkar replied shortly.

"I . . . I am just weighing the pros and cons," Ranjit replied.

Saralkar exchanged glances with Motkar and Tupe. They let Ranjit struggle with his thoughts.

He finally looked up, his face taut and grim, his whole demeanour sweaty and shaky. "I am ready to confess . . ."

*****

TWENTY-FOUR HOURS LATER

CP Arundhati Pradhan had listened to Senior Inspector Saralkar's briefing with rapt attention. Right at the outset, he had requested her to hear him out without interruption and reserve her compunctions, outrage, or questions till he'd finished. And she had kept her word despite many moments of aggravation.

"Along with Ranjit Sapatnekar's confession, we now have enough circumstantial and corroborative evidence. We conducted a thorough search of his bungalow and found Pranjal Bhatti's bicycle tucked away in an unused outhouse. It has been repainted but there are enough markers to confirm it is Pranjal's bicycle. Most importantly, we unexpectedly found footage of Pranjal in the bungalow in Ranjit's own CCTV cameras, on the date of his disappearance," Saralkar said, pausing for breath, then continued, "Also, now that we have established his identity, the Cyber Cell is confident of tracing the Bitcoin transfer to Mohnish Bhatti, back to Ranjit.

"Another piece of corroborative evidence is that the number from which Ranjit made the ransom call to Mohnish Bhatti had been traced to a dead individual, who used to work for Ranjit, about a year ago. All this unequivocally ties Ranjit Sapatnekar to Pranjal's death and we are confident of digging up more evidence that is incontrovertible."

Saralkar stopped speaking, having sensed that his boss's long fuse of patience had almost run out of length.

"What do you expect me to do, Saralkar?" the CP responded icily. "Pat you on your back?"

"Among other things, ma'am!" Saralkar replied. "With due respect, we have solved the case."

"And who gave you the right to use unauthorised, dubious tactics to do so? Without prior clearance from me?"

"That was just to ensure plausible deniability for you, ma'am, in case things didn't go according to plan or backfired."

"Don't patronise me, Saralkar . . . don't you play that card!" the CP snapped. "Don't you know how many fresh grounds for departmental inquiry and legal challenges by the accused you have created?"

"None, ma'am. It was a bona fide operation to bring a suspect to justice, given the exigencies of the case," Saralkar said.

"Bona fide! Exigencies! Don't use big words to talk crap, Saralkar! You used irregular means to whisk Sapatnekar's boys away and implicate him. You misled the suspect to believe his children's lives were in danger, to confess and self-incriminate!" CP Arundhati Pradhan said.

"But the kids were witnesses to the kidnapping and murders, committed by their own father. As witnesses, their lives were at permanent risk because they lived with the accused and so, as police officers, we were duty-bound to remove them from the risk zone, for their own safety," Saralkar argued back. "What's wrong with that even legally? Not to forget, the older boy, Gaurav, is eighteen and thus not a minor."

The CP glared at him.

"And as for the subterfuge played on the accused—let him prove that I did it. He cannot," Saralkar continued, "and if he does, I'll take the fall for it, because there was no other way it could have been done. Whatever happens, nothing can save Ranjit Sapatnekar from being proven guilty, given the evidence we have found."

Arundhati Pradhan shook her head, looking annoyed. Saralkar was right of course, but he needed raps on the knuckles. "And what about deploying the young girl, Namita, to confront Gaurav Sapatnekar? After the fiasco at Ahmedabad, how could you be so thoughtless?" the CP said. "As if that was not enough, you went ahead and used ASI Zirpe on the case, when I've still not made up my mind on her suspension. How dare you?"

Saralkar looked apologetically at his boss. It was time he threw her a bone. "I plead guilty on both counts, ma'am. That was reckless of me and I am ready to face any action you wish to take."

The CP was neither amused nor appeased, but she knew there was no point in admonishing the man in front of her beyond a point. Senior Inspector Saralkar was a maverick, not a rogue officer. Mavericks crossed lines but did not erase them. And they knew which lines never to cross.

"Maybe I will take action," Arundhati Pradhan said with put-on snarkiness. "Suspension, demotion, transfer, punishment posting—any helpful suggestions, Saralkar?"

Saralkar kept a straight face. He knew he was going to be let off the hook. "Well, ma'am, won't it suffice to continue keeping my promotion in abeyance?"

"Good idea," the CP said and broke into a wry smile. "Anyway, have both the boys been examined by a psychologist. I want no controversies. They have to be well taken care of."

Saralkar nodded. "They are, ma'am. I am conscious of that."

"Good. Well done. Make sure all loose ends are tied up," the CP said, signalling an end to the discussion.

Saralkar got up from his chair, then said, "One last thing, ma'am . . ."

"What?"

"ASI Sanika Zirpe has done a commendable job overall . . . I would be grateful if suspension or disciplinary action against her is waived," Saralkar said.

The CP didn't look up. "I'll consider your request."

*****

TWENTY-TWO HOURS EARLIER

"How could I do it?" Ranjit Sapatnekar said sardonically, repeating the question Saralkar had put to him, "Desperation."

"Desperation?" Saralkar mocked incredulously. Every fibre in his body itched to thrash the unremorseful bastard.

Ranjit nodded. "Do you know how my wife died, Inspector? She had her throat cut."

"What? Your wife was murdered?" Saralkar asked in disbelief. Nothing in the background check had revealed any such information.

"Yes, it was murder. Her lovely throat was slit just like that, one fine morning, a year after we shifted back to India from the USA. A day after Makar Sankrant festival . . . and yet they called it an accident! She bled to death on the road."

Saralkar glanced at Motkar, then Tupe. "How can that be? Why would a murder be passed off as an accident?"

"It can . . . It was."

"What exactly happened?"

Ranjit was quiet for a few seconds, either collecting his thoughts or making up a story, Saralkar reckoned.

"My wife had set out on her two-wheeler to drop Gaurav at his bus-stop, and before she knew it, a *manja*, the string used for kite-flying during Makar Sankrant, wrapped around her throat and lacerated her. By the time she realized and stopped the vehicle a few seconds later, it was too late and right in front of Gaurav's eyes, she just bled to death. An autorickshaw driver rushed her to the hospital . . . but she had lost so much blood, she died even before I could reach."

An involuntary shudder ran through Saralkar. Till a few years ago, infrequent incidents of deaths and severe throat injuries to two-wheeler riders, caused by these floating kite strings made of glass-coated nylon, known as Chinese manja—had become alarming enough, leading to a ban on its sale. It had always struck him as a terribly scary, freaky way to die in this country, where people died in all kinds of freak accidents.

To be riding a two-wheeler normally one moment and meet death suddenly by a floating string that was nearly invisible till one came too close, was a particularly horrible and unfortunate fate.

"Oh, I see . . ." he managed to say. "I sympathise . . . but what does that have to do with your crimes?"

Ranjit gave him a dark, bleak look. "Rohan was just a baby—about five—too young to understand anything, bewildered and missing his mother like crazy. But it was Gaurav who was unbearably traumatised. He had been sitting behind his mother when it happened. He had seen her throat slit open, blood gushing out—her terrified convulsions and death throes . . . all that blood. And he just went to pieces . . . he would have the most terrible nightmares and he would cry and cry—eating very little, inconsolable, getting thinner and sullen. His studies suffered and performance at school plummeted. He had been so good at competitive skateboarding, but he just stopped the activity. I took him to doctors and psychiatrists and it took me one long year to comfort and calm him . . . to regain some kind of normalcy. But he was still very fragile—the shock and trauma lay just below the surface, waiting to flare up . . ."

Ranjit stopped, his features distorted, his voice choked with emotion. If Saralkar knew anything about human behaviour, then Ranjit appeared to be telling the truth, not some invented story.

"Go on . . ." Saralkar said.

"The one encouraging thing in all the bleakness was that Gaurav had begun skateboarding again and was performing well competitively at city and district level competitions. It was the one thing that made him happy—when he would smile—life would return to his eyes and I would see zest and enthusiasm for life. He began to look set for being selected from the state to compete at the junior, zonal, and national level championships. And then it all came tumbling down again abruptly when . . . that other boy Atharva got selected from the state instead of my Gaurav. Imagine . . . the difference was just three bloody points and my son had been thwarted. Going by what happens at all levels of sports in India, I was sure there was more to Atharva's selection than met the eye. What makes all the difference is other considerations—contacts, favouritism, caste, religion—something or the other worked in that boy's favour apart from capability, and pushed my son back into the doldrums. Gaurav took it to heart and again became listless and depressed. I . . . I had to do something . . . I couldn't let him relapse into the depression and darkness I had pulled him out of . . . I was desperate."

Saralkar had been listening to him with increasing disgust, anticipating where he was going with the tale. And yet he couldn't help feeling sad at the gloom life bestowed on people, inexorably turning their desperation into something toxic and lethal. "And therefore, you thought it was okay to kidnap and kill Atharva Jambhekar to enable your son to take his place," he snarled at Ranjit. "You evil, cold-blooded brute, how dare you use the excuse of your misfortune to justify killing another innocent child?"

Ranjit gave him a long stare. "You are no one to judge me, Inspector. Wasn't what happened to my wife terribly unfair? Were the culprits caught? The people who used the manja knowing it was lethal and left it floating around? What that incident did to my son was even more unfair. All I did was to pass on the terrible arbitrary unfairness of life to someone else. So what if he was innocent? So was my wife, my sons, and I. God is horribly unfair, life is terribly unfair . . . so why should the onus be on me, a mere human being, to be fair? I did what I had to for my son . . . for his well-being, for his morale . . . for him not to lose that spark again, which had rekindled only because of his performance in skateboarding. And what I did, worked for him . . . it paved the way to give him the sort of luck he needed to build his fortitude. Gaurav has done well since then, winning several championships."

"Do you have no sense of right and wrong, Ranjit Sapatnekar?" PSI Motkar asked, with barely controlled rage.

Ranjit's reply was in a scornful tone, "Life is over-rated. It's no fun living it as a loser—unhappy, mediocre, ordinary. Only winners live well and every winner has benefited from someone else's misfortune at a key stage in their lives. I want my children to be winners and all I did is to set them on the path of winning.

"I wish it didn't have to be at the cost of the lives of the two boys, but they were in the way . . . in the wrong place at the wrong time. For instance, if my Gaurav was in a better state, he wouldn't have been so demoralised and I might not have felt so desperate to do something drastic to revive his spirits! The result—Atharva had to die."

"Atharva didn't die. You killed him, you piece of turd," Saralkar hissed. "And what about Pranjal? What desperation drove you to kill him? What desperation required you to help your younger son, Rohan? Surely Rohan was not suffering then as your older son had, six years ago?"

Ranjit looked away as if he needed to search for the answer outside, rather than within. "I had helped Gaurav at a critical stage. As a father I owed it to Rohan too. An opportunity presented itself . . . I merely took it."

A ball of fury blazed through Saralkar, but he controlled himself. "I wish we could subject you to third degree, Ranjit Sapatnekar. If someone deserves it, it is you, you kid killer," he said with quiet menace.

Ranjit nodded slowly. "I understand how you feel, but I am not a monster, Inspector. I inflicted minimum pain on those boys . . . I tried to compensate their parents."

"Really? What if those who have kidnapped your boys did the same and sent you compensation? Pay you back in the same coin? Would that be fine by you, too?" PSI Motkar asked, unable to hear the man's utterly callous words.

Ranjit's eyes flickered with anger as he shot a look at Motkar. "Please don't speak like that about my sons."

Motkar resisted the urge to twist the knife and say something hurtful to Ranjit. Instead, he said, "You can't bear to hear anything untoward happening to your sons, and yet you felt no qualms sexually mutilating and desecrating the corpses of Atharva and Pranjal . . .?"

For once Ranjit refused to look at either cop, as if his brazenness had deserted him. "I . . . I didn't do any unspeakable things to them . . . their little bodies . . . I swear! I . . . just created that effect with . . . with a . . . a tool," he mumbled shakily.

Saralkar had known the answer, but to hear it from Ranjit's mouth, threw up a vivid imagery of the deed. "Do your sons know what an evil slimeball you are? Do they know about the murders? Did they help you?"

"No way, absolutely not. They did not help me," Ranjit said, almost pouncing forward. "Don't try to implicate my boys. They are innocent. They didn't do anything!"

"So, you do know what you did was wrong and evil—that's why you are hastening to distance your children from culpability," Saralkar said bluntly.

"They had nothing to do with it," Ranjit said his eyes flashing. "Do not attempt to frame them for my crimes."

"But they knew about your gruesome crimes, didn't they?"

"No! No! I sent them away on some pretext before I drowned Atharva and Pranjal," Ranjit said. "And . . . and later I told them the boys had drowned accidentally in the pool."

"And they believed you?" Saralkar mocked. "How convenient!"

"Yes, they believed me. Why wouldn't they? I am their father. I . . . I then swore them to secrecy . . . and told them we had to keep it a secret otherwise we would be held responsible for accidental drowning," Ranjit said.

Saralkar regarded the man with loathing. "Well, they didn't believe you, because they saw you drown the boys."

Ranjit gaped at Saralkar in horror and began shaking as the implications of what he'd said sank in.

"Do you realize you killed those boys and gave your children horrible secrets to keep that they might never be able to purge their souls of, all their lives? You miserable, murderous wretch!"

Saralkar's hand struck with lightning speed across Ranjit Sapatnekar's face with such force that it knocked him off his chair.

*****

TWENTY-TWO HOURS LATER

Motkar wondered whether his boss was undergoing a rather prolonged dressing down than he had bargained for. You never knew with bosses and the new CP, Arundhati Pradhan, had a reputation for being a tough customer. Maybe after the Ahmedabad fiasco, Saralkar's high-risk, unconventional manoeuvre to entrap Ranjit Sapatnekar had proved to be the last straw for the CP and she'd really taken him apart for it.

Just then Motkar heard familiar footsteps pounding down the corridor and the next moment his boss walked in, looking exceptionally chirpy.

"Ah, Motkar, as you can see, I survived the skirmish," he said.

"I am relieved to hear that, sir," Motkar said with feeling.

He followed Saralkar into his cabin. "What a bloody case, Motkar," Saralkar said, sinking into his seat. "We nearly managed to disgrace ourselves and wreck our reputation, didn't we?"

"No, sir. That's an exaggeration. We were doing our best," Motkar replied.

Saralkar grunted and was quiet for a few moments. "You know, I thought human nature had lost its power to distress or disturb me, Motkar, but no . . . one only discovers new, stomach-turning depths to which it can plumb."

"You are right, sir," Motkar said. "Ranjit Sapatnekar's motive also bothers me greatly. How could a man . . ."

"Hmm . . . you know why I consider the Mahabharat such a great epic, Motkar? It's because it reveals the darkest impulses and nuances of human nature so well. Remember the Eklavya story? Dronacharya felt no scruples in asking Eklavya to cut his thumb off, just so that his own pupil Arjun could be the best archer. It was such a knowingly devious, immoral, cruel, underhand act that sacrificed Eklavya for Arjun's sake."

"Yes, sir."

"Didn't Ranjit virtually do the same thing? Wasn't his motive the same?"

Motkar nodded, fascinated by the parallels Saralkar had just drawn. "I didn't know you dabbled in the Mahabharat, sir."

Saralkar's eyes suddenly seemed to light up. "You want to know another curious Dronacharya connection to this case, Motkar? Funny, but it just struck me."

"What, sir?"

"Remember the name of Ranjit's bungalow?"

"Yes," Motkar said, startled, "Ashwathama."

"Correct. And who was Ashwathama?"

"Dronacharya's son . . ."

"Right, and he was infamous for being cursed with eternal life in which he would keep bleeding from his forehead injury . . . for having massacred the children of the Pandavas," Saralkar said. "Does that not describe Ranjit Sapatnekar too?"

Motkar smiled. "In a way, sir—the forever bleeding one."

Saralkar grunted. "I just hope his sons aren't cursed to forever bleed too, with the burden of their father's crimes."

Both the officers were quietly reflective for a few beats. Then Motkar spoke again. "Sir, you never got around to telling me why that man, Mahadik, kidnapped you. We were interrupted that day . . ."

Saralkar nodded and his face became troubled. "He was a father too, Motkar. His son, my school friend, Eknath, was afflicted with severe polio. Some fraud baba told Mahadik Kaka, Eknath would be cured if he sacrificed a boy of the same age, whose limbs were normal."

"Oh, my God, sir . . . what a narrow escape you had!" Motkar said, shocked.

"Yes, Motkar, just my luck he wasn't the kind of father Ranjit Sapatnekar is!"

*****

Acknowledgements

A big thank you to:

Readers and bookworms who love my Inspector Saralkar series enough to keep asking me when's the next one coming. Well, here it is!

My son, Sujay, for reading the manuscript and giving me incredibly thorough feedback on the narrative, right at home.

Vidya Sury, my editor, for deft editing, apt corrections, and a frank assessment of the story elements, which an author needs above all.

Shikha Sabharwal, Pooja Dadwal, and Neeraj Chawla—the original Fingerprint! team behind the publishing success of my first four Inspector Saralkar novels.

Salil Desai
January 2023

About the Author

Salil Desai is an author, columnist, and film-maker based in Pune. *The Kid Killer* is the fifth book in his much-acclaimed Inspector Saralkar Mystery Series, on the heels of *Murder Milestone* (2020), *3 and a Half Murders* (2017), *The Murder of Sonia Raikkonen* (2015), and *Killing Ashish Karve* (2014). The Inspector Saralkar Mystery series is currently being adapted into a web series by Jio Studios. Titled *Kalsutra,* the first season of the web-series is based on *Murder Milestone* and is due for release in early 2023. Salil is also the lead writer of the screenplay of 'Kalsutra'.

Salil's other popular books are *Murder on a Side Street* (2011), *Lost Libido and Other Gulp Fiction* (2012), as well as *The Sane Psychopath* (2018).

Over the years, Salil's books have received good reviews in *The Hindu, New Indian Express, The Pioneer, Bangalore Mirror, DNA, First City, The Tribune,* and many others. His work has been praised by veteran authors Dr. Shashi Tharoor, Shobhaa De, and film-makers Sriram Raghavan and Sujoy Ghosh.

An alumnus of Film & Television Institute of India (FTII), Salil also conducts intensive workshops in creative fiction writing, story and scenario design, screenplay writing and film-making at leading liberal arts institutions and media and communication colleges across India. As a newspaper columnist, over 400 articles, op-ed pieces, features, and travelogues written by him have appeared in *The Times of India*, *Indian Express*, *DNA*, *The Tribune*, *Reader's Digest*, *Deccan Herald*, and *The Hindu*.

Salil was also one of the four international authors worldwide selected for the HALD International Writers' Residency in Denmark, hosted by the Danish Centre for Writers & Translators in June 2016.

Know more about Salil at http://www.salildesai.com